AN

THE DARK SOLSTICE

"A compelling and addictive read, with mythology, romance, and betrayal. A must-read for fantasy lovers!"
-*Liz Konkel, Readers' Favorite*

"This is a wonderfully composed piece of work! The reader is brought into the story on every level with the detail that arouses all of your senses…the characters are so enticing, enriching, and unforgettable…I could not put this book down."
-*Jean Recha, Amazon review*

"An exceptional introduction to a series because it lays out the world so well. In the books that follow it will be easy for the reader to just dive in and enjoy."
-*Ray Simmons, Readers' Favorite*

THE HOUR OF EMBERS

"Truly masterful…the characters leap off the page with lush visual descriptions and lively dialogue, and the various gorgeous settings of the land set a high bar for atmosphere akin to Laini Taylor or Neil Gaiman."
-*K. C. Finn, Readers' Favorite*

"Reading this novel was like meeting old friends that I love and cherish. I enjoyed it so much that I read it once again immediately!"
-*Rabia Tanveer, Readers' Favorite*

"There is so much depth to this plot—politics, control, exploitation, subterfuge—that you fear to blink in case you miss something important."
-*K. J. Simmill, Readers' Favorite*

The Hour of Embers is a work of fiction. Names, characters, places, and incidents either are the product of the author's imagination or are used fictitiously. Any resemblance to actual persons, living or dead, events or locales, is entirely coincidental.

Copyright © 2018 Nikki Leigh Willcome
First Edition
Printed by CreateSpace, an Amazon.com Company
Cover photographs obtained through Shutterstock.com
Cover design by Nikki Leigh Willcome

All rights reserved.

ISBN-13: 978-1726301756
ISBN-10: 1726301753

The Hour of Embers

An Empyrian Odyssey: Book 2

N. L. Willcome

For Gabriel

Dramatis Personae:

Tamsin Urbane – daughter of Lord and Lady Urbane, real mother is Irin
Haven – Watcher, imprisoned
Mr. Monstran – Haven's captor, servant to the Master
Samih – young Watcher
Emilia Regoran – daughter of L. and L. Regoran, real father is L. Urbane
Sherene – former day maid to Tamsin
Lady Urbane – wife of L. Urbane
Lord Urbane – former Lord of Jalsai and Empyria, presumed dead
Georgiana Graysan – daughter of Mr. Graysan, servant to the Allards
Mr. Graysan – scribe to L. Regoran
Cornelius Saveen – Lord of Empyria and Captain of the Empyrian army
Brunos – manservant to Mr. Monstran
Tomas – servant to L. Regoran
Lord Regoran – Lord of Empyria, Emilia's father
Lady Allard – wife of L. Allard
Ysallah – Kazsera in the marsh lands, tribal color is red
Hazees – Kazsera in the marsh lands, tribal color is green
Poma – kazsiin to Hazees
Kellan – Watcher, friend of Haven
Oman – eldest Watcher
Numha – member of the Kor'diin
R'en – member of the Kor'diin
Calos – kazsiin to Bakkrah
Mowlgra – kazsiin to Hazees
Saashiim – member of the islanders
K'al – Kazsera of the marsh lands, tribal color is purple
Benuuk – member of the Kor'diin, brother of K'tar
Mora – seer
Enrik – Tamsin's friend, member of the Empyrian army

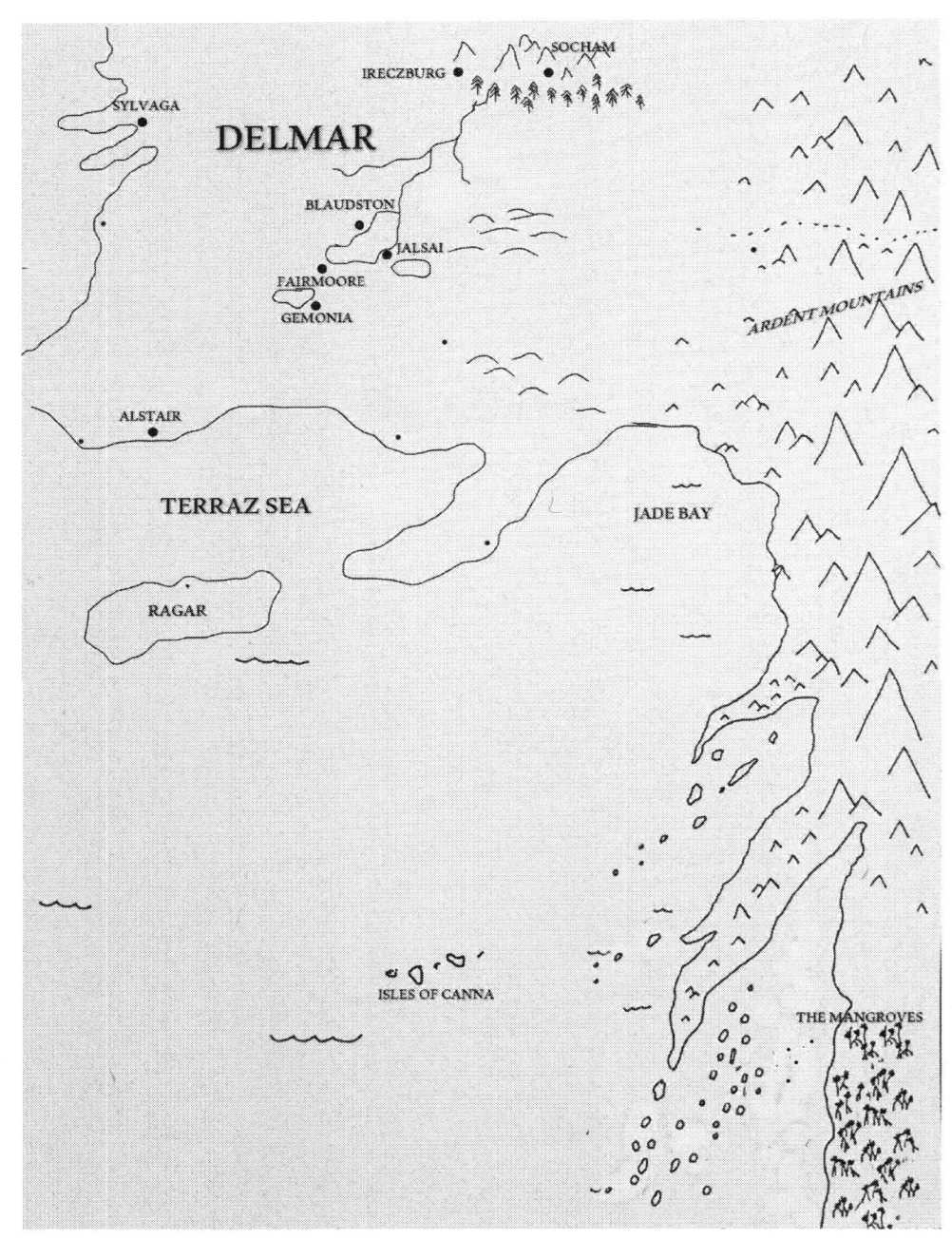

map design by Elizabeth Recha

EMPYRIA
THE HOLLOW CLIFFS

SINDUNE DESERT

ELGLAS RIVER

UNKNOWN REGIONS

RAVINE OF BONES   (ALAMORGRO)

ANASII HADA

THE MARSH LANDS

Hymn of the Lumierii

Together we fight
Together we rise
Together we burn
Together we die

To the Fallen

Under cloaks of black
Alone in the night
Watching, waiting, staying
Away from the light

To the Fallen

Born from the flame
We fell from the sky
Answering the call
Of the widow's cry

To the Fallen

Come from above
To end at last below
Buried by our oaths
The last river to row

To the Fallen

Honor to be found
Peace to be gained
Life to be lost
Soul to be saved

To the Fallen

Together we fight
Together we rise
Together we burn
Together we die

To the Fallen

Chapter One

There had been a time when the dark would dance before the light and it would sweep across the water like a feathered, black bird, letting the stars rest on its wings as it descended over the marshes. He would wait for it to take flight, watching the final folds of sunlight from behind a thin, black veil and when the last shades of orange and red had finally receded he would join that dark bird and blend into the shadows cast by its wings. Then it would consume him, refilling his limbs with necessary purpose and strength until it was time for the dance to end and the bird would relinquish its authority over the skies to the light once more.

But down in the tunnels there was no light. That familiar black bird had been captured and twisted into a tortured, unrecognizable thing. Down here, where narrow stone halls that were marred with claw marks and echoed with the screams of ancient horrors, the dark that he once knew didn't exist. There was no balance between the light and the dark, no cycle of moon rises and sunsets, and no dance between the night and the stars. It wasn't a partnership anymore, rather the dark was a constant oppressor here, like a fume strangling his lungs, ever present and sealing up the last of the cracks that dared to let any air through.

The light had never been his friend, nor had it been to any Watcher that came before him, but it wasn't until now that he realized that the light was as much a part of him as the dark was. He didn't need it to see and direct exposure to it meant certain extinction, but even so the light had never harbored any malice. And down in these hollowed tunnels and caves where all of his faults and fears were laid bare and there contained not even a hint of starlight, he was forced to acknowledge that what he desired the most was just to catch a glimpse of it. He had pretended for so many years that the light meant nothing to him, that he was a creature of the night and a willing participant of its games, but now the longing for clouds filled with golden light and stars that glimmered like crystals in the indigo sky was a torture all its own. Just a few stars; that was all he wanted to see. Even the broken ones of the Lumierii, reflected in the river water, patterned like honey drops on the soft skin of a girl...

"Now now," a slick, hissing voice said disapprovingly. *"What did I say about your old life?"*

A deafening pause echoed in the dark chamber.

"It's gone."

Then any thoughts of the dark or the light or tawny freckles disappeared with a crack of white-hot lightning up his spine...

Tamsin awoke to the sound of screaming and only when she felt the intensity of her pulse and her shortness of breath did she realize it was she who had been screaming. Her hands trembled as she gripped the edges of the blanket beneath her, feeling the smooth hide underneath the soft layer of fur. It didn't feel like she had woken up, that she had passed from the strange realm of dreams to the clear, crisp world of reality, but that she had only opened her eyes and was back to where she had been before she fell asleep. She looked up at the canvas tent, the *buurda*, above her, confirming that she was in fact back at camp. The canvas had a dark hue to it, letting her know that the sun would soon be descending below the horizon. She wiped her sweaty palms on her pant legs and rolled onto her side—and came face to face with a pair of black, lidless eyes.

The cream-colored lizard arched its long neck and its tongue slid out of its mouth, flicking up and down as if it could taste her fear in the air. It had a large horn protruding from its nose and a line of thin, pointed hair down its back.

Go away, please go away, she willed it, but the reptile made no such move. Her knife was underneath the blanket she laid upon. Nostrils flaring, she slowly started pulling the blanket up with her fingers, scrunching the fur up in her already slick palms until she could see the hilt of it out of the corner of her eye.

The lizard's tongue stopped flicking, but its tail started to slide back and forth, creating an S in the sand as if to distract her. A low hiss started to swell inside it.

Tamsin froze, sensing its decision.

Just as it opened its mouth to strike, a sword came plunging down from above, skewering the lizard's head to the sand. Tamsin jumped, feeling her heart quit for a moment as she beheld the dead creature, its tail still writhing on the ground.

A hooded figure knelt down in front of the opening, a smile spreading across his face as he lifted his sword back up, displaying the lifeless reptile still impaled on the end of it. "Breakfast," he said triumphantly.

Tamsin grimaced. The idea of eating the thing that had just wanted to eat her made her stomach turn. She collapsed down onto her back, putting her arm over her forehead. "I'm thrilled my almost killer will appease your appetite, Samih," she said, throwing as much sarcasm as she could into it.

Waking up from a nightmare just to come face to face with the tongue of that *thing* was not how she wanted to start her day. She had been just a waif of a girl when they started, not fully recovered from her grief when she thought both Haven and her father were dead, and the barren conditions of their journey had not improved that, but she did have something she had not had in months: an appetite. Her hunger was like a well, deep and never quite sated, but it fueled something else, something that made her feel alive and vulnerable. Samih was a good fisherman and for a while the catch had been bountiful. Tamsin got over her initial hesitation of touching the slimy creatures quicker than she expected and could now clean and prepare them while Samih caught more, but a lizard was something she wasn't willing to try just yet.

Samih just chuckled and shook his head. "He hardly would've killed you," he said. "The bite from a shriiski is not poisonous. He probably just wanted to keep you qui—." He stopped suddenly and averted his eyes, but Tamsin knew what he was going to say.

Her screaming had probably woken him. She took a deep breath and sat up, feeling guilty. "I'm sorry Samih. You should've wakened me."

Seventeen days ago they had left Empyria and had headed south to the marsh lands. Every day since they had left the Hollow Cliffs there had only been an endless sea of sand. Leagues of desert lay behind them and who knew how many more lay ahead. The Elglas River on which they rowed was their only indication that they were making any progress. Rowing was a much better alternative than hiking through the dunes, but even so, Tamsin had never been so physically tested like this before. She knew she was the reason why it was taking so long to get to the marsh lands. Blistered hands, aching shoulders, and sore muscles forced Samih to do most of the rowing by himself and what she could do took its toll on her, leaving her feeling exhausted every morning when they stopped on the banks to rest. The journey was not for the faint-hearted, Samih had warned her, but right now her heart was the only thing keeping her going.

"Another nightmare?" Samih asked her.

She nodded, rubbing her temples with her palms. That was another thing that seemed ever present, like her hunger. They slept for a few hours during the hottest parts of the day that usually lasted from early afternoon to just before dusk and every time she slept she was visited by vivid dreams. She didn't know if they were a product of the strange sleeping hours or the heat or the stress of their situation, but they came within minutes of closing her eyes and left her breathless and disoriented when she awoke again. These were different than other dreams she had had in the past, where even though they seemed real at the time, there was always that nagging sense that something was strange about them. Those dreams were harmless and disappeared like the wind. These ones terrified her though, and left her with a wary feeling that stayed with her long after she woke up.

But what worried her the most was the lingering feeling that these weren't *her* dreams. Almost like she was looking in on someone else's.

"I can see if I can find some more *haava*, if you think it will help?" he said.

"No, that's alright. It's just a dream, right?" Tamsin said, trying to sound nonchalant while she used her shoe to push sand over the spot where the lizard's blood had spilt.

She had stopped telling Samih about her nightmares after the first few times it happened. He would get very nervous and ramble to himself about evil omens. He was her lifeline out here and seeing him uncomfortable only made things worse, so she stopped telling him about the sense of dread that endured and decided it was best if she bore it herself. He had given her some herbs once, the *haava* of which he spoke, to try and help her sleep, but they only seemed to paralyze her in her own mind. She remembered that particular one clearer than the others, though the details of the dreams were already more vivid than she wished. She had vomited as soon as she had woken up.

"Of course," Samih said letting the matter drop, though his tone was worried. He took the lizard away and started preparing it.

Tamsin saw that his buurda was already rolled up and she had no desire to look at the lizard anymore so she started packing her own things. She took her knife and slid it in her boot then rolled up her animal skin blankets and tied them together with a leather strap. Then she started undoing the ties around the buurda, which consisted of one rectangular piece of coarse, burlap-like fabric adjoined by two triangular pieces on either side. They were attached to four, slightly bent reeds that served to hold up and connect the fabric and gave it its appearance of a half-open cocoon when it was assembled.

It was work of habit now, putting it together and taking it down every night, and her hands moved adeptly, but it left her thoughts free to turn to other things, like the fact that the buurda was not hers, nor were the blankets or any of the other supplies with them. Not even their reed canoe. They were Haven's.

Samih had told her that he and Haven were going to leave that night of the ball at the Armillary. They had constructed boats, gathered supplies, and were all set to leave, but Haven had insisted that he had one more thing to do. He had to go back to the city one last time, and Samih was to go without him and he would catch up. But Haven never came.

Tamsin bit her lip, trying to focus on untying the straps around the reeds.

Samih had found Haven's canoe where he had hidden them in the cliffs when he came back with Tamsin's father from the dam, packed with his buurda, his blankets, and a few of his weapons. She hadn't known when they set out that they were his; it wasn't until they had stopped to rest that first day. Samih helped her set it up before he constructed his own buurda and when Tamsin had laid down on the soft hide she instantly knew. Haven's scent was so strong among the blankets it had nearly taken her breath away. She cried herself to sleep that day, overwhelmed by everything.

If Samih had heard her he didn't say anything. Maybe because she hadn't cried since then. There was no point. It didn't make her feel better, so why waste time and energy on tears? That's what she kept telling herself anyway. She had to, otherwise every time she tied the straps on the buurda she would think about Haven tying these same straps, his gentle, calloused hands going through the same motions that she did now, or when she used one of his knives to clean the fish her mind would imagine him doing the same.

She rolled up the reeds in the canvas pieces to protect them and then put everything in the canoe, save for the bag that contained Haven's firestone and her mother's cloak, which she wore. Then she joined Samih and waited until he had finished with the lizard. When he was done and had wrapped the rest up for later, they put the last of their things in the canoe and set out once again.

They paddled well into the night, until the cool white sliver of the crescent moon was high above them and the chill of the air had taken permanent roost around them. It astounded her how cold the desert got at night compared to the sweltering heat of the day. Both were equally oppressive and it only made her admire Samih more for having endured multiple journeys through the unforgiving environment. And she also better understood why he had been so opposed to trekking across the desert to the Ravine of Bones after Haven.

Something suddenly flew past Tamsin's face and she shrieked in surprise, instinctively throwing her arms up to protect herself and dropping her oar in the water as a result.

Samih turned around quickly, his blade already in hand ready to defend against an attack. "What happened?" he asked, his golden eyes laced with alarm.

"I—I don't know," she said, lowering her arms cautiously and looking around, but she didn't see it. "Something's out there." She tried to control her breathing as Samih glanced around them.

They were silent for a few moments and then Samih pointed in front of them.

Tamsin squinted her eyes in the darkness and then saw it again as it swooped down several yards in front of the canoe.

"A bat," Samih said, lowering his blade as he relaxed again.

Tamsin breathed out a sigh and slumped her shoulders, both relieved and annoyed at this. "Well it had better stay far away from me," she said to him, and then muttered to herself, "This is so much nature today."

Samih chuckled. "It is a good sign," he said.

"How do you suppose?" she said crossly. "I've lost my oar because of it."

"Don't worry, you won't need it anymore. We're almost there."

And he was right. It wasn't even an hour later and the ridge came into view: a dark, jagged line in the distance outlined by the stars it concealed. Samih called it *anasii hada*, the honeycomb tomb, for he said those who travel its underground pools and caverns often get lost and never find their way out again. It was also the last barrier between the desert and the marsh lands.

"Do you know how to navigate these underground ways?" Tamsin asked him. Knowing that their time in the desert was nearing its end only made her anticipation to reach the marshes grow and she wanted to be certain that they could find their way through the *anasii hada* without any unwanted delay.

"I know only one way and it's the only one that matters to us. Just pray that it is not closed off to us already."

"Closed off? Why would it be closed off?"

"After your father was injured in the attack I hid him here, but one night I went back to the wall and it was nearly complete. That's when I knew that we could not wait for his leg to heal and we had to come back right away. But if they've finished it, then those caves will surely be flooded and I don't know that we'll be able to make it through."

Pray indeed, Tamsin thought grimly. "Is the dam close then?"

The dark hood nodded in front of her. "It is on the south side of the ridge. A little ways yet for the ridge is deep. We won't get close enough to be spotted, but we only travel by night now."

"Understood," Tamsin said, glad that Samih was seated ahead of her in the canoe so he would not see any disappointment on her face. Samih and the other Ma'diin had made it perfectly clear what they thought of the dam, "the guillotine" as her father had called it, but she could not deny that she wanted to see with her own eyes the massive structure, if only to put an image to the thing that had caused so much pandemonium in their lives.

They reached the entrance to the ridge: a gaping black maw that was fed nothing but darkness by the river that surged into it. The lip was about ten yards over their heads and once they passed underneath it, the light of the moon and stars disappeared completely and it was a darkness like Tamsin had only known in her nightmares. She fought hard against the childish fears that swelled inside her. Fear of the dark. Fear of the unknown. Fear of not being in control.

The sound of the water rushing over the rocks was amplified in the hollow space around them and helped mask the sound of her harsh breathing as they were swallowed by the maze that had swallowed and kept countless others before them.

Chapter Two

The sides of the wheelhouse shivered and moaned against the battering winds coming down from the mountains. The grunts from the horses and the jingling of stirrups and bits could not be heard over the unrelenting airflow, and the only way the inhabitants of the wheelhouse cabin knew that they had not been abandoned was the steady, rocking motion of the wheelhouse as they plodded on towards Delmar. The wind was surely bothersome for those on horseback outside of the cabin, but Emilia Regoran viewed it as a final sendoff, the last push away from the desert home that had held her captive since she was a girl and was as cold to her as any of the mountain passes that they had travelled through these last few days.

Leaving Empyra had been more emotionally difficult than she thought it would be and she realized very soon how alone she actually was. By some small miracle and a lot of carefulness on her part, she had somehow managed to keep up the ruse that she was Tamsin without anyone suspecting her true identity. She kept her veil down at all times and spoke to no one, which only enhanced her loneliness, though she did feel pity for Tamsin from time to time, thinking how deeply distraught she must have been over her father's death to where her mother and day maid seemed only a little concerned at her reclusive behavior, as if it were normal.

The space gave Emilia a lot of time to think and she often thought about what she would do or say when she finally had to tell Lavinia Urbane the truth. She was grateful that she had not been found out before crossing the mountains, for fear of being sent back, but she knew she must do it soon, before they reached the Cities.

They took refuge that night an hour later than usual, but they finally reached a small valley that offered them relief from the wind, of which both men and beasts were exhausted from. But even though it was late, the respite seemed to improve the general mood of the company and it wasn't long before the cooking fires were blazing and sizzling with the smell of roasted conies and spirits being passed around. Everyone seemed genuinely happy to put the mountains and the desert behind them.

Emilia, however, had only one thing on her mind since she stepped out of the wheelhouse: the grass underneath her feet.

Tufts of real, greenish-brown grass.

She had been only five years old when she had last felt grass between her toes, a notion that seemed absurd as she walked in slow circles around the wheelhouse, shoes and stockings in hand. But for the last 16 years all she had felt was scorching hot sand and rock beneath her shoes. There was no room for growth in that kind of environment. As soon as one arrived in Empyria any potential development was stunted and you were labeled an outsider. A trespasser. A *weed*. Unwanted in every way except by those that were under the same category and even then there was a hierarchy. She should've been married by now with children and a household of her own, but the existing pool of eligible candidates was dried up, which, she admitted, had led her to some less than honorable liaisons with men who were otherwise spoken for.

But seeing grass meant hope. Life could be built here. She remembered the love her aunt had for her and she knew she could find it here again. Maybe Lavinia would even help her find a suitable match; it was no secret that it was mostly by her hand that Tamsin and Cornelius were to be wed. Perhaps she could manage to do the same for Emilia.

Thoughts of weddings and cotillions and handsome gentlemen filled her head as she continued her path around the wheelhouse, which was why she didn't see the man standing around the corner in the shadows until she collided with him. The man was much taller and was barely startled by the impact, but he took a step back, favoring a bad leg.

"Oh, excuse me," Emilia said and when no apology was reciprocated she turned to go back, wondering how a man with a lameness had been included in the caravan at all, but the man grabbed her arms and turned her around to face him.

Most of his face was hidden by a turban that wrapped around his nose and mouth and was piled on top of his head like rolled dough, but the urgency in his eyes was unmistakable. "Tamsin," he said, his deep baritone voice slightly muffled by the fabric, "I know you are still unhappy about being here, but we must discuss what is to come next."

Emilia's heart beat forcibly against her chest as she contemplated what to say or if she should say anything at all. A servant had never spoken to her with such authority before and Tamsin had not mentioned anything about anyone other than her mother and her day maid who were to know about her.

The man's eyes changed from urgency to confusion and he pulled the wrap down from his face so it hung loosely around his neck. "Tamsin, what's wrong?"

Nothing had been wrong until about a second ago when Emilia realized she knew this man. She had seen him only once before, but it was enough.

It was Lord Urbane. Tamsin's father.

She gripped his arm to steady herself and as she tried to wrap her head around the fact that he was alive, that the arm she was holding was no ghost, she came to realize what Tamsin meant the night she came to her with her proposition.

Tamsin had told her that when her day maid, Sherene, found out to tell her it was time to tell her mother the truth. Emilia had assumed she was talking about her identity, but she knew now that Tamsin had not been talking about Emilia. Tamsin had known her father was alive and had been talking about him.

The time was now upon her. What was to happen now would determine her future. Emilia took a deep breath and lifted the veil back over her head so both of them, two people who were not supposed to be here, were unmasked. "I believe you're right," she said, sure her own face mirrored the nearly horrified look that stunned Lord Urbane's features. "We must discuss what is to come next."

Any sense of time that Tamsin had in the *anasii hada*, the honeycomb tomb, was lost. If Samih was right in his navigation through the watery tunnels, then they should be through to the other side before nightfall the next day. But how was she to determine the difference between day and night when everything was dark? Only when she had dozed off several times and woken to the same black surroundings did she realize just how long they had been going without rest.

Her night vision had improved a little and she was able to see shapes of the stalactites hanging from the cavern ceilings, which wriggled with the bodies of bats when they encountered nests of them above the slower-moving pools. Their loud chittering and scratching against the rocks echoed through the large chambers, making her skin crawl with the thought of even one of them getting close.

Samih remained unperturbed by them, but she could sense his agitation as the stalactites grew closer and closer to them. At first, she thought they were just getting larger, stretching out closer to the water, but then she realized it wasn't the rock formations getting bigger, it was the water.

Which meant the dam was working.

It was well that Samih's vision was better than her own for they soon had to maneuver around them, slowly making their way around the huge stones that more resembled pillars than cones now.

Samih stopped rowing suddenly and started taking off the straps and belts that held his weapons. He shrugged out of his cloak and removed his tunic, shoving everything down into the canoe.

His golden eyes pierced the dark like flames, but Tamsin noted briefly that he did not have the silver markings across his chest like Haven had, but she put the image in the back of her mind to ask him about later.

"Samih, what are you doing?"

"The water is getting too high," he said. He maneuvered the canoe over to one of the stalactite columns and instructed her to hang onto it.

She leaned closer and wrapped her arms around the moist stone, feeling the damp permeate her sleeves. It helped steady the canoe as Samih slipped over the edge into the water, letting out a puff of air through his lips as the cold water met his bare skin. He held onto the front so he could steer it and told her to lay down, his speech already trembling from the cold.

There was only room for one to fully extend in the canoe, but she didn't like the idea of him in the freezing water for lords knew how much longer. "Samih—."

"We're al-almost there," he said. "Lie down or I'll make you get out and swim t-too."

Tamsin did as she was told, feeling the tug as he started swimming and pulling the canoe with him. The going was much slower this way, but she soon understood why he was so adamant about it. Within a few minutes the ceiling had dropped even lower until it was only inches above the top of the canoe. In some places it even scratched the edges and Tamsin had to fight back the ball of dread that rose in her throat. *Anasii hada.* Honeycomb *tomb.* The name kept whispering in her mind. It was almost like being in her own coffin, pressed between the canoe and the cavern ceiling.

How many breaths could someone take in their own tomb before they ran out of air?

She was so focused on this that she almost didn't notice that they had stopped moving.

"Samih?" she whispered through the reed wall of the canoe. "Samih?!" she repeated, louder this time when there was no answer. She waited a few frozen heartbeats more and then heard a splash as Samih's head broke the surface and she heard his eager gulps for air. "Samih! Are you okay? What happened?"

It was a few moments before he was able to respond. When he got his breath back he said, "I'm alright. I had to swim below to see where to go next. I couldn't tell from up here."

"Thank the lords. I thought you had drowned!"

Samih actually laughed, though it was broken by the spluttering of water. "I grew up in a fishing village. I could swim before I could walk."

Tamsin assumed his light-hearted attitude was due to the fact that he had found out what he needed to below the surface. "How much farther?"

"Not f-far." And they started to move again.

Tamsin relaxed a little back into the canoe, though her heart was still beating too fast and little beads of sweat had started to form along her hairline. She could not shake the feeling of being entombed.

"Samih will you speak to me?"

"What do you wish to s-speak about?"

"Anything. I don't care."

He was silent at first, then he said, in a surprisingly rhythmic way, "Fear the dark and the murky d-deep, when water stills and lions sleep. Listen not to the demon's wail or fallen breath in wind's last sail. W-watch for eyes in the silver lake, but mind the stare of fury's wake."

Tamsin thought she had not interpreted the words properly for they were so strange. "What is that?"

"It's something my mother would tell me when I was a babe."

"What does it mean?" she said, replaying the words. She had been hoping he would say something a little more encouraging, but it had done the trick and distracted her nonetheless. The nursery rhymes Sherene had told her as a small girl were filled with talking bears and ducklings and flowery things, though Sherene had always been good at slipping messages in there about being punctual or minding one's manners.

"It means I should've listened to my m-mother more," he said with a sour laugh. "I would not have ended up like this if I had."

"It seems a rather frightening thing for a mother to tell her child."

"It is a lesson. Be aware of your surroundings. Be cautious of those that come out in the dark."

"So children are warned about the amon'jii," she said. *And the Watchers,* she thought silently to herself.

He remained silent for a moment and then added, "Seek the light and the halo's rise through clouded veil of shadowed skies. When dawn awakes and battles cease, let gods return with endless peace."

It was Tamsin's turn to be silent, understanding now why he had chosen this particular lullaby. She closed her eyes and imagined the sun, imagined the bliss its warmth brought. It was a little light in this dark place. Her heartbeat slowed and she found it was a little easier to breathe. "Samih," she said softly. "What is it going to be like when we get there?"

He knew she wasn't talking about the environment or the weather and when he answered he said, "I don't know. Life in the marsh lands is ruled by one law: survive or die. So I guess it depends on whether they see our cause as a threat to them or not. They will either fight with us or against us."

Tamsin was going to remark on how she wouldn't let their success hinge on so barbaric a law as basic instinct, but then a streak of white sliced through the thin space above the top of the canoe, illuminating the cavern ceiling. Slowly the ceiling began to grow farther away and the white spread and expanded. Once there was room, she sat up and shielded her eyes against the brilliant light until they adjusted. The tunnel had turned into a large cavern and on the opposite end there was a wide opening that gave way to the outside world.

A pair of birds flew out and disappeared into the warm blue sky as Samih pulled the canoe over the ledge at the cavern mouth that remained in the shadows yet. As he re-donned his clothes and weapons, Tamsin stepped out of the canoe and, a little shakily for her legs were cramped from being in the canoe for so long, climbed over the rocks to get a better look. She closed her eyes as she stepped into the sunlight, feeling the pressure leave her chest with each deep breath as the light and the fresh air embraced her again.

Samih joined her and surveyed the landscape, his eyes hidden under his n'qab, but the press of his lips told Tamsin that something wasn't quite right and he would not say what right away. They rested for a little while then at the mouth of the cavern, giving Samih a chance to recover from being in the cold water for so long. While he did that and made some small repairs to the canoe, Tamsin filled their water skins and brought out the last of the fish meat Samih had caught, giving some to him before taking a strip for herself. She would still not touch the lizard meat.

Once she was done, she started taking out the buurda rolls from the canoe, but Samih stopped her.

"I thought we were only to travel at night now," she said, puzzled. "It would do us both good to get some sleep while we can."

"I know what I said, but circumstances have changed."

"What do you mean?" She didn't know what could have possibly changed since they made it to the end of the tunnels, but she helped him push the canoe back into the water anyways.

"Look over there," he said, pointing to the left. They had come out of the tunnels on the southwest edge of it and a good portion of the marsh lands ran parallel to it to the northeast. "We have to go that way, which takes us closer to the dam and during the day that leaves us more exposed to the northerners. But since we know the wall is working and the *anasii hada* is filling up with water, there is less water between us and where we need to go."

Tamsin's eyes widened in realization. They had not been real until now; they had only been words and images put into her mind by Haven. But they were entering the marshlands now. They were in *their* territory. If they did not reach safer waters by nightfall then the threat from the Empyrians would be the least of their problems.

The amon'jii would be there instead.

Tamsin had no interest in meeting one of them, especially on her first night here. As Samih started rowing, she took apart the bundle that made up her buurda and with gritted teeth, for she was keenly aware that she was destroying something that belonged to Haven, cut a large patch out of the fabric with her dagger. She cut several smaller strips and a part of the strong reed frame into a shorter piece which she then fastened crossways with the strips to one of the longer reed poles. Then she fastened the patch to the cross so it looked like a large diamond on one end of the pole. On the other end she wrapped another strip of fabric for her hands. Then she stuck her makeshift paddle in the water and started rowing along with Samih.

He glanced back when she put her oar in the water and she caught him grinning as he turned away again.

"Do the amon'jii live in the *anasii hada*?" she asked, not caring if he found her attempt at helping him amusing.

The hood of his cloak shook back and forth. "There is too much water for them near the *anasii hada*. Usually," he added. "They come from the northeast."

The exact direction they were going. "Perfect," Tamsin muttered dryly. "Why would the Empyrians build so close to the marshlands? Why not build it closer to the city?"

"I would rather not waste my time trying to figure out why the northerners do the things they do," he said sharply, but Tamsin ignored his tone.

The answer to that question was important, she could feel it, but she was no closer to the answer than she had been when news about the dam's existence first came to her. Was it only just to keep it a secret from the other Empyrians? Or were they positioning themselves to take over the marsh lands and expand their power? Lord Saveen had set these events into motion, but without ever meeting him or knowing what kind of man he had been she couldn't begin to guess at his motivations. If he was anything like his nephew then she could only speculate that the reason had been a vain one and that was not an encouraging thought.

Survive or die.

They had survived the tomb. But as they set out into the open air, leaving the dark tunnels behind them and emerging into a completely different landscape, Tamsin had the distinct feeling that they were just getting started.

Chapter Three

Every day the sun rose in the east and every day Georgiana Graysan rose with it, went to work at the Allard compound, and then went home after the last candles had been blown out. It was the same routine she had grown accustomed to over the last few years, but these last weeks had been different. Something had been unsettled, as if someone had taken all the silverware and expected her to serve dinner without any spoons or knives. She had heard whispers from the Regoran maids that Lady Emilia had left with the caravan going back to Delmar. The Regorans were trying to appear nonchalant about it, saying she was merely going on holiday, but it didn't seem right to Georgiana. It had been the same caravan that took Tamsin away, but she could have sworn she had seen Tamsin in the compound kitchens that very morning, dressed like a maid, which didn't make any sense, and she hadn't even said goodbye. It was not like her. Not only that, but Enrik had disappeared. She knew he was busy now that he had been recruited by his father for the army, but any inquiries she had made about him came up empty.

And to put the topping on the cake, she had only seen her father a handful of times in the last couple weeks and each time he had said no more than a few words to her. He was haggard and barely eating. Some nights he never came home from the Armillary.

Something in Empyria had changed. And she thought she could pinpoint it to the night Captain Saveen became a Lord. A shift in power had happened and though there were still two other ruling lords in Empyria, Cornelius now controlled the majority of the city. The Regorans and the Allards and Lord Wohlrick's widow, for he had passed away only a week ago, were lords and ladies only to hold up a curtain so that no one would see who was pulling the strings behind them. But with the increased presence of soldiers in the compounds and in the streets (they had even shut down the docks on the west bank so all traffic and goods had to come through the Armillary), nobody was fooled. Especially those who worked in the compounds and at the Armillary where any gossip upstairs spread like a hay fire in the lower levels.

"I heard from Lady Regoran's maid that once Lady Wohlrick finally passes that Lord Saveen is going to take over the compound," one of the maids said as they were clearing the table one morning after the family had finished breakfast at the Allard compound.

"Finally?" another one of the maids exclaimed. "What a horrible thing to say!"

"Well it's true," said the first. "It won't be long now before she follows Lord Wohlrick into the grave and when she does Lord Saveen will snatch up that compound the same as he did with the Urbane's."

Georgiana found that she could not ignore the conversation, as she tried to focus on gathering the linens. She had heard rumors of this of course, though none of the servants had been allowed access to the abandoned compound so no one knew what he was using it for.

"Can't the other lords send word to the Cities? I'm sure they have an overabundance of lords that they could relocate here," the second one suggested. "Or send their handsome young sons at least."

"Who would want to come to this forsaken place? And besides, they haven't opened the gates since the last caravan left."

That last part was true at least. Usually when a large caravan departed they would send an extra rider to come back and verify they had made it to the mountains. But they had received no word. And no one had been allowed to leave. It left an edge in the air that everyone could feel, though nobody would look you in the eye and admit it. Either something terrible had befallen the caravan or Cornelius was shutting off Empyria from the Cities.

"They've shut the gate yes," the second maid said with exasperation, "but there are other ways to get information out of the city."

"Penelope!"

Georgiana nearly knocked over the glasses next to the napkin she was folding because she had been listening so intently. She looked up to see the Matron Maid standing in the doorway, glowering at the three.

"You three would get more work done if you gossiped less. Penelope," she addressed the second maid, "Lady Allard is visiting Lady Regoran today so I need you to go to the Regoran compound and drop this off for me. Give it to Mrs. Parson; she knows about Lady Allard's allergy and how to prepare her tea." The Matron Maid handed her a small basket with some herbs.

"Of course mum." Penelope said, blushing fiercely.

The Matron Maid reminded the girls again after Penelope left of the importance of focusing on their work before leaving herself to check on the kitchen maids.

Georgiana waited a half breath before she darted after Penelope, hastily apologizing to the first maid and promising she would be right back. Penelope had already made it to the front of the compound before Georgiana caught up with her.

"Penelope, wait!" And then she lowered her voice as Penelope stopped to face her. Georgiana pulled her over to the side by the top of the front stairs away from any curious ears of the other servants as they passed by. "What did you mean back there? About getting information out of the city?"

A mischievous expression replaced Penelope's confused look. "Why would you need to get information out? And to who?"

Georgiana shook her head. "That's not important. I need to get a letter out."

"To the Urbane girl, right?" Penelope guessed. "You were friends with her, weren't you?"

"Yes and there's been no word from her or the caravan. Please, Penelope. Do you know how?"

Penelope seemed to sense that Georgiana's intentions were more out of desperation than curiosity. "Not how, but rather *who*." She shoved the basket the Matron Maid had given her into Georgiana's hands. "Take this. When you get there, find Tomas, Lord Regoran's butler." She glanced around, making sure no one was in earshot. "Tell him I sent you and that you need to see the Hare."

"The Hare?" Georgiana raised her eyebrow. "Who—."

"Tomas will take you to him, but you can't say a word to anyone else, do you understand? I could get in big trouble for this."

Georgiana took Penelope's hand and squeezed it in thanks. "I understand. Not a word."

Penelope smiled, pressed her finger to lips and walked away.

Georgiana wasted no time and rushed down the stairs, clutching the basket tightly. She stopped at home first to retrieve the letter she had pre-written to Tamsin. Though nothing left the city, she had held onto it anyways in case the embargo was ever lifted. She hastily scrawled a few more lines at the bottom endearing Tamsin to reply at the earliest opportunity. She had to hope that Tamsin would find a way to get a letter back to her.

She then went to the Regoran compound and dropped off the basket for Mrs. Parson, enquiring where she could find Tomas. She was directed to the upper levels where it did not take her long to find him, for he was in the process of chastising two other servants quite loudly for forgetting to tie down a section of canvas over the veranda the previous night, which was now covered in a decent layer of sand.

Tomas was of average height, but held himself straight and proud, which made him seem taller than he was. His brown hair, though tinged with grey, was a shade darker than his tanned skin and pulled back in a tight bun. The vertical gold stripes that adorned his light blue vest signified him as the highest ranking member of the household staff, though Georgiana noticed that his wrists were tattooed with the symbols of the old religion: on one, a man with a snake wrapped up his arm and the other, a woman holding a vase.

Georgiana watched quietly and waited until it was done before walking over to him. "Tomas?" she asked, a bit more timidly than she would have liked.

He acknowledged her without a smile, the ire of the previous scene still in his narrow, black eyes. "Can I help you?" he asked, his tone indicating he would like to do anything but.

Georgiana decided it was best to get right to the point. "I need to see the Hare."

His stern expression melted instantly into surprise, but he quickly covered it with suspicion.

"Penelope sent me," she said before he could question her.

He thought a moment before he replied. Gauging if she was telling the truth or not, she guessed.

"I need to get a letter out of the city," she continued, pressing forward. "I—."

"Stop speaking," he said, looking around sharply. Then, "Follow me." He moved away without warning and it was all so abrupt she stood there dumb for a few seconds before she lurched forward as if a hand had shoved her and she had to nearly jog to catch up to him. He led her up one of the outer stairwells to what she guessed was the Regoran family's living quarters. He took her through the main chamber and into a smaller parlor-style room. He told her to wait and then disappeared back through the main chamber.

Georgiana knew better than to sit in any of the family's furniture so she stood awkwardly next to a brown and tan high-backed chair, brushing smooth the waistline of her dress while she wondered why Tomas had brought her to the family's private quarters. She glanced around the room; there was a square window letting in sunlight from the east and on the opposite wall was a portrait of Lord and Lady Regoran and their daughter Emilia. It must have been painted many years ago for the girl in the portrait was no older than six or seven.

She briefly wondered what Emilia was doing right now; if nothing had befallen the caravan, then had they reached Delmar already? What was it like there? Why had she gone? Tamsin had told her a little of Delmar; describing some of the places she had been. The rolling green hills and the trees that stood like towers amongst the buildings, of wide cobbled streets with a fountain or garden on nearly every corner, and the houses that stood side by side instead of piled on top of one another like stacked dice.

She could see the appeal, she concluded, especially for someone like Emilia who had never been satisfied with desert living, so leaving must have been an easy choice.

She heard footsteps and the man from the painting appeared before her, followed closely by Tomas.

She had a moment of panic, thinking for a moment that Penelope had tricked her and she was now going to be punished for trying to circumvent the ban on exportation. But then she remembered that there was little love between the Regorans and the Saveens and now that the other Lords were being pushed out of power by Cornelius, maybe it wasn't crazy to think that Lord Regoran… "You're the Hare?" she blurted out.

Lord Regoran kept his composure rather well, though he did let the corner of his mouth slip up into an amused smile. "If that's who you were expecting, then I'm sorry to disappoint," he said. "Tomas says you need to get a letter out. With that I can help at least. Do you have the letter?"

Georgiana retrieved the letter from her pocket and handed it over to him. He tucked it away in his vest. "I'll get this out for you, but you must never speak the name 'the Hare' again, do you understand?"

She nodded, but couldn't help from asking, "If you're not the Hare, then who is?"

A funny smile graced his face. "Never again. Be on your way now."

Georgiana knew she would get no more out of him so she thanked him and quietly left the room, though her curiosity was far from abated. She knew three people now who knew about the Hare, whoever he was, and she was determined to find more. If Lord Regoran was involved, then the situation with Cornelius had to be more serious than anyone was letting on.

It was difficult not to think about over the next couple days, but Georgiana couldn't help but wonder if in fact Lord Regoran had kept his word and gotten her letter out. She had not been back to the Regoran compound since and it was probably for the best for she would have had a hard time not questioning him about it and she did not want to press her luck. She vowed to put it out of her mind, because even if her letter did make it to Tamsin, with the ban going on it would probably be impossible for Tamsin to send word back. That was until one night at the Allard compound.

She had been cleaning up the table after Lord and Lady Allard had supped and had dropped a napkin on the floor. She crouched down to pick it up and just as she was about to stand back up she saw Tomas creeping silently across the veranda. She froze, wondering why he was here, though he had not seen her. Penelope was making her way back to the table with an empty tray to clear the dishes and Tomas changed his course abruptly to intercept her. He grabbed her arm and pulled her away from the light of the candelabras, though her expression was her only protest. Georgiana stood up and silently followed them, making sure to stay out of sight.

Their voices were hushed and she could not catch everything, but she did hear Tomas say "tonight" and "the Archive building." They must be meeting, tonight, and possibly with the Hare, Georgiana thought. She slipped away before they spotted her and continued her work at the table, keeping her head down nonchalantly when Penelope returned. Penelope set the tray down and sighed deeply and when Georgiana lifted her gaze, Penelope pouted firmly and told her she suddenly wasn't feeling well.

"Will you be able to manage without me?" Penelope asked.

Georgiana frowned, but nodded.

Penelope thanked her, whirled on her heel and left. Georgiana wanted to follow her, but there would be seven hells to pay from the Matron Maid if the table was left in such a state. She hurried through the cleanup, though it seemed to take longer than usual. Luckily it was the last of her duties for the night. Lately she had been helping the kitchen staff, since her father was not often home until after she went to bed and she preferred not spend her evenings alone, but tonight she dashed out with a sincere, but hasty, apology to them. It wasn't home that she hurried off to, but the Archive building.

The Archive building was not too far out of the way from her usual route home, so no one still out in the streets had any reason to suspect her, though she still felt the extra adrenaline tickling her veins when she passed a soldier or saw the wall through a cross section of a street. The Archive building was dark when she arrived there, but she caught the faintest movement at the top of the stairs leading up to the main chamber. She watched the figure for a few minutes, but he didn't move. He wasn't a soldier, but he was obviously the lookout for whatever was going on inside.

It was the only way up. Georgiana bit her lip. She would have to try and bluff her way through. She took a deep breath and tried to be confident as she strode forward. The figure picked up her movement almost immediately, but she kept going. She had barely made it up the first few steps when he stepped in front of her, blocking her way.

"Can I help you with something Miss?" the man said.

Georgiana recognized the voice, but it wasn't Tomas', to her relief. She pulled her hood back a little so he could see her face more clearly. "Aden?" she said.

Aden blinked a few times. "Georgiana?" Then he chuckled. "I didn't recognize you for a second."

Georgiana knew Aden who worked down at the fishing docks. She usually bought her fish from him. She smiled, relaxing a little. She enquired how he was doing and applauded him on the excellent catch he had last week. Before he could get too deep into his reply, another man came around the veranda. He must've been watching the other side.

"Aden, what's going on?" he asked.

"It's my fault," Georgiana interrupted. "I was running a little late. I'm sorry." She tried to take a step up, but the man blocked her way.

"What's the password?" the man asked.

"C'mon, this is Graysan's daughter. She's good," Aden said, but the man stayed rooted.

"Password," he repeated, his suspicious gaze threatening to uncover her.

Georgiana met his gaze, hoping the darkness would conceal the heat she felt rising in her cheeks, and decided to take a chance. "I would tell you," she said, "But I've been instructed never to say the name aloud."

Aden burst out laughing again, much to the irritation of his friend whose nostrils flared. But Aden waved her up and this time she was permitted to pass. He told her he had to remain out here, but she could go in.

Georgiana dared not look back at the other man so she went inside as quickly as she could, only now thinking how odd it was that Aden trusted her without hesitation. There were about two dozen people packed in the main chamber, and only a few heads turned when she entered, but the room was lit by only a single candle on a desk in the center of the room and nobody questioned her as she took a place near the entryway. They were far too entrenched in the conversation happening.

Most of the people were standing and she could not get a clear view of the speakers, but she recognized Lord Regoran's voice.

"Cornelius hasn't completely cut us off from the Cities," he said. "There's a shipment expected in a few days."

"Then how come none of us have heard of it?" someone asked, followed by a murmur of agreement.

"The army has seized control of all correspondences, including those concerning shipments for the marketplaces, which means Cornelius controls the flow of goods and information."

"But he's sharing this information with you?"

"No. It was only by chance that Tomas was able to learn of it, otherwise we've been unsuccessful in finding a mole in his regiments."

"The army is loyal to him. If we press too much we risk giving ourselves away," Georgiana recognized Tomas' voice.

"In one month, we'll have a firewood shortage," someone else spoke up. "In two, it will be fruit and vegetables. By the fourth it will be meat because by the third we will have run out of grain to feed the animals we do have. The people of this city will be pushed into poverty without outside help."

"Can't we wait it out? Ration what we do have until Saveen comes to his senses. The army will run out of supplies just like the rest of us and when they do they'll turn on him."

"The army's been hoarding supplies for weeks already."

"What does Saveen possibly have to gain from this?"

"He wants us to be desperate. If he controls the flow of goods, then he controls the people. The city is as good as his."

It was obviously an underground group on the opposite side of the army. And Georgiana could not blame them.

"Has there been any reply from your contact?" Lord Regoran asked someone.

A man stood up from a chair near the table, his back turned. "Not yet, but if they are on schedule they should make it to the Cities within the week."

Georgiana's eyes widened. Though she couldn't see his face, she would know that voice anywhere. She remained absolutely still as she watched her father take his seat again.

"And your courier? When is he expected back?"

Mr. Graysan stood up again, quickly, obviously having thought he was done speaking. "He has the best horses in all of Delmar, I'm sure he'll be here soon."

"Good."

The room had contained an anxious buzz when she first arrived, but now a stranger silence covered them. Lord Regoran was pensive for a moment and the others seemed to be expectantly waiting for what he was about to say.

"Graysan," he said finally, sending chills up Georgiana's arms. "You've been invaluable thus far in getting information out, but I need you to do something else for us."

Georgiana had to swallow her nerves. She couldn't deny the things that had been said here tonight, but it was dangerous to be here. And she wanted to grab her father and take him far away.

"I need you to be one hundred percent honest with me. It's no secret that Cornelius has taken a special interest in you." He let the pause hang in the air a moment. He leaned on the desk with fingers spread wide over the surface and looked at Mr. Graysan through his eyebrows. Then he continued, "Are you spying on us for him?"

A murmur went around the room and Georgiana took a step forward, but her father waved his hands.

"No! No! Of course not!" He turned his head from side to side and Georgiana caught the pleading look in his eyes.

"Then what *are* you doing for him?" Lord Regoran asked, his stance demanding an answer.

Mr. Graysan hung his head and for a pinprick of a second Georgiana wondered if the accusation was true, but what came out of his mouth next scared her even more.

"I am a spy of sorts for him, but," he added quickly for the incredulous looks he received, "I also spy against him."

Questions and more accusations flew around the room, but Lord Regoran held up his hand, silencing them, his disgusted expression showing the briefest curiosity. "Explain yourself."

Mr. Graysan took a second to collect himself. "A couple months ago, Cornelius wanted to know about the Ma'diin. I've been...educating him about them."

"Educating? About the Ma'diin?"

"Cornelius is in a contract of sorts—I don't—I don't know with who exactly, but I know it has something to do with Brunos and—."

"The big man always lurking around?" Lord Regoran interrupted.

"Yes, him and his lord: Mr. Monstran that was here. They have some kind of scheme against the Ma'diin."

Somebody hmphed. "After what they did they deserve whatever Cornelius has in store for them."

"But they didn't!" Mr. Graysan turned to the rest of them. His gaze scanned briefly over Georgiana, but he must not have seen her. "The tragedy at the dam was not what we think!"

"How do you know this?" Lord Regoran asked calmly.

Mr. Graysan hesitated. "I can't tell you."

Lord Regoran raised an eyebrow.

"It's who I am spying on Cornelius for. It's my contact. Please, I can't tell you anymore."

Lord Regoran's calm was vanishing quickly. "If our contact, the one we've been passing our information to, the one we're putting our hopes in, has been asking you to spy without the rest of us knowing anything, then how can we trust him?" When Mr. Graysan remained silent, Lord Regoran straightened up to his full height. "I'm ordering you to tell me."

Georgiana held her breath, wishing she could do something to help, but knowing if she revealed herself now that it would only make things worse. She walked slowly around the edge of the room so no one would notice her, but she needed to see her father's face.

"If a lord gives you an order, you obey it," another man said.

"Precisely," Mr. Graysan said, almost too soft to hear.

Confused glances were exchanged and someone asked, "Your contact is a Lord?"

Mr. Graysan put his face in his hands. Then he took a deep breath and explained what had really happened at the dam, how a truce had been reached, how a plan had been constructed to take it down, how Cornelius twisted the Commander's letter and sent a squadron of his men there, how they had attacked, how Cornelius had enlisted his knowledge of the Ma'diin to work against them, and how he continued to help him so he could spy on him. When he had finished, he slumped in his chair like a condemned man who had just confessed his sins.

"The Ma'diin are innocent," someone murmured and Georgiana immediately thought of the Watcher Tamsin had fallen in love with. He had been innocent. Her brow furrowed as she thought back to that night. Tamsin had been absolute in her intentions to tell Cornelius off at the Lord's ball, but then Georgiana had heard he proposed to her. At the time, she had no idea why Tamsin had changed her mind and agreed to marry Cornelius, and when rumors spread that Haven had kidnapped her, Georgiana thought that maybe they were running away together. But now…

She hadn't spoken with Tamsin since that night; Lavinia made sure of that, but what if Haven had figured out what Cornelius was really up to and warned Tamsin? What if they were going to the dam to warn them?

But Haven had died and Tamsin had gone back to the Cities and Cornelius was one step away from winning. If her father had been involved in that…Georgiana shook her head, forcing the thoughts away.

Lord Regoran sat down across from Mr. Graysan. "I didn't realize Saveen's treachery went so deep."

"They made threats on my daughter's life. I couldn't refuse him."

Georgiana's nostrils flared, angry at herself for thinking her father had anything but the best intentions.

"I'm sorry you've been put through that," Lord Regoran said, his eyes misting over slightly and Georgiana remembered his own daughter had left to go to the Cities. "Have you told your contact all of this?"

Mr. Graysan sighed. "He was the one that told me."

Everyone's foreheads knitted together. It didn't make sense…

"My contact, alive and on his way to the Cities right now…" he lifted his eyes to the ceiling as if asking some invisible deity for forgiveness, "…is Eleazar Urbane."

Georgiana waited outside of the Archive building as the meeting dispersed. People trickled out in twos and threes, taking different routes so as not to draw any attention though the only people awake at this hour were the guards on the wall. She thought she had missed her father when ten minutes passed after the last people had left and no one else came out. Even Aden and the other man standing guard had wandered off.

She took a peak back inside, tip-toeing in the dimly lit room. It appeared to be deserted. But she had been so careful and took note of everyone as they left. How had he disappeared? She sighed and rubbed her hands together. It would do no good to be seen lurking around here so she decided to go home and stay up as long as she had to.

She wished the walk home was a little longer, for when she got to her door she still had no idea what she would say to him. She was hurt by his keeping secrets from her, but it was overshadowed by her guilt for not knowing anyways. She should have pried more, made him tell her what was going on. This burden should not have been given to him. She went inside and closed the door behind her, but kept the latch open.

"Georgiana?"

She jumped at the sound of her name. She turned around and saw her father coming out of his room.

"Gia, where have you been?"

She crossed the room to join him. "I was going to ask you the same, but I think I've heard enough tonight to put the pieces together." She wasn't keen to take a harsh stance with him, but sometimes she needed to be tough with him to make him see clearly. He got so wrapped up in things sometimes that he wasn't able to step back and gain perspective.

Her father looked pale, even in the shadows. He stood up from his chair, suddenly animated and gripped her shoulders. "You cannot be involved in this Gia! I cannot allow it!"

She wanted to take a step back, her father's intensity was unexpected, but was held firm. "I'm not," she said. "And neither should you be."

His grip relaxed and he hung his head. "I cannot abandon them now. I've made promises."

"Well unmake them!" She lowered her voice then. "This is dangerous. The longer you play both sides the greater the chance is you'll be found out. And I can't let that happen." She went back over to the door and threw the latch on. When she turned around again her father's hopeless expression melted the rest of her anger. She realized it wasn't hurt that drove her emotion, it was fear for her father.

She drifted over to the kitchen. "Here, sit down," she said gently. "I'll make us some tea."

He slid into a chair and they were both silent as she prepared the water and herbs, putting an extra sprig of lavender in the boiling water. She put two cups on the table, filled them up, and sat down across from him. She let the relaxing steam float through the air a minute before she asked, "How did you get involved with this in the first place?"

Her father stared into his cup, his long fingers interlacing together around it. "It was my own fault," he said. "I went to Lord Saveen after that poor Watcher was killed because I wanted to warn him."

"Warn him of what?"

"I was afraid after what happened the Ma'diin would come back to Empyria and try to take Tamsin." He let go of his cup and flexed his fingers as if he needed to prepare himself for what he was about to say. He looked up and a fleeting grin touched his lips, but not his eyes. "I didn't think all of my secrets would come out tonight." He tried to laugh, but neither one of them felt it.

Georgiana motioned for him to drink his tea. "Why did you think they would come for her?" she asked. "Did they think she was responsible for his death?"

"No, and the Watcher isn't dead, that—that's why I have to do this."

Haven wasn't dead? As much as she wanted to find out how, she had to keep her father on track or none of it would make sense. "Go back to why you thought the Ma'diin would come for her."

"I saw you two, that night when Tamsin was showing you her...abilities with fire. I knew then that the Watcher knew who she was and if he knew then the other Ma'diin must surely know and if they knew—."

"What do you mean, 'who she was?'" Georgiana asked, confused despite her attempt to keep his story coherent.

"Tamsin is the daughter of Lord Urbane and," he said slowly, "Irin of the Ma'diin."

Georgiana's mouth fell open in spite of herself. "D—did Tamsin...?"

"Yes, well at the end, before they left she knew. And the Ma'diin knew. And I was afraid they would try to take her back to the marsh lands like they tried before."

"They tried to take her before?"

"When she was a baby. They lived here, in Empyria." He took a sip of his tea. "Do you remember when I told you about the massacre?"

Georgiana sifted through her memories, back to the night she and Tamsin were sitting right here and her father had told them about Lord Urbane's Ma'diin lover that came back with them from the expedition, the one that died. "The woman that came back, she wasn't just Lord Urbane's lover, was she? She was Irin."

"Yes. I also didn't tell you that I was there. I saw—I saw her body at the Saveen compound when I took you there to find the healer." He dipped his head and looked into his teacup, tormented, as if he could see the memories of that night reflected in the dark brown liquid. "We could hear the Ma'diin shouting, they were coming for the child, Irin's child."

He sighed deeply and Georgiana reached across the table and took his hand. "You were afraid they would come back again," she said softly.

He nodded. "I was only trying to protect her. But it's my fault. All of this is my fault."

Georgiana squeezed his hand, making him look at her. "This is not your fault. You did what you thought was right. No one can blame you for that."

"But I do," he countered sternly. "I tried to warn Lord Saveen, but then he started asking questions about the Watchers and the Ma'diin and I didn't know that he had already made plans to get Tamsin out of the city…." He continued, explaining how they kept sucking him deeper into their circle until finally showing him where they were keeping Haven alive. Where they were torturing him. Her father told them that he wanted no more part of it, but they threatened him.

"Did they hurt you?" Georgiana asked. "You told me you hurt your wrist because you fell." Several weeks ago he had come home cradling his arm and she had to put a splint on it because it was so bad.

"No, that um, was from the Watcher." He held up his hands to explain when Georgiana raised her eyebrow. "I helped him, brought him food and things when I could, but he got…confused sometimes. I do not blame the poor fellow."

Georgiana shook her head. "It's too dangerous to be a part of this. You can't play both sides anymore. Promise me you'll have nothing more to do with them."

"Gia…"

Georgiana knew exactly why he thought he needed to do this. As atonement. He had helped the wrong side and he believed he needed to make up for that.

"Promise me," she repeated. "You've paid your debt, Dad. Let your contact know that they can deal with someone else from now on." She couldn't help the emotion that bubbled to the surface as she spoke. She would not lose her father in a war that was not his to fight.

"Ok, Gia, ok." He grasped her hands firmly in his. "I'll promise to be done with it, if you promise never to get involved in it."

Georgiana smiled and happy tears filled her eyes. "Done."

Chapter Four

Emilia sat next to Sherene in the wheelhouse that was rocking gently side to side. Sherene had not spoken a word to her since Lord Urbane showed her the truth of who she was, not that they had spoken much before, but Emilia found it astounding how Sherene seemed to care so little that her lord was back from the dead and more that Emilia was here and Tamsin was back in Empyria somewhere. Lord Urbane had been a little more sympathetic, though the fear in his eyes had been constant for the last two days and he was not ready to talk about what was going to happen once they reached the Cities, which they would be arriving to today.

Lavinia had been dozing off for the last half hour or so in the seat across from them, her head lolling slightly from side to side with the movement of the wheelhouse. Emilia watched her for a few minutes, then turned to Sherene.

"You can't ignore me forever," she whispered. Even a whisper felt good. She had endured most of the trip in silence to keep her disguise intact.

"I can ignore you for as long as I wish," Sherene said stubbornly, still not looking at her.

"Once we get to Jalsai—."

"Once we get to Jalsai you will be expelled from this wheelhouse and from there you may go where you choose. I would suggest Ireczburg…"

"Tamsin assured me I could stay with the Urbanes. I sure as seven hells won't go to Ireczburg," she spat the name of the icy northern city with disdain.

Sherene snapped her head around at Emilia's profanity. "Watch your tongue miss. Your britches aren't too big where I can't throw you out right here."

The stout older woman probably could too, Emilia thought, so she held her tongue…but just for a moment. Then she whispered, "Lord Urbane will let me stay. Plus, how long do you think you could keep up the ruse that Tamsin is in fact here and not in Empyria without me?"

"Foolish girl!" Sherene hissed. "We don't know where Tamsin is!"

Emilia wrinkled her brow. "But I thought she and Cornelius were going to get married and—."

"Tamsin would never marry that selfish oaf. She was in love with the Watcher!" Sherene pressed her hands together and began kneading her knuckles anxiously.

"I don't understand. The Watcher was killed wasn't he?"

"No, he wasn't! And before we left Tamsin found out he was taken somewhere else, somewhere in the wilds. I know in my heart that that silly girl fooled us all to go after him. But Lord Urbane disagrees with me. He thinks she wouldn't after her experience with the sandstorm."

Emilia shut her mouth. She knew Sherene was right. She had not thought much about why Tamsin had wanted her to take her place, but now she knew it was the only way that Tamsin could have left. Lord Urbane would have never let her stay otherwise.

The wheelhouse jarred to the left, nearly throwing Emilia in Sherene's lap. Sherene gave her an accusing look and then mumbled under her breath about the driver hitting every rock and hole within a hundred yards. Emilia smoothed her skirt and looked up—right into Lavinia's wide-open eyes.

Lavinia's nostrils flared and her eyes glistened on the verge of tears, though her lips were pressed into a thin line. Her arms were straight as she gripped the edge of her seat and Emilia knew she had heard every word.

"You will tell me where my daughter is," Lavinia slowly snarled, "or so help me even the gods of old won't save you."

Emilia was more than ready to be out of the wheelhouse when at last it came to their final stop and she reached for the door, but Lavinia was faster and held it shut. After two hours of enduring Lavinia's accusations and Sherene's consoling babbling, Emilia was not in the mood for any more lectures.

"My lady?" one of the coachmen asked from outside.

"One moment," Lavinia barked back. Her feral eyes turned back to Emilia. "Put your veil back down. You are to continue to pretend until I tell you otherwise. Understood?"

Emilia covered her face once again and Lavinia released the door to the coachman. Emilia followed the two women out of the wheelhouse, her eyes searching for Lord Urbane among the coachmen and footmen scurrying around unloading trunks and taking the horses to the stable, but she did not see him. The walkway leading up to the massive oak front door consisted of white and grey pebbles that crunched when she walked. Standing just outside was a line of servants, footmen, and maids waiting for them. One man stepped forward. He was an older gentleman, with dark brown hair cut close to his head, bushy eyebrows, and a warm smile. He bowed and kissed Lavinia's hand.

"My Lady," he beamed. "You are a welcome sight for a heavy heart. When we heard of what befell our Lord we were heartbroken, but I must admit I am glad that you have returned to us in this terrible time."

Sherene and Emilia exchanged a glance. They had not told Lavinia yet about Lord Urbane.

"Mr. Brandstone," Lavinia addressed him, a friendly smile planted on her face, "it is good to see you again. I hope it was not too difficult to reopen the house?"

"No, my Lady. And all but two of the household staff have come back. And Lady Tamsin—" he started, but Lavinia cut him off.

"Is still in mourning and shall not be disturbed."

Mr. Brandstone nodded slowly and then motioned to the nearest footman and the door was opened.

As he led them inside, Emilia's jaw dropped. From the outside, the house was large, but plain-looking, only three stories tall and all the windows were covered with glass panes. But inside, the entryway opened up to two grand staircases, covered in burgundy rugs, on either side of the hall and a row of chandeliers hung from the high ceiling, glittering with crystal jewels. Marble pedestals flanked more doorways where Emilia could see rooms full of ornate chairs, plush couches, shelves brimming with books and golden trinkets, large paintings over fire places set right into the walls, and tables lined with silver platters and porcelain teacups.

There were two glass doors at the end of the hall and as Emilia got closer, she could see they led outside to a stone patio. But beyond the patio was the most beautiful garden she had ever seen.

"All of the rooms have been freshened," Mr. Brandstone was saying, "and the pantries have been stocked. I made it quite clear to the staff that it should be as if you never left at all."

"Thank you, Mr. Brandstone. I have sorely missed your appetite for order," Lavinia said. "Speaking of appetite, please have our lunches sent to our rooms, but dinner should be served in the formal dining room."

"Of course, my Lady. We can go over the estate's affairs when you have rested from your journey."

Lavinia nodded in thanks then went over to Emilia. "Sherene will take you to Tamsin's rooms," she whispered. "Stay there until I come for you." Then she walked away with Mr. Brandstone.

Sherene led her up to the second story, where the family's living quarters were. Tamsin's rooms were spacious and overlooked the front driveway. Heavy drapes outlined the windows and there was a large, four-poster bed on the opposite wall of the fireplace. The ceiling looked hand-painted with patterns of curving vines and blue and purple flowers. The shelves and wardrobes were bare, but the staff would be bringing in the trunks of Tamsin's things soon.

She flopped down on the bed, sighing as she sank into the soft cushions. It was much preferred to sleeping on bedrolls on the ground.

"Don't get too comfy miss," Sherene said, her hands crossed over her chest. "I'm sure Lavinia will find you *proper* accommodations quite soon."

Emilia propped herself up on her elbows. "What, upstairs with you and the other servants?"

Sherene's eyes flashed. "You will mind your tongue while you are in this house," she snapped back. Then she took a deep breath to calm herself. "If you choose to behave like a child, then you will be treated like one. But may I remind you that we have larger problems other than your living arrangements."

"If you would have told her from the beginning that Lord Urbane was still alive, then it wouldn't be a problem," Emilia retorted. "I only found out a few days ago so don't put that on me."

"And we only found out you were not Tamsin a few days ago. Don't bandy blame with me child, you will not win."

"Now who's acting like a child?"

The two women stared at each other a long time, each waiting to see whose resolve would waiver first. Finally, Sherene uncrossed her arms and put her hands on her wide hips. "You are as stubborn as your mother."

"No, I'm stubborn like my father," Emilia said, sitting up fully.

Sherene furrowed her brow. "Lord Regoran is a kind man. You did not get your poor qualities from him."

Emilia let out a laugh. She was so frustrated with the whole situation that she didn't care who knew her secret now. Her *real* secret. Coming to the Cities was supposed to be liberating for her, not another cage.

"You're right," she told Sherene. "None of my traits came from Lord Regoran. They came from Lord Urbane."

Sherene's irritation transformed to bewilderment. "What did you say?"

Emilia knew she should take no pleasure in this, but she couldn't deny the satisfaction she got from the look on Sherene's face as she told her the same story she told Tamsin on her last night in Empyria. She explained her mother's affair with Lord Urbane, how her aunt had raised her after she was born, and how five years later Lord Regoran found out and had taken both her and Lady Regoran to Empyria, where no one would question Emilia's heritage. When the news came to Empyria that Lord Urbane would be returning there, Emilia overheard her parents fighting about it and confronted her mother, who confessed everything.

Sherene sank down into the nearest chair after she had finished the telling, her hand over her mouth.

"You've been with the Urbanes a long time," Emilia said. "You know it's true."

Sherene stared at the open space in front of her. "I worked for Lord Urbane's mother, before he took me on. He was young back then, impulsive. His father decided to send him to Empyria in hopes he would get his fill of adventure. And it seemed he did. He came back a different man."

"One that wanted nothing to do with me," Emilia said.

Whatever this room had been used for before had long since vanished. When he had the strength to, he could lift his head up and see the black scorch marks scarring the walls. But more often he barely had the strength to open his eyes. When he did, he could see the ground. And it was covered with bones.

Curved ribs curled around a spine like a cage. Claws scattered about like thorns on the ground. Skulls with long snouts and teeth like saws with horns curled back over the holes where ears had been. Sometimes when he drifted towards unconsciousness, he could almost see the smoke rolling slowly out of its mouth. The black holes that filled the empty eye sockets stared at him. His imagination and fear and past experiences worked against him here, giving the inanimate bones a new imminence that terrified him. Even dead, they still had power over him, maybe even more so now. Time was a fragile conception, but sometimes hour after hour would pass and his only companions would be the bones.

It was only a strategy by the white-haired man, his elusive rational side would argue. Prolonged solitude forces the mind to use its imagination. And he had enough memories yet intact of the amon'jii to adequately animate the lifeless skeletons.

"How long do you think you can resist? You're only prolonging the inevitable."

His stomach trembled uncontrollably as his mind imagined tiny tendrils of smoke snaking through its teeth. He struggled to keep his rationale intact, but it was a losing battle. "Long enough."

"For what? What do you think is going to change?"

For a while, Haven had thought that they would come for him. His brothers would not abandon him. She would not have abandoned him. Every day he endured, he fought, and he hoped that someone would come. But time passed and no one came. Only the white-haired man came to see him now, breaking up the hours of his isolation.

The white-haired man. Mr. Monstran. That's who was talking now, not the amon'jii remains, he repeated to himself, grunting with the effort of holding onto his sanity.

"Only you can change, Haven," Mr. Monstran said. "Changing, adapting, that is how we survive. If we don't adapt, we don't survive."

"Then let me go," he said.

"I can't do that Haven. Not until you've accepted the truth."

He had considered it: just playing along with his game. But it went against everything he believed in. His very nature balked at the idea and would not let him go that easy. It would feel too much like giving up. And still there was a thorn of hope.

"You think someone will come for you yet? That is a foolish waste of time."

This man's words were poison. He knew it, but he was forced to listen to it. There was nowhere for him to go.

"Those people you think are your brethren; they are not your friends, Haven. They have left you behind."

Hanging, suspended five feet off the ground by his hands and feet made it difficult to focus on anything, to believe that something would change, that someone would come. Every breath, every thought was an effort. The pain contaminated everything, cast everything in a red haze.

The smoke drifted across the mouth, giving the illusion that it was smiling, its white teeth gleaming as if to boast its victory of being dead, of no longer living in the confines of an inferior body.

Red haze. White teeth. Blackness everywhere.

He closed his eyes. Just keep breathing...

Chapter Five

Tamsin doused her face with water, trembling not from the chill of it, but from the nightmare she had woken up from. She kneeled on the edge of the mud flat, several over from where they had made camp earlier that night. She didn't want Samih to see her this way. She stared at her reflection as tiny drops fell from the tip of her nose and chin back in the water and recalled several weeks ago when she had been doing the same thing in the bathing level in the compound the day of her father's funeral. The same sick feeling drifted over her now, but there was another, something close that wanted to overwhelm her. A feeling of such hopelessness that she wanted to curl up on the flat and never move again. But the longer she stared, the less insistent the sensation became and the shadows of the nightmare began to fade.

She looked up, wiping away the excess water from her eyes, and saw a pillar of smoke rising into the sky some ways off in the distance. She squinted, trying to make out if that was in fact what it was, but the smoke was the same color as the overcast sky. The only distinguishing thing was its slow motion upwards. She stood up and walked back over to where Samih was gathering their things. He didn't even glance at her when she returned; he knew what she had been doing. He had woken up to her screams.

She pushed down her embarrassment and asked him if he had seen the smoke.

His head jerked up abruptly, this time looking at her fully. "Where?"

She pointed over to where she had seen it. His hood was down and she could see the muscles in his jaw tense when he located it. He tossed the bundle he had been holding into his canoe and told her to hurry. They had their camp taken down and were off towards the smoke in minutes, but it still took them some time to get there with the winding waterways around the reed patches. More columns of smoke appeared the closer they got and when they made it around the last bend, Tamsin got her first look at a Ma'diin village. Or what was left of it.

There were piles of blackened debris everywhere and only a few skeletons remained of the huts. There was no one in sight.

Samih threw his hood back; safe from the sun by the overcast sky, and his anxious golden eyes darted back and forth quickly, taking in the scope of what was in front of them. He was visibly shaken. He edged the canoe on the nearest flat and started running from one flat to the other, scouring the ground and looking around as if he had lost his bearings. She couldn't help but compare him to Haven, and she immediately regretted it. Haven was always calm and strong, even near death, but Samih was just a kid.

"Samih, what happened here?" she called out to him as she carefully stepped through the ashes and mud after him.

His eyes were still wide. "I've never seen this kind of destruction before. Maybe it was just a fire," but even as he said it he knelt down and his fingers brushed a deep impression in the dirt. It was wider than both her hands put together and had four long lines sticking out of it on one side. "The amon'jii," he said. "I've never seen one take an entire village before."

"Is there any chance that they could've escaped?" she asked, horrified even though she had never seen one of the creatures personally. The stories Haven told her about them and the destruction around them was enough to send shivers up her spine.

He looked up and around slowly and then nodded. "If they noticed the water level dropping they would have fled deeper into the marshes."

She could see where the water level had dropped on the surrounding reeds that circled the burned village like a fence. There was a thick, dark circle that ran along the bottom of the reeds where the water had once been. Now the water was barely ankle deep.

"This is what your peoples' dam has done," he said, his chest heaving with emotion.

She closed her eyes against the swampy wasteland. She wanted him to see that she felt the same way he did, that she shared the same hurt and anger, but it was starkly clear that he still viewed her as a northerner. She realized for the first time that their alliance was only temporary. This was his home, not hers, and she could see he was not comfortable having her here.

"Tamsin." Samih's tone instantly switched from anger to a warning.

Tamsin snapped her eyes open and looked in the direction Samih was looking. Standing next to a smoldering pile that was once a hut was a man, his ruddy skin silhouetted by the rising smoke. His head was completely bald and he wore only loose fitting pants that ended in frayed tatters just below his knees, but he had a strap around his shoulder that held a water skin and a curved knife. He held a spear in his hand. His expression was made of stone save for the questioning look in his eyes as he tried to figure out the presence of these two in this wasteland. "It is not often we catch one of the Lumierii unawares," the bald man said.

"Or in the daylight," another Ma'diin stepped through the smoke. He wore a vest similar to the ones the male servants had worn in Empyria. He had a thick wad of braids tied back from his face.

"Here to see the aftermath of your neglect?" The bald man said, the emotion behind his accusation contrasting strangely with his stony face.

Samih flipped his hood back up. "We've just returned from the north," he said, displaying an extraordinary amount of self-control for what Tamsin thought was a very brazen introduction on the two men's part.

The man with the braids took a few steps forward, his eyes widening in recognition. "You know Ysallahkazsera?"

"Yes, she was once my Kazsera. I went to the north with her. Did she make it back?"

"Yes, but she was wounded. Then the water started dropping and the amon'jii attacks started increasing until…" He didn't need to finish.

"Are there more survivors?" Tamsin could almost hear Samih's heartbeat as he waited for the answer.

"Yes, we started getting refugees about a week ago. We came back to look for anyone who may have been left behind. And see if anything could be salvaged."

"There's nothing left," Samih shook his head. "Where have the rest gone?"

"Come. We will take you to them." The braided-haired man paused then, looking uncertainly at Tamsin.

"I'm responsible for her," Samih said, reading his hesitation. "She goes with me. And she can't go back now. The way to the north is closed."

Neither of them were going to challenge him. "Well, I'd rather have one of the Lumierii watching my back than not," the braided-haired man said.

"We had one, another Watcher," the bald man said, "but we haven't seen him since the attack."

The statement hung in the air like a fly trapped in a spider's web until the bald man finally shook his head and started walking back. Samih and the braided-haired man grabbed their canoe and carried it to where they had docked theirs not too far away. Samih and the braided haired man talked in hushed tones and too quickly for Tamsin to catch all of what was said, but she thought he asked about the missing Watcher. Someone named Sakiim. She didn't have to hear everything to know that a missing Watcher, especially with active amon'jii in the area, was not a good sign.

Samih had already warned her that he couldn't guarantee what would happen once the Kazserii got involved, but he also told her he wouldn't let anything bad happen to her. Bad things had already happened, she had told him, and she wouldn't hold him responsible for what might happen. She knew she was responsible for her own fate from the moment she decided to leave Empyria. It was good to have someone she could trust, though, even if he didn't trust her back. If Samih, one who had been with her for the last couple weeks, still viewed her as a northerner, then how could the others think differently? Sure she was a woman and she knew the dominant status they held in Ma'diin society, but she was still an outsider and she didn't know how the Ma'diin dealt with outsiders.

She allowed herself a few moments to breathe and take in the change in scenery, but she knew the hardest part was still ahead of her. The water was not very deep, for tall, slender grass still poked through the glassy surface and though the water was too dark for her to see clearly to the bottom she could not imagine the long grass could be much taller than her below the surface. As it was, it rose out of the water a good two or three feet in some places, making a gently waving curtain as they bent to the breeze. They parted as Samih guided their canoe through them, reminding Tamsin of the blue-vested servants in Empyria who would hold back the gauzy white curtains to allow her into the makeshift rooms they would create.

But the marshes were not a civilized place, at least not compared to her past experiences. The farther they went, the deeper the water became and the swampy mess of grass and weeds gave way to bamboo-like reeds that stretched up to the sky in thick clusters, some twice as tall as the men pushing the canoes. Others were thin and wispy with feathery white tassels at the top. There seemed to be a constant breeze that rustled the tops of these reeds and nearly bent them completely over so the tops sent ripples in the water. Tortoises jumped off of the muddy reed beds as they passed and a flock of rooks took flight with the thunderous surprise of a spooked turkey. Tiny bugs skittered across the water leaving ribbon-like trails in their wake. The river twisted around the reed beds and often broke off into narrower waterways that were dark under the canopy of the reaching reeds.

They passed a small mud dune, naturally patched together it seemed from plant roots that decided they had enough of the water. A long-legged white bird stood perched atop it, watching them closely as they went by, occasionally bending its long neck to pick at something on the ground. It picked its feet up carefully, as if it was sneaking across trying not to make a sound.

"The white crane is a good sign," Samih commented. "It means there are many fish nearby."

A question came to Tamsin then. "What did you do before you became a Watcher, Samih?"

"I was a fisher," he said openly, proudly even.

Tamsin was used to Samih's openness now, after having travelled with him for several weeks, but it had been hard earned. Neither knew anything about the other in their first few days together and Tamsin's nightmares made conversation awkward at best sometimes. But now, she couldn't imagine the young Watcher anything but talkative. Even if he did lash out in anger sometimes. It was much different than Haven.

"I was part of Ysallah's tribe," he continued. "She has been very kind to me since. Many Kazserii are not so gracious. She even invited me for Pa'shiia last season. I used to catch much of the fish for Pa'shiia."

"Did you go?" Tamsin asked, though she didn't know what Pa'shiia was.

"No," Samih shook his head. "It was very kind of her, but I was not ready."

She could sense it was a difficult struggle for him yet. "You are a very good fisher Samih," she said, and it was true. Someone who was mediocre at fishing could not have taught a Lord's daughter, one who had no survival skills, how to catch, clean, and prepare her own fish.

Then she remembered something she had seen back in the *anasii hada*. "Samih, can I ask you something?"

He nodded.

"When you became a Watcher, were you…marked?"

Samih was sitting in front of her so she could not see his expression, but his head turned back slightly. "Marked? How do you mean?"

"I've seen Haven's scars, they're—they're all over him. And when we were in the *anasii hada* I saw that you didn't have any."

He stopped paddling and twisted around so he could see her. His n'qab was down for the sun was blocked by the cloud-covered sky and the look in his eyes made her regret her question. "I didn't do that so you could compare my scars to his. We've all been through our own battles."

"I'm sorry Samih," she said, hoping he heard the sincerity in her words. "I didn't mean to imply anything. I was just curious I guess."

He blew air out of his nose quickly. He went to turn back around, but then paused and when he faced her again his expression was more patient. "I've been a Watcher a little over a year," he said. "Haven's been doing this his whole life. And he has a...zealous side when it comes to the amon'jii," he added with a sly smile. "You're bound to acquire a few battle wounds if you hang around with him."

Though she knew he hadn't meant it, his words punched her right in the gut. Yes, she knew all too well the kind of wounds one received with Haven, though hers marked her heart and not her skin.

Her face must have betrayed her thoughts for Samih opened his mouth to say something, but then shut it quickly. He lowered his gaze. "I didn't mean that," he said softly.

"I know," Tamsin replied, though it still hurt. She closed her eyes after Samih turned around and continued paddling. She breathed in slowly through her nose, trying to ease the ache that swelled in her throat when she thought of him.

"Tamsin," Samih's voice floated from the front and she opened her eyes again, but Samih was still facing forward. "Why did you ask about my scars?"

"I guess I assumed all Watcher's had them. It's not every day you see glow—."

She was cut short as one of the Ma'diin in the canoe ahead of them shouted something. Tamsin peered around Samih and saw the man signaling. They turned onto one of the narrower streams and were suddenly submerged in shadows. Rare streaks of daylight managed to break through gaps in the reed canopy, illuminating bands of bugs hovering above them in the denser air. The stream curved lazily between two reed beds, beds that were so close Tamsin could reach out her arms and brush the hard stalks of the reeds.

The cover broke and daylight poured over them again. The stream merged into a wide lagoon that was strewn with mud flats, too many for Tamsin to count, but these were not laden with reeds. Instead, they were covered with large reed houses. Most of the houses looked to be about the size of her bedroom in Empyria, and round too, not made of the burlap-like material of the traveling buurdas the Watchers used, but large stalks of reeds tied and woven together. The roofs were slanted with holes in the centers for smoke to escape. The doors were made of fabric and as they made their way through the flats Tamsin saw that each was dyed a dark green color. These reed houses were called *muudhiifs* Samih told her.

There were a few Ma'diin out: some in canoes, others weaving reeds together and wetting them in the water at the edge of the flats, some layering giant leaves in smoking piles, and a few appeared to be constructing a new mud flat. She couldn't tell who the refugees from the other tribe were and who was not for everyone was working hard.

Until they spotted Samih. His posture stiffened in the canoe; he was instantly recognized as a Watcher and some of the glances cast his way were curious, but not kind. Some were openly alarmed and rushed into their muudhiifs almost like they were afraid that Samih would suddenly attack.

It was unfair, she knew, but Tamsin couldn't help feel a little relief. She had been anxious about this for a few days, about finally being in Ma'diin territory and what people's reactions were going to be towards her. But all the focus was on the Watcher suddenly in their midst.

Her relief was short lived, however, when their canoe ran up against the largest mud flat yet. Samih jumped out and pulled the edge up so Tamsin was able to step off right onto the flat. It was three times the size of the others and had wooden ladders laid horizontally on the edges like the spokes of a wheel connecting it to several other flats. The muudhiif itself was intimidating and Tamsin didn't need anyone to tell her that this was the Kazsera's. It resembled the others she had seen, but there was a second, smaller room built into the back and the green fabric she had seen in the doorways was draped over the roof and down the sides in wide strips that were tapered on the bottom. The green fabric also made up an entryway that was held up by two poles and formed a small tunnel into the hut.

The braided haired man disappeared into the tunnel while the rest of them waited outside. When he emerged, it was with a girl. She had a delicate build, with onyx hair and gentle features. Her tan clothing was loose and flowy and Tamsin blushed at the parts that were more translucent than others. The girl also wore long earrings that could have rivaled the best emeralds in Delmar. She was not what Tamsin had expected the Kazsera to look like.

When she spoke, the girl had a clear, birdsong voice. "Watcher Samih," she addressed him. "I am Poma of the Hazees'diin. Hazees is not here, but I will give her a message for you."

So not the Kazsera, Tamsin realized.

Samih replied, "These men," he indicated the two, "will discuss what they need with you, but we are not here to talk to Hazees."

At the word *we* Poma glanced at Tamsin and looked her up and down, though she hid whatever she was wondering about her well. Tamsin had not thought about her appearance much since leaving Empyria, but now she frowned thinking about the toll the journey had exacted. She hadn't exactly been in top form before leaving either.

"We were told Ysallahkazsera is here. We must speak with her," Samih continued and Tamsin was impressed with the authority behind his tone.

"Ysallah is in no condition to receive guests. I can——."

"No! We've come too far! We need to speak with her now!" Samih's youthful willfulness and weeks of hard travel betrayed him and he took a few steps forward.

Faster than Tamsin's eyes could follow, Poma suddenly had a knife pointed at Samih. He could have easily swatted it away with one of his own, but instead he froze, just as the other two were about to draw their own weapons. Poma's face, gentle before, was now focused on Samih with the intensity of a bird of prey.

Samih made a frustrated sound, but took a step back. He bowed his head, but he wasn't about to give up. "Why don't you let Ysallah decide?"

Poma considered and then finally put the knife down. "Stay here Watcher." Then she disappeared into the muudhiif.

Tamsin thought it was awfully brave of Poma to stand up to a Watcher, but she agreed with Samih. They had come too far to be made to wait now. But then her mind raced back to those early days, when Ysallah had wanted to take her back to the marsh lands. Back to her mother's people against her will and before she had any knowledge of Irin. Was she walking right into Ysallah's hands? Would Ysallah even help them get Haven back?

"Tamsin, are you alright?"

She heard Samih's voice, but he sounded farther away than she knew he was and she couldn't tell if the edges of her vision were going black or if it was his cloak. "I just need to sit I think," she mumbled, though she was already sinking to the ground. Her hands felt numb as they dug into the mud. The world was reduced to a pinhole, but she felt Samih's hands on her arms holding her up. Her breaths quickened as it became harder to draw air in and she heard the words *slow, slow* and it sounded like Haven telling her to drink slow...

The thought of him sent a hailstorm of needles at her, setting her skin on fire and bringing her back from the edge. Her vision cleared suddenly and she saw several figures rushing at her. Samih was yelling and someone lifted her off the ground. She watched the green fabric darken the sky overhead and then she was inside the hut. Poma's emerald earrings glistened in front of her and she was handed a water skin to drink from.

Tamsin drank, but then heard a voice that she had not heard in months. Tamsin lowered the skin and saw a woman sitting across the muudhiif, a bandage across one eye and an arm in a sling. The arm stopped at the wrist and ended in another round bandage.

"Tamsin Urbane, what are you doing here?" Ysallah asked.

Chapter Six

Tamsin hadn't realized how exhausted she was until someone wrapped a blanket around her shoulders and put a warm bowl of soup in her hands. The soup was a mead color, with colorful beans and lentils and pieces of dark meat. She could only stare at the steaming liquid in amazement, her mouth watering at the smell, but too tired to lift the wooden spoon to her lips. Samih, on the other hand, was already on his second bowl.

"You do not like cavahst?" Poma asked.

Tamsin smiled gratefully. "It is not fish."

She heard Ysallah chuckle from across the muudhiif, but did not look up. She tried lifting a spoonful, but was still feeling groggy from her spell earlier and the warmth inside the muudhiif was making her eyelids and movements heavy.

"Your accent is quite good," Ysallah commented.

Tamsin finally got the spoon to her mouth. She savored the warm broth on her tongue a moment before she swallowed. "Thank you," she replied quietly. Then she ate another spoonful, then another, each easier than the last.

Ysallah was patient and waited until Tamsin could eat no more before starting their inevitable conversation, though Tamsin guessed she was less eager than Ysallah to begin. Ysallah looked like she had been through the seven hells and Tamsin made it a point not to look at her severed arm and missing hand. Lords only knew what she had been through to receive that.

"I expect that you being here means you know," Ysallah said.

"If you mean that I know who my real mother is, then yes," Tamsin replied.

"And your northern mother let you come?" A smile twitched at the corner of her mouth.

"No, but if she doesn't know I'm here by now she will soon." Her thoughts raced back across the desert and beyond the Ardent Mountains for a brief moment. She pushed down the rise of longing for home.

Ysallah's eyes were bright. No doubt she was thinking about the sh'pav'danya. "We thought Samih was dead. We never expected him to go back to the northerner's city, especially after what happened."

"Samih didn't come back to Empyria to honor the exchange," Tamsin said. "He doesn't know who I am. He rescued my father and brought him back to Empyria."

Ysallah's eyes widened and glanced over to Samih's sleeping form. As impatient as he had been to talk to Ysallah, his body would not be denied it's rest anymore. Ysallah's expression was more cautious when she turned back to Tamsin, who knew she was too practical to believe in things like luck. But Tamsin interrupted her before she could speak.

"Don't be angry with Samih. My father is a good man, and you know it wasn't his fault for what happened at the dam. If Samih hadn't come back I probably wouldn't be here right now."

"Alright. Then tell me why you are here."

Tamsin suppressed a shudder when she said his name aloud. "Haven." She put down the bowl, not trusting herself to keep it steady. She glanced wistfully at Samih; she had hoped he would've been awake for this part, but she could not deny him the rest that he had earned. She had practiced this moment many times and every time Samih had been there to reinforce her argument, to help the Kazserii see the justness of her request. Samih had warned her once not to let them know just how deep her affection for Haven went for the Ma'diin would immediately question her rationality.

Ysallah's expression was unreadable. "We thought Haven dead as well."

Tamsin took a quiet breath, tempering her emotions. "The Empyrians tried to kill him, but they did not succeed."

"I knew he would not let the northerners get the better of him, but it troubles me that he is not with you."

"He took your decree to protect me seriously, believe me. If he could be here now he would."

Ysallah's eyes narrowed and Tamsin realized she had to be even more careful. Admitting she knew of Ysallah's request of Haven revealed that she and Haven talked. If Ysallah suspected the relationship was more than ward and protector, she would start to ask questions.

Tamsin began again, mindful of her words. "Haven saved my life on more than one occasion. Though it was as you instructed him to do if the need arose, I am indebted to him."

"Watchers are appointed guardians by the gods. If they demanded debt on every life they saved we would all be their slaves."

Tamsin didn't know if the Ma'diin honored life debts. Delmarians surely didn't, and it was an unstable system even under the Ottarkin regime before the Lords Council. But Tamsin was playing all of her cards on the hope that Ysallah knew none of this.

"I gathered as much. Even my gratitude seemed to make him…uncomfortable." Which wasn't a lie, Tamsin thought. "But in Delmar we have what is called a life debt." She watched Ysallah, trying to read her expression.

Ysallah seemed to be buying it. "I have heard of this concept. It is not something the Ma'diin are fond of. It blurs lines between tribes."

"I am half Delmarian," Tamsin said, "and under their laws I am held to honor that life debt to Haven."

She could see Ysallah trying to puzzle it out. "You say Haven is alive, but he is not with you and he is not here. How do you expect to honor your life debt?"

Tamsin explained how Haven was captured, his release to Mr. Monstran, and Samih's return, without mentioning herself involved in any of the scenarios. She told Ysallah that Cornelius had orchestrated the attack at the dam and that they believed Mr. Monstran had taken Haven to the Ravine of Bones. She suspected Mr. Monstran had given Cornelius something in exchange for Haven, though she didn't know what his interest in him was.

Ysallah's nostrils flared at the mention of the Ravine. "They took him to the Alamorgrian ruins? I didn't think there were any left alive." She straightened herself, and Tamsin saw genuine concern tightening the corners of her mouth.

"I know the debt is mine," Tamsin said. "But I came here to ask for your help. If what Samih tells me about this place is true, I need to get him out of there."

Ysallah nodded, but her eyes were distant. "I remember my mother telling me stories of the Alamorgrians. They would come down to the marshes like vultures—they were blood stealers."

She elaborated at Tamsin's confused look. "Blood stealers—they would scavenge the marshes for Watchers that had been killed and collect their blood. They would use it to induce visions for their demonic rituals. They were a disgusting race—that is until the amon'jii invaded their territory and wiped them out."

Tamsin pulled the blanket tighter around the chill that crawled over her skin. The amon'jii had wiped out an entire race. Well, almost all of them.

"The Ravine is controlled by the amon'jii now," Ysallah said. "I respect the Watchers and recognize their sacrifice…"

Something stirred out of the corner of her eye and Tamsin saw Samih lift himself up and dust off his cloak.

"But you won't risk one of your own for one of ours," he finished, his eyes a dangerous shade of gold. "What if it was me? I used to be of the Ysallah'diin. If it were me in the Ravine would you help?"

The air in the muudhiif was suddenly crackling with tension. But Ysallah was too smart to fall for his trap.

"Will you help your people now, Samih? The amon'jii are pressing our borders back every night. *Your* sha'diin are dying. I ask you what you are asking me: are the lives of many less important than the life of one?"

The muscles in Samih's jawline were so tight he could barely get the next words out. "I know what my duty is. I've spent the last three months in the desert waste because *you* asked me to! And now when we need your help, you have none to give?"

Ysallah was on her feet faster than Tamsin thought she was capable of. She held out the stump of her arm, her face strained. "I have given. I have sacrificed!" she spat. She panted heavily for a few breaths, re-gaining her composure. "You should leave, Watcher Samih. Hazees only tolerates your presence because of me. Do not test her hospitality. Or mine."

Samih seethed, but the sight of Ysallah's bandaged arm stopped anything else he was going to say to her. He picked up his things and motioned to Tamsin to follow him.

"She stays with me," Ysallah said.

Samih whirled and laced his fingers over his sword hilt, but Tamsin jumped up and put a hand on his elbow.

"It's okay, Samih," Tamsin said gently, trying to bring the Watcher back to himself. She had spent weeks with Samih, had shared his frustrations, and could very much relate to the enmity building within him, but she had also witnessed the young adolescent display great amounts of self-discipline and reason. "We will discuss this later. Don't go far. I'll find you," she said, pressing his elbow lightly.

He jerked his arm away and stormed out of the muudhiif. He would sulk for a little while, but Tamsin believed he got her message. This wasn't over. They would do this with or without Ysallah.

Ysallah groaned and hobbled back over to her bed of cushions. Tamsin hadn't noticed Poma leave, but she must have been waiting right outside for she appeared at her side before the door flap had even settled from Samih's exit.

"You realize I will not let you follow through with it," Ysallah said.

"You can't stop me."

"I claimed you in the sh'pav'danya and if you honor your northern side you must honor your Ma'diin side. You belong to the Ysallah'diin."

Tamsin held up both her palms, her heart beating fast. "No claim was made. I belong to no one."

All movement in the muudhiif ceased and it seemed the very air held them fast. Tamsin wished now that Samih was still here for the look in Ysallah's eyes was enough to make her hands shake. She lowered them back into her lap before it became noticeable. But Ysallah was not satisfied and motioned for Poma to check. Poma quickly came over and turned both Tamsin's hands in her own. Then she looked back at Ysallah and shook her head.

Tamsin took what momentum she had, for she feared one signal from Ysallah and Poma would strike her dead. She had witnessed her loyalty to her Kazsera before and had no wish to witness it up close. "We've talked a lot about honor tonight. I hope you are still the Kazsera I met in Empyria. She was formidable, but she was also just."

The corner of Ysallah's mouth twitched. "I saw your blood with my own eyes. How——." Then her eyes widened. "It was Haven, wasn't it?"

But Tamsin didn't need to answer. Ysallah knew the truth now.

Ysallah tightened her fist and pressed it into her forehead. "Vas'akru, that fool."

"He was just trying to protect me. From *you*," Tamsin said, irked by Ysallah's cursing. On the slim chance that she ever did make it to the marsh lands, Haven hadn't wanted her to be slave to Ysallah.

Ysallah looked at her again and laughed causing both women to jump, then she looked up at the ceiling of the muudhiif. "The one time he should not have protected you," she said, speaking into the air above.

She closed her eyes and when she opened them again she looked at Poma. "You will speak nothing about what you heard tonight to anyone."

Instead of complying, Poma dropped to her knees and flicked her fingers over her hand. "I am afraid I have already broken that," she said, bowing her head. "Hazeeskazsera asked me who she was and I told her."

But Ysallah was not angry. She seemed resigned. "News of her return will spread quickly then. I will not be able to protect you, Tamsin."

Something was off. "Protect me from what?" Tamsin imagined that being bound to Ysallah's tribe was the worst case scenario, but what if there was something else even worse?

Poma sunk even lower under a weight of understanding. "I am truly sorry Kazsera."

Ysallah nodded, the only forgiveness Poma was going to get. "There are more claims on your life than you know," Ysallah said to Tamsin.

Tamsin was about to ask who else could possibly try to claim her when Hazees burst into the muudhiif. She was a tall woman with dark hair that was pulled back tightly from her face and hung down in three long braids. Her eyes were equally striking, with the severity and focus of a feline. "It's true," she breathed. "The resemblance is…" Then she shook her head. "Poma, take her. She is in your charge now. See her needs are met. I need to speak with Ysallah alone."

Instantly, Poma was on her feet and pulling Tamsin along with her. Tamsin barely had time to glance back at Ysallah before she was ushered around the tower that was Hazees. Both women's expressions indicated the following conversation was not going to be pleasant.

Chapter Seven

I can teach you how to use it, so you will not be held back by it. You don't have to be a slave to it anymore. Pain doesn't have to be a weakness.

"I do not fear pain."

And you shouldn't. But you fear being weak. And that is just as crippling. Once you get past the fear, you realize that pain is an inherent part of who we are. Suffering is human nature.

"But you can't control what causes the pain."

Sure you can. It's up to you what does and doesn't cause you pain because pain is an entity unique to every person. It's etched into your soul like those scars are a part of your body.

He gritted his teeth. "I don't think you would say that if you were in my position."

But I am, Haven. I feel everything you feel. I think everything you do. The only difference between you and I is that I have learned how to exist beyond our physical limitations. Let me help you.

Sweat dripped onto the floor from his forehead. "Why? Why are you doing this?"

Because you could be so much more than you are Haven. You have so much potential. Wouldn't you rather be unburdened from all the troubles of the past? Don't you dream of being free?

He tried to ignore the burn that was slowly creeping down his arms and legs. He tried to picture her face: her big brown eyes, the pout of her bottom lip when she was concentrating, the warmth in her cheeks when she looked at him. 'Stay with me,' he thought, trembling with the effort of keeping her image there.

You're thinking of her now, aren't you?

His eyes snapped open. He looked around, but he was alone. The white-haired man was not here. "Get out of my head."

Yes, you think you can keep her safely locked away, hidden from me, something to hang onto, far away from this place.

His words pervaded his mind like a snake, coiling around his thoughts tighter and tighter until her image faded away completely. He yelled out and clenched his fists.

You have no secrets that you can hide from me Haven.

The ropes tightened. The burning spread. She was the only thing strong enough to keep him tethered to reality and as much as he needed to remember her he knew that he could not think of her any more. He had to keep her secret as far from the darkness of this place as he could, even at the expense of his life.

The amon'jii and the Watchers are intrinsically linked, locked in a predatory circle made of blood and fire. I wonder, if we opened one up, what would we find? Is there a firestone in that chest? Something more human? Something less? That's what you fear, isn't it? That beneath that tough, loyal exterior is the heart of a monster. That what your people whisper is true. Well, I'm going to ease your fear Haven, because fear has no place in your life now. Realize what you are. Realize the truth and accept and the fear will go away. It will vanish, just like that. Wouldn't you like that?

He felt the pain taking over again. He let it. He had to let his mind go. And as terrified as he was to do that, he knew it was the only way to keep her safe. Perhaps this was the last choice he could make. Every ounce of blood within him, every fiber of instinct in his being screamed, begged him not to, but he could already feel himself disappearing. Would he be able to find his way back?

It won't matter by then, a voice whispered in his head.

Tamsin awoke to the sounds of screaming, but she could not recall the nightmare she had nor was she panting out of breath. And these screams were not sounds of fear, but of agony. The screaming wasn't hers, she realized slowly. She rolled over, her muscles stiff from lack of movement all night, and onto her feet. She stumbled out of the muudhiif as if the screams were a siren call she could not ignore. The bright morning sun momentarily blinded her, but it gave her the moment she needed to dispel the disorientation she felt upon waking up in a strange place. She was neither surrounded by hills of sand nor the damp rocky walls of the *anasii hada*, but wide streams of open water and irregular patches of tall grass and reeds and foxtails.

Another scream shattered the rest of her confusion, as if it rode along the sunbeams and cut through the air like prisms of glass. Her legs protested at the sudden movement as she forced them into motion towards the source of the screams, but the implied distress of the person making the sound compelled her forward. Someone close by was in pain.

She jogged across the mud flat and the little wooden bridge over to the next flat and repeated this until she came to the source. A few other people were gathered around the muudhiif, concern and even a little anger displayed across their expressions. Some glanced over at her, but two of the men seemed to be in a heated argument, her presence making little difference to them as they paused only when another scream pierced the muudhiif walls.

"What's going on?" Tamsin asked one of the silent ones, but before he could answer, the door flap was flung open and Samih stepped out, his hands and the front of his robes covered in mud and blood. She had never seen him truly angry before, but the expression on his face told her he was barely keeping himself in check.

The others took an involuntary step back at his sudden emergence and Samih's golden eyes focused on the two who were arguing. Though he was shorter, his black cloak and fiery gaze was enough to intimidate them.

"I will find better uses for your tongues on the end of my knife if you two don't keep quiet," he hissed. Then he disappeared back into the muudhiif.

Tamsin was about to follow him, when someone touched her elbow. It was Poma, the woman whose muudhiif she shared last night. She must have followed her. "Don't go in there," she said.

"Why not? What's going on?"

"A Watcher must have been attacked last night."

An amon'jii attack. What kind of damage could the amon'jii cause to produce such a gut-wrenching sound? She fought back the sick feeling that was rising and the urge to cover her ears. "How do you know it was a Watcher?"

She nodded towards the others and lowered her voice. "They would be in there helping Samih right now if it was anyone else."

"But Samih's not a healer," Tamsin said, her confusion and horror growing. "Why aren't they helping him?" She did not bother to lower her voice and few of the others shot her incredulous and offended looks.

Poma's grip on her elbow tightened. "They would—*we* would if we could," she said, "but Watcher's blood is nothing to mess around with. We will wait—."

But Tamsin had heard enough and shrugged out of her grip. She had seen blood before; she could handle it. She pushed past the others and into the muudhiif. Samih glanced up quickly and though he looked surprised he did not look unsurprised either and did not tell her to leave. He returned his attention to the figure lying on the ground. The hard edge she had seen only moments before melted from his face as the wounded man moaned. Samih removed a bloody cloth over the man's leg, revealing three deep gashes and white bone, and quickly replaced it with a fresh one. "Easy Sakiim, the healer will be here soon."

The injured Watcher, Sakiim, jerked his head into a nod, which seemed to be the only body part that wasn't covered in blood. He had been butchered.

Tamsin wanted to run. She had not been prepared for the carnage before her.

Then the man's glassy eyes found hers. They were bright blue.

She knelt down next to Samih, near Sakiim's head. His hand was trembling at his side so she took it and grasped it firmly.

"Sakiim, this is Tamsin," Samih said. "She looks like your sister, no?"

Sakiim nodded again and in a pained voice said, "Reyja got married while you were gone."

"Married? I didn't think she was serious with Col."

Sakiim let out a gurgling laugh. "Not Col."

Samih raised his eyebrows and asked him some more questions. Tamsin realized he was trying to keep Sakiim talking to take his mind off the pain a little, though Sakiim's grip on Tamsin's hand never lessened.

After a few minutes the door flap was opened again and the healer came in. Poma followed him, her face as pale as flour. She stayed near the door and kept her gaze firmly rooted on Tamsin, though the healer moved about without any hesitation or glimmer of emotion, like he had seen this all before. He wore a long, sleeveless robe that was tied around the middle with a thick cord. From this cord hung dozens of small pouches and sprigs of leaves. He started mixing herbs and things right away, surveying the extent of the damage as he did. He poured a little water into his mix and then made Sakiim drink it. After a minute, Sakiim's grip relaxed and his eyes became unfocused.

"Sakiim? Sakiim?"

"It's alright. It will help with what we have to do," the healer said. He started instructing Samih on cleaning the wounds, but never lifted a finger to do it himself. Instead he began making more poultices and creams.

"Tamsin," Poma croaked nervously and Tamsin knew it was time to go. From this point on she would only be in the way, though she wished she didn't have to leave Samih, who had thrown off his cloak and rolled up his sleeves, for he had gone pale.

Poma led her out of the muudhiif; more people had gathered outside, but they gave them a wide berth as she led Tamsin down to the water. From there, she made Tamsin kneel and then plunged her hands into the cold water, reminding her of when Mora had held her hands in the basin of water at the seer's dwelling. Poma rubbed them furiously until all the mud and blood was gone and Tamsin's hands were left feeling raw. Sakiim's moans could still be heard and she cringed every time.

"I should go back in there and help. There must be something I can do."

Poma shook her head vigorously. "You will not. I am entrusted to care for you. I will not fail."

"But who will care for Sakiim? Samih is not trained for this!"

"The healer will tell him what to do," Poma said assuredly.

"Why won't he do it himself?" Tamsin was disgusted by the Watcher's treatment thus far. Did the bigotry really go so deep that the Ma'diin wouldn't even give them life-saving aid?

"I told you: Watcher blood is nothing to mess around with."

Tamsin hadn't caught that before, but she asked why now.

"Because it could kill you."

This caught her off guard and she was unable to form a response, but Poma didn't need prompting and continued to explain how Watchers' blood was like poison. Death was the rarest and most extreme effect of coming into contact with it, but there were instances where some went blind and others went mad.

Tamsin swallowed the sick feeling forming in her stomach, but found her voice again when she remembered that she had already been exposed to Watcher blood. A long time ago it seemed now, Haven had cut his hand over hers in the sh'pav'danya. But if he had known what his blood was capable of, why would he have done that?

As if hearing her thoughts, Poma said, "If it got into your blood, there is little anyone could do."

Tamsin recalled her hand itching furiously after the exchange. Haven hadn't known about the scratches she had received from Mora. Luckily, they had been healed, but the skin had still been new and pink.

Tamsin let Poma finish washing her and listened to the sounds of distant birds singing and the wind as it whispered to the reeds. Across the water, a long-legged grey bird tip-toed silently through the water, picking its feet up high as to avoid causing ripples.

Tamsin jumped up and spun around. It was too quiet. Only moments ago the air had been filled with the sounds of a dying man…

Samih stepped out of the muudhiif and Tamsin could see his hands trembling from where she stood. She ran back over to him as the crowd began to disperse.

"Samih?" She put her hands out to stop his from shaking, but stopped herself. She wrapped her arms around herself.

He bent his head and blew out a long breath. "There's nothing I could've done," he said in a low voice. "He had already been exposed to the sunlight."

"I'm so sorry, Samih."

He shook his head. "I have—I have to take care of his body. But I have to tell the others. This can't go on."

"What can I do?" Tamsin asked earnestly. It killed her to see Samih this way.

He shook his head again, as if to dispel the awful images he had seen so he could think clearly. "Stay with Ysallah. I'll be back in a few days." He turned and went back inside before he had even finished the last word.

Tamsin almost followed him, but Poma was at her side instantly and led her away. Back in the muudhiif, Poma started cooking a batch of padi and the aroma made Tamsin's stomach growl. She could not deny that she was hungry, even after the horrific start to the morning. Poma's three children gathered around as bowls were dished out and Poma was kind enough to give Tamsin extra. But as she looked at her full bowl, she thought of Samih and was saddened. He had nobody to look after him.

"Who is your Kazsera?" Poma's eldest, Mikisle, asked, interrupting her thoughts. He was the tallest of them and though he couldn't have been older than seven or eight he was nearly as tall as Tamsin.

"I have none," she replied.

Mikisle and Miah both looked up at her with wide, incredulous eyes, but Cairn, too young to understand any of it, continued to spoon padi into his mouth.

"Kor'diin?" Miah asked and then looked to her mother.

"No, not Kor'diin," Poma said, patting the top of her head. "Tamsin is from the north," she said, before Tamsin could ask what Kor'diin was.

"How far is that?" Miah asked.

Tamsin let herself smile. "It is a long ways."

"What's it like there?" Mikisle asked, but Poma snapped her fingers at him.

"Finish your food and take your sister to Senna's. You'll be helping them with the thatching today."

Both children wore frowns down to the ground, but mumbled affirmative replies and ate their food.

Before they left, Tamsin leaned over to Mikisle and whispered, "There's sand as far as you can see and muudhiifs made of stone that almost reach the sun. And beyond that there are mountains so big they touch the clouds."

Mikisle's mouth hung open in astonishment and then he dashed out the door with his sister, eager to tell his friends.

Tamsin then helped Poma take the bowls outside and clean them. She looked over to the muudhiif where Ysallah was staying and watched several people go in and out. One woman stopped and looked directly at Tamsin before marching into the muudhiif, her expression a mixture of disdain and distrust.

"When can I see Ysallah again?" Tamsin asked.

"She will summon you," Poma said.

"But I—."

"I know Tamsin. I know why you've come here. What you've given up." Poma put a reassuring hand on her arm. "But you don't know the rules here. I will help you, but you must listen to me."

Tamsin knew she was alone here. Samih wouldn't be back for a few days. And here was Poma, offering to help her. It was only one person, but it was a start and she knew if she was going to gain any support here she had to do it on their terms.

"Why do you want to help me?" Tamsin asked. She was grateful for Poma's guidance, but was unsure of its source.

Poma gathered the bowls and laid them out to dry in the sun. "I have always taught my children to be honest and kind. I have taught them to do what is right." Then she pulled the flap open to the muudhiif and waved Tamsin in.

It was just before the evening meal when Tamsin was summoned again to the Kazsera's muudhiif. There were plates of steaming dishes and baskets full of purple fruit. Many women had been invited, but no men. Tamsin recalled being intimidated by the Lords Council, but that was nothing compared to this. At the Council at least she knew she wasn't the focal point. Here, all eyes were on her.

Poma stayed next to her and whispered names to her, who was in Ysallah's tribe and who was in Hazees's, the names of the foods being served, and what the rituals being observed meant.

The rituals and prayers were the most foreign to her. Before a crumb was eaten or a drop served, each woman took out whatever weapons they had brought with them and placed them in front of the fire in the middle of the muudhiif with the blades pointing inward. Some of the weapons were quite impressive, but Tamsin only had her small knife with her. She put it quickly with the rest and backed away and sat cross-legged next to Poma. It's presence inside her boot had given her some comfort amidst all these strangers, even if it was dwarfed by the others, and without it she felt rather vulnerable.

Both Kazserii were there and Hazees deferred to Ysallah to begin and she started what Poma whispered was a special prayer. She said it was because there had been a death that day and Tamsin knew she was referring to Sakiim. It lifted her mood a little knowing that his death had not been just swept under the rug.

"We offer these gifts to the First
To the makers and the givers
By the blood of the believers
And the waters of the living
We honor those that were
Those that are and those that will be
Protect us from the night
Deliver us to light
Until the fight has ended."

When Ysallah had finished, she began it again, and this time everyone joined her. As the women continued to chant, someone brought forth a small bowl and sprinkled some red powder over the fire. A shimmering golden hue emanated from the flames and filled the tent with a soft haze like that of a summer morning.

"The Q'atorii are with us tonight," Hazees said loudly and the chanting ended.

Then the feast began. Tamsin ate and drank and kept to herself, though quickly gave up on the two wooden needles they had given her for the round, potato-like vegetables when she noticed more than one barely concealed smirk from her attempts. She was too anxious anyways to waste time and filled her belly before the others were even halfway done. She suspected that questions would be thrown her way as soon as the others had finished. But the mood in the muudhiif seemed light, despite the gravity of the reality around them, and as the others conversed Tamsin stared at the fire and found herself lulled into a strange, relaxed state.

The glow of the fire seemed to ebb and flow like light seen from below the surface of a pool and though it wavered, the glow never went out. And as Tamsin watched it, it seemed the colors began to change. The gold started to turn to blue in the center and then spread out like a star shape. The blue shimmered even more than the gold until it seemed to form almost solid edges and then the star shape began to grow.

Tamsin's eyes widened as the blue star lifted itself up out of the embers. But it wasn't a star anymore. It was a person.

Tamsin slowly rose to her feet, but no one seemed to take notice. The blue woman she had seen as a little girl was standing right in front of her. She was exactly as she remembered her: skin sparkling like sapphires and a cloak made of the cobalt night sky.

"Who are you?" Tamsin managed to ask through her mesmerized astonishment.

With a voice that rang out like wind chimes in a breeze, the blue woman said, "Have you forgotten me already?"

Tamsin shook her head vigorously. "No, I remember, but I don't know your name."

The blue woman smiled and her teeth were like diamonds. "You know my name little one. You just don't recognize me."

Then she looked back over her shoulder like she had seen something out of the corner of her eye, but Tamsin couldn't see what. In fact, everyone had disappeared. It was just Tamsin and the blue woman in the muudhiif.

"I must go now, but I warn you," the blue woman said, "your journey is not a safe one. Keep your eyes open, for the assassin's are as well."

"Wait!" Tamsin pleaded. "What do you mean?"

But the blue woman had already started to shimmer and Tamsin had to shield her eyes from the brilliant white that followed.

"We can't let him win…"

Those words were echoing in Tamsin's ears when she snapped her eyes open. But the blue woman was gone. And she was lying on the ground. She propped herself up with her elbows and blinked a few times. She was surrounded by darkness, but she could see she was no longer in Hazees's muudhiif. She heard breathing next to her and whipped around, but it was only Miah, sound asleep. She was back in Poma's muudhiif.

Tamsin got to her feet, careful not to jostle Miah. She pinpointed the sleeping forms of Mikisle and Cairn as her eyes adjusted, but she did not see Poma anywhere. She tip-toed over to the door flap, but stopped just before she opened it, hearing voices on the other side. She listened for a few moments and then slowly pulled back a corner of the flap.

Through the opening she saw Poma and Ysallah speaking in hushed tones.

"What do you think it means?" Poma whispered.

Ysallah shook her head. "It is too early to say. The gods have their hands on her, that much is clear at least."

"Yes, but which god? Some are scared; they think she is here to deliver a message of evil."

"You and I have both heard her," Ysallah said defensively. "The evil is already upon us. She is not responsible for this."

"Yes, we know that, but others are skeptical. Hazees has already sent word out."

"Sent word out to who?"

Poma paused before she replied. "You know who will come for her."

Ysallah made a hissing sound through her teeth and started pacing. Then she looked directly at Tamsin.

Tamsin dropped the flap and scrambled back to Miah's side, her heart beating furiously. She heard their voices outside yet, rushed, but too low for her to hear. Then she heard the flap being pushed aside and Poma came back in.

Tamsin squeezed her eyes shut and tried to even her breathing out, pretending to be asleep. After a few moments, she heard Poma lie down, but she was too restless to fall asleep herself.

Samih had told her to stay with Ysallah, that she would be safe. But someone was coming for her, and she didn't know if she wanted to find out who.

Poma must have guessed what Tamsin's thoughts were, for the next day she wouldn't let Tamsin out of her sight. Though the urge to run and try and go after Samih was strong, Tamsin knew she would never find her way through the marshes on her own without getting lost. Mikisle and Miah were thrilled to have Tamsin with them all day and their unceasing questions made it nearly impossible for Tamsin to talk to Poma about the previous night.

It wasn't until the evening meal that Tamsin got her chance. They hadn't been invited back to Hazees's muudhiif—intentionally Tamsin assumed—so they ate in Poma's. Tamsin was growing quite fond of the children, for they were the only ones completely honest with her and weren't put off by her 'foreign' mannerisms, but she was glad for their silence as they ate.

"Poma, you said you wanted to help me."

Poma kept her gaze fixed on her bowl, so Tamsin continued.

"What happened last night?"

Poma set her spoon down. "You fell asleep."

"I don't believe you." It was quite possible that she had fallen asleep and she had dreamed everything...if her dreams had been normal, but they had been anything but lately.

A heavy silence hung in the air. Mikisle and Miah glanced back and forth between the two like they were watching a fencing match as the women stared at each other.

Tamsin decided to play her cards. "Who's coming for me?"

Poma's eyes flashed. Apparently she hadn't known Tamsin had heard their conversation last night. "Your journey has taken a toll on you," she said evenly. "We will talk later," and she tilted her head just slightly in the children's direction, indicating what she had to say she didn't want to say in front of them.

"We have to get her strength back," Mikisle said brightly, missing their silent exchange.

"That is a very good idea Mikisle," Poma said. "I've found that hard work is as good a remedy as any. The harvest is going on, so you will take Tamsin to the water fields tomorrow and help the harvesters."

Mikisle and Miah bounced up and down and Cairn clapped his hands, oblivious, but joining in his siblings' excitement, but Tamsin knew Poma was deflecting. She knew there was no danger in Tamsin running, but still needed to keep eyes on her and keep her occupied while she did…what? Poma's unwillingness to discuss things with her only made her uneasiness grow. She decided if she didn't get answers soon she would confront Ysallah, invitation be damned.

Tamsin awoke later that night to Mikisle poking her in the shoulder. She rubbed her sleep-filled eyes. "What is it, Mikisle?"

"My water skin is empty."

Tamsin squinted, trying to comprehend while not fully awake yet. "Ok…"

"I'm thirsty. Mama doesn't let us go outside by ourselves after dark." He shifted from foot to foot.

"Ok," she said, understanding now. "Where's your mom?"

"She's not here." Mikisle's bottom lip started to quiver.

Tamsin sat up, any lingering grogginess gone now. She looked around, but Mikisle was telling the truth. "Alright," she said calmly, hoping to have that effect on him, "I have to fill mine too. We can go together." She grabbed her water skin and then led him outside.

Mikisle looked around first, listening for any errant sounds, then went down to the water's edge.

While they were filling their skins, Tamsin asked, "Do you know where your mom went?"

"Probably to Hazeeskazsera. Mama helps her a lot."

"Do you know what they're talking about?" she asked innocently.

"You."

Tamsin was surprised by his candor. "What about me?"

"I heard Mama say Hazeeskazsera is afraid of you." Mikisle looked up at her, the slight tremor in his voice indicating his confusion on the topic.

"Are you afraid of me?"

He rocked back on his heels, staring at her quite seriously for one so young. "I don't think so."

"Why do you think Hazees is afraid of me?"

"She says you are *jiin mughaif.*"

"I don't know what that means."

"It means that bad things follow you." Mikisle picked up a stick and started poking a hole in the mud at the edge of the water. "My father was called *jiin mughaif.* The sha'diin said bad things happened when he was around and there was a curse on him."

"What happened to your father?"

"Hazeeskazsera brought the Havakkii and they killed him."

Tamsin could only sit there in response, horrified. Mikisle's father, Poma's *husband,* had been killed because of superstition. Her gaze drifted over to Hazees's muudhiif, where the faint shadow of smoke could be seen drifting from the top. Hazees had left Poma to raise three children on her own and still demanded loyalty from her. It was enough to make her blood boil. She had been here less than a week and the more she found out about Hazees the less she cared for her.

Tamsin reached over and rubbed Mikisle's back, who hastily rubbed under his eyes.

"I'm sorry that happened," Tamsin told him. "My mother used to tell me that bad things happen to people not because they are bad, but to make them stronger."

"Mama always tells me that we must have bad thing happen in order to grow," Mikisle looked over at her, his eyes glistening. "It is like the rain. It is scary when it storms and the gods roar in the sky, but then we wake up and Baat's light is shining on all the beautiful flowers and it is okay again. And everything is better." He said all this in one breath, like he had heard Poma say it numerous times. Then he raised his eyebrows mischievously and shook his finger. "But pray to Mahiri that there is a roof over your head when it does rain!" His white teeth gleamed in the darkness and they both shared a laugh. Mikisle chuckled some more, amused by his own rendition of his mother's teachings and Tamsin was glad. He would be alright.

"Is your water filled?" Tamsin asked.

He nodded and they made their way back to the muudhiif.

"If your mother catches you mocking her you're on your own," she added, lifting up the flap for him.

He grinned and stepped inside.

Tamsin looked back to Hazees's muudhiif for a few moments. "Hey Mikisle," she whispered, "who are the Havakkii?" She looked inside when he didn't answer and saw he was already curled back up on his mat.

She made sure he had fallen asleep before she left Poma's muudhiif again. There was no one else outside and smoke still rose from Hazees's muudhiif so she carefully made her way across the wooden planks to Hazees's mud flat. She already knew of Hazees's distaste for her, but other than bringing the truth about what was going on to them, Tamsin did not see herself as *jiin mughaif* and if Hazees was building a case to kill her, then she wanted to be prepared.

The Kazsera's muudhiif was built quite sturdily and Tamsin could find no gaps between the reeds. On the back side, however, there was a smaller muudhiif attached to the main one. She circled it, but there was no door that she could make out. This one was made with smaller reed bundles and when she inspected a binding that had broken off she found the reeds were loose. She was able to pry them out of the way just enough to squeeze through.

It was completely dark inside and she had to be extra careful not to run into anything, but from the dark shapes she could make out she figured this was Hazees's private quarters. She stood still for a long minute, too nervous to breathe, but it appeared to be empty. Then she noticed a door flap across the room with a sliver of light shining through the bottom and crossed over to it. She crouched near the side and ever so slowly pulled back the tiniest bit of edge she could.

A figure walked right past the door flap and Tamsin almost gasped in surprise, but the figure did not seem to notice her. It was Poma. Tamsin watched her cross the room and pour a steaming liquid into a shallow cup held by Hazees.

There were six women in the main muudhiif: Hazees, Poma, Ysallah, and three other women Tamsin did not recognize, two of which had their backs to Tamsin. The third was a brute of a woman, with muscles as large as a man's and thick, braided hair pulled back in a ponytail that accentuated the squareness of her face. When she opened her mouth to bite off a piece of meat Tamsin saw she was missing a front tooth.

"If she were one of us," Hazees replied to something Ysallah had said, "it would have never unfolded. She should go back. She doesn't know our ways or our people. We are too different. She will only do more harm than good."

"She's not here for us," Ysallah said.

"That's right, you mentioned the Watcher. You believe she came all this way to repay a debt? You are more foolish than I thought Ysallah."

One of the women whose back was turned stood up suddenly, her hand at her side where Tamsin assumed a weapon was. But Ysallah snapped at her to sit down, which the woman eventually did. One of Ysallah's people, Tamsin figured, though Ysallah was smart enough to know not to rise to any bait Hazees may throw out.

Hazees barely contained a sneer. "The girl is in love with him. One does not forsake her country for a man she does not love."

"So what if she is?" Ysallah continued. "She is determined to go after him. If we help her, she may be able to help us in return."

Hazees surprised her by smiling. "If she truly knew about his kind she would not rescue him from one hell just to deliver him to another."

"Now it is you who is being foolish Hazees," Ysallah retorted, heat rising in her voice. "She is our link to the northerners, the same people that are building that wall. Showing her some good will might prompt her to convince her people to do the same." She sighed heavily and restrained her tone. "I know of your aversion for the Watchers, but Haven is a good hunter. And we can't afford to lose any more."

"The number of Watchers has dwindled significantly," Poma commented. "Some are praising the gods. Others think it is an ill omen; that the gods are turning their backs on the Ma'diin and letting Ib'n's demons take over. What do you think?"

All eyes turned to Hazees. "I think—."

But she was interrupted as another woman rushed into the muudhiif, flicking her fingers furiously across her hands.

"The Havakkii have been spotted," she said breathlessly. "Less than a day away."

"They're coming here?" one of the women asked.

Hazees waived her off. "They are coming by my invitation. Welcome them when they arrive. They can do what they wish with the girl."

Whoever the Havakkii were, they were coming for her. She had just arrived in the marsh lands and she was already out of time.

Chapter Eight

No fire had burned like this before. It wasn't angry red whips anymore. It was white and cold, casting his bones in a freezing cauldron. It was as if all of his nerves had been stretched and slit and now the white fire had found an opening. It was as if his own heart pumped it through his body and his blood had turned into a river for it to flow into every curve and corner. It went deeper than flesh, deeper than muscle, deeper than bone. It was there all the time; it never relented. He could feel it while he slept and it was there when he awoke. It consumed him and yet he remained. It was becoming a part of him, more than that, it was becoming him. It was getting harder and harder to distinguish himself from the white fire. Each time he awoke to its presence, it was more difficult to extract himself from it, to draw the line between man and fire.

Let it in, a voice said.

He wanted to shake his head, but he couldn't tell if he succeeded or not. "No," he said.

Why not?

Why...why not? He tried to remember, tried to remember a time when the white fire had not been there. He was sure it hadn't always been there. But he couldn't remember when or what it felt like. "I don't know..."

Do you want me to take it away?

Take it away? The white fire? What would it be like without it? He wasn't sure he wanted to know. He was afraid. If he took it away there would be nothing left of him. He would be nothing. "I don't think I would like that..."

Then why do you fight it?

He considered. There was something else, something he couldn't quite name. It wanted him to keep fighting, to push back against the white fire, but it was small and he couldn't quite figure out where it came from. Sometimes, when he thought of giving in to it, he would see a face out of the corner of his eye, a woman's face, but when he tried to see she would disappear. "Who is she?"

She's the one holding you back. She's in your way.

"She's from before."
Yes.
The white fire flared until he was blinded by its power. It left him breathless.
Send her away. She makes you weak.
"But she is special."
"Special? How?" *a new voice emerged. The white-haired man's voice.*
He couldn't remember. He couldn't remember why, but the fire made him think of her. Was she controlling the white fire?
"No, she is not. Why would you think that?"
"Because she can. She is special." *He lifted his head and blinked, and for a moment, he could almost remember something...something about the dark room he was in, about the blurry shapes in front of him, but the white fire was too strong. It held him tight and pulled him back under, back into its depths.*
Tell me what you know.
The white fire suddenly relented, like a snake recoiling and he was nearly overwhelmed by the unexpected release. He could feel himself melting into the floor beneath him and an abrupt fear gripped him. He could feel his hands and arms rippling like water and he could see the red pool of his blood around him. He was falling apart. Without the white fire he would come undone. He would be nothing. He pleaded and his tears joined the red pool.
"Please, make it stop."
"Only you can make it stop Haven."
"How?"
"You have to accept the truth."
"And what is the truth?"
"You're dead Haven."
Haven's breath caught in his throat and for a long, cold moment he couldn't feel his heartbeat.
"You died a long time ago, Haven. You were just a boy. Don't you remember?"
Haven closed his eyes as he shook his head, but that did not stop the bursts of images lancing through his mind. He felt like he was being held down and then there was a sudden pain in his chest and then he couldn't breathe, like he was underwater. Then flashes of metal and of bodies falling to the ground and more pain in his chest and then...he was

the one falling. And someone was screaming…a girl. She was holding his face…

He opened his eyes and their luminescence only heightened the terror and confusion Monstran could see dancing across his face.

"But I survived. I remember…"

But he couldn't remember. There were just clusters of images and pain that he couldn't make sense of.

"You're confusing your memories, Haven. When you accept the truth, the pain will go away. Then I will take you to meet Him."

Monstran saw surprise flash across Haven's face before he turned and walked away.

"WHO ARE YOU TALKING ABOUT!?"

Monstran could hear his frantic calls, but he merely smiled and kept walking.

Mr. Monstran sometimes preferred to come out into the open and meander along the walkways and stairs that caressed the inside of the canyon. The parts of the city closest to the inner hollow of the canyon remained mostly untouched, its cone-shaped burrows and painted galleries intact, but empty. The sights and smells he remembered of a great city, once thriving in the days before the Purge with merchants selling pigeon wings, black roti, and vision blood, and artists molding vases to look like embracing lovers and making feathered chimes whose high rings would echo across the canyon, now escaped him, but it gave him a small bit of pleasure to reminisce. The only echoes now were the ones in his mind and the wind as it searched for a banner to whip about. But the banners of the old houses of Alamorgro were long gone.

The past was always easier to see than the present and he found it easier to pick out truths of the present by allowing himself a little time to linger in days long gone. The patterns were easier to see, just like it was easy to navigate the winding curves of the ledges and know which archways led further into the canyon and which led down to the dried up riverbed a little over a half mile below. He had studied these patterns for years. He had studied the ripples caused by small stones and the waves caused by large ones and what happened when the two coincided. He watched these happenings and contemplated the relationships of actions and reactions. The behavior of men fascinated him; how they responded to things they perceived they couldn't control based on unsubstantial and imaginary ideas like hope and loyalty compared to things they actually could control, but were convinced otherwise due to fear, stubbornness, or a simple lack of understanding.

He must have wandered the windy walkways for hours only noticing the time when the shadows cast on the opposite wall of the canyon had changed drastically. Sometimes he forgot that not everyone was gifted with as long a life as his. He had come out here to ponder his latest study, for he was often denied the time and space to do so in the burrows. The amon'jii did not venture here, the walkways being small and too precarious for their larger bodies and his attendants had not yet figured out where he went when they could not find him, for there was always someone looking for him to discuss some irrelevant matter. It was well that the plan was working and the young Watcher was finally succumbing to his will, but Mr. Monstran now wished that he had had a little more time to interrogate him before he had begun the transformation process. It had been necessary to keep him sedated on their journey to Alamorgro and it was nearly impossible to influence a mind numb to its own consciousness, but dealing with a fully aware Watcher would have been a worse alternative. Even as weak as he was coming out of the Empyrian dungeons he was still a threat and dangerous cargo to the Empyrian soldiers that had accompanied him back. And then when they had arrived Mr. Monstran had immediately begun working, for breaking a Watcher took twice the effort and skill than the average man and he had half the time to do it.

The Master was growing impatient. And even with his extended time in the world, Mr. Monstran was still a babe compared to the Master's understanding of time and the speed at which events needed to unravel.

Haven had not been able to tell him anything about the girl that darted in and out of his thoughts, which meant Mr. Monstran's ministrations were working and he was leaving that part of his life behind, but he had mentioned something the last time Mr. Monstran had visited him. Something that made him wonder. He thought the girl was causing his suffering, causing the *white fire*, as he called it. That's what the other Watcher had called it as well, but it was just the Master flexing his influence. But why did Haven think the girl had something to do with it? He called her special. Again, *why*? He had thought nothing more of her than Haven's lover, a girl who had ensnared his heart and only made it more difficult to pull him away, but this time it was different. Something odd in the tone of his voice maybe that made him question if Haven believed she was special to him or special for another reason.

He turned away from the sight of the canyon and went into one of the deserted burrows, pacing in a large circle around the room, though he paid no attention to the murals on the walls. There was something about the girl. He had seen her once in Empyria, though he could recall nothing about her that struck him as noteworthy save for the fact that she had ensnared a Watcher's heart. But what did Haven see in the girl?

He made one more circle, then making up his mind on a course of action, left and made his way down to the lower apartments where the soldiers that Cornelius Saveen had sent with him were staying. The apartments were spacious, though rudimentary. Equipped with enough to provide for their basic needs, but not much else in the way of comfort. They used to be lodgings for the slaves, though the soldiers were not treated as such now. The soldiers were still under orders to remain with Mr. Monstran until told otherwise, but he doubted they would stay for much longer, orders or not, for light lovers cracked easily when confined underground for so long. Claustrophobia grew in the mind like ivy until rationale lost control to primitive fear. And judging from the wary looks he received as he passed, it was already starting to take root, though he had not lifted a finger to help it spread. Indeed he had not visited the soldiers down here since they arrived, the familiarity of these rooms reminding him of things he would rather forget. But he rather hoped these men were smart enough to realize that if they left without his consent they would not make it through the first night. They knew creatures roamed the tunnels throughout the canyon and Mr. Monstran had made sure the amon'jii knew to stay well away from them, but if the soldiers chose to leave, then he would not deny the amon'jii the blood they craved.

He reached their commander's quarters and sat down across from the startled captain, an unpleasantly tall man with a head too small to possibly contain anything useful. He appeared to have just finished his evening meal and scrambled to clear off the tiny table.

"No need for that my dear Captain Larin," Mr. Monstran said. "I am already sitting down and I have something important to discuss."

Captain Larin ceased his actions and nodded eagerly, making Mr. Monstran fear his round head would just roll off his neck. "Of course, of course," he agreed enthusiastically.

A little too keen for Mr. Monstran's liking, especially since his men were only a few feet down the hall probably with scowls on their faces yet. But if Captain Larin was willing to help then he would take advantage of it. "What do you know of Tamsin Urbane?"

Captain Larin's enthusiasm was quickly replaced with confusion and his eyebrows rippled together. "Tamsin Urbane? The daughter of the late Lord Urbane? This is what you wanted to talk about?"

Mr. Monstran kept his face neutral. "Yes. Now what do you know of her?"

Captain Larin shook his head. "Only that she was to be married to Cornelius. I only saw her a couple times, uh, once during the Lords ball and again at Lord Urbane's funeral. I never spoke with her though. I think her and Cornelius maybe had a falling out."

Maybe Mr. Monstran was right and Captain Larin's head was too small to hold anything useful. "Would your men know anything?"

There was a grunt behind him and Mr. Monstran turned to see another Empyrian soldier leaning against the doorway, his arms folded across his chest. "I'll tell ya anythin' ya want to hear if ya just let us leave this hole and go home."

Mr. Monstran stood up and faced the newcomer with a speculative eye. "And that's why I couldn't trust the information even if you gave it to me. I'm sorry Captain," he nodded his head, "I am in search of truths not tales."

"Wait!" Captain Larin jumped up, banging his long legs on the table. "Enrik, Lieutenant Riggs' boy, could tell you something. He and Tamsin were acquainted." He motioned and Mr. Monstran followed him down the narrow hallway to the bunks.

They stopped at the last one and a boy, no more than seventeen, appeared to be drawing on a piece of parchment with a dozen more spread out on the thin mattress around him. His uniform was too big and seemed to not have been washed in weeks, but his face was strong and focused, the face of an intellectual who had more important things to contemplate than clean clothes.

Captain Larin coughed loudly and Enrik looked up. His eyes widened at the sight of Mr. Monstran and he hastily gathered his parchment together.

"Please, do not let me interrupt your work," Mr. Monstran said, sweeping over to the bunk and plucking up one of the papers. It was covered in lines and curves with illegible notes scrawled in the corners.

"Just, uh, something to pass the time," Enrik said, swallowing thickly like a servant who had been caught stealing from his master.

"A puzzle or maze I see," Mr. Monstran said, handing the parchment back. "Something to keep the mind sharp."

Enrik nodded slowly and took the parchment, putting it in a small leather satchel with the rest.

"Can I help you with something, Sir?" Enrik asked.

"I sincerely hope so," Mr. Monstran replied, ducking his head to sit down on the bunk next to him. "What can you tell me about Tamsin Urbane?"

The boy's expression was confused so Mr. Monstran explained. "I'll be completely honest with you Enrik, if you are honest with me."

Enrik nodded slowly.

"Good. You remember the man you helped bring here? Well, I've been trying to help him, but I'm afraid the trauma he experienced in Empyria still plagues him. He was close to Tamsin, whom I've learned you were acquainted with. I'm hoping that if I knew more about her I would be able to help him more sufficiently."

"I only knew her for a short while," Enrik started. He seemed hesitant.

"Was there anything...special about her?" Mr. Monstran pushed. "Anything unusual you noticed about her perhaps?"

"Unusual?"

The boy was nervous. He knew something.

Mr. Monstran smiled. He was a patient man. And the Empyrians weren't going anywhere soon.

Chapter Nine

Tamsin pushed her fists into the small of her back and arched in a satisfying stretch, taking a moment to look across the marshes as the waning light spread across it. It looked as if the world had forgotten about this small bit of it. The sky was tinged a soft pink and the surrounding reed patches were cast in a blue and grey haze. The farther they went the less defined they became as if they were only shadows of a time long gone, blending into the past like memories.

The day's work had been hard, but rewarding; harvesting the huge water lily leaves that were used to hold the cooking embers included much stooping and wading through mud that tried to turn her feet into permanent roots, but she found it a rather pleasing and welcome distraction. She and the other harvesters had set out in the early morning; Poma had agreed to let her go since she was busy with the Kazserii all day. Tamsin had been given a sickle and woven basket that floated nicely in the water so she could place the leaves in after she had cut them off at the top of the thick stem. They would do much harvesting over the next few days she was told, for it was the peak of the season to stock up on them, and at first she couldn't imagine how they could spend several days doing the same repetitive motion without getting worn out, but she learned there was much more to the process than she had first assumed. The first step was to harvest the leaves and then once the basket was full she would take it back to the mud flats where they would pull the seeds out of the center where the leaves connected. Then they would go back out and reseed the area they had just harvested by dropping the seeds, which sank surprisingly quickly, back into the water before moving on to the next section to harvest. They repeated this several times throughout the day; Tamsin with much help from the children of the tribe who had seemed to take a liking to her. Whether they were just curious about the northern girl or because she was closer to their height than most of the adults she didn't know, but she was grateful for their help nonetheless and seeing them cheer when they filled a basket before the others made the work less toilsome, though after a few hours their interest was diverted to chasing each other through the reed patches instead.

She had also been given new clothes to wear, ones that were more in keeping with the Ma'diin's own garb. What little clothing she had brought with her had been unsuitable for the trek through the desert with Samih and the servants clothing she had worn getting out of Empyria had just about lived out its use. Poma had given her some of her own garments to wear and at first Tamsin had balked at the idea, for it was even more revealing than the Empyrian servants clothing. The pants were loose and flowy and tied at the ankles and also had a green, belt-like sash around the hips, but the shirt was little more than a strip of tan fabric wrapped around her chest leaving her stomach and shoulders exposed. She thought about wearing her cloak, but it would be more of a hinderance working all day in the water fields. So she improvised and used what was left of her blue servants shirt to wrap around her stomach and over one of her shoulders like a sash. Tamsin had seen other Ma'diin who wore long, straight dresses that were draped over one shoulder and though she didn't want to complain, she asked why she couldn't wear something like that. Poma explained to her that the kazsiin, the Kazserii's personal attendants, were not required to wear the traditional long dress of the other Ma'diin that symbolized the laborers and though she would be working in the fields today, she was still a guest of the Kazserii which demanded a certain level of honor. It was funny, Tamsin thought, that even though it was backwards from that of Empyria, that even here in the marshes they had a caste system that was recognized by what one wore. Poma let her keep her blue sash however, for it branded her as a northerner.

Tamsin heard her name being called and realized that there were only a few men and women left gathering the leaves as evening set over the lily pad fields. They were headed back to the mud flats before night fell upon them. She called out that she just wanted to finish this batch and she would be right behind them. They acknowledged her with a wave. She cut off one last head of leaves and put it in her basket, looking over her shoulder at the retreating forms. When she was sure they weren't looking, she stuck the sickle through her belt loop and began digging through the leaves of her basket. She pulled out her pack and swung the strap over her shoulder.

She had made up her mind last night after leaving Hazees's muudhiif. Ysallah was in no position to help her it seemed and Hazees was intent on handing her over to these Havakkii people, whom Tamsin had no desire to meet, especially if Hazees had summoned them. And she could not wait for Samih any longer. So she had gone with Poma's children to help in the water fields all day, far enough away from the village so when she made her escape, it would be too dark for anyone to risk following her.

She adjusted her pack and started off.

"TAMSIIIN! TAMSIIIN!"

She heard her name again, but it was not coming from the other adults, who were already on their way back with their full baskets. She looked towards the reed patches and saw two pairs of tiny feet sloshing hurriedly through the shallow water towards her. There was something alarming in their tone so she hurried towards them.

"Mikisle, what's wrong?" she asked, recognizing them, though he and Miah were both red-cheeked and wide-eyed when they reached her.

"Cairn!" Mikisle cried and in a series of jumbled words and hand gestures told Tamsin that they had been playing out in the reeds and Cairn, Poma's youngest, had wandered off and couldn't be found. Mikisle then sunk to his knees in such a despairing way that Tamsin had never seen in a child before. Miah's bottom lip quivered and her eyes filled with tears seeing her older brother on his knees.

Fear slid its fingers around Tamsin's spine. She knew what was out there, as did Mikisle.

"I was supposed to watch him. But I only looked away for a minute, I swear!" Mikisle cried.

Tamsin knew she had to do something, despite the danger she could potentially face and the hollow, sick feeling forming in her stomach. There was no time to go back for help so she pulled Mikisle back onto his feet and urged him to take his sister and run. She pointed to the retreating forms of the other lily pad harvesters in the distance and he nodded. He grabbed his sibling's hand and started pulling her away, but paused and Tamsin could see the terror in his eyes and knew he was genuinely frightened.

"I know," she replied to his unspoken concern, but she had already made up her mind.

She watched the children splash away across the water field for a moment and then took off herself towards the reed patch they had come from, running so her fear would not catch her and turn her feet around to the mud flats. Maybe she would get lucky, extremely lucky, and find Cairn right away and they would make it back before the sun set completely. But if she didn't, then he was on his own until she could find him. If the three year old survived that long. She didn't know if anyone else would come after them after dark. That was the fear she had seen in Mikisle's eyes. If you were caught out in the reed patches after dark, then it was up to you to get out.

She couldn't abandon that little boy. Every instinct in her body was telling her to turn around, but imagining little Cairn out there alone after dark was enough to propel her forward. With that, all thoughts of escaping disappeared.

She made it to the reed patches, but instead of pushing her way through the thick forest she had enough wits about her yet to stay in the water. She slowed down a little as she waded through the channels between patches and stopped only so she could hear for a response when she called his name. But she heard nothing. She pressed on, her hope sinking with the descending light.

She came to an impasse in the channel where it split off in three different directions. The reeds were taller than she was by a few feet and she could not see where each led beyond the split. Mr. Graysan's table flashed into her mind, littered with drawings and maps of the marsh lands, and she remembered him telling her that they had been lucky that the Ma'diin had found them for they had gotten lost in the maze-like marshes. But she didn't have time to worry about getting lost, couldn't or she would never choose and become a frozen statue.

She knew she had to trust her instincts in here and she pulled the sickle from her belt as the twilight sighed and gave way to the night at last.

Her fear of the dark and dangers it kept waned with the passing hours as she continued through the meandering waterways, though her fear that she would never find Cairn grew exponentially. Her voice had finally cracked from calling out for him and now all she was able to do was whisper hoarsely through the reeds. Her weeks of traveling with Samih (and the nights with Haven before that she thought briefly) had prepared her better than most for being able to endure the long hours and stretches of silence that only seemed to lengthen in the blackness when one was accustomed to sleeping through those hours. But after a long day of harvesting lily pads, her body was starting to shake from weariness.

Come away from the water...

Tamsin spun around, sending little droplets of water flying around her. Eyes wide, she scanned the water and the surrounding reeds, but she saw nothing. Goosebumps shivered up her arms as she realized that she was still alone. She was sure she had heard somebody whisper. She let the water settle around her and listened, but all she heard was the wind picking up and rustling the reeds. She switched the sickle to her left hand and wiped her moist right one on the top of her pants sleeve and then rubbed her goosebumps away.

No fear...

Those first words he had told her in the sandstorm reverberated through the reeds like an anvil right to her gut. The sickle slipped from her hand and into the water. The *sploosh* sound it made shook some of her sense back though and she dove her hand in after it before it could sink too deep. She winced as her hand grabbed the blade a little too tightly, but she held onto it and brought it out of the water. She couldn't see where the blade had cut her, but she could feel it. She gritted her teeth and cursed under her breath, the pain momentarily making her forget why she dropped it in the first place, but the chill in her bones that had nothing to do with the cold water reminded her.

It's all in my head, she told herself. It's not real. He's *not here*.

It was just her body telling her she needed to rest, she decided, so she took a few deep breaths and waded over to the nearest reed patch. She pulled herself up, matted a few of the thinner ones down, and sat down on the edge of it so she could still see across the channel, but was not in the water anymore. Her pants were soaked almost to her waist from a particularly deep stretch of water for these parts so she took off her blue sash, ripped a large strip off and wrapped it around her bloody hand, discarding the rest in the water.

What would Haven think of her now? she wondered. Wandering off at night, cutting herself with her own blade, hearing voices in the wind. Being out here alone, she couldn't figure out if it was the perfect time or the worst time to go mad. She rubbed her temples with her good hand and forced herself to just breathe a moment and let her mind and body rest.

The reeds and foxtails brushed against her arms as the wind pushed them back and forth and she watched them sway across the water on the patch across the channel as the moon appeared from behind the thick layer of clouds that had covered the sky all night. She was grateful for the little sight it gave her.

Until she saw something move across the channel on the opposite reed patch that was neither reed nor foxtail.

It happened so swiftly, so silently, that at first she wasn't sure she had seen anything until she caught another glimpse of it as it moved a few yards to the right. Just a dark shape, nothing distinguishable, but it was big. Bigger than the buffalos that migrated across the shallow water fields, but not taller than the reeds themselves. And then it disappeared again.

She didn't need to see it completely to know what it was. There was only one thing that the Ma'diin feared out here after dark and her fear spiked like the hairs on the back of her neck seeing firsthand how stealthily it had moved through the reeds. If she had chosen the other shore…

Tamsin knew she should get back in the water immediately, for it was the one thing that would protect her. But she had no idea if the amon'jii had seen her and she had no wish to draw attention to herself now if it hadn't. Nor did she wish to get any closer to it. The reeds brushed against her arms again, making her shiver. She slowly got up and did a slow circle, scanning her own reed patch for any sign of movement, though it was nearly impossible to see anything but the slow swaying of the thick brush. She wished passionately for the wind to stop so she would be given the chance to discern between its whistling touch and what would be the lethal kiss from the cloaked predator. At least she was downwind from the one she had glimpsed, though she knew nothing of the amon'jii's sense of smell, and she would use that as long as she could.

Clutching the sickle tightly, she set off through the reeds, finally understanding the dangerous "game" Haven had spoken to her about when he used to refer to hunting the amon'jii. It was like the game she had played with her childhood friends: Seek and hide. One of them would go hide while the others would search for the one hiding. Whoever found the hidden one would become the next hider and on and on until they were called in for lunch. But no one would be calling her in for lunch here. If she was found by the amon'jii, then there was a wicked chance that nobody would ever find her again. She admitted that she had never truly given the credit that was due to the Watchers, or Haven, when they spoke of the hunt. It was always something she had to imagine, having never experienced it, and somehow the imagining made it less threatening. She wondered if that was how the other Ma'diin thought; they knew the looming threat of the amon'jii and sometimes witnessed the horrific aftermath of an amon'jii attack, but did the protection of the walls of the muudhiifs make it less real? The feeling of being hunted was very different when one didn't have a moat separating them.

Thinking of Haven now didn't hurt like it usually did. She felt close to him here, closer than she'd felt in months and it gave her an odd kind of strength, even though every footstep seemed to fall with doubled weight and she couldn't remember the last after she'd taken the next. But this was Haven's world; the one he had warned her about. She had been so willing, so *eager*, to give up hers and embrace his. She allowed herself a small moment to wonder: if they had escaped that night and made it to the marsh lands, knowing now the all-encompassing fear he faced, would she still have come? Would she have been able to endure watching him leave every night and wondering if she'd see him again in the morning? Would she have been able to resist following him, putting both of them in danger? She put an end to this line of thinking, afraid of what the answers would be. But she finally understood. Haven's diffidence in the beginning had been to protect her and sacrificing his happiness to ensure her safety was the only way he knew how; it was the only thing he knew how to do well.

"Stay with me tonight," she whispered, echoing the words he had spoken many weeks ago in a cold, dark cell beneath the Armillary.

Mr. Monstran did not look forward to what he had to do. He had made a mistake and now the Master would know. But it was the only way to correct it. To try and go behind the Master's back was unthinkable. He had made sure to run every word, every scenario through his head before he made his way to the Dread Chamber. The Master would not be pleased, though Mr. Monstran hoped he would be in a forgiving mood.

The boy, Enrik, had not shed as much light on the subject of Miss Urbane as Mr. Monstran would have liked, but it had been enough to give him the pieces to connect for himself.

Before Mr. Monstran had left for Empyria, the Master had a disturbing encounter, one that convinced him there was a threat in Empyria. A *she-hunter* he had called it. Mr. Monstran, in turn, had sent a message to his contacts within Empyria. They had used the late Lord Saveen for many years to help carry out their plans, but upon learning of his death, Mr. Monstran knew they would need a new mole. Word had reached him that Saveen's own nephew, Cornelius, was a prime candidate. He ranked high in the Empyrian army and was in negotiations to be married to a Lord's daughter. Mr. Monstran knew his type:

ambitious, highly-motivated, clever, and eager to make his mark on the world. Power: that was what men like Cornelius craved and Mr. Monstran could give him the illusion of power. Mr. Monstran thought it was time to meet his new target so he sent word back with one of his men, Jediah Harvus, to prepare for his arrival.

But then the Master found out that there was a threat in Empyria and told Mr. Monstran to deliver another message immediately. Mr. Monstran didn't understand what would cause the Master to fear a female Ma'diin, for Jediah had reported a group of them entered the city, but it was not his place to question the Master so he sent his fastest man with another message. Well, a message and a warning. An eyeball would be sufficient to get Cornelius's attention he imagined.

The warning seemed to work a little too well, for when he arrived in Empyria it was to the news that all the Ma'diin had perished at the dam site. But Cornelius had proved his cleverness and cunning and brought Mr. Monstran to where they were holding the Watcher they had caught. This feat in itself was something to behold, for even Monstran himself had only ever captured one Watcher in his long lifetime. The owner of the eye he sent to Cornelius, in fact. An endeavor which ended in failure, but with a direct descendant of the Lumierii right before him, he knew the Master would overlook the she-hunter's death. Monstran's arrival to Empyria had been glorious indeed.

But as Mr. Monstran stood before the doorway to the Dread Chamber, he knew his glorious achievement had only been a half-victory. And in the Master's eyes, half a victory was not a victory at all, but a failure. He had made an *assumption,* connecting the information Jediah had brought him about the Ma'diin and their Kazsera and the *she-hunter* the Master so desperately wanted.

But he had gotten it wrong. Ysallah was not the she-hunter the Master sought. It was Tamsin Urbane. And she was halfway across the world on her way back to the Cities.

Mr. Monstran had the brief thought to mention using the afain'jii, but he knew the Master would not rush their maturation. They were essential later in his plans, the Master had said, but did not elaborate what those future plans were. The afain'jii had been destroyed to near extinction. What was left took refuge in the caverns or had fled to the east beyond Mr. Monstran's knowledge. Their descendants were abandoned and left too long in the wild. They were weak, untrained, and savage. But since the Master's return, he had been cultivating them, *nurturing* them, and grooming them to his great purpose. Using them too soon, before their loyalty was absolute, would be a mistake. The amon'jii had their uses, but they were nothing compared to the potential of the afain'jii. The afain'jii were not hindered by land or light and once they were unleashed all other threats would be obsolete.

But until then, Monstran had to ensure all the pieces on the board were precisely where he wanted them. His last pieces were Haven and Tamsin. His control over Haven was nearly complete; there would be no more opposition there. But for Tamsin, his only hope was Brunos. The Empyrians were firmly in his grip so he could send Brunos after the girl to retrieve her. This is what he would propose to the Master.

Mr. Monstran tugged at the cuffs of his scarlet robe and then entered the Dread Chamber.

An hour later, Mr. Monstran returned to the Empyrians' quarters, dabbing the last of the sweat off the back of his neck with his white kerchief.

Captain Larin greeted him immediately. "Back so soon Sir? You—you look unwell. Is everything alright?" He offered him a seat, but Mr. Monstran refused.

His meeting with the Master had left Mr. Monstran feeling rather ill, but he had neither the time nor the patience to indulge in self-pity. "I come with good news, Captain. You're free to go. But first, I have a few questions yet for Enrik. May I see him?"

"Good luck tryin' to find him," another soldier said. The same dull-witted brute from earlier. "He left about an hour ago."

"And you didn't think it important to tell me?!" Captain Larin fumed, quite put out that one of his own would delay their chance to leave this place.

"Left? Where did he go?" Mr. Monstran asked.

"Dunno. He's been sneakin' off a lot lately. Always came back in an hour or two so I never asked him about it and he never said anythin' when he got back. Just went to his bunk and kept to himself."

Mr. Monstran moved past them both towards Enrik's bunk, ignoring the hasty footsteps of Captain Larin and the other man behind him. Mr. Monstran scanned the bed carefully when he reached it, separating the everyday necessities from items that could be informative.

He quickly zeroed in on a stack of parchment pieces haphazardly piled on the bed and crossed over to them, though the satchel was gone.

"Should we go after him?" Captain Larin asked.

The other man laughed. "He's probably long gone Cap'n. Either found a way out or the boogeyman got him."

Mr. Monstran paid no attention to them. It only took a minute of him looking over the curving lines and little notes scribbled into the corners of the pages to know exactly what the boy had been doing. These weren't puzzles or mazes as he had first thought. The patterns of the tunnels were undeniable, for Mr. Monstran knew them well and Enrik had even marked the ones to avoid. Ones that were more well-traveled by the amon'jii. Men twice his age sat here picking at their teeth and cursing their misfortune while Enrik had been systematically mapping the tunnels. And had gone undetected by the amon'jii and Mr. Monstran's own servants.

Mr. Monstran would have been impressed by the boy's ingenuity, but then he noticed something curious. There were multiple pages of the surrounding passages and burrows, but there were two pages in particular that had marked out routes and neither one led from their quarters to the outside world. At first Mr. Monstran thought the boy had made a mistake; that he didn't know the ways as well as he thought, but then he read the marks on the pages and the feeling he had entering the Dread Chamber returned.

One page had a route drawn from their quarters to a place deeper in the tunnels. The very place where he kept the Watcher.

And the other was a route of the way from Haven's cell to the outside. To the southern gap. And to Ma'diin territory.

The boy had lied. He knew more about Tamsin than he revealed. Enough to know that leaving here without Haven was not an option.

"Excuse me," Mr. Monstran said. "I suddenly have a sour taste in my mouth." He made to leave.

"Wait. What about Enrik?" Captain Larin asked. "Do we wait for him or should we go after him?"

"To seven hells with Enrik," the other soldier said, earning an annoyed glare from Larin. "What about us?"

There were two possible scenarios in motion right now. Either Enrik was on another scouting mission and would return soon barring the discovery from any amon'jii, a theory supported by the fact that his maps were still here, or he had memorized the routes and was escaping with Haven right now.

Mr. Monstran was not willing to risk the latter being true.

He scanned Enrik's pages a moment and selected the one he was looking for. "This page contains the instructions to your departure. You can either try to find Enrik or you can take this page and go home and leave Enrik's fate to me."

He held out the page.

Captain Larin stood frozen, the terrible weight of the choice evident on his face.

The other soldier scoffed at Larin's indecision and snatched the paper from Mr. Monstran. "Enrik's death was tragic," he said gravely, making known what they would be telling the others, "but his *sacrifice* allowed us to go home." He clapped Larin on the back and left to break the bad and good news to their counterparts.

Captain Larin remained in a deadlocked stare as he came to terms with his guilt, but Mr. Monstran knew he would go with the others all the same.

"Thank you for your service Captain. May your travels be safe," Mr. Monstran said, moving past him and down the hall. "And your death be swift."

Chapter Ten

Tamsin could still see her breath condensing in the night air in front of her, though sunrise was only less than an hour away, by her guess, and would soon dispel the nighttime chill. She had found a small clump of reeds that formed a small peninsula off of a larger patch where she was able to leave her back to the water so she only had one direction from which an attack might come. She knew she should keep moving; she had not yet found Cairn and it would help keep her body temperature up. But she would rather shiver from cold than fear. She had found the spot several hours ago and though she had seen nothing since, she had not been able to work up the courage necessary to leave until the sun came up. She had dozed off once and she knew she could not let her guard down, but it was so hard to fight the heaviness of her eyelids...

The breeze across her neck felt good, blowing and pulling back across her skin in a curious, rhythmic way. The sensation gave her goosebumps. She became aware of her little peninsula bed underneath her cheek, made soft and spongy from the stream surrounding it. Her fingers flexed into the soil as life returned to her limbs and she stretched lackadaisically, humming in sleepy contentment.

But the humming didn't stop when she did. In fact, it seemed to pulse with the breeze. Her forehead wrinkled in confusion and she grudgingly opened her eyes.

She heard a rustling next to her in the reeds so she rolled onto her back and propped herself up with her elbows—

Right into the snarling face of an amon'jii...

Tamsin cried out, the sound snapping her eyes open to full awareness. She shot up, her chest heaving with the intensity of her heartbeats, ready to defend herself. She blinked and looked around, but there was no amon'jii. She whirled around, but there was nothing. She was alone with the reeds.

Her stomach lurched as she realized that she had dreamt it all. But worse, she had fallen asleep. The amon'jii could've been real and she would've been too late to stop it from killing her. She splashed water on her face trying to dispel the nausea, clutching her sickle tightly.

A couple hours must have passed at least. The sun had not quite come up yet, but it was close. The sky was a light grey, giving the illusion of fog across the marshes. Even the water was dull, adding even more to the wraithlike aura.

"Mamaaa!"

Tamsin whipped around once more, water still dripping from her face. Her eyes widened as she searched the reeds.

"Mamaaa!"

She heard the cry again. The cry of a child. She darted forward, forsaking her small oasis. "Cairn!" she cried out. It didn't matter now if she yelled. If there were any amon'jii around they would've heard Cairn already. "Cairn!"

Cairn cried again and Tamsin altered her course to the right, charging headlong as the reeds clung to her face and arms. She could hardly see any further than her hand, but she kept running. Cairn's cries grew louder until he was outright wailing.

Tamsin's heart pounded in her ears and her breaths came in quick bursts, desperately hoping that she could find the small boy. She nearly fell as she burst through a clump of reeds and splashed into a wide stretch of river. She stopped, trying to steady herself and get her bearings.

There, across the deep stream on the other side, stood Cairn.

Their eyes met at the same time and Cairn instantly burst into more tears. Tamsin plunged into the water, droplets spraying around her. It was already at her waist before she even reached the middle.

Then she saw the reeds move off to Cairn's left, as if something had pushed them all aside and was making a path towards the small boy.

"Cairn! Get in the water! Come to me!" Tamsin shouted as she continued to strain against the water.

Cairn, shaken by Tamsin's outcry, immediately stopped crying. His fearful eyes were wide and puffy, it seemed from crying most of the night. His face was smeared with dirt and tears and he hugged his arms around his tiny torso, shivering. He took a few steps into the water, but stopped when it reached his knees. His bottom lip quivered.

"Cairn, come to me!" Tamsin urged again. The reeds were cracking and whipping apart as the amon'jii moved closer. Tamsin was too far yet; she wasn't going to make it before the amon'jii did. She tightened her grip on the sickle, tracking the moving reeds for a few moments and then stretched out her senses. There. She felt it: the amon'jii's fiery heart. The creature was only a few yards away…

Tamsin raised her arm and flung the sickle over Cairn's head. With a great stroke of luck it didn't hit Cairn, but reached its intended mark. A shriek loud enough to send ripples across the water erupted from the reeds. The sound seized Tamsin's heart and threatened to shred her resolve right there, but she charged ahead, trembling with momentary relief when she finally reached Cairn and felt the tiny boy's body in her arms.

"Sshh, you're okay, it's alright now," she murmured, but she knew they had to go. She picked Cairn up in her arms and started wading back into the deeper water.

She had only taken a couple steps when she heard a piercing snarl and the next thing she knew she was shoved forward into the water, a searing pain erupting on her shoulder blade. Through the pain though she managed to stay conscious of Cairn and made sure the boy was not under the water more than a few seconds. She kicked with her feet, shoving against the riverbed and away from the reed-line. They both came up, spluttering, and though the water blurred her vision she saw they were out of harm's reach. But she also got her first look at the amon'jii.

In a moment she realized why Haven had been hesitant to let her come. It was unlike any animal she had ever seen before and much larger, as if the stone creatures guarding the entrance to Empyria had come to life. She took in the rows of teeth led by two large incisors protruding from a long, thick snout. A bulging forehead sloped into two horns that twisted back behind the holes where the ears should have been. Its oily skin stretched tight over its bones as if its spine and ribcage were on the outside instead of inside. It's torso looked as if a lizard had mixed with the stealthy movements of a cat and grown to the size of an ox. It's slanted eyes fixated on her with calculated intent… and in the next moment she felt the pressure in its heart building and she knew what was about to happen.

She was a second too late and a cloud of black fire shot from the creature's mouth. Its distance would have been impressive had it not been aimed at them. Tamsin dove back into the water with Cairn, seeing tiny bubbles burst over the surface from the heat as the fire sizzled over the spot they had been. Instead of resurfacing, she kept them under, until she felt she had control over the amon'jii's heart and clamped down on it. Cairn squirmed in her arms and she knew they had to come up for air.

They broke the surface, Tamsin desperately hoping her power worked. They were near enough the other shore now where Tamsin could sit and still be in the water. Hanging onto Cairn with one arm, she dragged them closer to the reeds with the other.

The amon'jii opened its mouth of razors once again, but nothing came out and it made a choking sound in its throat. It snapped its mouth shut and zeroed in on Tamsin with its yellow eyes once again, as if reassessing the intelligence of its prey. Then its eyes darted momentarily to something just over Tamsin's head and then it turned and fled.

Tamsin felt something grab her arm and haul her out of the water. She cried out as the pain in her shoulder exploded and she swung her fist, but a hand flew out and caught her wrist.

She froze, except for her chest as she panted for air, and followed the hand up a cloaked arm into the dark hood of a Watcher. She did not recognize the glowing mahogany eyes that looked back at her right away, but this Watcher stared at her in disbelief as if he had just ensnared a faerie or a ghost. He seemed familiar somehow, but her mind could only focus on the fact that a Watcher was here now and the amon'jii was not.

The Watcher's gaze slowly pulled away and he looked behind his shoulder and whistled. A moment later another whistle echoed his, somewhere off to the right, and he pulled Tamsin in that direction. They slinked quickly through the reed patch—rather the Watcher slinked and Tamsin plodded, exhausted and soaked with water—until they emerged into another section of river where two canoes were waiting for them.

There was another Watcher there; the source of the other whistle, Tamsin concluded, and she almost sank to her knees when she saw who it was.

"Samih!"

"Tamsin!" Samih rushed over to her, his golden eyes widening when he saw Cairn. "Almighty Q'atorii of all, you found him," he breathed.

"We need to leave. Now," the other Watcher said, ushering them all into the boats.

A shiver ran down Tamsin's neck, making the pain in her shoulder flare as all her muscles tensed. His tone was different; more velvet than edge, but the cadence of his speech was nearly identical to Haven's, almost as if they were brothers. She found herself staring at him as they rowed away, but he kept his gaze pointedly away from her.

Cairn was trembling from head to foot so Tamsin hugged him tightly, rubbing his arms and legs to warm him and murmuring that they were safe now.

"Is he alright?" Samih asked from behind her.

Tamsin nodded. "How did you find us?"

"The dead could've found you, with all the noise you were making," the other Watcher said prickly. "You were lucky there was only one amon'jii."

Cairn whimpered into her sleeve. Tamsin cooed softly, though her irritation rose at the other Watcher. "And how was it that I found Cairn before you? Is that not your job?"

"Tamsin," Samih admonished gently.

"And where have you been?" Tamsin turned to Samih, wincing at her shoulder. She was exhausted and hurting and she knew it wasn't helping her anger. She was genuinely happy to see Samih, but she was in no mood for a lecture.

"He was looking for me," the other Watcher replied. "And the others."

"And who *are* you?"

The Watcher blew air out of his nose and turned to face her. "I'm the one who's pulled you from the water twice now to save your life."

"What are you talking about?" Tamsin's forehead wrinkled in confusion, then those mahogany eyes burned through the fog and she realized she did know him. She had remembered wrong. She had always thought it was Haven who pulled her from the Elglas before following her into the sandstorm. But now she remembered. "You. It was you."

The Watcher's gaze softened slightly at her recognition of him. "I am Kellan." He pointed at something inside the canoe. "We found this. I assume it belongs to you."

It was her pack. She had forgotten all about it in the chaos with the amon'jii. Tamsin's anger melted into the canoe as her shame rose, but she could not form a reply other than her name and a thank you. Luckily, it did not take too long to get back to the Hazees'diin. The canoes had barely touched the edge of Hazees's large mud flat and people were rushing towards them. Poma was one of the first to reach them and she helped Tamsin out of the canoe. Cairn started crying again as Poma scooped him in her arms. Everyone was shouting, and Tamsin couldn't distinguish between the exclamations of relief and the calls to alert others of their safe return. Poma gave her a look, simultaneously scolding her and thanking her, and Tamsin replied in like silence, too tired to form words.

Samih and Kellan stepped up next to her and Tamsin could almost feel the tension radiating from Kellan by the proximity to the sha'diin, though no one seemed to notice the Watchers' presence. Samih spoke up, "Tamsin's wounds need tending."

It was then that she noticed Ysallah next to them and her eyes flashed with concern at the same time as Kellan's, who had not noticed before, but before Tamsin could protest Ysallah was already ushering them away. "Come with me," she told them and they followed her away from the group and into the large muudhiif. Hazees was not there, but she told one of her kazsiin to fetch water and cloth.

"Was she burned?" Ysallah asked the Watchers.

"Not that I know of," Kellan said, kneeling and rifling through a pouch underneath his cloak. "Though it was close."

"It's her shoulder," Samih said.

"It's nothing," Tamsin said, uncomfortable with all the attention turned her way, especially when Ysallah's own wounds still looked quite painful. Samih tried to hide a smirk, already knowing Tamsin's affinity for privacy from traveling together so long.

Kellan shot him a look and then pulled out a clump of moss from the pouch. The kazsiin returned with the water and cloth, which Kellan took and then poured the water onto the moss and began making a greenish-grey paste in his hands.

"You're sure you weren't burned?" Ysallah asked her, peeling back the fabric around her back to see where the cuts ended.

"She would've known if she had," Samih said. "Trust me."

"I wasn't burned," Tamsin confirmed. "And neither was Cairn. Why do you keep asking that?"

"There's only two ways to become a Watcher," Ysallah said. "Either the gods mark you or the amon'jii do."

Tamsin recalled the black fire that had spewed from the creature's mouth. A fire so hot it had instantly made the water's surface boil. It made her wonder about Haven's markings and Samih's lack of.

"Which happened to you?" she asked Samih.

"I was caught in the fire," Samih said, his expression darkening at the memory. "Imagine being burned from the inside instead of out. All of your blood is suddenly on fire—."

"Enough," Kellan said, taking the paste and smearing it on Tamsin's shoulder.

Knowing she did not have to suffer burning alive from the inside made the pain of her shoulder more bearable, but his words chilled her. She had a good imagination, but that was something she could not envision, nor did she want to.

Ysallah waved the kazsiin over, instructing her to wrap the wound. Once that was done she told them all to leave so she could speak with Tamsin alone.

"I need to speak with her first," Kellan said.

Ysallah was reluctant, but at the look Kellan gave her she conceded and followed Samih and the kazsiin outside.

"What did you do?" Kellan asked when they were alone.

It was the first time she was able to get a good look at him aside from his mahogany eyes. He was larger than Samih, and though his cloak hid most of him, Tamsin could tell that he was a fighter just from the way he stood. His face was lean, though his cheekbones were wide and his dark hair rested on his shoulders. "What do you mean?"

"With the amon'jii. I didn't stop its fire."

"You think I did?"

"I know you did. I felt it."

Tamsin resisted the urge to bite her lip, but she knew she was already found out. She hadn't planned on telling anyone. She hadn't even told Samih. But those mahogany eyes of Kellan's would not be lied to.

"Don't tell anyone, please."

He rocked back on his heels. "I wouldn't know what to tell them even if I wanted to."

"Haven recognized it in me first. I believe he knew who my mother was, knew what she was. That's the only way I can explain it."

"Irin was your mother?"

"You knew her?"

He shook his head. "Knew of her. A female Watcher is rarer than a white halcyona. But you are no Watcher." His eyes lost their focus and he seemed to turn inward, connecting dots that Tamsin couldn't see.

She gave him a moment, then asked the question that had been burning inside her since she first heard him speak. "But you knew Haven?"

He slowly came back. "Samih told me what has happened. Why you're here." His expression was tightly controlled, as if he was afraid of some emotion that would leak out and betray him. "He is my best friend. I've known him since we were Cairn's age."

The pain of hope tightened her throat. "Samih told you what we plan to do?"

He nodded.

"You will help us then?"

Even Kellan could not hide the ache in his coffee cream eyes. "*Why* would you fall in love with him?"

Tamsin blinked several times, surprised at the hurt in his voice. It wasn't a question as much as an accusation, as if she had willingly decided to forfeit her heart to a Watcher.

"I told you."

Hazees's voice startled them both and they looked to see her standing in the doorway, still holding the flap open. Several others were standing just behind her, in neither the Hazees'diin nor the Ysallah'diin garb.

Kellan stood up and brushed his fingers in the sign of respect, but she ignored him, staring at Tamsin in something akin to disgust.

"For Cairn's life you may remain another day. But you are the Havakkii's by next sunrise. May the Q'atorii be merciful." Then Hazees marched out of the muudhiif.

Tamsin got a glimpse of the others before the flap closed again and a heavy pit formed instantly in her stomach. She had only seen Haven carry so many weapons, but these men wore their knives like a second skin. Their first being covered in white tattoos and piercings.

One man stepped inside, nodding towards Kellan. "May we speak with her Watcher?" His voice was softer than Tamsin expected and she wondered if it was to give her a false sense of safety. The man's white tattoos were covered only by strips of black cloth tied in necessary places and his weapons. His long hair was adorned with feathers and had small bones interwoven through it. When he smiled he did not show teeth.

"No, her wound needs time to heal. I gave her the root of haava. She'll be asleep in minutes," Kellan lied. He gave Tamsin a quick look, telling her to keep quiet.

"We can wait," the man said respectfully. He left and urged the others to stay outside, though some looked less than pleased to have to acquiesce to a Watcher.

"Those are the Havakkii, aren't they?" Tamsin whispered to him, though they were alone again.

He nodded once. "Does anyone else know what you are capable of?" he asked.

"No. Just you. And Haven."

"You must have done something to bring them here." He dug in his pouch and pulled out a small tuber that looked like a tiny brown carrot. The root of haava, she mused. He pulled out a knife and shaved a few strips off the side of the tuber, making it look more like what Samih had given her, then put the small pieces through the mouth of his water skin.

"Who are they? What do they want with me?" Tamsin asked.

"The Havakkii are—."

"Assassins?" Tamsin interjected.

Kellan gave her a funny look. "What makes you say that?"

"I was…warned," she said.

He furrowed his brow at her, but inquired no further. He handed her the water skin, instructing her to drink and she took a hesitant swallow, remembering the last time she took the powerful herb, though it was no herb at all. The tuber gave the water a bitter taste, like a harsh tea, and she hoped maybe it would work better this time.

"No, not assassins," he continued, "but that doesn't mean they aren't dangerous. They deal with evil spirits and religious disturbances. If they think you harbor jiin they will try to cleanse you."

"But it's not true," she said, though she wondered if even he had heard of her spectacle in the muudhiif the other night.

"Tamsin," he said sternly, "You must let them take you. They'll most likely head for the shaman stones. That's where they like to do their cleansings. But we won't let them get that far."

"Wha…?" Tamsin was going to protest, but suddenly her tongue felt heavy, like it had forgotten how to form words. Kellan's words alarmed her, but she was quickly losing focus as the drink's effects took hold. Kellan gently eased her down to the mat. She should have felt terrified by how paralyzed she felt, but sleep sounded so good…

"You should get some rest while you can," he said. He walked to the door, but paused before he went outside. "Samih and I won't let anything happen to you, I promise."

She wanted to protest, but her will was no match for the tiny brown tuber and Kellan's dark silhouette was the last thing she saw before her eyes closed.

He wished he could become like the stone beneath him. Cold, yet incapable of feeling. Hard and impermeable. Strong and unmoving. Cracked, but that was okay because it was not alive.

Dead.

As Haven's cheek pressed against the floor he wondered if that was what he really wished. Death had never scared him before, but he had always had the will and the instinct to prevail, to survive. But now, the thought of death sparked no such instinct and he wondered if that alone should scare him. But he felt no fear. No sense of obligation to this body or this rocky prison. No loyalty to the light or to the dark. Had Monstran's words finally pervaded his mind? Had he lost the fear that was holding him back? Or had he lost something greater? His mind? His soul?

Or was Monstran right? Was he already dead?

He had watched a tiny, rounded line of blood (out of his nose or mouth he couldn't tell) form a curving path over the uneven rock until it formed a small pool in between his fingers. He had watched it lose its liquid glisten as it dried, until it was just another dark stain. Maybe if enough of his blood faded into the rock, his body would do the same.

Haven!

The sound of his name cracked through his skull. He peeled his eyes away from the floor and saw something moving towards him. Something...it looked like a boy.

He felt his legs drop and then his arms as the chains were loosed from the walls. The young boy pulled the loops out from the shackles and heaved the iron away. The sudden lightness awakened Haven's senses, scratching the back of his mind. The strangeness of the boy's presence and the urgency at which he worked gave life to his curiosity.

"What are you doing?" he asked the boy, his tongue scraping the inside of his mouth like a cactus leaf.

The boy glanced up when he spoke, but didn't stop pulling the chains out. "Sorry buddy, I'm not catching that. Seven hells, they did a number on you didn't they?"

Funny, he could understand the boy, but the boy couldn't understand him. The scratching in his mind intensified, some memory trying to break its way to the surface. Something to do with his father...his father had taught him the boy's language.

The boy pulled the last chain out, his skin shining with sweat. He put one of Haven's arms over his shoulders and hauled him to his feet.

They were roughly the same height, but the boy was scrawny and lacked muscle.

"C'mon, you got to help me out buddy. I can't carry you the whole way."

Carry him? Where were they going? Haven tried to comply and move his legs, but he seemed to have less strength than the boy did. It felt awkward, moving like his joints had turned to stone, but something screamed inside him that he had to do it, to go with the boy. He tried again, staggering as each step fell, but forcing himself to remember where his legs were supposed to bend, how to grip the stone with his feet to keep from slipping. Slowly, his joints began to warm and with the boy's help made it to the doorway.

The crude hallway was just as dark, but the air...oh the air! The air in the cell was oppressive, like he was buried in mud, but walking into the hallway had removed all the pressure. He filled his lungs, feeling the spark burn throughout his body, igniting his limbs. The air was...good. He wanted more of it.

"That's it," *the boy encouraged him, adjusting Haven's arm to accommodate his weight.* "Only 782 more like that and we're home free."

Something hissed in the darkness and Haven looked up to see a bent old woman standing off to one side. Her eyes flashed maliciously. "We'd go a lot faster if we weren't taking him."

The boy grunted. "We'd go a lot faster if you helped us. Or did you already forget who got you out of that cell?"

The woman snarled and twisted on her heels, making no move to help them, but she was never more than a few paces ahead as they trudged down the hall. She paused when they reached intercut sections of the hall, peering down each way before motioning them forward.

Haven set the pace, one which a statue could beat, but the boy challenged him and encouraged him to keep moving. Every now and then they would hear high-pitched howls whispering against the rocks and Haven would get the tingling sense of familiarity, as if he had been here before. Flashes of images of swords and claws clashing together, of blood dripping from his hands, echoes of screams and crashing rocks scratched at his vision. This was a place of death. It made him falter.

The woman paused and turned around slowly to look at him with an expression of concealed horror. "This one is marked. He will only bring misery," *she whispered."*

"Stop your ramblings Mora!" *the boy cried.*

"He's too slow! They'll catch us!" the woman quietly screeched.

They weren't going to make it. Not at this rate. He tried to form his lips into the boy's language, struggling to pull the words from his memory. "Go. She right. You go."

The boy glanced at him in surprise, but shook his head. "I'm not going anywhere buddy. If Tamsin knew I left this place without you she'd have my head."

Tamsin. The name crashed into him like a gale-force wind, knocking the air from his lungs as the memories came streaming out. His knees buckled and the two of them crashed to the floor.

"Hey! No, no, c'mon buddy. We gotta go!"

Haven pressed his hands into the side of his head, trying to keep the memories contained, but they rushed out like a flock of birds released from a net. Everything that he had so carefully locked away came back: the sandstorm, watching her plant the pla'naii seed, seeing the glow of his Lumierii marks reflected in her eyes, the first time she created fire, sitting on the ledge overlooking the river, holding her hand as they jumped off the Armillary, her face in the darkness, tears streaming down her cheeks...

"Just leave him!" the old woman hissed.

"Hey, don't give up now. We're nearly there," the boy's words were gentle, but they cut through the images. "C'mon. I'm not leaving without you." He took Haven's hands and slowly removed them from his head.

Haven looked at him, trying to catch his breath. The boy was kind, just like... "Tamsin." The last shackles on his memory melted off with the warmth of her name.

The boy allowed a smile. "Yeah, we'll get you back to her. You ready?"

Haven nodded once, pressing his lips together in determination. The boy hauled him to his feet and they started off again. They plodded on for what seemed hours, and Haven had to start using the wall for extra support to stay upright. But on they went until they rounded a corner and they saw it.

Up ahead, the tunnel turned sharply to the right, but on the far wall were streaks of light.

They headed towards it with renewed energy, even the old woman seemed to have lost her fearful scorn. But as they got closer to the light, a darkness grew in Haven's thoughts and he slowed. He had been in the *light before; it burned him. He was a Watcher. He did not belong in the light.*

"What's the matter? C'mon," the boy urged, almost begged.

Just then, a shadow passed over the wall, dimming the light, but the hall must have been close to the outside for a new kind of air drifted in. One of space and pine trees and water.

Haven kept going and they made the turn. The hallway widened even further and he got his first glimpse of the outside world. There was a wide plateau stretching out under the overhanging cavern ceiling. There was a stone bridge that traversed the gorge and connected the plateau to the other side of the canyon, which was peppered with scraggly bushes and the skeletons of trees.

The woman made a dash for the bridge, but only got a few feet before jerking to a stop. She reached down and touched something, then brought it to her lips.

Haven and the boy slowed, but continued to limp towards her. When they finally got to the opening, they saw what made her stop. Scattered across the plateau were the dead bodies of a dozen or so men. Their blue and brown uniforms were almost unrecognizable from the amounts of blood that stained them. Glossy red pools marked the final graves.

The boy was visibly upset. He let go of Haven and staggered though the ruins searching for any sign of life. One hand covered his mouth in horror, but the breath that escaped came out ragged and harsh.

That was the first time Haven noticed the boy's clothes. He was dressed similarly to the dead men. These were his comrades, he realized. Haven had seen death before. He looked at one of the upturned faces. Despite the blood still dripping from the corner of his mouth, there was no tension there. No struggle, no pain. Dead men all had the same eyes. Even Watchers. There was no more fire trapped there.

The sun had reappeared from behind the clouds, sinking heavily into the western sky and casting a long shadow from the cavern's overhanging ceiling across the carnage. Haven took a few unsteady steps towards the edge of the shadow, stopping just before his feet crossed over the line into the light. Even Watchers who wanted to die didn't go that way. There were faster ways to get to that peace like he saw on the man's face.

"Leave them!" the woman hissed at the boy. *"There's nothing you can do for them now."* She crept over to the edge of the bridge, sniffing the air as if to gauge any danger in the vicinity.

"You won't get very far before nightfall," an oily voice emerged from the tunnel behind them.

The woman and the boy's heads both jerked up in that direction, but Haven didn't need to turn around to see. He knew that voice.

The woman shrieked and fled across the bridge, obviously willing to take her chances against the beasts of the night than the man behind them.

Haven watched her go. A part of him wanted to run after her, to be free from all the torments he had endured. And Tamsin was out there somewhere. But even though his chains were gone, he found himself unable to move. Every muscle in his body tensed with the conflict. His nostrils flared and his chin quivered as the woman grew smaller and smaller in his sight.

"Haven," the serpentine voice slithered over his skin like the legs of a crawling centipede. *"Step back into the darkness. You know it's where you belong."*

"Don't listen to him!" the boy's voice had risen an octave from emotion. *"He doesn't control you!"* He picked up a sword from one of his fallen comrades, gripping it with both hands and pointed it at the white-haired man. *"Leave us alone!"*

"He can barely walk. How far do you think you will make it?"

More footsteps emerged behind him—no, not footsteps. Claws scraping against the rock. The ground trembled beneath their feet. They were the culprits of the destruction strewn around them. The boy stepped into his line of sight, his eyes wide with fear as the amon'jii edged closer.

"C'mon buddy," the boy was nearly pleading now. *Confusion swept across the boy's face as he beheld the struggle in Haven's eyes. He stepped over until he was right in front of Haven.* *"We can do this. Come with me."*

But he couldn't. Like the amon'jii, he was stuck in the shadows. He wanted to apologize to the boy; he was going to die because he couldn't leave. Even if the boy ran, the amon'jii would hunt him down. He could sense their anger, their lust for blood, and the pulse of their restraint. The white-haired man was right; his heart was not his own. He felt like he was simultaneously being torn apart and squeezed together. He could feel the pull of the white fire drawing him back like a familiar hand. The white fire was strong; it made him strong. Here, on the edge of the light, on the edge of freedom he was weak, shaking like a foxtail in the wind. Sinking. Down into indescribable depths. He was drowning, though the hands that held him under were no longer the white-haired man's. They were his own. He tried to fight back; he was horrified at what was happening, but the last remaining rags of his life were being smothered by something more powerful. The boy had brought memories back to the surface, but now they slipped from his grasp again. His name. Her name. Her name was Tam...

Strength and weakness. Darkness and light. Life and death. There was a certain space between each of them where one was neither and both at the same time. White fire burning in a heart of darkness.

The amon'jii's hunger pulsed in the air around them. Even the boy could feel it as he turned to face them defiantly once more.

Using the last piece of himself he had left, Haven straightened himself as best he could. He could feel the fire burning in the amon'jii, just waiting to be released. But if he could do one last thing, it would be to choose how to die, and being burned by the amon'jii was not what he chose. Haven grabbed the boy's hands and turned the sword towards himself.

The white-haired man's eyes flashed in surprise. He raised his hand and the amon'jii opened its mouth.

"Haven, let go of the sword and I'll let the boy live. Don't, and the boy will die."

Haven's resolve faltered and it was all Monstran needed. He flicked his fingers and the amon'jii struck. It didn't release its fire, but swiped at them with its massive claw, knocking Haven and the boy to the ground and the sword uselessly out of reach. Monstran's human attendants rushed out from the tunnel, grabbing both of them.

"Take Haven back to his cell," Monstran said. "And bring the boy with me. The Master may have use for him yet."

When Tamsin finally awoke, she was surprised to find both Poma and Ysallah in the muudhiif with her. Poma handed her a water skin and a bowl of padi, which she gratefully accepted as her stomach rolled with hunger.

"I feel as if I have slept for days," Tamsin said. She stretched her sore arms and legs. Her shoulder was stiff, but the wound wasn't as tender as it had been, though it remained bandaged.

"You have been," Ysallah said, her eyebrow raising over her good eye. "The Watcher gave you quite a strong dose of haava."

Her conversation with Kellan came rushing back to her, though she couldn't be remembering it right. "The Havakkii, are they still here?"

"And making everyone nervous," Ysallah said. "But Poma convinced them not to take you while you were unconscious."

Tamsin nodded to Poma in gratitude.

"Hazees has been on the warpath about it," Poma said, "but they would have a hard time expelling any jiin from you while you are asleep."

Tamsin tried not to let her frustration show. "I'm not possessed or haunted by evil spirits or whatever else Hazees accuses me of."

"But something haunts your dreams," Ysallah said quietly.

Tamsin stiffened slightly. It was something she and Samih had stopped talking about so she had forgotten how jarring it had been for him to see her that way and to hear her screaming in her sleep. She hadn't realized it had been happening here. The strong dose of haava had worked; she couldn't remember anything. What if—what if she was possessed? It was the first time she had entertained the thought. The nightmares had only started recently, but she had seen the blue lady three times now. But the two seemed unrelated. No, she couldn't be possessed, she thought. But was that why Kellan wanted her to go with the Havakkii? Had Samih told him of her nightmares?

"Have you ever heard of pak'kriin?" Ysallah asked, interrupting her thoughts. At Tamsin's silence she continued. "In its simplest form it means *tribesmen stealing*. Some members of tribes are coveted by others because of their skills or strength. It usually ends up causing war. But since you are not Ysallah'diin I cannot keep the Havakkii from taking you."

"Hazees is the one that wants me gone and I am not Hazees'diin either. What right does she have—."

"You are in her territory and you are tribeless. She has every right," Poma said.

"I am prepared to protect you, but only if you become Ysallah'diin," Ysallah said.

The weight of her words sunk in sharply. Ysallah's priorities were not Tamsin's, and understandably so, but they did not align with Tamsin's purpose here. Ysallah had been trying to claim Tamsin since they first came to Empyria and Haven had risked a lot to prevent that. But the Havakkii were here wanting to take her away and do lords knew what. Kill her? Or at the best isolate her from the rest of the Ma'diin. She doubted very much that a "cleansing" was something she would enjoy.

"I don't think you understand who the Havakkii are and what they are capable of, otherwise you would not hesitate to join me," Ysallah said.

"It doesn't matter," Tamsin said. "Either way I lose my freedom."

"You'll lose your life if you go with them. I can protect you."

"Like you protected your people?"

Ysallah's expression went cold. She stood up, with some effort, but even as beat up and bruised as she was there was no mistaking who the Kazsera in the muudhiif was.

"You will regret your decision." Ysallah limped towards the door.

"Why do you want me to join you so badly?" Tamsin asked.

Ysallah paused, her nose flaring. "I made a promise to your mother." Then she left.

Tamsin did her best to seem confident, but her doubts were quickly consuming her. "Where are Kellan and Samih?" she asked. Kellan seemed to think staying here with Ysallah and Hazees was more dangerous than going with the Havakkii and she wanted to trust him, but everything in her was telling her going with them would take her even farther away from Haven. Samih had warned her when they arrived that he couldn't guarantee her safety, and it seemed he may have been right, though she hadn't quite expected this.

"They had to leave, Tamsin."

Tamsin's stomach dropped. "W-what?"

Poma frowned, the only outward sign of sympathy she offered. "You should have run when you had the chance," she said, though there was a tremor to her voice that made Tamsin think she was truly sorry for how things turned out. But she left too, leaving Tamsin with the gravity of what was happening.

It was hardly a minute after Poma left that the Havakkii came to take her. Gone were the gentle expressions and soft words. There was a greed in their eyes as they entered the muudhiif, an eagerness that set her instincts to flee on fire. But there was nowhere to escape to. Two came forward and grabbed her arms, pulling her outside where a third waited for them down by the canoes. He held a circle of thick rope, but it was not tied to any of the canoes. It was for her.

"I forgot my pack," she said quickly, but it was a feeble attempt too late and they both knew it.

"You will not be needing it," the Havakkii with the rope said.

Tamsin looked around for Poma, for Kellan, for anyone that could help her, but she recognized no one in the crowds that huddled together from the safety of their own mud flats. Except for Hazees, who stood triumphantly in the entrance of her muudhiif, barely able to conceal a smile.

The rope was shoved around her wrists and tightened, pulling her attention back to the Havakkii.

"Please," he said, indicating the canoe, and though this man still feigned politeness Tamsin was not fooled. Mikisle's tale the other night was a warning and she knew if she stepped into that canoe it could be the last time she ever did so.

Giving in to her instincts, Tamsin lashed out with her foot, connecting with the man's knee. As he fell, she reached out and snatched one of his many knives. She whipped around and the other two Havakkii jumped back to avoid the blade. But the first one had never let go of his end of the rope that was tied around her wrists and her kick had not been strong enough to make him abandon his wits. With one yank, Tamsin was thrown to the ground, and she lost hold of the knife.

The man with the rope was smiling. He picked up the knife where it had fallen and planted a foot on her back, shoving her further into the dirt.

Tamsin struggled to free herself from the man's weight, but then she froze, feeling the sharp point of the knife pushing into her wounded shoulder.

"It's funny," the man leaned down closer, "the man whose knife this belonged to had a jiin that resisted us too. That man needed a strong cleansing." He dug the point in a little deeper, turning it slightly.

Tamsin held back a moan, but tears exploded at the corners of her eyes.

"The shaman stones won't be enough for this one," the man said loud enough for his comrades to hear. "No, I think we'll take you to the mangroves instead."

Chapter Eleven

Tamsin could smell the mangroves before she could see them. There was a salty scent to the air and something else in the breeze that she hadn't come across since she left the Cities: trees. The pungent, woody smell that accompanied a lush forest, dense with vegetation and life. But the brush of nostalgia quickly passed as their canoes emerged from the reeds of the marshes. A wide channel of water opened up before them, as if the reeds refused to grow any closer, revealing the edge of the mangrove forest on the opposite side. The burst of green was in stark contrast to the tawny brown of the reeds and the leafy canopy extended twice as high. But it was the trees' roots that made the mangroves so unique and strange. They spread out like gnarled hands at least two feet above the water, giving the illusion that the trees were floating on top of the water. It was refreshing to look at the intertwining roots and how the wide, palm-shaped leaves reflected on the water, but the further Tamsin looked into the forest, the more the canopy choked out the sunlight and the darker and more intimidating it became.

The Havakkii guided the canoes to an opening in the trees and within moments of entering the mangroves it felt as if they had entered a completely new world. As other worldly as the marshes had seemed to her after months in the desert, the vibrancy of the mangrove trees was almost dizzying. The sound of birds and insects echoed throughout the branches, creating a steady hum of activity. There were other sounds too: creatures moving through the trees, branches being snapped, something splashing in the water, some animal howling in the distance…and the chanting of the Havakkii.

It had begun just before they entered the mangroves and Tamsin had thought it just a boat song, for she had heard other Ma'diin singing to pass the time along the waterways, but the words were neither melodious nor were they any Ma'diin words she was familiar with.

Suddenly a cover was thrown over her head and her view of the mangroves disappeared.

"What are you doing?" She turned her head slightly to the one sitting behind her in the canoe. None of them had given her their names, but this one seemed to be the leader and had a scar on his left foot so she had taken to calling him Scarfoot.

He paused, though the other two continued chanting. "We are preparing the way for your spirit so that it may be joined with the gods once it is cleansed of the jiin. Your spirit knows the words and will use them to find its way out of the mangroves, but the jiin will be trapped in the forest."

"Could you chant a little more clearly then so I can find my way out?" she muttered into the dark cloth. She was trying not to sound afraid, but she knew that she was hopelessly alone. Kellan had thought the Havakkii were taking her to the shaman stones, whatever those were. But even if he had been planning on rescuing her it didn't matter now, because he was going one way and she another.

Scarfoot chuckled. "Your body will not be leaving this place."

Sweat trickled down Tamsin's neck. "How exactly do you propose to get the jiin out?" She didn't particularly want to know the details, but maybe he would give her something that would help her come up with a way out of this mess. And right now talking was the only way to keep her fear in check.

"The Q'atorii will give you three tests. If you survive the first, then you will be given the second and then the third and final test, though it is quite more merciful if your jiin leaves by the first, especially since it ends in your death anyway."

"The Q'atorii? Did it ever occur to you that maybe your gods are the ones meddling with my life and not some jiin?" Until now it hadn't occurred to her either because her old self didn't believe in gods or magic. But that girl hadn't seen the things she had seen. That girl couldn't control fire.

She had thought about setting the canoes ablaze and the rope that held her captive to the prow, but she couldn't chance the Havakkii being better swimmers than she and one swipe of one of their many weapons would end her.

"The Q'atorii only speak through the chosen," Scarfoot said. "And you are not one of them."

"And I suppose you are?"

Scarfoot was silent, but Tamsin imagined he was smiling.

Suddenly the chanting ceased and the boat came to a stop. She felt it sway as Scarfoot stepped out and then the pull of the rope as he untied her hands from the prow. Arms lifted her out of the boat and set her down on spongy ground. The tug of the rope propelled her forward and she immediately tripped over a root, landing nearly shoulder deep in water. She scurried back up before she went any further and used the moment to whip the cover off her head.

She squinted against the sudden light, but that was all she could do before hands were on her again, holding her firmly in place.

"It's alright," Scarfoot said to the other two holding her. "She won't need it anymore."

He tugged the rope again and moved her off of the spongy patch of ground and towards the tree he was standing next to. There was a wide gap in the roots where they reached down into the water. Scarfoot lifted her up and put her in the gap; the water came up to his waist, but was already chest deep for Tamsin. He held her back against the trunk as the other two starting pulling out rope from the boats.

"You never told me what the three tests were," Tamsin said.

Scarfoot smiled. "Your first test will come in the form of an animal."

"An amon'jii?" Tamsin's stomach dropped. She had no wish to encounter another one so soon.

"No, the amon'jii have no interest in the mangroves, but there are other animals that live here. Hungry animals."

One of the Havakkii came back with some rope and ducked under the water. Tamsin felt the rope tighten against her ankles, securing her feet against the trunk. She squirmed, but Scarfoot's grip on her was like iron.

"If you survive them, then the Q'atorii will send the second test, in which your height will be a disadvantage."

The Havakkii then grabbed her arms, pulling her back against the trunk as Scarfoot cut the rope binding her wrists. They pulled her arms behind the trunk and re-tied them beneath the water.

"And the third?"

Scarfoot cupped his hands under the water and then brought them back up to her lips. "Drink, for this will be the last time you do."

She stared at him hard for a moment, trying to discern what he meant, but he raised his eyebrow and brought his hands closer. Finally, she tilted her head and took a sip. Her eyes widened in realization. The salty smell in the air was from the water. It was saltwater.

Scarfoot nodded. "We will come back in seven days for your body, or what's left of it."

Tamsin's nostrils flared. She wanted to say something. She wanted to scream. But her anger and fear paralyzed her voice as surely as the ropes paralyzed her body.

Scarfoot grinned one last time and then stepped away with the other Havakkii. Tamsin could hear them sloshing through the water, then the scratching of the reeds as they got back in their boats, and the dip of their paddles in the water.

After a minute, all she heard was the drumming of her own frantic heart.

Emilia tapped at a stubborn raindrop on the windowpane. The rain was finally letting up after three days, but it did not matter. Emilia had not been allowed to leave the great house since they arrived. She was finally free of Empyria, but what good was it when she was forced to remain behind the doors of the Urbane manor? It seemed she had escaped one set of walls only to be detained by another.

At least she could do away with the wretched veil she'd been wearing while she was in her bedroom—well, Tamsin's bedroom. No one other than Lavinia and Sherene were allowed in her private quarters. Lord Urbane too, but he had to be even more careful with his disguise and had not risked being seen in the house. Emilia did not even know where he was staying. She could walk about the house if she had her veil on, though she was instructed not to speak to the servants lest they figure out she was not really Tamsin. She had asked Lavinia how much longer they planned on keeping up the ruse, but her question was dismissed with a vague answer about getting things squared away with her future. Emilia didn't think Lavinia had any plans at all in place for Emilia; if she did she was being tight-lipped about it.

She didn't know how much longer she could keep up pretenses herself. The accepted mourning period had long since expired. But she knew no one here. She couldn't even send a letter.

There was a sharp knock on the door and Lavinia came in, followed by Sherene.

"Please, come in," Emilia said without luster, not bothering to move away from the window.

"Dull your tongue for a moment girl," Sherene snapped. "We may not be your favorite people, but Lady Lavinia is still the mistress of this house and—."

"It's alright Sherene," Lavinia interjected, holding up a consolatory hand. But what was in her other was what piqued Emilia's interest. That and the strain on Lavinia's face looked like she was about to break some unpleasant news.

"What have you got there?" Emilia asked.

Lavinia held up a piece of parchment. "My letter never made it. It came back."

"Came back?" Sherene asked. "What does that mean?"

"Wait." Emilia finally moved away from the window. "What letter?"

"I sent a letter to Cornel—Lord Saveen," she corrected herself. "I wanted to ask him if Tamsin was there or if—if she was really gone. But the letter was returned. It's the second time I've tried."

"Why are you telling me this?"

"That's not what I came to tell you." She paused, taking a deep breath.

Emilia unconsciously straightened, bracing herself for whatever Lavinia was going to say.

"I came to tell you that I've been making inquiries about your aunt, the one you said lived in the Cities."

Emilia barely dared to breathe. "And?"

"And...I'm sorry Emilia. Your aunt passed away two years ago."

Emilia was dumbfounded. Two whole years. And her parents hadn't said a word.

Lavinia's face was truly sympathetic. "I'm so sorry Emilia. I have a meeting with your aunt's estate steward tomorrow morning to see if he knows of any other family members in the Cities."

This jarred Emilia out of her stupor. "Please let me come with you. I won't say a thing, I swear."

"It's too risky. If I find anything out I will let you know, I promise. I'll be leaving right after noon, since it is all the way in Fairmoore. Sherene, please tell Mr. Brandstone to have the coach ready by then." She looked as if she wanted to say something more, but instead she turned and left, followed by Sherene.

Emilia went slowly back to the window, trying to keep her emotions in check. She had thought about writing a letter to her parents, letting them know she was safe and well-looked after, though she had wondered why they had not written to her. It stung far more than she cared to admit. She had left them a note, as Tamsin had instructed her to do, but she didn't think they would abandon her completely. And maybe they hadn't. If Lavinia couldn't get a letter to Empyria, then maybe her parents couldn't get a letter to the Cities. The hurt she had felt lessened a little with that thought.

Suddenly an idea occurred to her. If she could get to the Lords' Council building, then she might be able to find out what was going on in Empyria and why there were no correspondences. She would've asked Lord Urbane, but he was keeping a low profile. She hadn't seen him since they arrived. He had mentioned that it was too dangerous for him to make himself known yet. But Lavinia was leaving in just a few short hours and with Lord Urbane in hiding that only left Sherene to get past.

She smiled. She already had the perfect disguise: herself.

It was easier than she thought, getting past the servants. Emilia had changed out of the mourning garments in favor of one of Tamsin's day dresses, a vibrant purple gown with a white petticoat that peaked through a slit in the skirt. She chose a white, wide-brimmed fascinator to match and donned a pair of delicate lace gloves as well. She then snuck downstairs and made it all the way to the front door and outside. But instead of simply leaving, she turned around and knocked. Mr. Brandstone answered a few moments later and looked rather puzzled seeing her there. But she was good at lying, as Tamsin had said weeks ago, and she told him she was a friend of Tamsin's, hoping to visit after hearing she had returned from Empyria. As expected, Mr. Brandstone said she was not receiving visitors, as Emilia had known was instructed by Lavinia. Emilia feigned disappointment, but instead of leaving right away she asked if she could borrow the carriage for it looked like another wave of rain might pass through and she would never make it home in time if she were to walk. Mr. Brandtone eyed the sky doubtingly, but conceded nevertheless. Once the open-air carriage was brought, for Lavinia had already left in the coach, she instructed the driver to take her to the Lords' Council building.

She felt slightly dizzy and giggled the whole way like she had had one too many drinks, but she didn't care about the funny looks the driver gave her because she planned on enjoying every second of her freedom. There was so much to see and it was all so different from anything she was used to. Every building, every brick, every tree was precisely placed along the streets and flowed seamlessly from one thing to the next. They passed little shops and gardens where people strolled arm in arm, statues of great men Emilia didn't know, and massive estates like the Urbane's whose circumferences took up entire blocks.

But the most impressive sight was the Lord's Council building. They passed underneath a square, white stone arch that towered over the neighboring trees and contained carvings of horses in each of its supporting legs. Beyond that was a cobbled courtyard where the carriages could turn around amidst tall pedestals that formed a half circle in front of the building. Each pedestal contained a flag with a Lord's crest on it and being the capitol of the seven ruling Cities of Delmar each Lord was represented. She recognized her father's, a plumed soldier holding a spear, but the next one, a deep red flag with an S emblazoned in an orange triangle, made her remember why she had come here. Leading up to the building was a waterfall of stairs and she took a deep breath as she got out of the carriage. The building itself was a wall of pillars stretching up four stories. It needed no other ornamentation, for its solid façade was enough to cast an air of authority.

There were others going in and out so Emilia walked up the stairs to the entrance, putting on her own air of authority. Nobody stopped her as she went inside, though she was aware of several looks glanced her way as there were not many women around. The inside opened up into a large hall, covered in marble and lined on each side with chandeliers. Smaller hallways led off on each side, tiled with glossy red stones and flanked by more statues.

Before she could even wonder where to go someone approached her. He was dressed similarly to how the butlers dressed here, but he wore a smart hat that was more military than service. He asked her if she needed assistance.

"Indeed I do," she said sweetly. "I have family in Empyria you see, and I'm quite worried because they haven't returned any of my letters. Is there someone I can speak to about this?"

The man eyed her carefully. "What is your name madame?"

"Emma Regoran," she said, holding out her gloved hand. "Niece to Lord Regoran."

The man ignored her proffered hand. "Wait here." Then he marched over to where another man dressed similarly was standing and they conversed briefly.

Emilia clasped her hands behind her back and looked around the room, trying to appear unconcerned, but the way the men kept glancing at her made her uneasy. Someone bumped into her shoulder as they walked by and she was about to say something, but the man looked back at her first.

It was Lord Urbane. And his glare was not happy.

The other man started walking back and Lord Urbane walked away, lowering his gaze under his turban. The man paid him no attention and addressed Emilia, who was trying to hide her surprise. "Come with me," he said.

Suddenly Emilia wished she hadn't come, but she had no choice but to follow. He led her down one of the red hallways until they came to a black door. He opened it and ushered her inside. There was nothing intimidating about the room, there were plush chairs and a large wooden desk and portraits on the walls, but the man behind the desk gave her goosebumps.

He was an older man, dressed in dark military garb, with a bald head and chiseled features to the point of extremity. He motioned for her to sit down while the other man waited by the door.

"I am Commander Garz," the man said. "What can I help you with?"

Emilia swallowed and repeated what she had told the other man.

Commander Garz clasped his hands on top of his desk. "You know, I don't seem to recall Lord Regoran having any siblings."

"A sister," Emilia lied. It was true, her father had no siblings. Emilia's aunt was on her mother's side. "Though she died several years ago and my father was never in the picture. So I kept my mother's name." She hoped she sounded convincing and Commander Garz would make the assumption that her birth had been unplanned and therefore kept hidden. If he thought she was actually Lord Regoran's daughter, she didn't want him sending her back to Empyria.

"Well, Miss Regoran, you know that there is unrest in Empyria right now." He stood up and started pacing around the room. "Rumors of traitors. Even Lords conspiring against the Cities." He paused behind her chair, putting a hand on her shoulder.

She wanted to shake it off, but she forced herself to remain still.

"If you receive correspondence from your uncle or anyone from Empyria you are to come back and notify me directly, is that clear?" he said.

"Of course," she replied, flashing a quick smile.

He squeezed her shoulder before letting go. "Good," said. "I hope to see you again soon, Miss Regoran." Then he motioned to the other man who opened the door behind her.

Emilia couldn't get out of the office fast enough, but she forced another smile and gave him her thanks before leaving. The man escorted her back to the entrance, but disappeared again as soon as she was outside.

Her chest heaved as she let out a deep breath and pulled her gloves off her shaking hands. *Damn, these dresses are tight*, she thought, wishing she had a flask.

Someone stepped out from behind the pillar closest to her and she nearly jumped, but it was only Lord Urbane. His expression reflected a barely contained storm.

He pulled her swiftly away from the entrance and out of earshot of anyone walking in or out. "What are you doing here?" he hissed.

"I'm trying to help you." She pulled her arm away.

"Help me?"

"Your wife has been trying to get in touch with Cornelius Saveen. Yeah, I thought that might get your attention," she said, correctly reading the flash of surprise in his eyes.

Lord Urbane shook his head. "That doesn't explain what you're doing here."

"I'm trying to get answers. Lavinia's letters keep getting returned. And I haven't received anything from my parents."

Lord Urbane sighed. "I'm sorry, but you shouldn't be here. You will have to go back and do as Lavinia says for now."

"I met with Commander Garz," she said quickly. "He said there's unrest in Empyria. He said there's traitors there."

"He told you this?"

Emilia relayed the whole conversation, as short and one-sided as it had been. "I think he thinks that my father is a traitor and that he might try to contact me."

"Saveen is the traitor," Lord Urbane said. "I've been trying to find out just how deep his connections here go. It doesn't surprise me that Commander Garz is one of them."

"What is going on in Empyria exactly?" she asked. "Can't we just send someone? Or ask Tamsin? She was supposed to marry Cornelius after all."

"We both know that's impossible. And it's your fault if she's in any danger."

This stirred Emilia's blood. "*We both know*," she fired back, "that she would have stayed with or without my help."

"And why did you help her? Hmm? Maybe because she was in this whole mess because of you in the first place!?"

Emilia felt tears spring to the corners of her eyes and it inflamed her anger even more. "Why is she the only one you care about!? How come you never cared about me!? How come you never cared if I was safe!?"

"What are you talking about?" Lord Urbane grabbed her by the shoulders, nearly lifting her off the ground. "Speak!"

Emilia's eyes widened. She hadn't meant to say that much; it just slipped out. But she couldn't take it back now. "You had an affair with my mother." She watched Lord Urbane's hard gaze soften to confusion. "I am the product of that affair."

As much as she pulled and strained, Tamsin could not get the ropes that held her to the mangrove tree to budge. It had been hours since the Havakkii had left her alone in the watery forest and she had gone through every wave of fear and desperation to finally exhaustion. She was emotionally and physically spent and the Havakkii's so-called "tests" hadn't even begun.

She sagged forward, shaking with fatigue. Her long hair melted into the water, framing her reflection. The image reminded her of another time she had seen her reflection in the bathing level pool in Empyria. She had not recognized that girl then, a pitiful shell of a person who had been struck down by loss. Did she recognize her reflection now? Was this the face of someone who had given up and succumbed to fear?

Haven would not have given up. He would not have given in to the fear.

She let out a shaky breath. She could not control the situation, but she could control how she responded to it.

"No fear," she said to her reflection through gritted teeth.

She saw it then just before she felt it. Just past her reflection, beneath the surface, something moved, then brushed against her leg. Her breath hitched and that fear drove through her again like a stake. The thing was long and oily, moving against her leg like a lover's caress. And then it disappeared.

Panic and fear of the unknown began to rise, but she knew she had to calm down if she was to think clearly. She focused on slowing her breathing. That was something she could control.

The creature emerged from the water a few yards away, coiling itself around a tree root. Tamsin had never seen a snake this close before and she had to swallow the sick feeling that came with knowing it had touched her just moments before. It's black body crept up the root slowly until it reached the trunk's base, then it flicked its tongue out as if it were tasting the air. It's girth was easily the size of her forearm, but it seemed to have no trouble maneuvering through the roots. It flicked its tongue out one more time and then began to descend back into the water once more. This time it stayed on the surface, weaving back and forth…aiming right for Tamsin.

Tamsin's eyes widened, realizing it was coming back for her. She pulled against her bonds and started moving as much as she could to try and scare it away, but it kept coming.

Just before it reached her it suddenly veered quickly to the left, meandering away from her through the water.

Tamsin let out a sharp breath and stopped her frantic movements. What was it doing? She watched it for a minute, but it continued to swim away. It's behavior was baffling. Either it had suddenly lost interest or— or something else had scared it off.

Tamsin slowly turned her head, trying to look behind her, but she saw nothing within the mangroves. She listened for a long minute, but again she could not discern any unusual noises. She did notice though how bleak the light had become. The reflections of the trees and the water were starting to blend together. Night wasn't far off.

Tamsin felt a sharp prick on the back of her neck then. She tilted her head to the side, wincing and wishing she could bring her hand up to rub it.

She gasped as she felt another prick close to the first. What was going on?

She pressed her neck into the trunk, hoping to dispel whatever it was. But then she felt another and another. She jerked her head to the side as she felt one pierce her shoulder and saw a tiny ant crawling across her skin. And then another joined it. Beyond her shoulder she could see a line of them skittering up the tree trunk.

She cried out, horrified as the pricking intensified, each sting leaving a burning sensation in its wake. As if she were on fire.

That was it.

Tamsin reacted to the thought instantly, foregoing any harm she might cause herself in the process. She called upon the familiar energy and a flame shot up the side of the tree trunk, scorching every ant and leaf behind her.

She subdued it just as quickly before she went up in flames too. Her neck and shoulders still burned from the ants' bites, but she no longer felt them crawling on her.

Panting from the sudden release, she looked around. Pieces of charred bark had fallen around her, sending little ripples out into the darkening water. Movement to her right caught her eye and she saw the snake again, making its way up another root system. She realized then that the ants were what had deterred it earlier. She didn't know if it had stuck around for another chance at her or to watch the ants finish her off.

"I swear I will set you on fire too if you come any closer," she panted at the snake.

It's lidless eyes stared back at her a moment and then it slowly moved away.

Tamsin didn't want to give much credence to the Havakkii's warning of three "tests" she would endure in the mangroves, and she certainly didn't want to stick around for the second if that had been the first. The encounter had been horrifying, but it had awakened her determination again.

And it had given her an idea.

Chapter Twelve

Tamsin had to hurry. The water was rising and she was running out of time. The Havakkii's second test was upon her and she had yet to accomplish her goal. The last several hours she had spent methodically using her power to burn parts of the tree down. Her idea to burn the entire thing down all at once quickly evaporated after her first attempt. She was sorely out of practice and attempting to bring down something so massive had nearly made her lose consciousness. So she had slowed down, taken her time with each branch and rested in between. Until she noticed the water level had reached her shoulders.

She didn't understand how it was possible at first, but then the pieces had clicked. Scarfoot had said her height would be a disadvantage and Tamsin was far from the tallest person in the world. And the water here was salty, which meant the mangroves were near an ocean.

Oceans had tides.

If she didn't get out of these binds quickly she was going to drown.

There were only a few branches left. The rest floated around the roots in severed pieces. But she was in no danger of the remaining ones falling on her so it was time to attack the trunk itself. She focused on the wood behind her just above the water line. She had tried multiple times to burn through the ropes themselves, but the water effectively suffocated her efforts.

She felt the tree growing hot behind her and the scent of charred wood filled her nose. She leaned away from it as far as she could and let the flames engulf what was left of the tree. She held it as long as she could and when she could stand the heat no more she released it.

Breathing hard from the effort she managed to stay awake. She gave herself a minute, though the water was creeping up over her shoulders now. When she had caught her breath she pushed back against the still hot trunk with her head, using all of her might to tip it over. Suddenly it gave way and crashed into the water behind her.

She cried out loud as happy tears spilled down her cheeks. But she had no time to savor her victory. She still had to get her hands over the stump which reached up to her shoulders. Her ankles were tied to the tree itself, but by some stroke of luck or error by the Havakkii her hands were only tied together, not to the trunk itself. She stretched forward as far as she could, her chin dipping into the water and reached her arms up behind her, but it was not enough to get over the stump.

She tried again, this time bringing her elbows up first, her muscles already burning from being behind her for so long. She leaned forward again, inching her hands up little by little until she felt the stump. Gritting her teeth, she reached up, up…

And fell forward into the water as her hands were suddenly freed. Her instinct to catch herself went unfulfilled and she struggled to right herself again. She grabbed onto the trunk again and lifted herself back out of the water, her legs shaking from the effort of keeping her upright. She hadn't realized just how much the tree had been supporting her until now. She coughed and spat water out of her mouth, taking only a moment to get enough air again. She took a deep breath and slid back under, working her way back down to her feet. She felt the ropes around her ankles, and where the knots were. She managed to find the ends, though it was difficult to work them with her hands still bound together.

She pushed back up to the surface, taking in a huge breath. The water was now up to her chin. She had to work fast. Taking another deep breath she dove back under, bending her knees and working her way down the trunk until she found the knot again. She pictured the knot in her mind, working the end through each loop until she had to go up for air again. She had to tilt her face up to get a good breath this time. This was it. It was now or never.

She plunged back down, fumbling to find the right strand as urgency set in. She found it and started working it through again. Then she felt the ropes loosen around her ankles. Hope sparked in her and she tried to move faster as her lungs screamed at her for more air. She pulled on the loose rings until there was just enough space and she was able to wriggle her feet out. She pushed off against the trunk with as much force as she could muster and to the surface.

She managed to gasp for one breath before she was back under. She curled up into a ball and wormed her arms underneath her butt and legs, somersaulting through the water as she worked to get her arms in front of her. Finally, she got her hands in front of her and she made her way back to the surface.

Coughing and spluttering, she kicked until she found a root to grab onto. She pulled herself up, climbing up the roots and not stopping until she was completely out of the water. She collapsed at the top, shaking from head to toe as water droplets fell off her skin.

Two tests down. One to go.

Emilia sat on the edge of her bed back at the Urbane house, wondering what in the world would become of her now. Tamsin had promised she would be taken care of, but how could she have known all that would transpire? It was funny how only this morning Emilia was wishing for the day when she could just be herself again, but now it was probably the only thing keeping her from being cast out onto the street.

Lord Urbane had practically done it already. After the shock of the news, he had brusquely escorted her back outside and to the nearest free coach to take her back to the Urbane estate without so much as a word.

So now Emilia sat here, hoping beyond hope, that Lavinia came back from her meeting tomorrow with some good news.

"I didn't know about you."

Emilia jumped at the voice and her head whipped towards the sound.

Lord Urbane stood in the doorway, his turban clenched in his hands in front of him. He took a step in, but stopped, his expression asking permission.

Emilia nodded rigidly, indicating the divan on the wall across from the bed. "It's not my room," she said.

He winced a little, though she couldn't tell if it was from her words or his leg as he limped over and sat down. He only took a moment to glance around the room, Tamsin's room, before focusing solely on her. "I'm sorry," he said. "I should've handled it better, but you caught me by surprise. I didn't know about you."

It still hurt, but she believed him. If he hadn't known about her, then she couldn't blame him.

"Aren't you afraid someone's going to see you here?"

"This is worth the risk. I want to make things right by you Emilia."

His words caught her off guard. "Even after all that I've done?"

"I didn't understand why you were so cruel to Tamsin when we first arrived in Empyria, but I do now, at least I think I do. And it's my fault."

Emilia shook her head. "It's not. How could you have known? I had just found out before you arrived and when I saw Tamsin…I don't know. I was hurt and angry and I took it out on her. And when she almost died, I couldn't bear to face her I was so ashamed." Her emotions were threatening to rise to the surface, for just being able to talk to someone about it felt like a release.

"I thought you wanted nothing to do with me because I was—because I was a bastard," she continued, dropping her gaze.

"Emilia, I'm not the man I was back then, but even so, I'd like to think that had I known about you I would have wanted *everything* to do with you. Becoming a father changed me for the better."

"But you had your nice little family. You had Lavinia and Tamsin and everything was perfect."

"It was far from perfect, believe me."

Emilia looked up at this.

Lord Urbane squeezed the turban in his hands. "Lavinia and I married right after I got back from Empyria. But I didn't come back alone. I had Tamsin with me."

Emilia felt her mouth drop open slightly. "But Lavinia…"

"Isn't Tamsin's mother," he finished.

Emilia's tongue felt as heavy as the mattress beneath her. "Does Tamsin know?"

He shook his head. "No, I don't think so." He continued on, telling her in more detail the events that took place after his affair with Lady Regoran, his time in Empyria, and how his mother had arranged the marriage to Lavinia. He had returned to the Cities with an illegitimate child and in an attempt to salvage the Urbane name his mother had negotiated the marriage between him and Lavinia, who could not have children of her own.

Emilia tried to swallow all of this information. "The marriage was a cover up."

"In essence, yes. Tamsin needed a mother, Lavinia had no other prospects, and I couldn't let my family down by letting our name fall into disrepair. Like I said, I was a different man before Empyria. I loved Tamsin's mother, but Lavinia showed me what it was like to be in a family. She took on more than she deserved, but she handled it with grace, and I learned to love her for it."

Emilia looked down at her hands in her lap. "I won't tell her who I am."

Lord Urbane furrowed his brow.

"Lavinia," Emilia explained. "I won't tell her about you and my mother."

"I appreciate that," he said earnestly. "But that's not why I came back. I truly want to do what's best for you. Until all this business with Empyria is sorted out though…"

"I understand. Anyway, Lavinia is going to my aunt's estate to see if I have any relatives that would put me up. I shouldn't be in your hair for much longer."

Lord Urbane's hands appeared on her own and she looked up to see him kneeling in front of her.

"Emilia, if you want to leave I'll see to it that you are taken care of, but you are my family too now. If you choose to stay, I—I would like very much to get to know you better."

"Are you sure?"

"I've judged you harshly and I wish to make up for it, if you'll allow me to."

Emilia sniffed loudly and wiped the corner of her eye. "You shouldn't kneel on your leg like that." He smiled and she helped him stand. "I suppose I could stick around a while longer. I mean, Tamsin is my half-sister after all, so if you need me to pretend to be her yet I can do that. Until she's safe." It was strange thinking of Tamsin that way, even after saying it out loud, but even if she didn't feel quite sisterly towards her yet she knew she had to try. If not for her sake then for Lord Urbane's. She believed him when he said she was family now too, but she wouldn't fool herself into thinking things would be honey from here on out. Not without effort on both their parts.

"Thank you. Tamsin was always keen on exploring and finding her own adventures to go on as a girl," he said fondly, "but the stakes are real in this one and she doesn't even know she's in it." His smile turned sad.

"Can I ask you something?"

He nodded.

"I get why Tamsin wanted me to pretend to be her, but why do you? Why does Lavinia?"

"I'm glad Lavinia's letters did not reach Cornelius, because he's unpredictable. He's had an iron grip on Empyria since we left and as long as he thinks Tamsin is here, then I know he won't go looking for her elsewhere. Sherene has filled me in on his courtship with Tamsin, but the Saveens have cost me too much already. I won't let him near Tamsin if I can help it."

Emilia had to ignore that last part in favor of what he said about Empyria. "How do you know what he's been up to in Empyria?"

He looked as if he didn't want to tell her, but he knew he had already given himself away. "I have a contact who knows who I am inside Empyria. He says Cornelius has complete control over Empyria and has cut off any correspondence with the Cities."

So she had been right in assuming her parents couldn't get any letters to her. "Why would he do that?" she asked.

"That," he said with a shake of his head, "is what I can't figure out."

Cornelius wasn't an idiot. He knew that it was only a matter of time before Mr. Monstran would call on him again. Or he wouldn't. He had a way of showing up uninvited, much like his manservant whom he had left behind to lurk around the corners to keep an eye on things. So when Mr. Monstran did decide to make another appearance, Cornelius would be ready, for when that happened he would make sure that his throne was protected.

He stood on the balcony of the top most level of the Saveen compound, surveying his kingdom. For it was his now. Mr. Monstran may have given him the means, but Cornelius was determined to rule it his way. He knew Mr. Monstran answered to another, just as Cornelius's uncle had. But that was not his destiny. He looked back at the full glass of Arak sitting on the desk. It was tempting, but he knew that was what had driven his uncle mad. That and his conversations with the Master.

Weeks ago, Mr. Monstran had revealed something to him. Something he called a firestone. He had procured it from another Watcher. What it was or how he had gotten it he didn't say, but Mr. Monstran told him that the Master used these to communicate with and control his subjects.

Cornelius hadn't believed him. Not until he had used it.

He didn't like to recall the experience for it made him feel weak and powerless. But afterwards, he knew that he had to protect himself. And Empyria. So he cut off any connection with the Cities because if word got out to the public and more importantly to the members of the Council that weren't in his circle of what was going on then they would send in troops and take power from him. But he was the only one that knew what was coming. He knew that the power he felt in that firestone, the Master, had his eye on Empyria. He knew that if that power turned against him then there was no hope. But if Cornelius cooperated, then he might just actually hold on to his reign in the coming storm.

Monstran had hinted that sacrifices would be needed for the Master, sacrifices in blood. He would sacrifice what he needed to, *who* he needed to when the time came, because Empyria itself was not the Master's endgame. The Master had not revealed his plans to Cornelius, but he hadn't needed to. The kind of hunger and thirst for control he had felt in the firestone went beyond a backwater fortress in the desert. It went beyond the mountains.

The Cities didn't stand a chance. But if Cornelius stayed on the right side of power, then maybe he did.

He looked out across the river, to the other side of Empyria. If it was sacrifices that needed to be made, then Cornelius had half a city for just that purpose.

The Watcher was still resisting. At this point, he should've succumbed to the mental manipulation, but his brief taste of freedom had given him a fresh wall to put up. And Monstran didn't know how to crack it. Until he realized what he had missed.

He had brought the boy, Enrik, to the Dread Chamber and indeed the Master agreed to keep him alive. But when Monstran relayed that Haven was still not ready for the transformation, the Master had demanded he bring him and his firestone to him.

They had not made it this far with the other Watcher before he had died of his injuries, but Monstran should have known that he would need the Watcher's firestone to complete the transformation. The firestone was very much a part of a Watcher and the Master would need it if he were to completely control him. But Monstran had overlooked it and instead focused on destroying the memory of the girl in the Watcher's mind, thinking that was the key to Haven's submission.

Haven had been trying to keep her hidden. Not as a safe refuge in his mind, but because there was something about the girl that he did not want Mr. Monstran to know. But Monstran had figured out that she was in fact the one the Master had felt. The she-hunter.

And she most undoubtedly had the firestone.

There would be no more mistakes.

Mr. Graysan had been at the Armillary and overheard Cornelius tell one of his lieutenants he was going to the compound and wished not to be disturbed for the evening. Neither one had seen him and Cornelius had left his office at the Armillary unlocked. He knew that he had promised Georgiana that he was done with all of this business, but he didn't know when this kind of opportunity would present itself again. And Lord Urbane was counting on him. Lord Urbane's last letter had specifically told him to get more information about who Cornelius's contacts were in the Cities. And crouched underneath the desk, he didn't have much choice. Either remain hidden or be revealed as a spy and killed. He had barely had a chance to look around before he heard footsteps coming. Large, heavy footsteps that could only belong to one person.

He watched Brunos's feet as he shut the door and walked over to the desk. He fumbled for something in his pocket and set it on top of the desk, but Mr. Graysan didn't see what it was. Brunos started breathing hard as if he were preparing to lift something heavy.

"What is your bidding?" Brunos said aloud.

Mr. Graysan furrowed his brow. They were the only two in the room. Who was he talking to?

"Yes, yes...I will do it...You're sure it's here?"

There was a long pause, interrupted only by Brunos's panting. He was listening to something, as if something, or someone, was talking back to him.

"The she-hunter?...She used it?...No. The she-hunter was killed...That wasn't her? Who then...?"

Another long pause ensued and Mr. Graysan tried to figure out what Brunos was talking about. A she-hunter? Were they talking about a female Watcher?

"…Of course, of course. I do not question. I will find it." Then with a loud exhale, Brunos staggered backwards. He stood in the middle of the room for a long minute, seeming to catch his breath. Then he walked back over to the desk, retrieved whatever he had placed there, and left the room.

Mr. Graysan himself took a moment to catch his breath before coming out from his hiding spot, slow to believe the large man had not seen him. There was no trace of whatever he had put on the desk. But he was looking for something. Something in Empyria.

He tip-toed out of the office, catching the back of Brunos as he turned down the hall. It wasn't often that he caught the large man unawares, or alone, for he was often with Cornelius whenever Mr. Graysan was summoned. But this was different. He had to find out what was going on. So he quietly followed Brunos down the hall. When he came to the corner, he peered around it and saw Brunos with another lieutenant, demanding to know where Cornelius was. The lieutenant replied that he would find out as quickly as he could.

But Mr. Graysan knew. He rushed back down the hall. If he hurried, he would make it to the Saveen compound before Brunos did.

A half hour later, he arrived. The servants were used to seeing him so no one questioned his presence there, but he tried to remain calm as he made his way through the lower levels. But he was stopped almost immediately as soon as he ascended the stairs.

One of the servants stopped him and asked if he was here to see Lord Saveen.

Mr. Graysan nodded. "He summoned me. I came as quickly as I could."

The servant looked puzzled. "Lord Saveen has asked not to be disturbed. Wait here a moment."

Mr. Graysan rung his hands together as the servant disappeared. How could he have been so careless? He thought about just leaving, but that would raise more suspicion and the servant would undoubtedly tell Cornelius he had been here.

A minute later he saw the servant walking back, but before he reached Mr. Graysan he was apprehended by another: Brunos.

The servant looked flustered as Brunos spoke with him, but in the end Brunos's hand on his hammer convinced him to take him to Cornelius. Mr. Graysan watched them go up another flight of stairs and to the top of the compound.

This was his only chance.

He snuck up the stairs after them, glancing around to make sure no one else saw him. Once he got to the top level he hid behind the doorway just in time for the servant to leave. He did not look back, but went down the stairs again, obviously eager to leave the situation.

Mr. Graysan stayed behind the doorway, wanting desperately to leave, but his conscience held him firm. He risked a glance inside, hoping the shadows would conceal him.

"I swear I don't know," Cornelius said to Brunos. "I never saw him with a stone of any kind."

Brunos was not the patient type nor the trusting, and shoved his hammer under Cornelius's chin. With his other hand he withdrew something from his pocket and held it up for Cornelius to see. It was a firestone. "Like this! It looks like this!"

Cornelius eyed the stone with caution, not seeming to care that the hammer was inches from crushing his windpipe. Then he looked directly back at Brunos. "No, never," he said steadily.

Brunos shoved the firestone back in his pocket and lowered his hammer with a frustrated grunt.

"I told you," Cornelius continued, straightening his collar, "we searched the compounds after the Ma'diin left. It's not here."

Mr. Graysan could see the veins bulging out of Brunos' neck as he struggled to reign in his frustration. He cracked the knuckles in his hammerless hand. "Not where," he said slowly. "Who."

"Excuse me?"

A spike of fear shot down Mr. Graysan's spine. They were looking for Haven's firestone, but he didn't have it wherever they had taken him and it wasn't in Empyria. And if they figured out who had it…

"Who," Brunos repeated. "The girl he was with. She has it."

"The girl…?" Cornelius started, but then it dawned on him. "Tamsin had one of those vile things?" He rubbed his hand over his hair.

"Where is she?"

Cornelius hesitated and Brunos swiped one of his massive hands across the desk in the room, sending a bottle and a glass smashing into the wall. "Where!?"

"She's not here anymore," Cornelius finally said. "She's in the Cities."

Mr. Graysan couldn't stick around to hear any more. He fled down the stairs, as swiftly and silently as he could, and didn't stop until he was back home. He hurriedly scrambled through the piles on the table for a blank piece of parchment, sending some fluttering to the floor and knocking over a clay vase in the process which crashed to the floor, though he paid it no mind. He snatched his quill and inkwell once he had found one and hastily scrawled a letter to Lord Urbane, notifying him of the new threat posed to them. He hadn't found out about Cornelius's contacts, but this was potentially worse so if he was able to get this letter out before any action was taken on Brunos's part then maybe Lord Urbane would have some time to prepare.

Mr. Graysan heard the door creak behind him. The letters and scrolls froze in his hands and a bead of sweat ran down his spine.

"Dad?" a soft voice called out.

The letters fluttered as his hands broke through the invisible ice that held them. He turned around and saw Georgiana standing halfway in the door. Her confusion quickly changed to suspicion as she saw the papers clutched in his hands.

"Dad, what are you doing." It wasn't a question.

He had wanted to keep his promise, but more he wanted Georgiana to understand why he couldn't. The remorse displayed on his face did nothing to change her stance however, so he turned back and began shoving the papers into the satchel. "I have to Gia. This is more important than me."

He finished packing them and turned to go, but she stood firmly in his path, blocking the door.

"Gia, I must!"

"No! It's not worth it! Do you know what could happen if you were caught?"

He slipped the satchel over his head and set it on the floor then took Gia by the shoulders. "People are counting on me. This is the second most important thing I've done in my life, after you. Let me do this." Hurt tears welled in her eyes, but he resolved himself to follow through with his task.

Gia broke from his grip and reached down and snatched the satchel, backing away before he could reach for it.

"If you insist on doing this, then I'm going with you," she said.

Mr. Graysan's heart dropped. "No——."

She clutched the satchel tighter to her chest. "Either I come with you," she said, moving closer to the fire, "or I burn it all right now."

Mr. Graysan moved to intercept her, horrified by both scenarios, but she held out her hand, his own resolve reflected in her eyes. He stopped, knowing she would do what she had to if he forced her.

He bowed his head, then grabbed a second cloak from the hook by the door and handed it to her. "Stay close to me," he said. "But I want you to run at the first sign of any trouble. You understand me?"

She nodded, taking the cloak, but she did not give the satchel back to him.

"Let's go then."

The streets were busy this time of day, especially in the market districts. Since the new embargo on goods, the usual bartering that took place had amplified to near frenzied levels. Everything from herbs and eggs were coveted like gems and the fishermen were having to hire men to guard their boats while they brought their fish in from the river. The crowds and commotion provided good cover for Mr. Graysan and Georgiana to cut through the heart of the city without drawing attention. But it also drew in more soldiers from the Armillary. They had to break up at least one unruly crowd a day, but as long as Mr. Graysan and Georgiana could avoid that, then they would be okay.

The crowds were especially thick today and her father leaned in close so she could hear him. "If we get separated, go to Aden's boat. I will meet you there."

Aden was a fisherman who Georgiana frequently visited at the docks. If she got there before he brought his first catch in in the early morning he would sometimes have an extra bundle to give her. She remembered seeing him at the Archive building. "Is Aden your contact?"

Her father shook his head. "No, but he can be trusted. He is with us."

Georgiana nodded and continued following him through the shifting crowd, her palms sweating as she gripped the satchel underneath her cloak. "Who are we meeting then? Do I know him?"

Her father shook his head, but didn't offer any more information.

She nearly ran into him when he cut in front of her and started looking at a display of scarves hanging from a vendor's canopy.

"What—?" she started to ask, but he silenced her by gripping her arm.

Then she saw a group of soldiers cutting through the crowd. They were getting closer, rudely shoving people who didn't get out of their way. One stopped and scanned the crowd, his eyes landing on the back of her father's head, then on Georgiana.

She hastily averted her gaze. Her father picked up an orange scarf and laid it across Georgiana's shoulders, beaming. He turned her slightly and she realized he wanted her to look at the soldiers. The soldiers were coming their way. One of them pointed at them and made a motion with his hands, indicating the scarf she wore. The look in her eyes must have betrayed her for her father quickly threw some money on the wooden counter and pulled her away.

"They're following us," she whispered urgently.

"I know," he said. "Don't look back. Go left at the next cross street. Meet me at the boat."

She could hear the *clink clink* as the metal buckles of the soldiers' uniforms rubbed together, getting closer.

They reached the cross street and her father suddenly grabbed the scarf from her and shoved her away. With the bright garment waving in the air he took off down the opposite street. She stumbled, but caught herself underneath the archway on the other side, looking up in time to see the trio of soldiers running after the orange scarf.

She wanted to go after him, to draw the soldiers away, but it was too late. Then she saw a fourth soldier, looking around through the confused mob of people. She turned, pulling the hood of her cloak up, and marched swiftly down the canopied street without looking back. She darted down another street, but ducked into a small alcove immediately in case the other soldier had spotted her. She pressed her back to the shadowed wall and stared at a disfigured statue of one of the old gods. It was Vainus, the goddess of many paths. Her face had been smashed with something, but Georgiana recognized her from the vase she carried.

Please hide my father's path from them, she prayed silently.

Just then she heard the *clink clink* again and pressed even further into the shadows. Peeking outside, she caught a glimpse of sunlight reflecting on metal as the soldier filed past. She waited a few breaths and then stepped slowly out of her hiding place. The soldier was far down the street in the midst of another throng of people.

She gently brushed her fingers on the goddess's stone toes in quick thanks and hurried out the other way.

A few minutes later she reached the docks. Aden was there, tying his boat to the stone anchor. He looked up as she rushed over to him.

"Hey Gia. Sorry, I don't have any extra t'day."

"That's alright Aden," she said, looking around. "Have you seen my father?"

He shook his head. "Nah. He's a scarce cat these days." He stopped tying the rope at the look on Georgiana's face. "Everythin' alright?"

Georgiana didn't say anything, but scanned the shoreline. Her father should have been here. She had taken a longer route to the docks in case any other soldiers had followed her.

"Get in the boat, luv," Aden said. His tone had dropped at least two octaves.

She turned to face him, a question on her lips, but he was already herding her towards the boat. It was a double-man skiff with a single-pole mast in the middle which Aden had built himself. Though she didn't question his craftsmanship, he had never invited her onto his boat before. His boat was his joy and fishing was something he preferred to do alone. But his tone moved her to comply. As she stepped into the boat, Aden began unwinding the rope he had just tied. Once it was loose, he tossed the rope into the skiff, shoved the prow away from the dock, and jumped in after it. He motioned for her to stay low and then grabbed the oars and started rowing out into the river. He started whistling a tune, relaxed and whimsical, but Georgiana could see his eyes carefully scanning the shoreline with eagle-like focus underneath his wide-brimmed hat.

Georgiana peered over the edge, trying to determine what had spooked him earlier. She saw fishermen hauling their nets onto the docks, civilians being turned away by the boat guards, women carrying pails of water up from the bank…and a squadron of soldiers marching up the shoreline from the south quadrant.

In between the moving limbs and shining armor she caught a glimpse of an orange scarf.

She gripped the edge of the boat, causing it to rock slightly. Had Aden not grabbed her arm she would have jumped in the water right there.

How had they known? Her mind raced as fast as her heartbeat as she tried to follow the bobbing scarf between the moving bodies.

"We have to go back, Aden," she pleaded.

"Was he doin' what I think he was doin'?" Aden asked slowly, ignoring her.

"Yes, but…" She pulled the satchel out from underneath her cloak and Aden's eyes widened slightly. "He doesn't have what they're looking for."

"Did they see you?"

"They were following me too."

"Then we are stayin' right here," he said, gripping both oars again in case she tried anything.

"That's my father, Aden. I can't just leave him!"

He continued rowing farther out until they were almost halfway across the width of the Elglas. "If you go back now, luv, everythin' he's been doin' will've been for nothin'. If he was daft enough to try and do this in the daylight, then my guess is whatever's in that bag is real important."

Georgiana felt frustrated tears springing to the corners of her eyes. Her father didn't deserve this. Yes, she didn't believe in what the Saveen regime was doing, but it wasn't worth her father's life to rebel against it. Not to her.

They rocked out on the water until well after the soldiers had disappeared, but Aden wanted to make sure no more were forthcoming. Georgiana jumped out as soon as they made it back to the dock, but Aden made her pause.

"My advice," he said, "Get that to your father's man, then lie low for a while."

She didn't tell him that she had no idea who that was or where to find him, but nodded and then ran back to the city with the sole intention of getting her father back.

"You know, the power to control water would be pretty useful right about now," Tamsin spoke to the air. She had been trudging and stumbling through the mud and mangroves for over a day now and she was about as close to finding her way out as she was to sprouting wings and flying. The roots of the mangrove trees made traveling in any kind of a straight line impossible. She had tried climbing one of them to see if she could gain her whereabouts, but as thick as the roots were near the water, the branches above were too thin to support her weight. She was leery about traveling solely through the water, already knowing that snakes preferred the speed of the waterways, but sometimes it couldn't be helped when the gap between trees was too great. So far though she had tried to stick to the roots that spread over the water to make her way through the forest.

Occasionally she tested the water to check its salinity, but she was always greeted with that salty taste on her tongue. She was already parched beyond measure, reminding her of the first time she met Haven out in the Sindune. Her body had not been prepared for the heat and dryness of the desert, leaving her feeling drained and vulnerable. But here, the humidity held underneath the canopy contained a new threat. Every ounce of energy she exerted making her way through the trees trickled out in sweat and she knew if she did not find a fresh water source very soon then she was going to be in trouble, because as much as she was suffering now, it was going to get a lot worse over the next 48 hours.

A rustling in the canopy above her made her pause. She looked up, but only saw some branches moving a few trees over, though she did not see what caused it. A monkey or a large bird probably. The mangroves supported all kinds of life it seemed, not just reptiles and insects. Tamsin had seen some small monkeys earlier and though they were curious about her, they weren't curious enough to come any closer, which was fine with her. It had gotten her thinking though. If the mangroves contained all these different types of animals, there had to be fresh water sources somewhere. And food. The trick was going to be to find them.

She sat down on the root of a particularly large tree, dangling her legs above the water. Without water, food, or sleep, she had to rest frequently. She hunched over, looking at her reflection in the water and wondering what kind of fool would let herself get manipulated into this situation. Leaving Empyria, she had made a vow that from now on the course of her life would be made by her own decisions and not by others. All day she had spent thinking about the Havakki and the Hazees'diin and Kellan and Ysallah and blaming them for what was happening. But as she sat looking at her reflection, at the grime and sweat that covered her face and the redness of her eyes, she realized that it was she who was responsible for all of this. She had chosen to come to the marsh lands.

She had chosen to listen to Samih and Poma and Kellan and let them take choices away from her.

Determination settled on her brow and though she struggled to push the desperation away, she made another vow to herself: she would find a way out of the mangroves and she would find her way to Haven.

Her reflection in the water rippled in response, but it wasn't her reflection that had moved. Something just behind her shoulder.

Tamsin didn't turn around to look. With a gasp, she dropped into the water and pushed herself underneath the giant roots, using them to shield herself from whatever was above her. She moved as far away from the spot as she could, but there wasn't much room and a massive paw plunged in between them, narrowly missing her head. Angry claws scratched at the roots above her, trying to break the wood apart to get to her. Heart in her throat, Tamsin plunged below the water's surface, knowing the roots wouldn't keep the predator at bay for long. She tried to stay as deep as she could, using the roots to pull herself along and out from underneath. Once free, she swam for as long as she could, until she could hold her breath no longer. Upon surfacing, she whipped around, trying to gain her bearings and the whereabouts of the animal that had just attacked her.

There, just off to her right on the tree she had just left, was a giant, striped cat. It was big enough to take down a water buffalo and yet lean enough to maneuver through the mangrove trees. Its yellow eyes locked onto her immediately and it started traversing the root system with a speed and grace that was terrifying.

Tamsin's stomach churned with fear, but there was no time to panic. The large cat paused, but only for a moment to calculate the quickest way to reach her. It was a few trees over with a wide water gap between them.

Tamsin turned towards the nearest tree, grabbing onto one of the roots to help keep her afloat. Then she heard a splash behind her. Not needing to look to know the cat had jumped in, she pulled herself up with all of her might as fast as she could. Once she was on top of the roots again she glanced back. The cat was swimming straight for her and had already closed half the distance. There was no way she was going to outswim the beast, and she couldn't climb up away from it.

She had barely thought it when the roots around her erupted into flames. Surprised, the cat turned away, choosing another tree to climb up. It perched on the roots, studying the fire with a raise of its nose.

Tamsin released the flames, hugging the trunk as some of the roots crumbled to ash around her, but she didn't take her eyes off the cat.

They remained that way for a long time it seemed, each dripping wet and focused on the other, trying to figure out who would be predator and who would be prey. But it was only mere minutes. Out of the corner of her eye she saw her arm was a watery, red color. She pressed her fingers under her nose and when she took them away there was more blood.

It was her power. When she didn't use it and got emotional it gave her headaches and when she used it too much her nose bled or she passed out. She had not used her power this much and for such large things ever. The adrenaline in her veins was keeping her from passing out at the moment, but what if that ran out? Then she would be at the mercy of the mangroves and the cat.

Her eyes darted back up, but the feline was gone.

Tamsin looked everywhere: in the nearby trees, the water, the canopy...but the cat had disappeared. And the forest had gone quiet. The smell of blood was in the air. Her blood. A knot formed in her stomach, telling her that she had lost the position of equal and was being hunted once again.

I've been a hunter long enough to know what it feels like being hunted.

So do I, she had thought, all those nights ago in the Hollow Cliffs with Haven.

But she had no idea. Not truly. Not until now. When every sinew and hair on her body was telling her to run.

So she did.

She took off through the mangrove, which was getting darker by the minute as the day ended. She jumped and scrambled and crawled her way over the roots like a deer escaping a wildfire. Every now and then she heard a rustle behind her, in the canopy, but she did not stop and she did not look back. Branches ripped at her arms and legs, but she kept going. She kept moving with every ounce of strength she could muster, pushed on by the pace of her frantic heart.

She clamored over a large root system, barely able to get her feet under her and saw the next one just a few feet away. She jumped, but miscalculated the gap in the roots and fell backwards into the water... landing only knee high in water.

The shock of feeling land underneath her paralyzed her for a moment as her brain struggled to catch up. But only for a moment. She darted up, taking off in a quick sprint, praying that her hunch was right and it was not just a lone patch of land that she had fallen on. And after a few yards she realized she was right. The water level started to go down even further until she was running through water that was only ankle deep.

She heard the creaking of branches behind her and then a splash of water over her own sloshing. It was close. Much closer than she had imagined. With a cry, she pushed herself harder, willing her legs to go faster despite the fear that made her progress jerky and on the brink of collapse.

There was a wall of leaves ahead of her, but it stretched far to either side and there was nowhere else to go. Her lungs ached for more air, but the air that made it felt like parchment down her dry throat. She panted for breath, not knowing how much longer she could keep going…

She burst through the leaves and then stumbled as her feet hit sand, falling to her knees and catching herself with her hands.

Sand…Dirty maroon grains mixed with strains of grey shifting under her hands as she flexed her fingers, not quite comprehending what she was seeing. A clear line of water appeared then and soaked her fingertips, retreating almost as quickly, pulled back by some invisible force. Tamsin looked up, following the line of water back to its home.

She was unprepared for the sheer expanse of the ocean before her and beyond that, settling on its furthest edge, was the most majestic sunset she had ever lain eyes on.

She choked back a sob, overwhelmed by the beauty of the sight before her. All her fears, exhaustion, and pain melted into the sand in that moment. Clouds of royal purple and lush pink feathered the crimson sky like wings, brushing against the nest of orange that harbored the golden sun as if it were protecting an egg from the glimpses of deep blue from the coming night sky. In that image there was only peace, an end to all her trials and suffering. If only the water were glass and she could walk into that sunset…

The water touched her fingers again, breaking the spell. She blinked and something moved out of the corner of her eye. She turned her head, weariness forcing itself upon her once more, and saw a wooden spear flying right towards her.

She flinched, but the spear missed her, embedding itself in something behind her. She turned to look and saw the giant cat that had been hunting her two feet away, now lying dead in the sand.

She had almost been the dead one. By animals, by water, too much and not enough, by the Havakkii, and the amon'jii before them. She was too exhausted that she could barely wonder who had thrown the spear when her world tilted, but something caught her before her head hit the sand. Fresh water touched her lips, but she wasn't aware of drinking it for her bleary eyes couldn't make out the man above her, offering her the water. Was it Haven, his hooded cloak a dark shadow against the desert sun? Or was it this stranger, his wild grey hair and knitted brow bathed in purple light?

She blinked hard and the grey hair formed the frame of a tanned face, wrinkled but strong. Liquid blue eyes squinted back at her, filled with concern and compassion. Steady hands held her, confusing her mind again with memories of the desert.

Then she wept. Uncontrollably and without shame, collapsing into the man who was neither her father nor Haven, but she was too weary to care. All she knew was at this moment, she was alive.

The old man held her, cradling her head into his chest. He whispered, "Shh, child, you are safe now. You are safe now," over and over soothingly.

The child had fallen asleep in his arms. For a moment he thought she was dead, but her breath steadied and heartbeat remained. She had just been too exhausted from what he imagined had been hell in the mangroves. Who knew the last time she had had peaceful rest. The forest was not for the weak. It devoured even the strongest of men.

"Saashiim?" the soft voice of his wife called out cautiously, blowing away his grim thoughts. "Who is that?"

"I don't know," he said, looking down at the dark-haired girl.

His wife sidled closer. "Is she alive?"

"Yes, though she needs care. Baagh nearly had her." He shifted his gaze towards the dead tiger.

His wife's eyes widened at the sight of the large cat. The man-eater of the mangroves was what they called him. "Saashiim," she said gently, "you know we don't interfere—."

"She was out of the mangroves, already on the beach," he said firmly. It was true, they didn't interfere with what the marsh people did, and most often if they came across anyone in the forest they were already dead. But the beach was their territory. He wasn't about to watch a child get slaughtered before his eyes.

"Alright," she said, conceding without argument.

The other fishermen on the beach had run over to them by then. He handed the girl over to one of the younger men as the others gathered around Baagh in astonishment.

Saashiim stared at the dead cat a moment, watching the tide leech its blood out as the sun settled against the sea line. He may be older and weaker than the others, but his aim was still true. He walked over and pulled his fishing spear from its side, then followed his wife and the others back to the boats.

Chapter Thirteen

Tamsin could not decide what was stranger: the fact that she was alive or that these Ma'diin were unconditionally friendly. She had been with her rescuers for three days now (the first of which she had slept through) and although they were somewhat reserved, there was no limit to their generosity and care. Her rescuer, a man named Saashiim, had taken her to his home, fed her, tended to her wounds, and even mended her clothes. And he nor his wife ever asked for an explanation as to how she had gotten on that beach or ended up in the mangroves in the first place. There were others that came to visit though, bringing baskets of fish or supplies, that were curious about the girl who had survived Baagh, the tiger. Saashiim's wife, Mala, always ushered them out politely, telling them not to remind the poor girl of her ordeal. Though they didn't ask, Tamsin figured they could guess what happened from the various cuts and scrapes she had.

Tamsin sat on the edge of the rocky, black cliff looking out at the beach and the edge of the mangrove forest, absentmindedly rubbing the skin around the rope burns on her wrists. It was hard not to replay everything that had happened, but having a hundred yards of ocean in between herself and the mangroves helped. These Ma'diin, though they said they were not part of the Ma'diin or the twelve tribes as Tamsin knew them, lived on the jagged islands that littered the coastline. They rose out of the water like giant obelisks, most of them easily bigger and taller than the compounds of Empyria. There were stairs and paths carved into them, leading up from the water and to the caves where these people lived. Though families retreated into the deeper, darker caves for more privacy, most of the communal living was done in the open, in tunnels that sometimes extended right through the islands. Some of the islands were even close enough where they had built wooden bridges connecting them. But it wasn't all rock; there were patches of vegetation, tiny trees with thick leaves, mossy growths that the islanders harvested and ferns that sprouted up between cracks above the sea spray.

Tamsin felt a presence behind her and Saashiim let out a long breath as he sat down next to her.

"You left quickly after mealtime," he said, implying a question with his statement.

Tamsin had eaten dinner quickly and then headed out alone to a more secluded area of the island. But it had not been to escape Saashiim's company.

"The bats," she replied. The caves were not only home to these people it turned out, but to legions of bats as well. And they all turned out just before sunset to hunt on the mainland. She had witnessed this the previous night and was keen not to repeat the experience. Usually Saashiim was out with the other fishermen at that time of day, but he had seemed nonplussed by the hundreds of tiny creatures flying around them nonetheless.

Saashiim smiled. "You'll learn to get used to them," he said, but saw Tamsin's eyes tighten slightly at this. "But you won't get used to them, will you?"

Tamsin shook her head. "I have to go back."

Saashiim sighed again and opened up his hands. Tamsin hadn't noticed him holding anything before, but now she looked and saw the charred remains of a branch in them.

"Some of the others went into the forest today. And found this. In fact, they found a whole tree had been burned down, but none of the others around it. Child, did those men try to burn you?"

His question took her by surprise. It was the first question about her experience he had asked her and the genuine concern in his voice touched her.

"We have seen the aftermath of what those wicked men do, but to do this…"

"No, Saashiim. They did not do this." She took the branch from his hands. This was her handiwork. "I did. It's how I escaped."

She could see the wheels turning behind his eyes, trying to figure it out, but he was too polite to ask outright.

"That seems like quite the story."

She turned the branch over in her hands. "If you have nowhere to be, I will tell it to you."

"If you want to, then I have nowhere to be," he said.

She thought for a minute about where to begin. Saashiim and his people had given her no reason to believe that they would do anything other than help her. If she asked to leave now, then they would probably give her a boat filled with food and tell her safe travels. If she wanted to stay, then they would probably give her one of the islands. It would be so easy for these people to be cynical, for theirs' was a hard way of life, but they weren't. They were truly selfless. And she owed Saashiim her life.

So she told him everything. About Empyria. About Haven. About her Ma'diin mother. About everything that had happened since coming to the marsh lands. And when she had finished, she felt no regret that she had told him.

Saashiim sat cross-legged with his eyes closed, his brow knitted in serious concentration. When he finally looked up, he said, "The blue woman you spoke of…I know her. I can take you to her if you wish it."

The weightlessness Tamsin felt after having told her story suddenly vanished. Her breath hitched in her throat. Of all the responses that had been the last one she expected. "She—she's here?"

Saashiim stood up and stretched out his sore muscles. "Come with me."

Tamsin got up as well and followed him up a path that led to a wooden bridge near the top of the island. The next island was close, so the distance wasn't too great, but being so high above the open water made Tamsin's palms sweat on the ropes. Her mind was buzzing with thoughts about the blue woman though, so not even a wind-ravaged old bridge could stop her. They made it across and then followed a tunnel down into the heart of the island. The end of the tunnel came out into a cave that opened up to the sea. They walked along the slippery edge that circled the cave, as water lapped up over their feet. There was a side tunnel that opened up and Saashiim paused here.

"We may only stay a few minutes," he said, "otherwise the high tide will trap us."

Tamsin nodded eagerly and followed him in. As haven-like as this place was, it was not without its dangers.

It opened up into a smaller, enclosed cave, reminding her much of her old room in Empyria, but it wasn't just the size that was similar. Saashiim lit the torch he had brought and the walls of the cave came to life with dozens of paintings. Crude images, even more archaic than the ones in Empyria, were painted right onto the walls. But there was no one here.

Tamsin's hopes fell. All the questions she had wanted to ask the blue woman disappeared into the air. "She's not here, Saashiim."

"But she is," he insisted, waving his torch towards the wall.

Tamsin stepped closer and realized what he had meant all along. There was a woman, painted right on the wall, as vivid as if she had been painted yesterday. Her arms were spread wide against a bright backdrop of orange and yellow and she was painted above a wide congregation of other people, most of them on their knees or with their hands raised. These other people were rudimentary in comparison, painted with basic white outlines, though one person, a woman, was holding up a vase near the woman's feet. The woman's face was the only part of her not ornately detailed. It was covered with a dark shroud.

"Who is she?" Tamsin asked.

"We call her *Kazszura'jiin*," Saashiim said.

"*Kazszura'jiin,*" Tamsin repeated in a whisper. The Ghost Queen.

"She is neither god nor spirit, but is believed to be made of the smokeless fire and was created when the first sunrise rose over the horizon. The goddess Mahiri was so moved by the sight that she cried and Kazszura'jiin rose up from where her tears fell in the ocean."

"So she watches over ghosts?"

"She is the guardian of the departed and keeper of spirits, yes. The soul, Tamsin, is the most precious part of a person and the moment of Kazszura'jiin's creation was so pure that it drew the departed souls to her. So she gave them a home in the world that she resides in."

"What world?"

"Oh, it is one we cannot see or hear or touch. But we can feel it, no?" He sighed heavily, like he could feel the air from this other world in his lungs.

Tamsin turned away, her thoughts cloudy.

"Has she appeared to others before?"

"Yes, though there hasn't been mention of a sighting for many years. The Ma'diin have twisted the memory of her and now she is all but forgotten."

"But your people have not forgotten her."

"No," he said. "We have not."

"Why is her face covered?"

"It is said that she has many faces and when she appears she takes the face of a loved one who has left this earth."

Tamsin's brow furrowed. She had never seen the blue woman's face, in any form, but more so she knew no one that had passed away.

Not now nor when she was a child. And there was another big difference.

"Saashiim," she said, "the woman in the painting isn't blue."

"As I said, she appears as a loved one."

She was about to tell him that she didn't know anyone who was blue, but he nodded towards the cave opening and said they should be going. So she followed him back to the dwellings and joined the others around the evening fires. Seeing the fires reminded her of something else he had said. She waited until all the others had gone to bed and it was just her and Saashiim.

"You mentioned the smokeless fire before. What is it?" Tamsin asked.

Saashiim gave her a funny look and a slight smile. "You've never heard of this?"

"We don't have religion in the Cities and I've never heard it mentioned by the Empyrians or the Ma'diin."

Saashiim rubbed his chin. "Tell me, Tamsin, do you believe in love?"

"Of course I do," Tamsin replied without hesitation.

"Then you have heard of the smokeless fire." He let her mull that over a moment before continuing. "There are more connections between the ungodly and the believers than you realize. I suppose that is why it makes sense."

"Why what makes sense?" Tamsin asked.

He tilted his head. "Why she decided to appear to you."

But it didn't make sense, not to Tamsin. She stayed awake late into the night, the questions brought forth from her conversation with Saashiim making it impossible to go to sleep. Saashiim seemed so at ease with the mysticism of it all, but it contradicted everything she believed, or thought she believed. The blue woman had always been a part of her story, since the unquestioning innocence of her childhood, which was probably why she had never really given the implications of it much logical thought.

Had it not all been happening to her, Tamsin would never have believed it. The moment she stepped into Empyria everything had changed. She hadn't known it right away but she had stepped into a world where gods and magic were very much real.

She stood up from the fire and extinguished the embers, but instead of going to bed she went out and climbed up the stairs around the island until she found a large boulder to sit on that overlooked the western horizon and the sea. The night air was cold and the waves rolled like thunder across the rocks below, but it brought a clearness to her thoughts that the flames in the fire had not.

She knew now that she had to leave behind the old rules of her life. The ones that were governed by civility and rationale. Without thinking about it, she had been clinging to them, clinging to a world where everything made sense. But she had to let them go or she wouldn't survive here. The marsh lands and the mangroves and the islands…these were places that were built from faith and pulsed with the blood of myths. And the evidence of its existence was all around her. Not just in cave paintings, but her very ability to control fire.

And her visits by the blue lady.

Maybe Saashiim was right. Maybe the blue lady and the Kazsura'jiin were the same. She was the guardian of the dead, but Tamsin could not tell if the blue lady was guiding her away from death or towards it.

Chapter Fourteen

The catacombs were a miserable place and knowing this was where he had helped keep Haven prisoner was an irony that only made his incarceration worse. But when they removed his chains and marched him upstairs into the main chamber of the Armillary, he felt a deeper kind of dread. In the catacombs at least he knew where he stood, but up here, his future was uncertain. It should have been the opposite, but the polished stone pillars and mosaic-patterned floor of the chamber held no comfort for him.

The light coming through the stained-glass dome blinded him for a moment; it had been several days since he'd seen sunlight. His guards placed him in the center of the room and he shielded his eyes until he could see. There were guards between every pillar and in every archway, but their presence was dwarfed by the enormity of the chamber. There was not one friendly face among them. Except for Lord Regoran, who stood next to Lord Allard and Cornelius on the balcony level in front of him. But from the tight line his lips were pressed into, Mr. Graysan knew that even with Lord Regoran on his side, this was not going to go well.

"Albon Graysan, you are brought before the Lords' Council of Empyria today to answer the charges for which you were arrested," Cornelius's voice rang out, cold and clear.

Mr. Graysan, being a scribe for Lord Regoran, had sat in on numerous trials. Most were done privately, in one of the smaller chambers that only required one lord to preside over and make a decision. The charges were read, the evidence presented, and then the offender was given a chance to either defend himself or repent. Then a decision would be made and the punishment read. Mr. Graysan would be a silent observer and document everything. That was the order of things and after sitting through several of them Mr. Graysan had built up an emotional tolerance to the proceedings.

But being on the other side of the readings eroded any walls he had erected. Listening to Cornelius read the charges—disobeying the exportation ban, inciting rebellion by breaking the law, conspiring with a suspected underground rebel group, and committing actions deemed to be traitorous against the Empyrian lordship and Delmarian law—was enough to make his knees shake.

Mr. Graysan had been a strong man once. But that was before his wife, Georgiana's mother, died. After that everything was different. The ground he stood on was not solid anymore. Something inside him had cracked and Georgiana was the only thing that kept the two halves together. He relied on her more than a father should and he wished he could have been stronger for her. He prayed that she was able to deliver the letters and that she wasn't caught.

He barely heard the next words as Cornelius listed the evidence against him; that man could spin any story he wanted to. Lord Regoran would only be able to oppose him to a point for if he defended Mr. Graysan too much then suspicion would be turned on him and Lord Regoran's position in the rebel group was too important. The thought that Lord Regoran was only here to make sure Mr. Graysan didn't give any names up flitted through his mind, but when he looked at him and saw the pity there he knew that wasn't the case. Lord Regoran looked at him like he was a …martyr.

His wife had practiced the old religion. In private, at their home she would thank the gods for their blessings and pray for the happiness and safe-keeping of their family. She used to recite the old sayings to him after they supped and it was just the two of them sitting by the hearth. She had asked him to write them down, for Georgiana, so that when she was old enough she could read the words that were so important to her. Mr. Graysan had gone along with it, but she had been the true believer. She had sacrificed everything for her family. She was the true martyr.

Mr. Graysan looked up at the stained glass ceiling, at the blue and green and gold light that shifted through. His wife had radiated light, as did Georgiana.

"Mr. Graysan?"

Mr. Graysan focused his attention back on the Lords. Cornelius was staring at him with narrowed eyes.

"Mr. Graysan," Cornelius repeated, "do you have anything you wish to say?"

Mr. Graysan looked at Lord Regoran. Despite his faith he knew Lord Regoran was anxiously hoping he would remain silent about the underground resistance. Cornelius wanted him to confess. He wanted him to betray them and give up names. But as Mr. Graysan looked at Cornelius again he knew he wouldn't. A strange peace settled on him and he straightened his shoulders. He would not betray anyone else. He was done with that.

"I have nothing to say."

Cornelius stretched his grip on the banister, his expression dark. "Then the vote will commence. Lord Regoran?"

A tight silence hung in the air. Then in a loud voice, Lord Regoran said, "Innocent."

"Lord Allard?"

Lord Allard, a robust man, seemed quite small and fidgeted in a very un-lordly way. He seemed torn, but under Cornelius's intense scrutiny he caved. "Guilty," he said.

Cornelius, barely working to conceal a smile, said, "Guilty."

Mr. Graysan hung his head. It had been brave of Lord Regoran to stick up for him, but it didn't matter now.

Lord Regoran knew it too. His tone was beaten when he spoke, though he did his best to cover it. "As the Council stands, the vote is guilty. In accordance to Delmarian law set forth by the Lords' Council for convicted traitors, you are sentenced to exile in the malachite mines of Ragar across the Terraz Sea. A transport will be arranged and then-."

"No," Cornelius interrupted, the word echoing through the room.

Lord Regoran went still. His gaze caught Mr. Graysan's briefly before turning to Cornelius. "It is the law, Cornelius. All traitors are sentenced to—."

"And is it not the law that all exports to the Cities are to be detained?"

Mr. Graysan barely dared to breathe and he could see Lord Regoran's jaw working even from where he stood below. He remembered how they had treated Haven; they had tortured him just shy of death and it made his stomach turn thinking what they would do to him. Treatment like that was outlawed under Delmarian law, but Cornelius had gotten away with it once, before he had seized control of the city, so who knew now what lengths he would go to get information from him.

"A law that *you* put into place," Lord Regoran accused.

"I think we should set an example," Cornelius continued, as if he had not heard him. "If the rebels think they can get a free pass out of here by conspiring against us, thus spreading their dissention to the Cities, then they are quite mistaken. No, we mustn't let that happen."

Mr. Graysan looked down at his left hand. It had gone cold, as if a corpse had suddenly taken hold of it. And he realized, with a clarity that he had lacked these last many years, that torture was not in his future. No, Cornelius had something much more permanent planned for him.

The light from the Armillary had always been a beautiful sight. Sometimes when she worked late at the compound, Georgiana would take a minute and lean against the wall of the veranda and gaze out across the Elglas. At night, the stained glass of the dome broke through the dark water surrounding it, sending glittering light across the surface like it was made of the scales of the rainbow carp that swam in its depths. The Armillary was the center of the city, the so-called eye of Empyria with the stained glass being the iris. Sometime she wondered if that's what the Ottarkins had planned when they built the city; if the Armillary was supposed to represent an eye always looking towards the heavens. It was certainly a transcendent view.

But tonight, Georgiana found the light as cold as the water surrounding it. It had been three days since her father had been taken. She couldn't go to the Armillary, in case the guards recognized her, but the guards were letting no one even get past the courtyards leading to the bridge. She had gone to the Regoran compound, hoping that Lord Regoran would get her past Cornelius's blockade of men, but she was thwarted there as well. The news of her father's arrest had spread even through the resistance and she had expected everyone to lay low for a while, but nobody seemed to be in contact with Lord Regoran or know his whereabouts. Georgiana was worried that he might be distancing himself. She didn't know him well enough to know if he would abandon the resistance if he thought it was compromised. She hoped not.

More than that, she was worried about her father. She had been taking care of him since she was young. These last few weeks he had kept his involvement in the rebel group and with Lord Urbane a secret from her. She had pleaded with him to stop, to not do another thing for them. It was too dangerous and had already taken its toll on him. He needed someone to look after him, someone that loved him. Not someone to accuse him and arrest him. She was afraid of what it would do to him.

"You're Georgiana, right?"

Georgiana turned away from the view to see Lady Allard standing behind her. Her hair hung in loose waves around her shoulders and her pink nightgown shimmered from the light of the cauldrons when she moved.

Georgiana dipped her head. "Yes. I'm so sorry my lady. I was just on my way home and I stopped—I didn't realize anyone was still up."

Lady Allard glided over to her and laid her hands on the veranda wall. She looked out at the Armillary, her eyes narrowing like she was trying to figure something out. "I used to think it was breathtaking, in a daunting kind of way. I used to stare at it for hours when we first moved here and I couldn't sleep." She turned to look at Georgiana then, though Georgiana couldn't tell from the shadows if her expression was sympathetic or probing. "It's all an illusion isn't it?"

Georgiana remained silent. Lady Allard was a kind patroness, but with her father imprisoned she couldn't be sure who she could trust.

"If people are looking at the Armillary, at the center of the city," Lady Allard continued, "then they aren't concerned with what's out there." She turned to gaze out beyond the wall, into the desert.

Georgiana's throat swelled a little. "I wish I could agree with you, my lady," she said softly. Her heart was in the Armillary. She couldn't afford to think beyond the wall right now. "If you don't mind, I should be getting home now."

Lady Allard nodded her head. "Of course. But would you do one thing for me? If it's not too much trouble."

"Of course, my lady."

"I need you to get something from the Urbane compound for me."

"The Urbane compound?"

"There is still a skeleton crew working there. You'll be expected."

Georgiana agreed to go, but with the strange feeling growing in her stomach as she made her way to the compound, it occurred to her that Lady Allard had not told her what it was exactly she was retrieving. And she had not seen her or Lord Allard that night in the archive building at the resistance meeting. She had no idea where their allegiance lay.

She shook her head, trying to dispel the paranoia. She didn't know how her father had managed it for so long.

The compound was dark when she reached it. It rose into the night like the horned head of a bull, its twin towers reaching towards the sky as if to skewer the stars. She had not thought to bring a lantern with her and the lack of light only made her uneasiness grow. She passed through the open arch, her eyes deadlocked on those foreboding towers, but paused when she got to the foot of the stairs leading up to the main level.

Something moved out of the corner of her eye, but before she could turn to look, a hand shot out of the darkness and clamped around her mouth. Her scream was muffled as she tried to pry the hand off, but the other person was much stronger and pulled her back. She twisted and turned and dug her heels into the ground, but nothing she did helped. Until the person flipped her around and she could see the face of her attacker.

It was Tomas.

Tomas held up a finger to his lips and then slowly removed his other hand from Georgiana's mouth. He waited a moment, his eyes piercing the darkness as he looked around. "Were you followed?" he whispered.

Georgiana shook her head. She had stopped struggling, but the shock of the abduction still had her hands trembling. "What in the seven hells of old was that *for*?" she hissed.

"Quiet," he hissed right back. He looked around again and, confident that they were alone, motioned for her to follow him.

He led her around the side of the stairs to the servants' entrance and went inside. The halls were eerily empty, but their footsteps seemed to echo louder than desired so Tomas made sure they hurried. They took the small, inner stairway up to the main level and Tomas paused at the edge as it opened up into the floor, peering carefully above.

"What are we—?" Georgiana started to ask, but Tomas shot her a look.

He peered over the edge again and this time Georgiana did too. Across the level, on the opposite veranda, a guard walked along the wall. He was recognizable from the silhouette of a sword hanging from his hip and the smooth curve of his helm. When he turned to go back on his route, Tomas grabbed Georgiana and pulled her up. They quietly rushed over to the stairway going up to the higher levels before they could be seen.

They made it up to the very top level; it seemed the guards only patrolled the main level. The room was circular, one Georgiana had been in before. It was Tamsin's room. Though not as she remembered it. White sheets covered the furniture, giving the ancient room a haunted feel. Shivers ran up her arms as the wind blew through from the balcony, ruffling the sheets' edges.

Tomas waved her over to a partition by the wall. She watched as he pushed a section of the painted wall and gasped when it gave way. He stepped through and she hesitantly followed him. He shoved the door shut behind her. A torch was lit on the wall and he grabbed it and headed down a narrow stairway, not pausing for Georgiana to wonder what this place was. She remembered Enrik had mentioned something once about secret tunnels throughout the city, but she hadn't given it much thought. Until now. She had to hurry to keep up with Tomas or risk losing the light from his torch. The light illuminated the tattoos on his arms and she wondered if he knew about the tunnels from associating with the religious sect. Enrik's grandfather had been a devout believer; she wondered if that was where he learned it from.

Her mother had been a believer. Had she known?

She shook the thoughts aside as they came to a large room. There were more torches on the walls which provided enough light to see everything.

Standing near a grate in the floor in the center of the room was Lord Regoran.

Tomas wasted no time and went over to him, not seeming to be surprised by his lord's presence there, and lifted the grate to reveal a large hole. He then began working with a pile of rope by the side of the room.

But instead of relief at seeing Lord Regoran she felt anger rising in her. "What is going on?" she demanded. "Lady Allard is expecting me back—."

"I asked Lady Allard to send you," Lord Regoran interrupted. "She knows."

"Knows what?"

Tomas had tightened the rope around a large boulder in the room and now flung the other end down the hole. He pulled against the rope, testing it, and then nodded.

Lord Regoran nodded back, but his expression was grim. Then he turned to Georgiana. "You have not been abandoned Georgiana. You wanted to see your father. Let's go see him." He held out the rope towards her.

Georgiana stared at the rope in his hands then into his eyes. He had a guard up, but she could see his intentions were genuine. Her heart swelled with gratitude that these men, and Lady Allard, had gone through all this trouble for her. But it also made her fearful. It was clear neither Lord Regoran nor Lord Allard had any actual power left if the only way to see her father was to sneak through secret tunnels like a thief.

She walked over to him and took the proffered rope.

"Grip it tight. I'll be right behind you."

She nodded and did as he said. Slowly she made her way down the hole until her feet landed on solid ground. She looked around; she was in another tunnel of some kind, but this one was more polished. It wasn't like the one she just came from. Lord Regoran came down a moment later, made some motion to Tomas who pulled the rope back up, and then led Georgiana down the corridor. He was wary, like Tomas had been leading her up through the compound, but there were no soldiers down here.

They were in the catacombs, Georgiana realized. She had never been down here before, but the alcoves carved into the stone were unmistakable in their purpose. Though, there were no stone coffins, or effigies, or cenotaphs to mark the tombs. There were piles of rocks and tools against the walls, as if the stone masons had been recently down here. Then she saw what they were working on: doors. As they went along, more and more of the alcoves had been sealed off. And if her father was down here…

It wasn't a tomb anymore. It was a prison.

There were narrow slits in the doors about eye level and Lord Regoran paused to look in each one. When Georgiana realized what he was doing she quickly went to the other side and started doing the same.

"How many are there?" Georgiana whispered, but Lord Regoran just shook his head.

"Georgiana?"

She heard her father's voice and ran over to the next sealed alcove. She looked into the slit and saw her father's face looking back at her.

"Georgiana what are you doing here? You shouldn't be here!" His voice was on the verge of panic.

"It's okay," Georgiana tried to soothe him. "Lord Regoran is here."

His eyes flitted over to Lord Regoran who stood a little ways behind her, giving them as much privacy as he could.

There was enough space in the slit for Georgiana to slide her hand through and her father took it tightly in his own.

A lump formed in her throat. "I'm going to get you out of here," she said. "I'll go to Cornelius directly if I have to. I'll get you a trial—."

Her father shook his head. "There's already been a trial, Gia." The dim lighting made it hard to see his expression, but she saw the sheen of tears on his cheeks.

"W—what did they say?" Her voice quivered when she asked. Her father smiled, but it was one *to* comfort, not comforting.

She turned to Lord Regoran, not letting go of her father's hand, and repeated her question. "What did you say?!"

Lord Regoran's expression frightened her. It was an expression of helplessness. He opened his hands in front of him and was about to speak, but her father squeezed her hand, turning her attention back.

"Lord Regoran was able to get me a good deal," he said firmly. His eyes were unwavering and Georgiana saw a glimpse of his old strength, like the kind he had before her mother died. "I'll be going to the Cities, to work in the mines."

Her heart sank. It was not a good deal to her. Her father would crumble under those conditions. "No." She shook her head. "They can't do that. They can't take you away."

"I'll be taken care of Gia. You won't have to worry about me anymore."

Georgiana closed her eyes, but the tears spilled over anyway. "I'll come after you. Once the ban is lifted, I'll come and petition the Council and—."

"Don't you think of it Gia," he said. "No good will come of it. You've always been so strong for me, but it's my turn now. I will be strong for you."

The words pulled at her resolve and she pressed into the stone. It hurt to think that this was the last time she would be close to him, to see his face, to hear his voice.

"I'll get to be an explorer again." He chuckled, but his eyes twinkled with sadness. "I've always wanted to see the Terraz Sea."

"That's a lie," Georgiana said, wiping the tears away with the back of her other hand.

"Hey, listen to me Gia. I know I haven't been the father that I should have, but listen to me now. Your mother believed in the old ways. She believed that we would all see our loved ones again after we die. We're not meant to see each other again in this world, Gia. Many years from now, after you've gotten married, and had a houseful of children, and your hair is as white as mine, then after that we'll see each other again."

She was a little girl again. He was the father and she was the daughter, as things should have been, but she would gladly give up a husband and children if it meant that he could stay. She would take care of him for the rest of his days in a heartbeat. He was her family.

"Do you really believe that?" she whispered, barely able to get the words out.

He squeezed her hand again. "I'll think of you every day," he said, "and I'll imagine what your life is like. Then, when the day comes, you can tell me everything."

Her tears were forming a flood beneath her feet and threatening to swallow her, but she clung to his hand and the hope his faith offered.

"We can't linger much longer," Lord Regoran said, putting a gentle hand on her shoulder.

She knew he was right; the longer they stayed the greater the chance they were discovered.

Her father squeezed her hand tightly, not letting go just yet. "The letters Gia! Where…?"

"I—I still have them—."

"Go to the south portcullis. My contact will be there. Those letters need to get to Lord Urbane."

The portcullis. That's where he was taking her the other day. "But it's been three days…?"

"If he is not there, look for the wild camels beyond the wall. You must find him tonight or it will be too late." Her father kissed her hand. "I love you, Gia. Go now." Then he let go.

"I love you too daddy."

She let Lord Regoran pull her away then, for she did not have the courage to do it herself. She saw him nod to her father through her tears, but she could not look back. She vowed then to not picture him in the mines, but as the explorer he was. As the loving, scatter-brained father he was. They reached the alcove and Tomas dropped the rope down for them. She did not think she had the strength to climb, but somehow she did it. When they had both emerged and were standing with Tomas again, Lord Regoran took her by the shoulders.

"We won't let Cornelius get away with this, I promise you. We will overthrow him."

She could hear the conviction in his words, but it was not enough. "I'll help you, but I need your help too."

"Whatever you need."

"I'll help you overthrow him, and then you'll help me kill him."

They waited for fifteen minutes. Tomas snuck down the narrow walkway to the portcullis, but he returned shortly after and shook his head. No one was there. No one was coming. And the longer they stayed there, the more chances they had that the soldiers would catch them.

"My father said to look for the camels," Georgiana said.

"Outside the wall," Tomas said. He pointed to the stairs leading up to the walkway. "We have to get up there, but the wall patrol has doubled. We'll have maybe a minute before we're spotted up there."

"I have an idea," Georgiana said, squeezing his arm. She motioned for him to follow her and she cautiously led him over to the stairway. The ascended the stairway and paused at the top, looking left and right down the walkway. There were two guards a little ways to the left and one to the right, so Georgiana waited until they were facing away from their part of the walkway, then hurried across with Tomas to the other side where the arched windows outlined the overhang of the wall. It was the very spot they had taken Tamsin to see the Hollow Cliffs. She shimmied through and up to the overhang's roof, Tomas close on her heels. She motioned for him to stay low and he gave her a look as if to say *how in the world did you find this place?* She shrugged and smiled, taking a bit of pride in knowing something that Tomas, the one who seemed to know every nook and secret tunnel in Empyria, did not.

She stole a glance out at the Hollow Cliffs and a wisp of nostalgia blew over her, but she quickly suppressed it. They had no time for the past.

Tomas nudged her shoulder and she looked in the direction he was pointing. Just off to the right, a little distance from the southwest bend of the wall, were about a dozen moving shapes. The shapes of plodding camels. She wished she had Enrik's spyglass right now, for it was difficult to make out if there was someone with them, but she felt a burst of hope ignite inside her. It was as her father had said.

But as she searched for human legs amongst the moving camel legs she noticed they were moving away from the river. They were leaving.

Tomas seemed to have gathered the same information for his eyes narrowed and his fingers dug into the solid stone beneath them.

We're too late, Georgiana thought. There was no way they were going to catch anyone's attention without drawing the attention of the guards. They were out of time.

Then Tomas grabbed her arm, forcing her to look at him. There was an urgency in his movement, but his eyes were resolute. "Find me at the Archive building."

Before she could even ask what he meant, he jumped back down the way they had just come. Georgiana heard his fast footsteps on the walkway. She scrambled over to the edge above the walkway and saw him running with a torch in his hand. He stopped midway between the overhang and the nearest guard. Then he let out a piercing whistle that was so loud it could have been heard clear across the city. Standing at the outer wall he began waving the torch frantically as he continued to whistle. The guard spotted him and seemed bewildered by Tomas's wild behavior. But his training kicked in a moment later and he raced across the walkway towards him. Tomas continued to wave and whistle and let out a kick just as the guard reached him. The guard stumbled and landed on his back. Then, before the guard could recover, Tomas flung the torch over the wall and it sailed in a large, flaming arc and landed in a burning heap in the sand a few yards from the river. He took off running then and Georgiana lost sight of him as he continued to make noise and draw the other guards' attention to himself.

Georgiana forced herself to look away and back out to the desert. The small camel herd had stopped.

Then a fast-moving shape caught her eye. It was lone camel with a rider on its back, cantering across the sand towards the flaming torch on the ground. The rider circled the torch a few times and the fire illuminated his desert clothing and the black cloth wrapped around half his face.

That was him, Georgiana thought. Her father's contact. It had to be. She glanced at the guard Tomas had knocked down. He had run back to his post at the extruded tower and was now lighting the massive cauldron perched atop the wall. At each of the towers dispersed along the wall was a large cauldron, that once lit, could be seen from someone at the Armillary. Then the troops could be alerted to trouble in that section.

Georgiana slung the pouch over her head and just as Tomas had done with the torch, flung it as far as she could. It landed several yards short of the torch, but the movement had caught the rider's eye and he circled his spooked camel over to it. He dismounted and knelt next to the pouch.

At the same moment that he looked up and caught Georgiana's eye the cauldron erupted into flames and both their gazes were directed towards the flames.

The rider snatched the pouch, tucked it away somewhere and remounted his camel. With speed that Georgiana didn't think the lumbering animals had, the camel shot away from the glowing torch faster than a racehorse and galloped across the dark sand away from the wall. A low, quick whistle burst forth from the rider and the heads of the small herd of camels that had lingered farther down the wall shot up. Seeing their companion fleeing into the desert, the herd took off after them with indignant snorts and bleats, kicking up sand in the moonlight.

Georgiana watched them a moment longer than she knew she should have, for the Armillary had been alerted to trouble in this area and soon the place would be swarming with soldiers. She had to get to the Archive building and find Tomas. She climbed down off the roof, careful on the steps for she feared the thundering beating of her heart would rock her right off. She paused in the arched window and once she was certain it was clear she darted across the walkway and down the stairs. She wanted to run as fast as she could away from that place, but she knew she still had to be careful to avoid being seen. She took every deserted side street and shortcut through empty courtyards she could think of until her eyes fell upon the most welcome sight of the Archive building. It was a dark monolith, standing slightly apart from the rest of the surrounding buildings, a lone beacon.

Fear and doubt ascended the stairs with her. The darkness and silence could either be hiding Tomas or it could be hiding nothing. In the latter case, she would be alone. And she didn't know what to do next.

She stepped into the main room and looked around. Even at night it seemed much larger than it had the other night when the rebels had gathered, filling the circular space with bodies instead of books. But now it was completely empty. There was nowhere to hide in the round room. There were a few scattered tables and chairs, but the shelves lined all the walls. There were no corners or crannies to hide anyone.

Her chin quivered slightly and she brushed a tear hastily from her eye.

Something creaked loudly behind her and she whirled to see one of the book cases moving. It swung out slowly, like a door, and she took a step back.

Then a figure stepped out from behind it. It was Tomas.

He held out his hand and Georgiana let out a breath. Another secret passageway. That's how her father had left the other night after the meeting without her seeing him. She hesitated only a moment before taking his hand. In that moment, she said goodbye to the past and steeled herself for whatever future that passageway led to.

She was a rebel now.

Chapter Fifteen

Tamsin waved goodbye to the islanders as Saashiim rowed their boat to shore. As restful as her stay had been, it had given her a lot of time to think and in the morning she had gone to Saashiim and asked for a boat. As expected, he complied without argument or questions, for he knew her whole story and knew why she had to go back. They had generously filled the boat with food and fishing supplies and were ready to go as soon as breakfast was over. It was a bright, clear day and Tamsin hoped it was a sign of a less troubling journey back through the mangroves. Saashiim said he could get her through to the other side without harm, but he had no knowledge of the waterways of the marsh lands in which to direct her. Her heart was lightened knowing that she wouldn't have to go through alone.

Two other boats accompanied them as well. Though Baagh was no longer a threat, the mangroves could still be dangerous. There was in inlet that cut through the beach and into the mangroves so they didn't have to carry the boats across the sand. Tamsin glanced one final time back at the islands, already wistful for the peace they had brought, but she could not linger there any longer. Her purpose was waiting for her.

Her lips pursed in a frown at the thought of Haven. Every day that passed was a mark on her heart, knowing that he could not escape his torment. He had no islands to rest upon.

Saashiim seemed to sense her change in mood as they entered underneath the forest canopy.

"Tamsin, we can wait, you know. We don't have to do this yet if you're not ready," he said, bringing his oar out of the water and turning towards her.

Tamsin shook her head no. "I have to Saashiim. I must be ready even if I'm not."

"You have a heart of courage, child." He smiled and started paddling once again.

It took them a fraction of the time to get through the mangroves as had taken Tamsin for Saashim knew the quickest routes. It was early evening when they emerged through to the other side and came upon the familiar wall of reeds. Saashiim made sure Tamsin had everything she needed in the boat and then nimbly climbed into one of the others.

"I wish you could come with me," Tamsin said, genuinely sorry to be leaving him.

"I have a feeling you won't be alone for long, Tamsin, *kazszura'asha, Baagh'dovuurii.*"

Tamsin shook her head at the titles. Tamsin, Queen of the Embers, Fear of Baagh. "Thank you, Saashiim. I would be dinner of Baagh if it hadn't been for you."

Saashiim bowed his head and touched his clasped hands to his forehead. "You may find rest with us whenever you need it," he said. Then, looking up, he said, "I hope you succeed Tamsin, and…may the gods be with you on your way." He winked and then they left, disappearing back into the mangroves.

Tamsin breathed deep and then grasped her own oar tightly, gathering her courage.

She looked at the oar in her hands. It had been her plan to go into the marshes until she found someone that could help guide her through. But looking at the wooden handle gave her an idea. Maybe she could get a guide to come to her.

She used the rest of the evening to harvest enough reeds for her plan using the fishing knife in her supplies. She planted her oar in the mud in the middle of the cleared flat and then tied the reeds using some fishing net to the top of the oar, making it taller than the surrounding reeds. If this didn't work, then the next morning she would take her remaining oar and do her original idea.

Once nightfall set and the sky was a solid blanket of darkness, she put her plan into action. She stood several yards away and then ignited the reed stalks attached to her oar. Immediately, the flames sprang up, illuminating the darkness like a lighthouse in the sea. If that didn't attract attention, she didn't know what would.

She walked a little ways away, to a spot she had picked out earlier, where she would be hidden but still able to see if anyone approached the fire. Now all she had to do was wait.

Luckily, that wasn't very long. It was about an hour, she guessed, after she had started the fire when it abruptly went out. She almost jumped up, afraid a gust of wind had put it out, but stopped herself just in time. The reeds had burned up quickly, but the oar had been more efficient at holding the flame. No, there was only one thing that could have put it out that fast.

She waited several minutes and then her patience was rewarded. A cloaked figure walked cautiously up to the oar, circling it as he studied it.

Tamsin's breath hitched, the sight stirring up memories, but she couldn't get caught up in that now. She was about to step out of her hiding place when she felt cold steel press into her neck. She froze, painfully aware of the fishing knife tucked uselessly in her boot. This had definitely not been a part of her plan.

"Out with you," the owner of the blade said sternly.

Tamsin rose, slowly, and walked out from her hiding spot into the open.

The first figure turned to them and walked over, confident in his stride. "Thank you, Rashu," he said. "I can take it from here."

The blade left her neck and the man stepped away. He wasn't a Watcher like the first, but had a dark, long-sleeved shirt on and hair to match. It was hard to see his features, but Tamsin could see the glint of beads in his hair and something shiny pinned in his nose. It was a wonder she didn't hear him sneak up on her.

Then it dawned on her. "How long did you know I was here?" she asked.

"Long enough to know you hadn't set any traps," the Watcher said. "Why did you light this fire?"

Tamsin squared her shoulders. "I don't know this part of the marshes very well and got lost. I was hoping someone would see the fire and help me."

"You're lucky Oman was with us when we saw it," Rashu said. "The amon'jii hardly travel this far in, but knowingly starting a fire after dark out in the open is a serious risk."

"I'm sorry if I put anyone in danger," she said, softening her stance a little. "That was not my intent."

"It's alright," the Watcher, Oman, said. "You may come with us. There is enough room in the canoe."

"Thank you, and I have my own boat. I can follow you." She went through the reeds, with the men following, to where she had anchored her boat to the shore.

Rashu ran a hand over the wooden surface. "This is not like our reed canoes," he said. "Where did you get this?"

Tamsin threw the rope anchoring it back into the boat. "Umm..."

"Rashu," Oman interrupted, "why don't you go ahead and tell K'al we are coming. She will want to be prepared for guests."

"Of course," Rashu said, flicking his fingers off the back of his hand respectfully. Then he disappeared back to their canoe.

"Do you mind?" Oman asked, indicating the boat.

"Not at all," Tamsin said. She climbed in, letting Oman give it a good shove into the water before jumping in after her.

Oman too seemed impressed with the craftmanship of the boat, taking a moment to study it before using Tamsin's remaining oar. "Rashu was right. This boat was made for much harsher waters than the marshes. You must have a very interesting story."

Tamsin did not want to divulge anything she knew about the islanders, or how she came upon them, but something in Oman's tone made her suspect that he already knew more than he was letting on. And she had been trying to put her finger on that sense of familiarity she felt when he spoke.

"You have not asked who I am," she finally said.

"No I have not," he said. "I already know who you are."

Tamsin spun around to face him, her hand hovering over her boot. She didn't know what her odds were against a Watcher, but if he was in league with Hazees or the Havakkii then she wasn't taking any chances. She wasn't going back there.

"How do you know me?" she asked.

"I met you a long ways away from here. First, by the cliffs of the walled city, then during the sh'pav'danya."

Tamsin's hand dropped. "You were there. In Empyria with Haven and Kellan and Samih. You were the fourth."

He nodded.

Tamsin tried to collect her racing thoughts. "Did Kellan send you here? To look for me?"

"No, but I had heard stories of the Havakkii being seen in these parts and I came to offer my assistance."

"Assistance?"

"The K'al'diin have been kind to me in the past. If the Havakkii were harassing them I would see to it they were dealt with."

"It's my fault the Havakkii were here. They took me to the mangroves and left me for dead."

Oman paused and lifted his hood away from his face. He was older than the others, with a short beard that showed a touch of gray in the moonlight and several small scars that cut across some wrinkles by his mouth. But his eyes glowed just as brightly as the younger Watchers, if not more so being a vibrant silver.

"The mangroves are an archaic form of punishment," he said, his expression on the verge of horror. "How did you survive?"

"I nearly didn't," she said.

He let her dodge his question, but he eyed the supplies in the boat before putting the paddle back into motion.

"You told Rashu to go tell K'al we were coming," she said, changing the subject. "She is the Kazsera of these parts?"

"Yes."

"How long before we get there?"

"We have a little ways, but we will be there before the night is half over."

"Oman," Tamsin bit her lip, pausing as she thought of how to say this. "I have not had the best luck with the Kazserii so far. I need to know whose side K'al is on."

"Side?"

"Is she allies with Hazees?"

"We Watchers do not get involved in the politics of the Kazserii," he said, "but if I remember right, then I believe that K'al holds no love for Hazees."

Tamsin breathed a sigh. "I like her already."

It was too dark to tell what colors the K'al'diin bore when their boat finally made it to the village, but there was one muudhiif that still had smoke rolling out of the top. This one they pulled their boat up to.

Tamsin had barely stepped out when the flap to the muudhiif was thrown open and several people stepped out to meet them. Rashu stood next to a tall woman whose wavy hair engulfed most of the space around her head and though her facial features were hard to make out in the shadow of the light coming from the muudhiif, the shine of metal through her nose and around her neck were quite visible.

"I am K'al," the tall woman said, her voice clear and animated despite the lateness of the hour. "You must be the one Rashu told me about. She is the reason the Havakkii hover nearby?" K'al asked, her eyebrows raised.

"The Havakkii took her to the mangroves, but the only thing she is guilty of is harboring foreign blood. And even that is not her fault," Oman said.

Tamsin bowed and flicked her fingers over her hand as she had seen done countless times from others when addressing the Kazserii. "I am Tamsin Urbane, daughter to Irin of the Ma'diin and Lord Urbane of Empyria, Queen of Embers, and Fear of Baagh."

K'al took several steps closer until she was directly in front of Tamsin, unable to conceal her astonishment. She took Tamsin's chin in her hand and lifted upwards slightly. From here Tamsin could see her eyes were a crisp blue and her face was wide but lean. She let go of Tamsin's chin and smiled.

"Rashu did not tell me you were Irinbaat," K'al said.

"I did not know, Kazsera," Rashu said.

"Nor I," Oman said.

"Forgive me," K'al said after a moment. "Please, both of you, come inside. Eat and rest. We can discuss everything in the morning."

"Go ahead, Tamsin," Oman said. "I still have work to do."

K'al nodded. "Of course. You are welcome to join us in the morning."

He thanked her and left in his own canoe, and though K'al seemed quite unthreatening, his absence left Tamsin feeling wary once more. But she accompanied them back in the muudhiif and true to her word, K'al had food ready and by the time Tamsin had finished eating a sleeping mat and blankets had been arranged for her. And though K'al had said they could talk in the morning, Tamsin had questions of her own she wanted to ask.

Before she retired, she asked, "Did you know her? Irin?"

"I knew her when I was younger. My mother knew her better. She was a great Kazsera, your mother."

A long pause hung between them, until K'al continued. "You are quite welcome here, Irinbaat. You have nothing to fear from me."

"Thank you," Tamsin said. "And I'm sorry if I have brought trouble to your tribe."

K'al smiled, it filling up the whole muudhiif. "Like Oman said, he has work to do. I suspect the Havakkii will trouble us no more after tonight." She winked. "You may sleep easy tonight."

And Tamsin did.

Oman and K'al were waiting for her when she woke the next morning, and they had breakfast together in the muudhiif. She told them more of her time with Samih and the Hazees'diin than she did about her time in the mangroves, saying it was not pleasant to recall, and they respected her wishes, though she could see the fascination in both their eyes that she managed to survive. She asked Oman if he knew what had happened to Kellan, but he didn't so K'al offered to send the sha'diin out to make inquiries. He did tell her that the Havakkii had been taken care of, though Tamsin didn't ask what exactly that meant for she had found him cleaning his swords this morning.

But he had come across something that made her extremely happy: her pack. The Havakkii had apparently taken it when they took Tamsin and Oman had gotten it back. He had assumed from the strange material it was made of that it belonged to her.

Tamsin looked inside. Everything was still there, including her shawl that was wrapped around Haven's firestone.

After breakfast Oman excused himself so he could retire for the day, but Tamsin wasn't afraid to be left alone anymore.

"So you know my story now," Tamsin told K'al. "Will you help me? Will you help me get Haven back?"

"I spoke to Oman earlier this morning," she said. "We have a plan, but you must be patient. And you must stay out of sight. At least for now. I've spoken to Rashu and my kazsiin. Your presence with us will be kept a secret for the time being."

"I must stay in the muudhiif? For how long?"

"Not just the muudhiif. You may go about the tribe as you wish. My people will not betray you. But anyone who passes through not wearing these colors," she procured a purple garment for Tamsin to don, "cannot be trusted as much."

Tamsin understood. "And what is your plan?" she asked.

"Oman will leave tonight. He should return in a few days and hopefully with answers for you, but he and the other Watchers have much to contend with as of late."

Tamsin knew all too well for she had seen firsthand what they were up against. The completion of the dam had already decimated an entire tribe by allowing the amon'jii to roam farther into the marsh lands. But she was still not happy about having to wait.

She was restless the rest of the day and took to learning about the K'al'diin to pass the time. They were a mixed tribe, she found out, of water buffalo herders and herbalists, skilled with both animals and plants for this section of the marsh was usually lush all year long. There were also groups of young men and women that came together on a cleared mud flat throughout the day and fought each other with long sticks. It didn't seem like they were out to harm each other, and when Tamsin asked what they were doing they said they were preparing for the Kapu'era. The Kapu'era, or *the Duels*, they told her happened every three years and was a chance for them to show their tribe's strength and even advance their position in the tribe.

Seeing them fighting made Tamsin even more anxious to do something, anything but this waiting. She had promised herself upon leaving the islands that she would be in control. So she made a decision and marched back into the muudhiif to collect her things.

K'al was talking to some of her kazsiin when Tamsin entered and immediately sensed something was out of place.

"What's wrong?" she asked.

"I'm leaving," Tamsin declared, grabbing her pack by the bedding. "You said you would help me so all I ask is a guide to get me through the marshes. But I'll be going with or without one."

K'al waved her kazsiin out of the muudhiif quickly.

"But why?" K'al seemed truly confused.

"Why?" Tamsin said incredulously. "Because I still don't have a clue about what you and Oman are planning and I am sick of waiting around while the man I love is still out there!"

"I think we weren't clear this morning," K'al said, furrowing her brow. "You said you needed an army to rescue your Watcher, yes?"

"Yes," Tamsin replied.

"Oman is going to get you one."

Tamsin's reply fell off her lips in silence. She paced the muudhiif a moment to collect herself. "Oman is going to get me an army?"

"A small one, but it's a start."

Tamsin couldn't contain herself anymore and threw her arms around K'al, hugging her tightly. Whether it was appropriate or not, Tamsin was going to celebrate the first good news she had heard in a long time. "Where?" Tamsin asked, still not quite believing it. "Who?"

"The Kor'diin."

Tamsin released her. She had heard that name before. Poma's children had asked if she was Kor'diin. "Who are they?"

K'al smiled. "Your mother's tribe."

Tamsin stayed with the K'al'diin for two more days. They were eating the evening meal when one of the sha'diin came in and whispered something to K'al.

K'al nodded once and waved the man away. She turned to Tamsin with a grin, her blue eyes shining even brighter from the fire they sat around. "They are coming," she said.

Tamsin didn't need to ask who. Two days ago she had been so eager to leave, but that was until K'al told her that Oman would be bringing back her mother's tribe. K'al explained to her that the Kor'diin were different than the other tribes for they had elected no new Kazsera after Irin's death. *Kor* was not the name of their new Kazsera, but rather it meant *headless.* They had broken thousands of years of tradition by choosing to remain leaderless and as a result were not even considered a complete tribe by the other Kazserii. But the Irin'diin had been fearless warriors and resisted any attempts from other tribes to absorb them into their own tribes.

This made Tamsin nervous and she wished the days had been longer, though K'al assured her that the Kor'diin would be ecstatic upon hearing of Tamsin's presence here. But Tamsin was still not so sure. She was not Irin. She couldn't even remember her and the Kor'diin harbored so much loyalty to Irin even so many years after her passing. How could she compare?

"Don't be nervous, Irinbaat," K'al said, as Tamsin had stopped eating as soon as the news reached them. "They are not so different from the rest of us. Not as different as the northerners."

Tamsin appreciated K'al's attempt at a joke, but it did nothing to take the edge away. "Will Oman be coming with them?"

"I imagine so, unless something diverted his attention. He wants to see you safe, Tamsin, and not just because of your affections for his oath-brother."

"How old is he?" Tamsin asked, glad to turn the attention off of herself.

"Oman? He is the oldest Watcher I know, though it does not reflect on his courage, for he is also one of the most brave. He is like a father to the others."

"At what age do they get their scars?"

The kazsiin stopped eating and glanced at Tamsin and then to their Kazsera, who looked at Tamsin curiously.

"Scars?" she asked.

"Yeah," Tamsin said, looking at the others and wondering what she had said. "Haven has silvery ones all over, and I've seen some on Oman, but Samih has none and I know he is much younger than Haven…"

All eyes were on her.

"Tamsin," K'al started slowly. "When you told us of your encounter with the amon'jii, you told us you had not been burned. Is that true?"

"Of course," Tamsin said, bewildered by the turn in the conversation. "The amon'jii only scratched me, nothing more."

"May I see it?" K'al asked.

Tamsin hesitantly agreed and K'al crossed the muudhiif to sit next to her. She was extra careful when pulling down Tamsin's shoulder strap, but Tamsin assured her it didn't hurt anymore. It had not been deep and felt nearly healed. But K'al's sudden interest in it unnerved her.

"Is something wrong?" she asked.

"No," K'al said, replacing her shoulder strap. "Merely curious."

"Please don't lie to me," Tamsin said.

K'al sighed and returned to her seat. "I'm not lying Tamsin. If you say you were not burned, then I believe you."

"Why is that so important?"

"The Watchers—their eyes are different. They see things differently," K'al said, and Tamsin could see she was searching for the right words to say. "It becomes that way when they become Watchers. I've known Oman my whole life. I've never seen any kind of silver scars on him."

Tamsin digested her words, but understanding eluded her. "But…" She scratched her temple.

"I wanted to make sure you were not burned," K'al said.

"You wanted to make sure I wasn't becoming a Watcher," Tamsin corrected. "But I saw Haven's markings when we were in Empyria. How is that possible?"

Before K'al could answer, the flap to the muudhiif was opened. One of the sha'diin came in followed by Oman. And behind him was Kellan.

A ripple of unease went around the kazsiin. They were accustomed to Oman and were tolerant of their Kazsera's affinity for him, but having two Watchers here, and in the muudhiif itself, was a bit more than they were used to.

But Tamsin had to sit on her hands to keep herself from getting up and going to him. She had so many questions for him and despite everything she had went through after he left, she was glad to see he was okay.

Oman flicked K'al the sign of respect and took a few steps further into the muudhiif, but Kellan stayed resolutely by the doorway.

"Welcome back, Oman," K'al greeted him. "And you," she looked over to Kellan, "you are welcome here as well."

A slight nod of his hood was all the acknowledgement he offered.

K'al raised an eyebrow, but continued. "I trust your hunting was fruitful then?" she asked Oman.

He nodded. "They are right outside." He turned to Tamsin. "And they are eager to meet you."

Tamsin could sit still no longer and stood up, hastily brushing her hands on her dress.

K'al got up as well and motioned for the kazsiin to do likewise. "We will give you your privacy, Irinbaat," she said.

Oman and Kellan moved out of the way so the kazsiin could leave, but K'al stopped by Oman.

"The sh'lomiin may be needed as well, Oman," K'al said quietly, indicating with a tilt of her head that she wanted to speak to him privately.

Oman nodded once and followed her out, leaving Tamsin and Kellan alone.

After a moment Kellan asked, "You are okay?" He kept his hood up and stood facing slightly away from her, but Tamsin could hear the shame in his voice.

"Yes, I'm okay," she replied. "Kellan—."

The flap to the muudhiif opened again and a man and a woman entered. Kellan turned and left before the flap had even come down.

Tamsin swallowed the conversation she knew she needed to have with Kellan and focused on the two people before her.

The woman looked like she could have been a faerie. She had flaming orange hair that twisted in a long braid that laid against her delicate shoulders. Her piercing green eyes were set perfectly in her equally delicate face that slanted up at just the right angles. But her beauty was edged with a fierceness that even Tamsin could see. Deep blue sashes were interwoven throughout and softened the tight leather jerkin she wore, but her pants were adorned with extra pockets and straps for blades.

The man was tall and had a darker complexion than the woman, but he was beautiful as well. He had short hair that allowed for his unassuming features to shine. Tamsin could imagine he smiled often.

The woman bowed her head slightly, not taking her eyes off Tamsin. "I am Numha, and this is Benuuk," she said. "You are really her." She seemed awestruck.

Tamsin straightened. "I am Tamsin, daughter of Irin. And you are the Kor'diin? I am honored to——." She went to flick her fingers in the sign of respect, but Numha crossed the space between them and took her hands.

"Please, no. The honor is ours, Tamsin." She bent her forehead down until it was touching Tamsin's hands. "We have been waiting a long time to meet you."

Tamsin was stunned by the adoration she displayed and she didn't know the right way to respond. She was used to a level of reverence back in the Cities that her family's position granted her, but here she was nobody. Unless she had underestimated Irin's rank in the Ma'diin. "I—I didn't know her," she said. "I didn't know any of you existed."

Numha smiled kindly, unoffended by Tamsin's ignorance of them. "Your mother was the greatest Kazsera I have ever seen. So great that she could have been Kaz'ma'sha."

"Kaz'ma'sha, what is that?" Tamsin asked.

"Kazsera of *all* tribes. The Great Leader."

"You knew her well then?" Numha couldn't have been very much older than Tamsin herself.

"I was a young girl, but yes. My mother was one of her kazsiin. Irin was always very kind to me. I was deeply saddened when she left."

"We all were," Benuuk spoke up.

"I am sorry for your loss," Tamsin said, slipping her hands away from Numha's, "and for any part I had in her decision to leave."

"Do not be sorry," Numha said. "For we are not. Her decision is why we are all here tonight."

"The gods have brought you back to us," Benuuk said. "From now on we will no longer be Kor'diin."

Tamsin took an involuntary step back and looked back and forth between the two. "Oman explained to you why I came here right?" she asked slowly.

"Yes," Numha said. "For your Watcher. Haven, right?"

Tamsin nodded, starting to erect again the walls she had taken down around her hope ever since K'al told her what they were planning. But if she was interpreting correctly what Benuuk was insinuating…

"I did not come here to be your Kazsera," Tamsin said.

Their faces did not betray disappointment, as if they had been expecting this response.

"We know you didn't," Numha said, compassion twinkling brightly in her green eyes.

Just then, Oman and K'al re-emerged into the muudhiif. Something was wrong.

"What is it?" Tamsin asked.

"I'd like to speak to Tamsin alone, if I could," Oman said.

"They can stay," Tamsin said. Whatever Oman needed to say, she didn't want to hear it alone right now.

Oman pressed his lips together a moment and then nodded, conceding. "I just spoke to K'al," he said. "I need to see something."

The muudhiif suddenly went dark as Oman subdued the fire they had just been eating around. He left just enough heat in the embers to give off a slight orange glow, but it was dark enough so he could remove his hood. His eyes flashed keenly in the dark and he walked up to Tamsin, pulling back the sleeve on his arm.

"Tell me what you see," he said.

"Must we really do this now?" Tamsin asked. "K'al said—."

"K'al said you can see things the others cannot. Tell me."

Tamsin shifted her weight. She had seen glimpses of the markings on Oman already and just as the ones on Haven, these ones shimmered up Oman's arms like he had lightening in his veins.

"I can see them," Tamsin said. "The silver markings. Haven had them too. I don't know how I can see them, but like I told K'al, I saw them before I ever came here. I wasn't burned by the amon'jii."

His vibrant eyes stared at her a moment longer before he rolled down his sleeve and released his hold on the fire. Flames sprung up once more, revealing the concerned faces of the Kor'diin.

Tamsin didn't know why she was under such scrutiny for this. She wondered if Kellan had mentioned something to him about what he felt in the marshes when she had controlled the amon'jii's fire. Maybe her ability to control fire and ability to see the silver markings were connected.

"You can see the *lumii veritaas*?" Numha asked.

"Not many know of the *lumii veritaas*," Oman said, turning to Numha.

"I knew a Watcher who told me," Numha said quickly. "He was Benuuk's brother."

Benuuk straightened and a stone mask fell over his features. He didn't say a word, but it was plain to everyone that it was still a painful subject. Tamsin wondered if his brother was still alive.

"Samih does not have the markings," Tamsin said, trying to dispel the silence.

"All Watchers can see them, but not all have them. Samih became a Watcher by misfortune, but Haven and I were chosen because of our markings. The light of the twelve original Lumierii runs through the bloodlines of the tribes. That light manifests itself in some individuals that only other Watchers can see."

Tamsin was beginning to understand. "So what happens when someone shows signs of these markings?"

"They are chosen to join the brotherhood of the Watchers."

"They are chosen, but they have no choice in the matter," Benuuk said with a hint of anger.

Oman was patient with him though. "It is unfair, but it is the way things work."

"And do these men go willingly?" Tamsin asked. "Do they just trust your word that they have these markings?" She didn't know if Benuuk's anger was rubbing off on her or if it was the fear of not knowing why *she* could see them, but for some reason the idea that these men, that Haven, had their futures taken away from them without a chance or a choice was unfathomable and unacceptable.

"No, most mothers do not trust us and do not give up their sons willingly. But—."

Sons? "You're telling me that you take children?"

"K'tar was only eleven when he was taken," Benuuk said.

Numha turned away slightly, glancing at the ground, but not before Tamsin saw a strange look pass over her face. It was familiar somehow.

Now it was Oman's turn to don a stone mask. "I take no joy in it. But the alternative is far more terrifying a thought. The younger they can be trained, the better their chances at surviving are. I myself was taken when I was only nine."

The silence that followed was as thick as the mud flat they were standing on.

Tamsin took a moment to reign in her feelings. "I'm sorry Oman," she said.

"Do not apologize. The anger you feel is how most of my people feel."

K'al stepped forward in between Oman and the Kor'diin, as if to shield them from one another. "Let us forget the past for tonight and focus on right now. Agreed?"

They all murmured their agreement.

Then Tamsin spoke up, the explanation for everything dawning on her. "I know why I can see the markings."

Everyone looked at her.

"I'm not a Watcher," she said. "But my mother was."

Tamsin had already guessed when she had found out Irin was a Watcher that it was connected to her ability to control fire, but she hadn't thought it affected anything else. But now she was beginning to question it all and wondered what else lay dormant that would emerge.

They all seemed to accept this with mild forms of surprise and awe, except for Oman who remained rigidly troubled. And Numha seemed to pick up on it more than the others.

"Is there any danger that Tamsin could become a Watcher from this?" Numha asked. "Is this a sign?"

Oman stood still, his nervous expression planted firmly on Tamsin and she felt a sudden stab of doubt that made her breath go cold, but eventually he shook his head.

"I don't think so," he said, but then he added, "Tamsin, have you experienced anything else like this? Any other…symptoms?"

Should she tell them? Kellan knew, but he was just one person. Her ordeal in the mangroves was still fresh in her mind. She wanted to trust the Kor'diin, but what if they thought she harbored *jiin* just like Hazees had? She wasn't ready to face that kind of persecution again.

She shook her head no, hoping he would not ask her again.

He watched her a few uncomfortable moments more and Tamsin remembered how he had studied the reed pyre she had built that had caught their attention in the first place. She wondered if he was remembering it now.

But then he looked away. "I have never heard of anyone inheriting the *lumii veritaas* from their parents, but I think it is a good idea to summon the sh'lomiin anyways."

Haven had told her of the sh'lomiin a little. Storytellers, he had called them.

"We wish to bring her to the Kor'diin as soon as possible," Numha said.

"We can send him there," K'al said.

"Wait," Tamsin said forcefully. "I have not said I would go anywhere." If the Kor'diin intended on making her their Kazsera and not helping with her own agenda, then it would be pointless to go with them.

"What?" K'al said, thinking the Kor'diin's arrival had set Tamsin's path.

But Tamsin would not be forced into anything that was not her decision. Ever again.

"I need a minute to think," she said and headed for the doorway.

K'al was about to go after her, but Numha shook her head. "It's alright. Let her go," she said.

Tamsin walked to the edge of the mudflat, letting the coolness of the night air fill her lungs and dispel the heaviness that had permeated the muudhiif.

Something made a sound off to her right, breaking the momentary calm and she turned to look.

The dark silhouette of a Watcher stood by the edge of the water.

Kellan.

Tamsin walked over to him. He acknowledged her presence with a slight turn of his head, but didn't say anything right away and for a long minute they just stood side by side, staring out across the calm water.

Finally, he said, "You do not join the others?"

She sighed deeply. "I needed a moment to think."

His hood rustled as he nodded. "I understand that."

"It's not your fault," Tamsin said, unable to avoid the topic any longer. And she believed it. What had happened with the Havakki, that was not Kellan's fault. And she didn't want Kellan believing she held a grudge against him for his mistake. She didn't want this awkward air between them.

"I shouldn't have let them take you," he said quietly.

"You were just trying to help me. I know that now."

"I thought I could get you out if they took you away from the Hazees'diin."

She put her hand on his arm. "It's not your fault," she repeated.

He looked down at her hand, his nostrils flaring underneath his hood as he saw the freshly healed ring around her wrist. "You could have died."

"I'm tougher than I look," she said, not wanting to reveal how close she had actually come to dying. Sharing that would only make things worse. "Please, you wanted to help me before. I need your help now. But that can only happen if we put this behind us. Can you do that?"

She felt the muscles in his arm tense underneath her hand, as he must've been struggling to bury his guilt, but after a few moments he relaxed.

"I will. Though," he paused, his lips pressed together to conceal a smile, "you look about as tough as a reed mouse."

Tamsin's own mouth fell open slightly. "Was that a joke? I didn't realize Watchers had a sense of humor."

He shrugged. "Some of us are more gifted than others."

She let out a laugh, the sound echoing across the water like windchimes. It felt good to laugh. It had been such a long time. Her brow furrowed. She couldn't remember the last time she had laughed, not truly.

He sensed her change in mood. "What did they say to you in there?"

"The Kor'diin want me to join their tribe and make me their Kazsera, but I don't know if I can. What if they just want to use me like Ysallah did?" To keep her in a glass box, displayed for everyone to see, but safe from the dangers of the world. Trapped by the prominence of her heritage, deemed too important to be taking such risks as rescuing a Watcher from the heart of amon'jii territory.

"Tamsin, other than the Watchers, for I want to get Haven back as much as you do, the Kor'diin's interests are the most similar to yours."

"Why do you say that?"

"Because Haven isn't the only one missing."

This took her by surprise.

"Another Watcher, K'tar is his name, went missing a while ago," he said.

K'tar. "That is Benuuk's brother. They mentioned him. He's missing?"

"We don't believe he's dead, but we don't know where he is either."

Tamsin believed him if he said they didn't think he had been killed by an amon'jii, but it seemed odd for a Watcher to just vanish. "Could he have left? I know how difficult your way of life is…"

"That's not likely."

"Why?"

"Because he and Numha were lovers."

Tamsin sucked in her breath. That was the look she had seen in Numha's eyes when K'tar was mentioned. She recognized it now for she was familiar with it. It was the same look that escaped her own eyes every once in a while. It was the pain of not knowing if the man she loved was alive or dead. That terrible space between hope and despair.

It seemed then that Kellan was right: the Kor'diin were her greatest allies. And if she became their Kazsera then she would have her army.

She knelt down and touched the water with her fingertips. "If I go, will you and Oman come with me?" She looked up at him.

His mahogany eyes simmered beneath his hood and she identified it as the same feeling she now felt, that now, finally, they would be making progress. He nodded.

She stood up then and walked back into the muudhiif. The others had been discussing something, but stopped when she entered. Tamsin looked at each of them, her gaze landing on Numha last. She hoped her decision would tip the scale towards hope for her.

She cleared her throat. "What must I do?"

Arriving at the Kor'diin's territory was unlike the rest of the Ma'diin tribes Tamsin had visited. The boundaries of the marsh tribes were unclear to her and in some cases, like the K'al'diin who followed the migrations of the water buffalo, the territory moved. But Tamsin knew immediately when they had passed the boundary. There were black cloth markers tied to reeds and manmade spears crossing over the waterway.

Tamsin inquired as to what their meaning was and Numha explained that they were warnings. The Kor'diin marshes were heavily guarded. Had been since Irin's departure.

As if on cue, something shot past her head and splashed into the water next to the canoe. Numha held up her fist and the boats stopped. Numha let out a short, fluttering whistle, which was quickly answered by another somewhere in the reed patches. The reeds began to quiver and several figures emerged at the edge of the water. They carried spears and knives and a young man had a crude slingshot dangling from his hand.

There was a tall woman next to him, taller than even the men who stood next to her. She carried more weapons than the rest of them, but they were all sheathed. She was so muscular she probably had no use for them, Tamsin thought. Her hair was cropped short, showing off her wide cheekbones.

This woman called out to Numha: "The haniis route is closed Numha. Best to go through the shafaii."

"And you were waiting out here to tell me that?" Numha replied.

The tall woman smirked. "I wanted to be the first to see her."

Tamsin realized she was talking about her.

The tall woman cocked her head to the side. "She's young."

"She is Irin's daughter, R'en," Numha said, steering the canoe towards the reed patch. "She cannot make time speed up."

"She may be young, but the young make better students," Oman said from his canoe.

The tall woman, R'en, noticed him then and smiled. She flicked her fingers over her hand in respect and Tamsin noticed that some of the others did the same. No one seemed put off by his presence.

"It is hard not to be a good student when one has a great teacher," R'en said.

Oman scoffed. "Who said you were a good student?"

Tamsin momentarily forgot about her nervousness about meeting the well-armed Kor'diin in lieu of the oddly familiar banter between the two. Never had she seen the Watchers treated so pleasantly, not even by the K'al'diin.

The look on her face must have given away her perplexity for Numha explained how the Watchers, Oman in particular, trained the Irin'diin. After Irin became a Watcher herself, she thought it best that her kazsiin be trained as well. And being so close to the amon'jii border made the need for trained fighters even more imperative.

"It's how we've managed to survive all these years," R'en said. "Not just against the amon'jii, but from Kazserii trying to conquer us."

She tilted her head, stepping closer to Tamsin. With the speed of a striking cobra, she shoved her hands against Tamsin's chest, who had been stepping out of the canoe and tripped backwards over the edge into the water. It was only a foot deep here, but before she could come up for air, R'en's foot stomped on her chest, pinning her under the water. Bubbles exploded from Tamsin's mouth as she screamed, or tried to, as she thrashed against the weight on her. She clutched R'en's leg, trying to shove it off, but it was like trying to move stone. Then her fingers felt something, and with the shred of rationale she had she realized it was knife, tucked in R'en's boot. She latched onto it, pulled it out and swung. With a lurch, the weight was gone, and Tamsin shot up, gasping in the free air.

She jumped to her feet, expecting a second attack, but when she cleared the water from her eyes she saw the others standing still in the reeds, watching her.

Oman smiled from beneath his hood. "She nearly got you, R'en."

"I told you she's spirited," Numha said.

"What in the seven hells of old was that for?!" Tamsin cried, still coughing water from her lungs.

"Her cursing could use some work, but I think she'll do," R'en said, inspecting the tear in her boot with a scowl. She dipped her head and flicked her fingers over her hand.

Tamsin's anger still hissed inside her; she had not expected to be tested by her mother's people, people that claimed to be loyal to her. "I've survived the Sindune, the anasii hada, an amon'jii, the mangroves and you still want to kill me!? Have I not proved myself yet?"

"I made a vow to your mother, to protect and honor her legacy until my soul flows into the great waterfalls of Edan. You are that legacy Irinbaat. You've shown me you are worth keeping that vow. But proving yourself is not a onetime act. Irin knew that."

"You have our loyalty," Numha said, a little gentler, and despite herself Tamsin felt her anger dissipating. "But it goes both ways."

Tamsin realized what she was trying to say. The Kor'diin would be loyal to her as long as she was loyal to them. They wanted to make her Kazsera, and that was a lifetime commitment.

They packed up their gear and the Kor'diin hauled the canoes out of the water, making a single file path through the reeds. Tamsin followed silently, looking forward to the moment when she would get some privacy to change out of her drenched clothes. Numha and R'en spoke together several paces ahead, and Tamsin wondered if they were concocting the next "test" for her. She would have to redefine her definition of adventure, she mused. It wasn't gallant gentlemen on horseback or sailing on white-sails through serene waters towards glittering caverns of treasure. It was traipsing through mud in soaking clothes after being nearly drowned, sleepless nights of scratching bug bites, and daydreams of velvet pillows and Sherene's raspberry crème de jene. Hearing the childhood versions of her father's travels had falsely glorified the notion of adventure for her.

Thinking of the past made her think of home, but she didn't dwell in memories. Instead she wondered about the future. Would she ever see the Cities again? She had come close to death several times already since coming to the marsh lands and she understood why Haven had been so hesitant to bring her here. It wasn't for the delicate natured or those short on courage. If she succeeded in getting an army, getting to the Ravine, and rescuing Haven, then what would become of them? Would he go to the Cities with her? Or would they stay in the marshes?

Her musing was interrupted by singing. They made it through the reed patch to another wide stretch of water and heard a choir of voices across the other side. The water was lined on either side with mud flats filled with muudhiifs and the source of the singing. They set their canoes back in the water and started off towards them. The waterway meandered through the rows of mud flats, narrowing the farther they went so they could almost reach out and touch them. The muudhiifs looked identical to the ones Tamsin had seen in the other tribes, but as they passed and more people saw them, the singing stopped and turned to cheers and whistles. People were soon flocking to the edges of the flats to see them. Some reached out to touch Tamsin as they went by, whispering 'Irinbaat' in awe and others rushed over with swags of flowers, food, and woven blankets to put in her canoe. Tamsin was glad that she still had the wooden one from the islanders for it was soon filled with offerings and she thought had it been made out of reeds it would have sunk. Children splashed in the water, sending sparkling droplets flying everywhere. No one seemed to notice the Watchers that accompanied them or else didn't care.

Tamsin's nostrils flared, overwhelmed by the reception. This was not what she had expected, especially after R'en's watery welcome. But it was true. She looked into their eyes as they went by and she could see the joy planted in them. To them, the lost daughter had returned home.

For the first time she understood what exactly she had inherited from her mother. Not just her looks or her ability to control fire, but the love of her people. This was Irin's family.

She stopped rowing, planting her oar in the shallow water until her canoe stopped completely. R'en and Numha turned to look behind them, but didn't stop her as she climbed out of her canoe. They simply watched as she stepped up onto the nearest mud flat. The crowd of Ma'diin there parted for her, but kept close, making the sign of respect with their hands and brushing their fingertips over her hair, shoulders and arms.

Tamsin walked over to an old woman who had caught her eye from the canoe and kneeled down in front of her where she sat in the shade of the muudhiif. Age had wrinkled the old woman's face and turned her hair a pure shade of white, but her eyes were bright with life. And the tears that streamed out of them were filled with happiness. The woman's shaking hands came up and cupped Tamsin's face and only then did Tamsin realize she had tears of her own running down her cheeks. The old woman smiled at her and nodded, as if she understood every mixed feeling that Tamsin had and was saying it was okay.

The crowd had gone quiet, but now erupted into loud cheers and joyful singing. They beckoned her away and she followed them across several more mud flats until they came to a large one at the end of the waterway. The faces around her seemed to hold even more delight as they ushered her forward and parted for her to reveal an enormous muudhiif. It looked as if it had been newly built with fresh, green reeds thatching the roof and flowering vines that wound up the support beams to the entrance. Vibrant blue fabric draped across the opening and down the sides in triangular strips.

Numha and the others pulled up to the edge of the flat with their canoes and joined her.

"They've been working day and night to complete it in time," R'en said, smiling at Tamsin's confused look. "It's yours."

Her own muudhiif. She walked up to it slowly, running her fingers along the edge of the blue door flap before stepping inside. It was quiet inside, the packed reed walls shielding her from the joyful celebration that continued outside. The Kor'diin had already adorned it with pillows, blankets, and anything else that she could ever need. She went to the very back where there was another blue flap. She pushed it aside to reveal a cozy annex. There was more bedding and a small outline of stones for a fire. It was just for her.

She returned to the main chamber and saw Numha standing inside the door.

"Do you like it?" she asked.

"It's more than I could've imagined," Tamsin said.

"I know it seems strange now, their devotion," Numha said, "but you are already the Kazsera in their minds."

It was strange, intimidatingly so. They didn't even know her. Yes, she was of the lording class back home, but as a woman her power was dictated by her father or husband and that power was privileged, but limited to the household. But Tamsin knew she had to push that mindset aside if their plan had any chance.

"I want to meet them," she said. If she were to be responsible for these peoples' lives, then she wanted to know who they were.

Numha held the door flap open and smiled. "Then let's begin. We have no time to lose."

The fires in the muudhiifs burned long into the night that night as Tamsin met the people of the Kor'diin and they exchanged stories. Oman and Kellan had disappeared, but Tamsin had enough to keep her distracted from thinking of their safety as they patrolled the marshes. There was a huge feast and Tamsin's new muudhiif was packed with men, women, and children, each eager to introduce themselves and hear Tamsin's stories of the north and her experiences in the marsh lands thus far. Some told her their favorite memories of Irin and Tamsin began to truly understand the depth of their affection for their departed Kazsera. And Irin's unwavering commitment to her people. Some offered their condolences and conveyed their pity that Tamsin never got the chance to know her, but no one mentioned Irin's decision to leave them outright, as if it were a taboo subject. As taboo as Tamsin's relationship with Haven.

Tamsin wanted to be honest with these people, and she had discussed this with Numha on the way from the K'al'diin. She wanted them to know why she needed their help. And what they planned to do about it. But she wanted them to have a choice. She would not force them down a path if it wasn't what they chose.

So that night, with the whole tribe present, Tamsin brought her plea before the Kor'diin and she and Numha explained their plan:

With the Kor'diin's approval, Tamsin would officially become their Kazsera. Then, any man or woman able and willing would follow them to the Ravine of Bones in a joint rescue mission with the Watchers.

There was a lot of murmuring and questions that arose, and Numha answered all of them as best she could, since she was more familiar with the tribe than Tamsin. Even though it was dangerous, the Kor'diin seemed open to the idea and one by one the commitment was made. But before a final decision could be made, a flaw in their plan was pointed out. To get to the Ravine they would have to cross through three other tribes' territories: the Lam'diin, the Zekkara'diin,…and the Hazees'diin.

Hazees was ruthless and had no qualms about getting rid of those she viewed as a threat. And the bad blood between the Hazees'diin and the Kor'diin went back to Irin's day. There was no way of getting through her territory without her knowing and if the Kor'diin tried to pass she would use it as an excuse to declare war on the Kor'diin. Together, the Kor'diin could defend their land, but if they were split up between those on the rescue mission and those that stayed behind they would be easily defeated on both fronts.

Tamsin looked to Numha, hoping there was a possible way to avoid this, but Numha's look was troubled. She had hoped that with the Watchers' help they could force their way through Hazees's territory if necessary, but the Kor'diin were right. Even if they did it would leave the Kor'diin's territory to be protected only by children and the elderly. And that just wasn't an option.

The Kor'diin eventually filtered out of the muudhiif until it was only Tamsin, Numha, R'en, and Benuuk. Dawn was only a few hours away and R'en stoked the embers in the fire. Everyone was exhausted, but determined to find a solution. Benuuk offered the idea of passing through the territories in smaller, less noticeable groups. R'en wanted to march right into Hazees's muudhiif and run her through with a sword.

But it was Numha's silence that Tamsin noticed and she asked her what she was thinking.

Numha rocked back on her heels, her gaze still locked onto the embers in concentration, as if the answer would reveal itself in the orange glow. She was lost in some thought, seemingly oblivious to the others.

Tamsin looked at R'en who shrugged her shoulders and then at Benuuk, but he merely shook his head.

Tamsin said Numha's name again and when she again did not answer, Tamsin felt the embers with her senses and sent a burst of sparks out of them. Numha sat back, blinking, the burst bringing her mind back into the muudhiif. She looked up at the others watching her.

"What is it?" Tamsin asked.

Numha breathed deeply. Her head was bent forward slightly, but her eyes locked onto Tamsin's now. "I have an idea, but you're not going to like it."

Three weeks. Three more weeks of waiting.

Numha was right, Tamsin didn't like the new plan, but she couldn't deny the small pleasure she took from the surprised glance Oman and Kellan exchanged when Kellan's first attempt to "teach" Tamsin how to wield a weapon ended in a swift *smack* on the arm from her stick. They used long sticks made of woven reed roots instead of swords because the Watchers assumed they were starting from scratch with Tamsin. Kellan had showed her where to place her hands and how to distribute her weight. He told her the Watchers often practiced against each other to stay sharp, but rarely did the need arise for man to man combat. So he had started *very* slow with her, expecting her to be uncomfortable with the motions.

Then she had went on the attack until her stick connected with Kellan's arm.

After their exchanged look, Oman started laughing. His laugh startled both of them making Tamsin think Kellan had never heard him laugh either.

"Haven taught you, didn't he?" Oman asked, moving his hand inside his hood to wipe tears from his eyes as the chuckles subsided.

Tamsin nodded, unable to stop herself thinking back to that first lesson they had together. It wasn't the first time they had been physically close, but unlike the sandstorm, it had been intentional. "He wanted me to be able to defend myself, if the need ever arose," she replied, shaking off the feeling of his arms around her. *If Ysallah succeeded in taking me to the marsh lands,* she thought quietly to herself. "How did you know?"

"He's the only one that could best Kellan in a fight. Until now," he said, smiling.

Kellan scowled and Tamsin knew that that was the last time he would underestimate her.

Oman seated himself on an upturned canoe. "Let's begin again."

The two faced each other again. "This is going to hurt, isn't it?"

Kellan's grin was her only answer.

They started again and continued on for the next two hours, but it only took a few minutes into it for Tamsin to realize how unprepared she was and how good Kellan was. Not once was she able to go on the offensive again and more often than not she ended up on her backside on the ground. After the end of the second hour, Kellan finally held up his hand and signaled to end. Tamsin dropped her stick and let her hands rest on her knees, breathing heavily.

Kellan said something to Oman then walked off, seeming unaffected by their match.

"Are we done then?" Tamsin panted.

Oman shook his head. "Kellan is going to get some sleep. I will take his place."

Tamsin groaned. She knew Kellan and Oman both needed their rest after being up all night patrolling the marshes, but she was spent and Oman would be fresh. "I had hoped we were done for the day."

His eyebrow raised. "We have less than a moon cycle to get you ready Tamsin. We need to make the most of it."

She nodded, understanding the logic of it, but also feeling the weight of an impossible task on her shoulders. Three weeks was not a long time. "Haven went easy on me, didn't he?"

But Oman shook his head. "No, he taught you what you needed to know, things it takes Ma'diin children years to master. He gave you a good foundation Tamsin. Now we need to sharpen you."

"Then why could I not get a single blow in?" Tamsin had been confident of her skills starting, but all that had vanished within minutes.

"Because he was teaching you how to defend. Kellan is a very effective attacker, but there are flaws to his methods, openings he leaves if someone is quick enough, quicker than him, to see them. I will teach you now how to do that."

Tamsin nodded again, too tired to do anything else. Oman gave her enough time to rest, but not too much where her muscles would get cold. When she had been dueling Kellan, he had made comments from the side, little things like moving her feet or protecting her face, but as they started again he started talking about connecting with the movements, about being in tune with the weapon in her hands and with the environment around her.

"You cannot think of a fight in terms of who is stronger or who is bigger, for you will always lose that battle Tamsin," he said as he easily parried one of her blows.

"Then what can I do?" she asked, sweat making her hands clammy.

"It's not what you *can* do, it's what you *must* do," he replied. Then he swung his stick wide and low at her ankles.

She jumped, only just in time for the move was unexpected, but when her feet hit the ground again, she dropped and rolled out of the way before Oman could take advantage. She rolled up to her knees, ready to ward off his next attack, but he was standing still, smiling.

"You must be able to adapt."

Tamsin knew he was right, for in three weeks she would be facing many others, all with different fighting styles.

Tamsin was going to the Duels.

Chapter Sixteen

Georgiana had to assume that she was now being watched by the Empyrian army, whether they knew of her actual involvement with the resistance or not. There was increased military activity and patrols everywhere throughout the city, but since her father's incarceration she had felt their shadows following her more closely. Tomas had told her that the rebels had people watching her home and there had been no sign that the army had anyone doing the same. She had been instructed to carry on as if everything was normal and she would be notified of the time and location of the next meeting.

But everything was far from normal. And though Tomas insisted that they would keep her safe, the feeling that she was being watched by either the rebels or the army or both tainted even the most habitual tasks with paranoia.

The only thing that kept her from succumbing to it was her need for justice.

A loud banging on her door interrupted her from her thoughts. She had just finished her shift at the Allard compound and had been staring at the untouched food on her plate in front of her, too anxious about everything else to eat. She took a candle to the door and jumped as another loud bang pounded from the other side. She opened it slowly and saw a guard standing there. Her heart stopped for a moment, but then she realized she knew the guard, though the last time she had seen him he was highly inebriated. It was the night she had met Tamsin.

"Reynold? What are you doing here?"

"Can I come in?" he asked seriously, though he walked in without waiting for an answer. He closed the door behind him.

"Is everything alright?" she asked, but he didn't appear to be drunk this time.

He scratched his head and ran his hand down the back of his neck, pacing back and forth in the small room like he was questioning his coming here.

"We don't have a lot of time," he said, "but I had to warn you."

A cold shiver ran down her spine. "Warn me? Of what?"

"Your name was on the list, Gia."

"List? What list?"

"The list of rebels. Lord Saveen has been compiling names of possible rebels and arresting them. When your name came up I volunteered to go to confirm your innocence. Because you wouldn't be stupid enough to get involved in that."

Georgiana was silent, trying to process all of this.

But Reynold looked dumbfounded. "Oh seven hells of old, Gia, how could you?"

"Because they took my father," she said. She was grateful to Reynold for warning her, but she didn't want to defend her reasons to him.

"Oh lords," Reynold said, running his hand over his face. "I can just go back and tell them that you weren't here. You'll have to leave."

"No," Georgiana said firmly, an idea hatching in her mind. "Take me to the Armillary. Pretend you're arresting me."

"What?! Are you—."

"I have to get a hold of that list, Reynold. There are good people who could get hurt. We have to warn them."

Reynolds argued for a few more minutes, but Georgiana reminded him that time was of the essence here, and they had none. So either he would help her or she would go alone.

Eventually he agreed and they gathered their composure before stepping out into the night air. He escorted her through the streets to the Armillary as discreetly as possible, but there were several wary glances thrown their way by passerby's.

Just before they passed the threshold of the courtyard that led to the bridge, two figures partially stepped out of the shadow of the wall, and the unmistakable glint of metal pointed at them shown in the moonlight.

Reynold reached for his sword, but one of the figures raised his higher, pointing the tip at his throat. Reynold froze.

"Let her go," the figure said.

"Tomas?" Georgiana said, recognizing the voice. "What are you doing here?"

Tomas stepped all the way into the light and his partner did likewise. "Someone told me there was a guard at your house and that you had been arrested."

"Put your sword down," she hissed. "He's helping me get in."

"Why?"

"Reynold says there's a list with the names of rebels on it. I'm going to get it."

"That's out of the question. You'd be going right into the wolf den."

"I'm going. There's no time to argue. You should warn as many as you can and then meet me in the catacombs. I might need a way out. Reynold let's go, before more guards come."

It was a tense moment before Tomas finally relented and lowered his sword. He nodded to his partner who then took off down the street to warn the others.

"You have one hour. Any longer and I'm coming in to get you."

She nodded, trying not to let her nerves show on her face and then let Reynold lead her into the courtyard. She glanced back, but Tomas had already disappeared.

"Are you sure about this?" Reynold asked as they were allowed to pass by the bridge guards.

"I have to try," she replied.

They didn't say another word until they crossed the bridge to the other side and were met by more guards. Reynolds briefly explained what he was doing and they were again waved on, though Georgiana's pulse was beginning to quicken.

The went inside and walked through a series of hallways and no one questioned them further. Glancing each way down a cross section, Reynold motioned her to the left and they hurried down until they got to a room with two double doors. Reynold rapped on the doors with his knuckles twice and when there was no answer he slowly pushed it open.

"He keeps it in here," he said, looking around to make sure no one was in fact in there. "I'll stay outside and keep lookout, but be quick."

Georgiana went inside and closed the doors behind her, going to the large desk that filled the room right away. There were a few scrolls and pieces of parchment scattered on top, but nothing that resembled a list. She pulled the drawers open, rifling through the contents, but again nothing. She slammed her palms on the desk in frustration. She looked up and scanned the room, and her eyes came to a stop at the portrait of the late Lord Saveen.

Pinned to the middle of the picture was a single piece of parchment, held there by a dagger.

Georgiana rushed over to it. She pulled the dagger out and scanned the contents.

This was it.

She recognized several names on there, including her own and Tomas's. Lady Allard was on there as well. Her stomach clenched when she saw her father's name on there. It was crossed out. There were several more names crossed off, some she didn't recognize, but one she did: Lord Regoran's. Did that mean he had already been arrested?

There was a rap on the door from Reynold. She dropped the knife, but stuffed the parchment in her pocket. She opened the door slowly, but Reynold waved her out.

"C'mon, there's something going on. Did you find it?"

"Yeah," she nodded, though she did not feel better after having seen it.

They hurried back down the hall and she heard the commotion from what Reynold was talking about. It was coming from the main chamber. People were arguing and she thought she heard…

"C'mon, let's get out of here," Reynold urged.

But she was drawn to the voices and went that way instead. She peered around the edge of the corner, her breath catching at the grandeur of the main chamber. The last time she had been here was as Tamsin's guest at the Lord's Ball. But the sight before her was much different from that night.

Cornelius Saveen stood at the head of a dozen soldiers in the center of the chamber. Mary Regoran was also there, standing slightly off to the side, her expression caught somewhere between fear and righteousness. And the reason for her expression was kneeling in front of Cornelius.

Lord Regoran looked up at Cornelius defiantly. "You've crossed a line, Cornelius."

"You're the one who crossed a line," Cornelius replied, "when you decided to help the rebels. At least your better half knows which is the right side."

"Leave her alone, she has nothing to do with this."

"No? But she has everything to do with this. She gave me a list of unusual guests seen leaving your compound. Some are known rebels."

Lord Regoran looked to his wife. "Mary?"

Lady Regoran raised her chin, but her righteousness wavered at the scene unfolding before her. "I'm sorry."

Lord Regoran's defiant look returned, though the sting of being betrayed by one's own wife hung on his slumped shoulders. "You won't get away with this," he said to Cornelius.

"With what? With this?" Then Cornelius drew out his sword and plunged it through Lord Regoran's chest.

Georgiana's mouth fell open, but it was Lady Regoran who screamed. One of the soldiers caught her before she collapsed on the ground.

"I just did," Cornelius said smugly, pushing Lord Regoran off his sword with his boot.

Georgiana covered her mouth in horror. She backed away and bumped into something.

It was Reynold. He grabbed her by the shoulders and spun her around. "You need to leave. Now."

She nodded numbly. "The catacombs."

Reynold grabbed her hand and pulled her down the hallway. They reached a stairway and went down it, passing a guard on the way up. He stopped them.

"Do you want me to take her down?" the guard asked. "I just locked a few up myself."

"Nah, that's alright," Reynold said. "I got this one. She's feisty." He clamped his hand on Georgiana's shoulder, for she looked anything but feisty after what she had just witnessed. She tried to look convincing as she tried shrugging his hand off.

The guard tipped his hat then and kept going.

Reynold and Georgiana flew down the rest of the steps and went by several cells until they came to the one she knew contained the secret tunnel to the Urbane compound.

"Wait!" She spun around. "My father is down here. We have to get him out."

Reynolds looked peeved, but rushed back down the hall, looking into the cells for her father. After a minute, he came back, shaking his head. "He's not here anymore."

A rope dropped down at her feet and she looked up the hole to see Tomas waving her up.

"I can't leave without him," she said. "Not if Cornelius is killing people."

"He's gone, Gia." Reynold took her by the shoulders again. "You can't help him anymore, but you can help the people on that list. Now go."

Torn, she hesitated for a moment, but she knew he was right. She thanked him and then grabbed the rope. Tomas hauled her up and when she came out the top they both sat there for a moment, breathing heavily.

Then she told him what had happened and the other names she had seen on the list. The news of Lord Regoran's death visibly surprised him and she could see him trying to sort out the future now without their leader. But their first step was clear to Georgiana. They had to warn the others before Cornelius killed anyone else. Warn them and get them to safety.

They made their way back through the secret tunnels and into the empty Urbane compound. Georgiana caught a glimpse of the Allard compound out the balcony window from the top level, Tamsin's old room, and knew what she had to do. She didn't know if Cornelius would hand out the same fate to the women as he had given Lord Regoran, but she couldn't let Lady Allard fall into that possibility.

Tomas was hesitant to let her out of his sight again, but she convinced him that she would be careful and meet him as soon as she could at the Archive building. Then they would figure out what their next steps would be.

She then took off for the Allard compound. It was late when she arrived and most of the servants had gone to bed, but some were still going around tying up curtains and blowing out candles. They smiled at her as she walked by, accustomed to seeing her there late at night. Their normalcy was a good sign that the soldiers had not yet been here. She had hoped to see Penelope and warn her as well, but she didn't see her anywhere. She made her way up the stairs to the Allard's private chambers.

She saw the soft glow of candlelight from within and went in slowly. But the scene was not what she had expected.

Lady Allard was there and so was Madame Corinthia. And there were suitcases and clothes strewn about the room.

Madame Corinthia made a slight gasp when she saw Georgiana in the doorway, causing Lady Allard to cease her hasty packing and turn around. But she breathed easily when she saw who it was.

"Georgiana, what are you doing here?"

"I came to warn you," she said.

"We know that Cornelius is looking for rebels," Lady Allard said, resuming her packing. "Lord Allard has gone to the Armillary to get special permission to leave Empyria. Under the ruse that Belinda needs special care for the baby that she can't get here."

Madame Corinthia sat in a high-backed chair across from the bed, cradling her round belly. "If everything goes according to plan, we'll be leaving in the morning," she said.

"But it won't," Georgiana said. "I was just at the Armillary. Cornelius killed Lord Regoran. I saw it happen."

The two women froze and Lady Allard dropped the shawl she had been folding.

"My husband…" Lady Allard started to ask.

"I didn't see him," Georgiana said. "But your name was on a list, Lady Allard. I fear you won't have until morning before they come for you. I'm sorry."

Lady Allard looked stunned and she gripped the edges of the suitcase for support, but then she took a deep breath and seemed to gather her wits again. "It's alright dear. Thank you for telling us."

"Cerena, what are we going to do?" Madame Corinthia asked. She was not much older than Georgiana, but she was the Commander's widow and had a baby on the way. The worry in her voice was plain as day.

Lady Allard went over to her and squeezed her hands. "We are going to get through this," she said confidently. "We will leave tonight. Right now. Tell me what you need. We'll bring only the essentials."

Madame Corinthia still looked worried, but she started telling Lady Allard what she would need. Lady Allard started repacking and then asked Georgiana if she could go down to the kitchens and start filling a bag with at least a week's worth of food. They would meet her down there.

Georgiana hurried down to the lowest level, to the kitchens, and did as she was instructed. No one else was down there so she was free to raid the cupboards and pantry unhindered. She filled up several water skins and put them in the bag as well. They would have to ration it, but it should be enough to get them to the mountain villages. Once there they would get help.

She spotted a quill and ink bottle on the corner of the cook's desk in the next room and she had another idea. She grabbed a piece of parchment used for filling out food orders from the market and started scrawling a letter on it. She had to get word out about what was happening here.

Lady Allard and Madame Corinthia came into the kitchen then and Georgiana quickly finished the letter, folding it up and putting it in the food bag.

"When you make it to the Cities," she said, "can you find Tamsin Urbane and give that letter to her? It's important."

"You're not coming with us?" Madame Corinthia asked.

Georgiana shook her head. "I'm needed here."

"Then of course we will," Lady Allard said. "We're indebted to you for helping us." Then she surprised them by walking into the pantry and lifting up the rug on the floor. Underneath was a wooden door. "There are some secret passages that are still a secret. This leads to the Hollow Cliffs," she said. "Promise me you'll use it before it's too late."

"I promise," Georgiana said, but another idea was already stirring as she watched the two women disappear. She closed the door behind them and put the rug back in place.

Now she had to go meet Tomas, and tell him she had the perfect hiding place for the rebels.

Chapter Seventeen

The next two weeks were rigorously scheduled for Tamsin, so much so that after Kellan and Oman left to make their patrols every night, she could barely keep her eyes open through the evening meal. Someone would eventually shake her awake, padi bowl still resting in her hands, and she would stagger back to her private room in a daze before collapsing on her mat. Oman woke her up every morning as soon as they returned and led her to the cleared reed patch they practiced at every day. There she would find Kellan making them breakfast and she and Oman would practice until it was ready. After they ate, Oman would retire and Kellan would take over for the next couple hours. Oman always used sticks when they practiced in the afternoon, teaching her how to wield it both from one end and from the middle.

But Kellan preferred not to use the reed sticks. He'd wait until Oman disappeared to rest, then would toss Tamsin one of his swords.

"They might be training you for the Duels," he said one day, "but I want to train you how to save your life."

She had appreciated that and she found she actually preferred using a sword to the reed sticks, but she had a nagging fear that she would feel differently if she ever had to use it against someone for real. Sticks left bruises. Swords left scars. Or worse.

She definitely accumulated some cuts and bruises from their sparring matches and Numha would always frown when she arrived for the evening meal with a new scrape or split lip. Her battle wounds seemed to garner new respect from the others, however, especially R'en who would chuckle and hand her a skin full of some bitter drink that left her belly warm and tingling. She and Numha had an argument about her once after Tamsin had come back still bleeding from a cut above her eyebrow that she had obtained from a poorly timed block. Numha thought the Watchers were being too harsh, that they needed their Kazsera in one piece, but R'en proclaimed that it was good for her.

"One can't get better unless one knows the pain of being weak," she had said.

Precisely two weeks after they had started, Tamsin came to her muudhiif and recounted her day as she often did, but this time neither

Oman nor Kellan had managed to touch her in their matches. A chorus of heartfelt congratulations went around the muudhiif, each knowing the level of skill it took to evade a Watcher's blade.

Numha beamed. "I think it's time we observed your prowess with our own eyes."

Several of the Kor'diin gathered the next morning to watch Tamsin's practice. The two Watchers seemed unfazed, but the extra eyes watching them made Tamsin nervous and she received several hits because of it. Oman knew exactly what was going on though, and coached her through, telling her to clear her mind of the unnecessary and focus on what she needed to do. Awareness of one's surroundings was paramount, especially when danger could spring up anywhere, but she needed to make lightning fast decisions of what was relevant and what was just background.

Having both Oman and Kellan to teach her was a blessing, she knew, for Kellan pushed her physically, but Oman stretched her mentally. She would need to master both to be successful.

She knew she had done well after Oman and then Kellan retired to rest and the Kor'diin remained with grins spreading all around. She was allowed a short respite as bits of flat *hiita* bread were passed around as well as stories from past duels and pieces of advice they had for Tamsin. Hearing stories of the Duels from the others though raised questions for Tamsin. She was starting to think that these weren't the same as duels she had witnessed in the Cities.

R'en had the idea then to simulate the Duels here, to help prepare her. Numha had already explained what the Duels, the Kapu'era, actually were, but knowing and doing were two totally different experiences. They were held once every three seasons, near the land tribes. At the Duels, the men competed against men from other tribes and women competed against other women, mainly as a demonstration of the tribe's strength and for pride, but the Kazsera of the winning side could choose to steal the losing combatant to join her tribe if she felt they fought well (though often it depended on the relationship of the Kazserii from the dueling tribes). The Duels were also a place where the Kazsera could choose a partner for any unmated kazsiin she had in her circle. Or the Kazsera could choose one for herself. Also, the women could challenge their Kazsera for her title. If the woman was not killed in the duel, and lost, the Kazsera could make her part of her kazsiin, or she could choose to exile her. If there was more than one challenger, than the challengers must duel each other before they had the right to challenge their Kazsera.

It sounded quite confusing when Numha had first explained it to her, but Numha assured her that it would be much simpler when she was there.

"All you need to worry about is winning as many duels as you can," she had said.

The plan was to garner as much support for the Kor'diin and their cause as they could. The Ma'diin valued strength. So Tamsin would have to be strong, and win every duel she engaged in.

R'en threw her a reed stick and picked one up herself. "The duels are fought with these," she said. "Real weapons are banned, unless you're challenging a Kazsera directly."

R'en planted another reed stick into the center of the flat and tied a long strip of cloth around it. Then she unfurled the cloth and walked about six paces away from the stick, still holding the cloth. Then she put an end of her own stick in the ground and proceeded to walk in a circle until there was a complete outline in the ground.

"There are only two ways to win," R'en said. "You must either force your opponent out of the circle or defeat them."

"Defeat them?" Tamsin arched her eyebrows. "You don't mean…"

"No, you won't kill them. Just so they can't fight back."

Before she could blink R'en had whipped her stick around and caught another Kor'diin behind the ankles, sending him sprawling onto his back in the dirt. Her stick was at his throat before he even stopped falling.

Tamsin didn't need any more examples and she hoped R'en wouldn't make one of her. The other Kor'diin formed a ring outside of the drawn circle to watch, adding to Tamsin's nerves. R'en was the unspoken best fighter among the Kor'diin. *'If I can just survive her…'* she thought.

R'en liked to surprise her victims, Tamsin had gathered that much, so as they entered the circle Tamsin made sure her eyes didn't waver from her. And her instincts were telling her not to anticipate anything, which she inwardly balked at, for figuring out what her opponent would most likely do next was crucial.

But her instincts were right. R'en's first move was a fake, a decoy to throw Tamsin off balance. She feinted to the right, but Tamsin wasn't fooled by it. Instead, she was more than ready when R'en switched her grip and swung from the left. Tamsin blocked easily and retaliated with a quick succession of underarm swings from the middle of her stick. Then she caught the end and swung wide, forcing R'en to jump back to avoid getting hit. She landed just inside the circle and charged. Tamsin dropped to the side and as she blocked R'en's stick with her own, she swung her left leg out and caught R'en's shin. R'en caved to her side and Tamsin jumped back up. Instead of swinging at her with her stick, Tamsin used R'en's move and charged, but she was so close already that she didn't have enough momentum (or sheer size) to off-balance her significantly, so she planted her stick behind R'en's feet and shoved. When R'en tried to step back, her feet caught the stick and she fell back, her shoulders and head ending up outside of the circle.

No one moved. Tamsin had gotten R'en outside the circle and bested her in less than a minute.

Tamsin's stick remained frozen hovering over R'en's chest. She didn't know if she had been more nervous before they started or now. So she extended her hand.

R'en's surprised gaze moved from Tamsin's face to her outstretched hand, slowly, as if she was contemplating chopping it off in retaliation. Then she grinned and grasped it tightly.

As Tamsin helped her to her feet, the others broke out in cheers and clapped them both on the back. Numha hugged her then took the cloth off the center pole and tied it around Tamsin's.

"You are truly Kor'diin now," R'en said proudly, but Numha interjected.

"No, you are not Kor'diin," she said, quieting the others. "You are Tamsinkazsera."

The rest of the day was spent celebrating, with short bouts of duels in between. Some wanted to test themselves against the new Kazsera and some engaged each other for entertainment, the spirit of the impending duels as contagious as the laughter that abounded. In between duels they would come up to her and praise her, praise the gods, and tell her how much of her mother they saw in her. Numha's declaration was slow to sink in for Tamsin. She had failed to realize that R'en's challenge had been her test for their loyalty, but she mulled it over after and it made sense. R'en was their best fighter and because the Kor'diin had no official Kazsera, it was the next best thing. The thought left her dazed. Fighting

R'en had seemed almost…*simple*. She almost wanted to take it all back. She should have lost. She didn't feel equipped to lead these people.

It was with relief that she welcomed Oman when he came back for their afternoon session. The others left to make their preparations for the feast that night in her honor. Tamsin was exhausted, but she felt lighter after the others left, free from the expectations and hopes they pinned on her shoulders.

Oman nodded knowingly when she told him all this as they sparred. "Do you remember how inadequate you felt when we first started?" he asked.

She did. She still had some of the bruises to prove it.

"I knew your mother," he said, catching her off guard. "And I could tell you how much of her I see in you. She had the spirit of a fighter. Of a *Lumierii*." He put down his reed stick and relaxed his stance. "But it would mean nothing to you."

Tamsin's brow furrowed. "It doesn't mean nothing."

"As much as the water buffalo want to know how high the leopard can climb. It makes no difference to them."

Tamsin wanted to rebuke his words, but she didn't know what to say. Because it was true, she realized. Her mother was a mystery to her and the more she wanted to know about her and the more people praised her and exalted her, the farther away she felt. As much as her mother was beloved, her path had ended in tragedy. Every time someone proclaimed Tamsin Irinbaat, she wondered if she was getting closer and closer to that path. And it frightened her.

"So I will tell you this instead," Oman continued and Tamsin could see the passion in his grey eyes. "Yes, I see Irin in you. I see the Q'atorii working through you. But most of all I see a woman who chooses to fight for my friend."

His gaze and his head dropped then in a rare display of emotion and Tamsin's throat tightened. They spent a minute like that in silence until finally Tamsin could bear it no more.

"Will you join us for the evening meal tonight? I want to show you something. Kellan may come too."

He nodded and that night they did both show up to the mudhiif. There was only a momentary pause in the conversations when they arrived, but the Ma'diin accepted their presence there. It was a celebration after all and the Watchers had helped build their new Kazsera. Sometime during the meal Kellan managed to slip away. Tamsin had invited everyone though, and had enough attention on her where she could not go and see where he'd gone.

They made it official that night. Tamsin was the new Kazsera and the Kor'diin were no longer called that, but now they were the Tamsin'diin. They all said a prayer for her and solidified their allegiance with the sign of respect across their hands. Numha told her that it was custom to offer gifts to the new Kazsera. At first Tamsin was confused by this, since no one had brought gifts, but then she remembered when she had first arrived. Her canoe had been filled with gifts and offerings. These people had thought of her as their Kazsera from the beginning. It was also custom for her to name her kazsiin, those who would protect her, serve her, and advise her for as long as she reigned. This choice was easy for Tamsin. She chose Numha without hesitation and R'en. Numha accepted with a grateful smile and Tamsin was pleased when R'en seemed surprised by her name being chosen. R'en, often prickly and unpredictable, was not easily surprised. Tamsin also named Benuuk, as he had been with Numha initially, but this earned more than a few giggles from the others and she asked what was so funny.

Numha politely leaned in and said, "The kazsiin are usually always women, unless the Kazsera wishes to…" She trailed off and raised an eyebrow suggestively.

Tamsin spit out her drink. "Oh lords no! No, no."

This earned another bout of laughter around the mudhiif. Tamsin apologized to Benuuk for her ignorance, but he was gracious about it and said not to worry.

It was later than she wanted when the mudhiif emptied, but eventually everyone left until she was alone with Oman, who had patiently waited while everyone celebrated. She apologized for keeping him from the hunt, but he said it was fine, that there was rain on the wind and the amon'jii would be scarce tonight. She asked him to wait one more minute and she went to her private room and retrieved her pack. She took out the shawl that Haven's firestone was wrapped in and brought it back into the main chamber. She handed it to Oman.

"Sometimes I forget that you know Haven," she confessed. "But you probably know him better than any of us. So I want you to have it."

Oman's brow knitted slightly, but when he unwrapped it, the shock on his face nearly made her step back. It was a long moment before he finally spoke.

"How did you get this?" he asked slowly, deliberately.

"Haven gave it to me," she said, unable to interpret the look on his face.

"Tamsin, do you know what this is?"

"It's a firestone." She couldn't tell if his shock was from the fact that she had it or that Haven had given it to her in the first place. "It's the heart of an amon'jii."

"Is that what Haven told you?"

Tamsin nearly answered yes, but then his words came back to her. "He said it was the heart of a monster." Had she been wrong to assume that the amon'jii were the only monsters in the marsh lands? "I just assumed it was from the amon'jii. Is that not true?"

"What Haven told you…I suppose that is how he truly feels. But no, the firestones are not the hearts of amon'jii's."

"Then what are they?"

"I will let Haven tell you, after we get him back." He wrapped the firestone back in her shawl and folded her hands around it. "But know that Haven giving this to you means he cares for you a great deal. It is perhaps a Watcher's most guarded treasure. Do not part with it lightly."

Tamsin could not ask more without revealing her abilities with fire and what had happened with the firestone after Haven had given it to her. So she nodded, but thought maybe Kellan could shed some light on it for her, since he already knew of her ability. Thinking of him, she asked where he had gone to.

"He is right outside," Oman said, surprising her. "He is not used to social gatherings, but he didn't want to go far."

"Why is that?"

"He's stayed on your flat every night Tamsin."

Tamsin sucked in her breath. "Why?"

Oman pressed his lips together for a moment like he didn't want to tell her. "Your nightmares, Tamsin."

Tamsin still had them, but she hadn't realized anyone else had been aware of them. Usually she woke up in a cold sweat, but she had been so exhausted from training lately that she couldn't remember them upon waking.

"The first night," Oman said, "he heard you screaming and went to check on you, but he said you were still asleep. From then on he hasn't left your flat at night."

"They're just nightmares," Tamsin said, trying to sound nonchalant, but the fact that Kellan had witnessed one made her cheeks flush. And she did not know what to think about him not leaving her side.

"As you say," Oman said, tilting his head. "But perhaps you should speak with him."

Tamsin nodded and Oman bid her goodnight. Tamsin returned the firestone to her pack, parting with it with a new appreciation and uncertainty. It was important, Oman confirmed that much, but what was it if it was not the heart of an amon'jii? What about it made Oman and Haven both reluctant to tell her?

She went outside and found Kellan near the water sitting on a rock and sharpening one of his swords. Seeing him that way reminded her of how Haven would do that at the Hollow Cliffs. She sat down next to him, crossing her feet in front of her.

"Would you like me to help you?" she asked. Kellan had taught her how after their sparring matches and told her that knowing how to take care of your weapons was just as important as knowing how to use them.

But he just grunted and kept on sharpening. "You're Kazsera now," he said. "You don't sharpen swords." The corner of his mouth curved up.

"Oh give me that," Tamsin said, snatching the whetstone from his hands and holding out her other for a blade.

He smirked and pulled out a long knife from within his cloak and handed it to her.

"In the Cities," she said, "women don't even touch swords."

"It is a very strange place you come from." He pulled out another whetstone and continued with his own blade.

She smiled, but she thought of something else that had been in the back of her mind for a while. "Why are there no women Watchers?" she asked, running the whetstone slowly across the edge of the knife.

"There have been some in our history," Kellan said and they both knew he was referring specifically to Irin, "but never from the Lumierii line. Most that are unfortunate to cross paths with the amon'jii do not survive the transition." He glanced up at her, trying to gauge her reaction.

She had heard Haven mention it before and Samih as well. "What happens," she asked, "during the transition?"

He let out a quick snort like he was amused by her question, but she could see his shoulders stiffen. "There are some things that even I won't tell you Tamsin."

More secrets. She was starting to get sick of being in the dark, but his reluctance to say made her believe it had something to do with the firestone. "But my mother survived it. I want to know what she went through."

"No, you don't and do not ask me again." There was a sharp, defensive edge to his tone.

She understood there were many secrets within the Watcher brotherhood, but her mother had been one of them and it was important to Tamsin to understand what she went through. What Haven had gone through. "Fine, then I'll ask Numha or Benuuk."

Kellan threw his sword and whetstone off his lap and stood up in one bursting motion, causing her to drop hers, startled. "Please Tamsin! Trust me!" He turned away, his fists clenched tightly and she could visibly see him trembling. When he spoke again it was softer, under control, but still laced with emotion. "I do not keep this from you only for your sake. I do it for theirs, and for mine."

She stood up and walked over to him slowly, letting her knife lie where it was. She took his hands in hers, hoping the act would garner his forgiveness. His head was bent and his eyes were squeezed shut, but at her touch he opened them again. "I'm sorry Kellan. I'm sorry," she said. "I had no right."

The look in his eyes pained her. "You have Haven's firestone," he said. It was a statement, not a question.

She nodded. Oman must have told him.

That fiery emotion was returning to his mahogany eyes and she could see him struggling to control it.

"It's not fair," he said quietly, but sharply. "You've spent more time apart than you have together."

The statement hit a nerve and now Tamsin was the one feeling the flames. She let go of his hands. "So, what? You're asking me how can I possibly love someone I barely know? Because I do know him! I may not know about his childhood or how he became a Watcher or what the damn firestone even means, but I know who he is and it doesn't matter how much or how little time we've had together! I love him." Her chest heaved with emotion. She would not bridle her anger if he was going to question her like that, whether she was Kazsera or not.

His nostrils flared and she could see he wanted to say something, but he held back. Instead, he took a step closer to her. He brought one of her hands up and placed it over his heart.

Her own thumped wildly as she felt the thunder of his under her palm.

"Can you feel that?" he asked.

"Yes," she said, swallowing thickly.

"No. Can you feel it, like you feel fire?"

She looked at him, confused, but he was serious, so she took a doubtful breath and then focused...

She pulled her hand away and took a step back reflexively. She stared at him in alarm. "Kellan," she breathed, "...how is that possible?"

His eyes locked onto hers under the edge of his hood, but only for an instant. Then he went over and picked up his sword, glancing over his shoulder. "That, Tamsinkazsera, is why I won't tell you." Then he sheathed his sword and walked off.

She stared after him, but her feet and head had sprouted roots—of awe or fear she couldn't tell yet—and she couldn't move. She had felt his heart with the same sense she used to control fire and it—it had felt exactly like the heart of an amon'jii.

She looked back at her mudhiif, imagining Haven's firestone through the walls. If the Watchers had hearts like the amon'jii, then the firestones were...

"It seems I have arrived just in time."

Tamsin whipped around at the voice and saw a man standing in a canoe just off the edge of her flat.

"Who are you?" she asked. She felt a presence behind her as well and knew Kellan had returned. Even as angry as he was he wouldn't leave her alone, especially with a stranger at her doorstep.

"I am called Zaful," the man said. "I am the sh'lomiin."

Tamsin, Kellan, and the sh'lomiin sat inside her mudhiif around a fire, though it was small enough so Kellan would not be uncomfortable. Zaful had accepted Tamsin's offering of food and drink and while he ate Tamsin had the chance to study him. He was something of an oddity, though Tamsin couldn't quite put her finger on it. He seemed slightly younger than Oman, but his voice was hoarse with age. His blue eyes held the same years that his voice did, though his bearded face had strong features. He wore many layers of fur and animal skins, making his already broad shoulders wider. He had left his belongings in his canoe, but carried a thin walking stick that was embellished with polished stones that hung from braided rope or hair.

He thanked her when he had finished and folded his hands in his lap. "I heard a little of yer conversation before," he confessed. "Yeh have a firestone of yer own?"

"I have one."

"May I see it?"

Tamsin went and retrieved Haven's firestone, unwrapping it from her shawl. She saw Kellan shift slightly.

"Were yeh ever told the story of where the firestones came from?"

Tamsin glanced at Kellan, though he refused to look at her. "Not entirely," she said. "Though I think I'm starting to understand."

Zaful leaned his stick forward and picked out one of the stones held by a string of rope and turned it over in his fingers. "It is a—tricky topic," he said. "But do yeh know where the first ones came from?"

Tamsin shook her head, looking at him quizzically.

"Many, many years ago, long before yer grandmothers were born, there were traders that came up from the south. They had crossed the great river from the Isles of Canna. These Isles, they said, were made of sea-mountains that spewed fire so hot that it ran down the sides like tears. When this fire met water, though, it turned to stone. Obsidia, they called it. Dark as a cat's mind and slick as rain." He held up the stone between his thumb and forefinger and then held out his other hand, which Tamsin then carefully placed Haven's firestone into.

"They say Canna is where Ib'n went to create fire and the amon'jii and he used the liquid fire to create their hearts," Kellan said.

"Yes, that they called Red Obsidia," Zaful said.

Tamsin opened her mouth and was about to ask why he was telling her all of this, but Kellan seemed to sense her question and put a calming hand on her shoulder. He shook his head ever so slightly and mouthed *wait*.

Zaful closed his eyes for a long moment and he kept them closed when he spoke again. "I know many stories, lady hunter," he said, and Tamsin thought he sounded wearied, as if the amount of stories he knew were an actual weight on his shoulders. "I have treaded through their histories and mulled over their meanings for a long time." He paused here and opened his eyes.

Tamsin blinked. She could have sworn that both of his eyes were blue, but as he held her gaze she saw that one was blue and the other was brown. She ignored this, however, as his next words sent ice through her veins.

"Red Obsidia is the seed from an evil fruit." His eyes glanced briefly to Kellan. "Once separated from its hearth, it takes root in a new host. The sons of the Lumierii are usually strong enough to control them and can find use in their strange powers."

So it was true. Shivers ran down Tamsin's arms and she tried to control her expression, knowing Kellan was watching her every move, her every response.

The Watchers had the hearts of the amon'jii.

She took a slow breath to calm her nerves. "So when these men become Watchers" she said carefully, hoping she understood all of this correctly, "they are given the Red Obsidia, the amon'jii hearts."

Zaful nodded, his expression urging her on.

He wanted her to say it, she realized, to make the connection. But it was scary and she understood why everyone had been so reluctant to tell her, because its implication was horrific. If she was right, then every Watcher alive right now…had already died.

"The Watchers have the amon'jii hearts inside them," she said, forcing herself to hold Zaful's gaze, but she broke it and looked at Kellan, "and the firestones are the Watchers' hearts.

Kellan's shoulders rose and fell as he took a deep breath. "Now you know," he said quietly.

Tamsin felt sick, though she pushed the feeling down with all her might. She had wanted to know so badly about the firestones and the transition to becoming a Watcher, but talking about it now seemed cruel. She didn't need to know how the Watchers' hearts were preserved and turned to firestones, nor did she want to know how they survived with amon'jii hearts in their chests.

"I was told that women don't often survive the transition," Tamsin said, thinking back to her conversation with Kellan.

"When *daughters* of the Lumierii possess them…" Zaful's voice dropped an octave lower, "the Red Obsidia becomes unpredictable. Most often it rejects it's new host. Even I do not know why."

For some reason her mother survived. Tamsin could not imagine what she had endured.

"Yer nightmares, lady hunter, describe them to me."

Her nightmares? The demand shook her from her thoughts. How had he known about those? Even Kellan inched closer to her, almost protectively.

She took a deep breath and began. She told him what she could, describing the darkness and the pain and the disorienting sense that these atrocities were happening to someone else. She told him of the panic she was left with upon waking and the sense that she was running out of time.

Her cheeks grew hot as she spoke, keenly aware of both Zaful's furrowed brows and Kellan's concerned stare, but she kept going, knowing that Zaful believed it was important. And no matter how much it terrified her to admit it or how ridiculous it sounded, they had happened over and over too many times to be discounted as a restless mind manifesting its worries in disturbing nightmares.

"It's like there's a ghost living inside my head, coming awake when I sleep and it's his life I'm dreaming about. But it's awful. Terrible things happened to him."

Zaful had been studying the firestone as she recanted and when she had finished he asked, "This does not belong to yeh, does it?"

"What does that have to do with it?" she asked fearfully.

"Have yeh not heard anything I have said?" Zaful asked indignantly. "There are forces at work in this world, lady hunter, that cannot be explained simply or with reason." His tone was serious, though his eyes said that she was going to have a hard time believing what he was about to say. He watched her a moment longer, then nodded. "Firestones are powerful," he said. "There is ancient history in them, powers whose capabilities and understanding has been lost to us over the years. But there are some stories that linger yet, about powerful Watchers and soothsayers who could do strange things. Some of them were women. So I'll ask yeh again: does this belong to yeh?"

"No," she said, matching his steely gaze, but then her voice wavered. "The man it belongs to..." She stopped suddenly, feeling as if she had been struck by a hammer.

"He is in yer mind," Zaful said.

Kellan looked up sharply. "What do you mean?"

But the sh'lomiin's gaze rested on Tamsin and she knew what he meant with the look that was exchanged between them. She knew as well that buried deep within her this thought had occurred to her because he was forever on her mind, but her fear of it had made her discard it immediately and replaced it with her stubbornly logical thinking of the west.

She felt tears welling in her eyes and quickly suppressed them, but she could not stop her bottom lip from trembling. "I'm seeing Haven in my dreams, aren't I?"

Zaful did not answer and she didn't need him to.

There was a gathering the next night on Numha's flat. All of the Tamsin'diin had come to listen to Zaful's stories. Some had moved their flats closer, cooking fluazan in steaming pots and passing out bowls of it and skins filled with the Ma'diin equivalent of wine to the others who sat contentedly in their canoes with their families. Each canoe had a swag of pentiyan flowers over the bow and as the sun disappeared behind the swaying hedges of reeds, the tiny insects that were attracted to the flowers began to creep out, blinking into the air as if they had come to see the sh'lomiin as well. Soon, every canoe was bathed in a soft blue halo from the insects' luminescence, casting an ethereal glow across the water and surrounding flats.

It was breathtaking, Tamsin thought, seeing the world cast in a cerulean hue and the serenity it depicted was enough to make her forget everything else for a moment. There was a peaceful anticipation in the air and when Zaful finally came out of Numha's mudhiif, a hushed calm descended over everyone. Even Oman seemed relaxed as he sat next to Tamsin on the edge of her mudflat and the others seemed to evoke no wariness to his presence.

Zaful first told a story about the sh'lomiin, how they were charged with keeping the histories, the laws, and the stories of the Ma'diin. That because they were blessed with long life, it was their responsibility to see that these stories were remembered and passed down through the generations. Their peoples' past was a map to their future.

He told a story of the Q'atorii, very similar to the one Haven had told her and even though Zaful's was very descriptive Tamsin still preferred Haven's version. The next story Zaful told was of the halcyona, a small bird of blue and purple with a green throat that hunted the waters of the marshes for fish. He told them that one day the white halcyona would emerge from the green mountain and bring peace to all the lands.

The next story he told was quite different.

"They fell from the sky, with a purpose, with a path.
They breathed in the wind and fire
Through broken clouds of choking ash
And buried their wings in the soil.
No longer free, no longer high.
They rose like gods to join the fight.
Immortal light doomed to die."

Oman leaned closer. "It is the story of the fall of the Lumierii," he whispered, just loud enough for Tamsin to hear him.

"The cause was right and just
And they held no malice.
Incapable of wickedness
Though sorrow they cried at the fall of their creator
Even though the forsaken they had become
And buried his wings next to theirs.
The ones they watched, delicate and tender
Stay, they begged, foul breath still burns the land
But by the rise of the daughter's gift
They were branded.
Slaves to the betrayer's prison
Their wings nowhere to be found.
They wept for life and light destroyed
They could not go back, could not move forward.
They could only fight, but only to flee with the morning's light.
But a dawn will rise
When they will catch the wings of the sun and fly once more."

Some of the Ma'diin flicked Oman the sign of respect, but he made no move to acknowledge them. He sat as straight as if he had a spear pole strapped to his back and his eyes were glued to a spot near his feet.

Tamsin thought for a moment that he had been offended by the story, but when he said, "Not all of the sh'lomiin tell it so eloquently," she realized that he was not offended, but proud. The moments were rare when the Watchers were publicly praised.

But the story reminded her of all that she had learned the previous night and she slipped quietly away back to her mudhiif. Everyone was enraptured by Zaful's stories and wouldn't miss her. He was indeed a great storyteller, but she wanted to be alone.

Knowing that Haven was still alive fanned the flames of her purpose. But as she lay down, she thought of all the nightmares she had. It was endless dark and suffering and confusion. Knowing the truth of those nightmares made her break out in a cold sweat. The more she thought about it the more images came back to her. Visions of bones and blood and screams. Knowing that it was a constant for Haven in that terrible place made her feel sick with guilt. She had been so angry and annoyed to be vexed by those visions to the point where she had wept on her knees and prayed to whoever was listening to make it stop.

Some nights she slept sound, though it was an uncomfortable sleep, as if the threat of pain cloaked her like a blanket, just waiting for her to wake. But the sense of an impending threat always faded when she woke. She wondered now if those nights she was seeing Haven sleep. It broke her heart to think that she got to wake up to the sun and escape that dread when he did not.

Pushing herself up off her sleeping mat, she made her way outside to the edge of the mud flat. Zaful had long since retired for the evening as well as the rest of the Ma'diin. She knelt down and cupped her hands in the water, then rinsed her face. She shivered at the cold, but that and the open night air seemed to shake off some of the shadows that haunted her. She rocked back on her heels and looked up at the stars, her breath condensing in front of her as she breathed out.

"Kellan told me what the sh'lomiin said."

Tamsin turned her head around at the voice and saw Numha sitting several feet away. Her legs were crossed and she appeared to be weaving something in her hands, but Tamsin could not tell what in the darkness.

Tamsin slowly turned back to looking at the stars. She didn't know if she wanted to talk about it or not, but she thought it rude to ignore her completely. Presently she said, "Yes, the sh'lomiin said many things didn't he."

"Do you believe him?"

Tamsin turned her gaze from the stars to the waters in front of her. To the reeds and mud flats and somewhere beyond the edge of the marsh, to the Ravine.

"Yes," she breathed.

The urge to just take off in a canoe towards the Ravine was suddenly so strong that she jumped up from where she sat like a metal spring. She moved no further however, but just stared out into the distance, hands clenched and chest heaving.

"What am I doing here Numha?"

"You mean, why are you here wasting your time when you could be getting your Watcher back."

They were both silent for a moment, then Numha spoke again. "Your time is not being wasted, Tamsinkazsera. You must be strong if you're thinking of marching into the Ravine and you will need strong people by your side. You came to get help. You came to get an army. Well, an army doesn't happen overnight. The Ma'diin need to know they can trust you Tamsin. They need to believe that you're someone they can follow. Only then will they help you."

"It's taking too long. Haven could be dead tomorrow."

"He's held on this long. If you believe what you see at night, then you know there is still time. Have faith Kazsera."

Tamsin turned to face her. "I have no faith in your gods to help us Numha. I've seen nothing to show that they're on our side."

"Have you not?" Then she went back to weaving whatever was in her hands as Tamsin could only stare, struck silent by frustration. She was tired of fighting. Tired of arguing. She started walking back inside.

"Have faith in your Watcher, Tamsin. He needs it right now."

Oman gave her the day off from training as preparations were made to leave for the Duels the next day. The mud flats were a hive of activity before the sun was even up. Swords and spears were sharpened, canoes were patched, buurdas were rolled up in large bundles, pot after pot of padi was made, and meat was wrapped up in the giant leaves from the water fields. There was a constant murmur of excitement in the air. Everyone wanted to be prepared for the Duels, as they were the first they had attended in nearly twenty years. Sparring matches broke out occasionally as a brief distraction from the work. Some of the young boys and girls had been eagerly awaiting this day ever since news that the Tamsin'diin would be going was announced.

But Tamsin found the busyness of packing a poor distraction from her thoughts and concerns. Her hands itched to hold a blade. Which was why she was almost excited to see Oman come back to her mudhiif before it was even midday.

"Have you changed your mind?" she asked.

"No, I came back to tell you that we are leaving."

This halted her excitement abruptly. "What?"

"Kellan and I. The Watchers do not attend the Kapu'era. But even so, there's been news from the north and we must go."

The north. "What news?" she asked.

"We've had scouts patrolling the northern border, near the dam and the Ravine. Samih has sent word—."

"You know where Samih is?" Tamsin had wondered what had happened to the young Watcher after they left the Hazees'diin. There had been no word of him or from him and she had feared something had happened to him, or worse, he had gone off to the Ravine without her.

"Samih volunteered to lead the patrol. And he's sent word back of some strange activity."

"What kind of activity?"

Oman shook his head. "I'm not sure. His message wasn't clear. But whatever it is, it doesn't sound good."

Tamsin knew she couldn't stop him from going, but she could ask a favor. "Will you send word to me when you find out?"

He nodded. "Of course." Then he went back to his canoe and pulled something out of it. It was as long as her arm and wrapped in a thin reed mat. He handed it to her. "Open it."

She laid it on the ground and unraveled it to reveal a long, curved sword, though it was unlike any she had seen before. Inlaid into the blade itself was a row of stones, opalescent in color, that followed the slight curve of the blunt edge. They were smooth to the touch and as thin as the blade itself, but did not appear to weaken the integrity of the metal as Tamsin picked it up and inspected it. It was not only beautiful, but perfectly balanced and light.

"A gift for the new Kazsera," Oman said. "It was my mentor's before it was mine and his mentor's before him."

"I can't accept this, Oman," Tamsin said. "It belongs to the Watchers and should stay with a Watcher."

"Think of it as an alliance then. You carry with you the strength and loyalty of the Watchers."

She clutched the handle of the sword tightly, unable to say anything due to the tightening of her throat.

Oman flicked her the sign of respect across his hand before getting back into his canoe. "May the gods be with you at the Kapu'era," he said, pushing his canoe away.

Chapter Eighteen

The moon that rose above the trees of Jalsai was different than the one that rose above the walls of Empyria. Emilia took no lantern or candle with her as she tip-toed down the damp stone steps leading out to the gardens behind the Urbane residence. She didn't want anyone to see the light and come out after her and the moon offered enough to see by. The paths were neatly trimmed and well-kept so there was no danger of being scratched by a wayward branch or stumbling on a loose stone. Being surrounded by shrubs and trees and flowers of all kinds was a strange kind of intoxication, but Emilia craved it. It was like stepping into a completely different world. She couldn't even name half of the foliage there, but it didn't matter. She came out here to enjoy their mere existence, and her presence amongst them. It wasn't the solitude she wanted, just the opportunity to breathe in the fresh air without having to hide her face.

She was sure half the staff already knew she wasn't Tamsin, but Lavinia still insisted that she keep up the disguise. And as long as Emilia played along, she would still have a roof over her head. But maybe sleeping out underneath the stars wouldn't be so bad, she thought as she sat down on the crescent-shaped bench at the edge of the pond and looked up at the sky.

Yes, the moon was definitely different here.

She let her thoughts wander to what it would be like when all this business was over. She had plans to find herself a husband and an estate of her own, but that could take time. She couldn't do anything, however, until Lord Urbane made his move. He had yet to go to the other Lords, though she didn't know what he was waiting for. Coming back from the dead was a tricky matter apparently.

She heard a rustling of leaves nearby, but there was no breeze. Then she saw movement through the bushes across the pond. There was a gap in the hedge that circled the pond on the opposite side. She slowly got up and went over to investigate, but just as she reached the gap, two people came through. She flattened herself in the shrubbery and luckily they went around the other side of the pond and didn't see her. It was a man and a woman, walking with their arms linked tight together.

Emilia thought for a moment she had stumbled upon a secret tryst between two of the staff, but even from behind she could see the woman was dressed elegantly. She decided not to confront them, for she wasn't wearing her veil and would create a bigger problem for her rather than for them, but followed them instead. She stayed close enough to see which ways they went, for the hedges were taller than she was in some places, but their path was obviously leading back to the house.

The two paused just before the stone steps going back up and faced each other.

It was Lord and Lady Urbane.

Emilia's lips parted in surprise. Lavinia *knew?* How could that be? Lord Urbane was still dressed as a servant, with his turban piled on his head, but the way they embraced each other, like lovers reunited after years of forced separation, told Emilia that the disguise was no longer a disguise. How long had she known? Did Sherene tell her or did Lord Urbane tell her himself? Why hadn't anyone told *her?*

Lord Urbane kissed his wife's hands and held them to his lips for a long moment before letting go. Then he drifted away into the dark shadows around the steps. Lavinia lingered a moment longer, staring at the spot he had just left before turning to go back in the house. She slipped inside the wide glass doors and shut them behind her with a delicate hand.

Pretending to be someone she wasn't was like getting sand in one's hair and not being able to wash it out. For weeks she had put up with the grit, but suddenly it was too much. She wanted to be clean. She wanted to be Emilia again.

Emilia wasn't going to let Lavinia get away. She gathered her skirt in her fists and raced across the yard and up the steps. She whipped open the glass doors in time to see Lavinia ascending the inner staircase. She slammed the doors shut with a force that would've made the ghosts jump had there been any haunting the place. It made Lavinia jump and she might have fallen had she not been gripping the banister. Emilia could see the whites of her eyes even from across the hall. She must have looked positively eerie standing in front of the glass, silhouetted by the moonlight.

Emilia let the intimidating image sink in a moment longer and then marched forward. "We need to talk. Now."

Lavinia rushed over to her, glancing from side to side as if she expected to see someone lurking in the dark corners, but when she reached Emilia her glare was as tight as a violin string. She grabbed

Emilia's elbow and directed her into the reading room. There were no books in the room (one had to go down the hall to the library for that), but there were several pieces of lush furniture well-suited to spend an hour turning pages and soaking in the southern sun from the tall windows that stretched the height of the room.

Lavinia lit a lantern from the small table near the door, dispelling the cold ambience the moonlight had created. She shut the door behind her, crossed the room and shut the doors on the other side.

"What are you doing down here at this hour?" Lavinia asked, pressing her back to the door a moment before crossing back over to her.

"I could ask you the same thing," Emilia replied, "but I don't need to because I saw everything."

Lavinia's eyes fluttered briefly in surprise, but she must have realized there was no point in denying anything now. She composed herself and sat delicately in one of the chairs. She indicated Emilia to sit, but Emilia was too angry. Lavinia's poise only fueled that.

"You need to understand, Tamsin, that the situation—."

"Stop calling me that! There's no one here! I'm sick of pretending."

Lavinia folded her hands across her lap. "Alright, Emilia," she deliberately paused after her name, "you must understand that the situation requires discretion, on all our parts."

"But I don't understand. What are you afraid will happen? That your friends will ask where Tamsin really is? I'm sure you've already conjured a hundred excuses to tell them."

A shadow fell across the room and out of the corner of her eye Emilia thought she saw something move outside, but it appeared to be nothing. A stray cloud perhaps.

Lavinia lifted her chin. "We've been receiving letters from Empyria. Eleazar has sources that are telling him the situation there is increasing. Cornelius Saveen has taken almost complete control of the city."

Emilia crossed her arms. So Cornelius was a little power hungry, everyone who knew him knew that. He was a Lord now and if he was throwing his weight around a little more than he should then that was one thing, but she still didn't see how it affected them here in the Cities.

"It was Cornelius who ordered my husband to be killed."

Now that was something she hadn't expected.

"Cornelius could have connections here in the Cities, even on the Council, that is what Eleazar is trying to find out now. So as long as Cornelius thinks Eleazar is dead, then he won't make any moves towards us here. But if word gets to him that you are not Tamsin, he will get suspicious and contact his people here. If they start digging and find that Eleazar is still alive, and planning a coup against Cornelius..." Lavinia's eyes glistened slightly, the only crack in her composure. "Well, we imagine that they won't make the same mistake twice."

Emilia sank into the chair, processing everything. "Are we in danger here?"

"Not as long as we keep up the appearance. Eleazar told me he was meeting with his man again tonight, so hopefully it won't have to be too much longer."

"Has there been any news from my father?" Her voice wavered a little as she confronted the gravity of it all. If Cornelius wanted power and had already tried to remove Lord Urbane, what was stopping him from going after the other lords?

"Your father is alright. He's one of Eleazar's contacts in fact. We figure Cornelius won't do anything to your father or Lord Allard as long as the Cities still believe Empyria's trifecta council is still intact."

That was right. Each city needed at least three governing lords to uphold the system. If the appearance was still up that Empyria was still functioning under the law, then her father was safe. But something else dawned on her.

"If Lord Urbane exposes what Cornelius is doing to the Council," she said slowly, "and word gets back to Cornelius, then there's nothing left to shield the others."

Lavinia didn't say anything. She didn't have to. It was clear to Emilia now why they needed to keep up the act. She was sorry and ashamed and had she realized lives were at stake—.

There was a loud thud behind the door then, as if something solid had fallen on the rug. Emilia started for the door to see what it was, but Lavinia stopped her, motioning that Emilia didn't have her veil on. If it was a person, they couldn't risk her being seen. Especially after what she knew now, Emilia thought.

Lavinia cracked the door open to look out and barely had time to utter a startled cry before the door flew in and knocked her away. She stumbled back, but Emilia was able to catch her just before she would've fallen.

The lantern had tipped off the table and shattered, casting the room into darkness once more, but the moonlight coming through the window illuminated it enough so Emilia could see a giant man standing in the doorway. He filled the entire width and had one massive hand on the door. He grabbed something off his belt and held it out. It looked like a hammer. He took a step into the room.

Clutching each other's arms, the two women stepped back instinctively. Emilia felt Lavinia straighten next to her, but the man towered over everything in the room. They bumped into one of the chairs and moved behind it, so it was between them and the stranger.

"Who are you? What do you want?" Lavinia asked, sounding a lot braver than Emilia felt.

"Tamsin Urbane."

Emilia's blood went cold. She could feel it freezing her veins, making the hair on her arms stand up.

"You need to leave," Lavinia told him, but she nudged Emilia hard and nodded slightly towards the door on the opposite side of the room. "Immediately."

Emilia bolted for the door, but she hadn't taken two steps when the man's hammer *wizzed* by her head and embedded itself in the door. She froze.

"I'm looking for Tamsin Urbane," the man said.

Emilia's chin trembled and she yearned for a sip from her flask. It would have been so easy to say no, to tell the truth, but she couldn't. Not after everything Lavinia had told her.

"I'm Tamsin," she said.

The man charged forward without hesitation, shoving the chair and Lavinia aside like he was swinging a machete through a jungle. Emilia didn't have time to scream before his hand enclosed around her throat and she was shoved against the wall, her eyes level with the hammer in the door.

But her feet were only off the ground for a moment, then she was released. She dropped to the ground, gasping for breath and looked up. Two more men had come in and were wrestling against the large man. One of them had his whole arm around his neck and was trying to pull the man backwards while the other struggled to contain his arms. Limbs and furniture flew everywhere as each tried to gain the upper hand. The man clinging to his back was smashed against the wall and slumped down, unmoving.

The large man then grabbed the other man and flung him across the room, collapsing him into a table and sending wooden shards across the floor. He grabbed one of the broken table legs and raised it up, about to finish off the other man.

Emilia only saw a blur next to her, but then saw the large man stagger back like he had been struck. Lavinia stood in his wake, breathing heavily, the large man's hammer trembling in her hands.

Blood glistened down the side of his face in the moonlight. His mouth twisted into a snarl and he lunged back at Lavinia. He wrenched the hammer from her hands and pushed her down to the floor, stepping over her to get to Emilia.

Everything had happened so quickly she had no time to react. Once again Emilia was shoved against the wall, the man's hand around her throat and his hammer at the side of her head.

"You are a liar," he growled. "I have seen the girl and you are not her!"

"Please! Don't hurt her!" the man lying in the broken table said. It was Lord Urbane. He was trying to stand, but his bad leg wouldn't support him.

"Where is the girl!?" the large man demanded, pushing his hammer harder against Emilia's face.

"She's not here," Lord Urbane said.

"Eleazar, no," Lavinia urged.

"Tell me where she is or this one's pretty little face will be all over this wall," the large man said.

"She's not here," Lord Urbane repeated. "We don't know where she is."

Emilia gasped as the hand tightened around her throat.

"I swear it!" Lord Urbane said. "She never left Empyria. She never came with us."

Lavinia let out a sob on the floor just as shouts were heard outside the room. The large man released Emilia with a grunt and headed for the opposite door. And just as reinforcements arrived the large man disappeared.

Emilia stared at the steam floating up from her mug of tea as she sat wrapped in a blanket near the fire in the retiring room. It was the room the men would go to after dinner to smoke their cigars and discuss the day's events and things too delicate for women's ears. It had been unoccupied since they arrived, but the white sheets had been removed and the fire stoked to a respectable blaze. Emilia didn't mind because she was having a difficult time thawing the ice in her blood after what had happened. The piping hot tea just wasn't helping.

She pushed the blanket off and got up, sizing up the room. This was the retiring room after all; there had to be something useful.

The two men that had come to their rescue, Lord Urbane and his horse master, stood around a low table that was scattered with scrolls and letters. Lavinia sat on a divan next to them, readjusting the shawl around her shoulders every few minutes. Sherene flitted in and out of the room with different trays of food, tea, towels, bandages and ink wells, but her anxious expression stayed the same. The whole staff had been awakened by the commotion, some of which had scared off the large man, but only Sherene and the butler were allowed in the room.

Searches were being made for the large man throughout the city, as the butler had alerted the authorities, but they had had no word yet of the outcome.

Emilia spotted a wooden cabinet inlaid with glass doors between two bookshelves that contained what she wanted. She went over and pulled out a decanter of some amber-colored liquid. She poured a little in her teacup, aware that the conversation had stopped. She met their raised eyebrows with her own, then went over to Lavinia and poured a teaspoonful in her cup as well.

"So, do we know who that man was yet?" she asked, instantly feeling warmer as the liquid gold ran down her throat. Her neck ached and she could still feel where the man's fingers had squeezed against her skin, but the drink helped.

"Brunos, I think his name is. He's mentioned in them," the horse master said, indicating the pile of scrolls. The horse master, whose name Emilia had forgotten, was of a tanned complexion with black hair hanging down to his chin in loose ringlets. He had thick, bushy eyebrows atop his deep brown eyes. Eyes that matched the horses he cared for: observant, intelligent, and a hint of wildness about them. "Most of these are letters to the Council from members of the resistance. Lord Regoran thought it would help bolster our argument when we decided to approach them. One is from Lord Regoran himself. He also agrees that we need to move on this." His accent was thick with rolled R's, burning like her accented tea, but his movements were suave and sure.

"Regoran wrote directly? Has Graysan been compromised?" Lord Urbane asked.

The horse master's expression seemed to cast shadows into the room like a dark storm. He took the decanter Emilia had brought out and poured some into his own glass. "Graysan has been executed."

Lord Urbane looked up sharply. *"Executed?"* He rummaged through the papers until he found the one he wanted. He quickly read through it, then dropped it on the table. He sat down and ran a hand over his eyes. "Cornelius is hunting traitors." He reached over and took Lavinia's hand. "We're out of time."

Lavinia nodded, wide eyes shining with tears.

Emilia took another sip. She was afraid, but her father was a strong man. She believed he would get through this. Though she didn't know how the rest of them would fare.

She cleared her throat. "I don't mean to sound insensitive; I'm sure this Graysan was a good man, but we also have a problem here. I don't know what Tamsin did to piss off that guy, but I don't think I'm comfortable pretending to be her anymore."

"You won't have to," Lord Urbane said seriously.

"You mean...?"

"Yes, I'm going to the Council. It can't be avoided any longer." His eyes connected with hers in silent understanding. The charade would be lifted with the morning sun. There was no point trying to protect the others by pretending anymore. Cornelius was on the scent. As Lord Urbane said, they were out of time.

"Emilia is right though," Lavinia said. "Why would Cornelius send someone for Tamsin? He let her go."

Lord Urbane turned to the horse master. He hadn't had time to go through all the letters when they met earlier; they had rushed to the reading room as soon as he got there.

The horse master pulled out another piece of parchment from inside his vest and handed it to Lord Urbane. "This is Graysan's last letter. It's why I came here myself," he glanced at Emilia, "but I was almost too late."

"What does it say Eleazar?" Lavinia asked.

Lord Urbane started reading the letter aloud, though most of it was jumbled together like Graysan had written it in a hurry. Graysan detailed what he had overheard from Brunos, the man that tried to kill her, and what his intentions were. The horse master was right: he had almost been too late. Graysan had tried to warn them about Brunos coming, but it was unclear still as to why.

Lavinia went rigid when Graysan mentioned the Ma'diin. In a super-controlled tone she said, "I warned her about her relationship with that Watcher man. I knew the Empyrians wouldn't look kindly on her involvement with him."

"Is that why they tried to kill me—her?" Emilia asked. "Because they think she's a traitor too?"

Lord Urbane's eyebrows furrowed though as he read on, silently. After a moment, he gave the letter to Lavinia to read then went over to another table that had a chessboard displayed. He plucked a few pieces and brought them over.

He held up a polished, wooden Bishop, then placed it on the table. "This is us." Then he held up the Rook, a solid tower that reminded Emilia of… "Empyria," he said, placing it next to the Bishop. He put the Knight down next to them for the Ma'diin. But then he held up the King, right in front of his nose, and studied it a moment. "There's a fourth party in play," he said. Then he set it next to the rest and it seemed to tower over all of them.

This fourth party, he explained, was somehow connected to Mr. Monstran. He remembered Tamsin talking about him, how he had an interest in Haven and, she had suspected, his imprisonment. But this Mr. Monstran was not the fourth party Graysan discussed in his letter. Brunos and Mr. Monstran were working for someone else. Someone who had yet to make themselves known. But whomever this person was, he very much wanted Tamsin dead. Somehow she was a threat to him.

Lavinia put down the letter. "And now Tamsin is in even more danger. Why did you tell him, Eleazar?" Her teary eyes were burning angrily now. "You risk our daughter's life for her's?" She motioned towards Emilia.

Emilia clenched the cup in her hands, but Lord Urbane limped over to her and put a hand on her shoulder.

"She is my daughter, too, Lavinia," he said quietly.

Lavinia's eyes widened, as did everyone else's in the room, including Emilia's.

Lavinia's lower lip trembled. "Is it my fate to take care of all your bastards?"

Lord Urbane's shoulders slumped and he went over to his wife. "Please, let me explain," he said gently.

Emilia sat down near the fire with her drink as they discussed everything, quietly and with great restraint. She must have lost track of time for when she looked up again Lavinia was gone and Lord Urbane and the horse master were huddled around the stack of letters once more.

Lord Urbane dropped the last letter on the stack and rubbed his head. "Nothing. They haven't seen Tamsin anywhere. Sherene was right. She's not in Empyria anymore."

"Well at least Brunos can't get to her here or in Empyria," the horse master said.

"True, but if he's able to get word out to whoever he's working for before he's caught…Tamsin doesn't have any way of knowing or being warned."

"Where is she?" Emilia asked.

They both looked up. "Our best guess is she's looking for Haven," Lord Urbane said.

Emilia stared at them both incredulously.

"What's wrong?" Lord Urbane asked.

"Tamsin is looking for Haven," she said. "Didn't you say Mr. Monstran was the one who took Haven? And Brunos was working with Mr. Monstran."

The horse master covered his mouth and Lord Urbane went pale.

"This means," the horse master said, "that either Mr. Monstran is going to find Tamsin or she is going to find him. It's just a matter of who finds who first."

"And there's nothing we can do," Lord Urbane finished.

Emilia stared at the chess pieces and couldn't help but think: it wasn't the Bishop, the Rook, and the Knight there. They were pawns. And the King, still hidden behind his own line, was outmaneuvering them all.

Chapter Nineteen

It was strange to see so much solid land after having been in the marshes for so long. Tamsin felt like she had stepped out of the canoe and into another country, but she was soon bombarded with the familiar sights and smells of Ma'diin culture, as it seemed not a single inch of land was unoccupied. They tied up the canoes, gathered the supplies, and headed into the throng of activity. There were clusters of buurdas and muudhiifs as far as she could see and hundreds, if not thousands of Ma'diin walking around, setting up, practicing their combat skills, dishing out bowls of padi, and trading various items like weapons and clothing. They found an empty patch of land and began setting up their own buurdas around a vacant muudhiif, but as they worked Tamsin couldn't help but notice more than one curious glance thrown their way.

The first three days of the Kapu'era were spent setting up the individual duels. It all seemed quite chaotic to Tamsin, with members of every tribe trying to set up times and competitions. Often, the duelers would send messengers out to accomplish all of this and the Tamsin'diin were no different. Men and women would return to camp and let them know when and who Tamsin would be dueling. Tamsin would have preferred to meet her competition before the actual fight, but Numha explained that their time needed to be spent "wooing" the other Kazserii, for their cause was greater than winning the duels.

"The Kazserii will not support a weak Kazsera. They will expect to see you fight," R'en told her.

Tamsin realized they had a lot of work to do and she must keep her composure through all of it. Numha kept a steady expression throughout and R'en even seemed eager, but even their busy schedule could not keep Tamsin's self-doubt at bay. Everyone here was a hardened fighter and had alliances within alliances that Tamsin would have to try and squeeze her way into. She knew the odds were against them. She was a young outlander whose only claim to be here came though her dead mother. And the Kor'diin had slowly been shunned over the years for their regular association with the Watchers and their unheard of refusal to elect a new Kazsera.

Until Tamsin showed up.

Some of the Ma'diin still harbored antipathy towards the Tamsin'diin, but most were quite curious. Those that denied a duel with the Tamsin'diin's new Kazsera were outnumbered a dozen to one and word spread quickly throughout the camps. At times, messengers from the other tribes had to wait for others to finish before they could propose a duel. Many were eager to see what skills the Tamsin'diin's new Kazsera possessed. By the end of the first day, Tamsin's schedule was so full that she was afraid she would not remember them all. But Numha assured her that all she needed to concern herself with was winning. Practicing with Oman and Kellan eight hours every day had prepared her for the rigorous days ahead.

Tamsin made sure to get some sparring time in after they had finished setting up duels for the day. She did not want her muscles to grow cold and forget their movements and it helped channel her nervous energy. Though R'en and the others were good, she missed Oman and Kellan. They challenged her and often beat her, which drove Tamsin to make herself better and not only avoid her mistakes, but to learn what their mistakes were as well. Kellan was especially good at changing his fighting styles to keep her on her toes so she would have to quickly assess what weakness he was displaying and exploit it. Though he would often realize she had figured it out and change his style again, making their matches last until both were sweating and barely able to lift their arms.

She remembered what he said: "Adapting is your greatest weapon, and once you've mastered it, you are unbeatable."

"Has anyone ever mastered it?" she had asked him.

"No," was his answer. Not him, not Oman, not even Haven.

She remembered smiling as she said, "Then I shall be the first."

But she had fought well that day and had let her arrogance talk. Here, surrounded by fighters who had been fighting for years, she felt less sure. She would face someone new every time she turned around and that would test her ability to adapt like nothing else.

And she quickly discovered that treating with the Kazserii was just as unpredictable. The second day after they arrived she met with three more of the Kazserii. They had visited K'al the first day, though there was no need to confirm her alliance with them.

They had discussed how to approach the Kazserii thoroughly and though R'en would have liked to see her defeat all the Kazserii and sha'diin, Tamsin was adamant that the Kazserii remain leaders of their tribes. Their goal was to unite them, not to conquer them. As good advisors as Numha and R'en were, Tamsin did not have the understanding of the tribes and marsh lands that would be needed to rule and the Kazserii would be more open to a unified proposal if they were able to keep their tribes intact. Truthfully, though Tamsin did not admit it out loud, it made her nervous enough to lead the Tamsin'diin, and now they were discussing the entire Ma'diin culture. Not even the Delmarian lords had that kind of power. It was too much for one person.

So she had proposed alliances. Get all the Kazserii and their tribes to align with them and their cause, name no Kazsera greater than the other, and work together until the dam was destroyed and Haven was rescued.

That was the second part of the plan. Realistically, they all knew that the Kazserii would not risk marching their tribes into the Ravine to rescue one Watcher, especially when a bigger threat loomed at their doorstep. The dam was quickly drying up much of the northern marshes already. Hazees and Ysallah's tribes had not shown up yet to the dueling grounds, being from the northernmost territories, and their absence worked in the Tamsin'diin's favor as it fueled their argument for united action. Two enemies: the dam and the amon'jii. One united Ma'diin army could eliminate them both.

Some of the Kazserii were willing to make an alliance to take down the dam and restore the marshes, but intentionally marching upon the Ravine of Bones gave them great pause. Numha tried to reason with them, explaining how it was in all of their best interests to take this opportunity to wipe out the amon'jii for good. There had never been a solid alliance between all twelve tribes since the beginning days and the Ma'diin had never had the potential for more greatness. And Numha was very convincing. She knew the Kazserii well and knew what drove them.

But by this point, the Kazserii would say the Watchers were responsible for keeping the amon'jii in check.

And this was where Numha would pause. They had arranged it with Oman and Kellan before they departed. The price to pay for a single massive attack that could rid them of the amon'jii for good was less than a lifetime of endless fighting. Having the Watchers on their side was a great asset, but some of the Kazserii were less inclined to view it that way. Fighting side by side with a Watcher was akin to inviting a thief to stay in one's muudhiif, as one Kazsera put it.

By the end of the second day, the best they had gotten was the Kazserii had promised to "wait and see" what the other Kazserii would do.

Tamsin was on edge that night. She sparred so aggressively with R'en that none of the others wanted to take her on, which fueled her foul mood. After supper, she took to walking throughout the camps. They were deep enough in the marshes that the Ma'diin did not fear the amon'jii. Many were still awake, swapping stories of past duels, speculating about the outcomes of the new competitors, cooking over open fires, and enjoying the company of friends. Tamsin was small and walked quietly and few took notice of her, though she watched and listened as she walked by and heard her name mentioned more than once.

"Did you hear? The Kor'diin have a new Kazsera! I never thought I'd live to see the day."

"I heard its Irin's daughter."

"She's said to have Watcher's blood."

"But I heard she came from the north. Beyond the desert waste."

"Fasahan told me she married a Watcher. Or killed one. I can't remember which."

The last comment was followed by a bout of raucous laughter that made Tamsin stop dead in her tracks. She didn't care if they were superstitious or they thought the Watchers were demons or if they had a son taken away from them to be trained. She was sick of it all. She turned around, bent on unleashing her temper on them and maybe a flame or two, but just before she stepped into the firelight someone bumped into her and grabbed her arm, pulling her away.

"Let it go, Tamsinkazsera," a soft voice whispered. "Those men are nothing more than gnats."

Tamsin yanked her arm away, but didn't go back for the voice belonged to Poma. She looked up into Poma's elegantly chiseled face and felt her irritation fading. She was glad to see a familiar face.

"I didn't think I would see you here," Tamsin said.

"Nor did I."

Even in the dark Tamsin could see the shadows haunting Poma's face. And her hair was different. "Poma, did something happen?"

Poma glanced at the ground. "Ysallah is dead."

Tamsin grasped the handle of her sword in one hand and the blade in the other, slowly squeezing until just before it broke skin. Numha, R'en, and Poma sat next to her. Poma had just finished relaying to them what she had told Tamsin. Hazees had told them that Ysallah had fallen ill from her injuries about a week after Tamsin departed and had not survived. But Poma had seen Ysallah nearly every day and she had not seemed ill. Normally after the death of a Kazsera, it is custom to elect a new one, often by combat, but the Ysallah'diin were barely recovering from the amon'jii attack and loss of their tribe land. Hazees took over before they even burned Ysallah's body. Hazees had the manpower and strength to do it without opposition. Poma gathered her children and left after that. She told them she would rather break her oaths to Hazees then follow a Kazsera like that.

"She pretended to help them, but she only wanted to conquer them."

"Is she coming to the Duels? We have not seen her yet," Numha asked.

"She is already on her way. I wanted to warn you first. I fear she will not make your task easier."

Tamsin stopped gripping her sword and looked at Poma. "If you go to the Ysallah'diin while Hazees is here, do you think you can persuade them to join us?"

Poma's eyes narrowed, but in a thoughtful way. "They are in no condition to fight Tamsinkazsera. What you plan to do—."

"I don't plan to make them fight. I don't want to conquer them. I want to give them refuge. The heirs of Ysallah deserve that much."

They were all silent for a moment and then Poma smiled. "Then I will go gladly." She unsheathed her knife and laid it in the palms of her hands, offering it to Tamsin. "I give you my allegiance, Tamsinkazsera, now until Mahiri's arms take me. You are worthy to follow."

Hazees and her tribe arrived the next morning and only after Tamsin eavesdropped on some of the conversations throughout the camp did she understand why the other Kazserii were hesitant to pledge their support. Rumors had already spread about the animosity Hazees held for the Tamsin'diin and their new Kazsera. But the Kazserii's hesitation came not just from rumors, but from past Duels. Hazees had a reputation for being a fierce combatant and for raising her tribe in the same image. Poma was an excellent fighter and if she was any indication as to the rest of them then Tamsin had her work cut out. But Hazees also had a reputation for pak'kriin, *tribesman stealing*, though during the Duels it was not considered stealing if one lost. She pitted her best fighters against those she wanted and when they lost, she claimed them for her own tribe.

Tamsin bristled at her arrogance; thinking she could just take Ysallah's tribe without any resistance or consequence. Poma had left that morning to fulfill her errand of bringing the Ysallah'diin into the fold.

She must have had a brooding look while she was watching the Hazees'diin parade through the camps for Numha nudged her elbow and gave her a reproachful look.

"Don't worry. Poma will do her part," Numha said.

"It's not Poma I'm worried about."

Numha nodded in agreement. "Hazees will be hard to convince, but her lands will be next if she chooses to ignore the dam."

Tamsin continued to rub the stones in her sword where she sat in front of her muudhiif, though her mind was still on Hazees. "I have a bad feeling about this," she muttered.

Hazees was a conqueror. More than land, more than the safety of her people, she wanted power. Tamsin had not been a threat when she first arrived, half-starved and weary to the bone, but now she was stronger. And smarter. She didn't need her instincts to tell her that Hazees wouldn't bow down to an upstart Kazsera, but she could feel that Hazees would make a play before the Duels were over.

It came sooner than Tamsin expected. It was barely noon before a summons arrived for Tamsin to meet at Hazees's buurda. Hazees already thought she was bewitched or possessed by demons. If this did not go well, she could easily influence the others against them. And that's what Tamsin was afraid of as she walked into the Hazees'diin camp. They had erected a large makeshift buurda for their Kazsera while they made repairs to the more solid muudhiif. It was open on four sides and had green banners striping the back. There was a man on each corner, a long spear in each hand.

Hazees was in the center. She motioned Tamsin, R'en, and Numha to join her. As soon as they were beneath the tent, Hazees made a motion and the men reached out their arms and crossed their spears with the men on the adjacent corners, creating large X's over the openings.

"No one shall bother us now," Hazees said pleasantly.

But R'en wrinkled her nose at the blatant display of intimidation. Hazees wanted them to know that they were there until she was done with them.

Numha remained ever calm and flicked her fingers off the back of her hand. "Welcome to the Kapu'era, Hazeeskazsera. It's been a long time."

"It's been eighteen years since the Kor'diin participated in the Duels," Hazees said. She walked slowly around the tent, sizing them up.

"We are no longer Kor'diin," R'en said. "Tamsin is our Kazsera."

"Kazsera…" Hazees let the word hiss out like steam. "You bring a child to the warrior's ring. A foreign child and you put a sword in one hand and a title in the other and hope she comes out a fighter."

"One doesn't have to be a fighter to be a leader," Tamsin said, growing increasingly annoyed with the conversation. Hazees was acting like nothing had happened, like she had never summoned the Havakki, never killed Ysallah.

"You think you know what it means to be Kazsera?" Hazees stopped in front of Tamsin, looking down at her. "Oh that's right. You can talk like us, wear our clothes, and love one of us so that must mean you're an expert. Please tell me, what makes you worthy of being Kazsera?"

"I know the difference between right and wrong," Tamsin replied, glaring back up at her.

Hazees narrowed her eyes, then after a moment let out a slow smile. She turned and walked back towards the center of the tent. "You have a fiery spirit, lu'Kazsera. It's too bad you will not survive the Kapu'era."

"Like I didn't survive the mangroves?"

Hazees whipped around to face her once more.

R'en put a hand on her sword hilt. "Are you making threats against our Kazsera?"

"Not a threat. A prediction." Hazees grinned.

"She's trying to intimidate you," Numha whispered to Tamsin. "Don't let her—."

Tamsin held up her hand, stopping the rest of what she was going to say. She knew a bully when she saw one. She took a step forward. "May I make my own prediction?"

Hazees raised her eyebrow curiously, but nodded.

"You arrived at the Kapu'era the leader of two tribes. You will leave with none."

Hazees's chin raised slightly. "I have heard rumors from the other Kazserii of your intentions here. I see they are true. Let me save you a lot of trouble. The Kazserii will never follow a half-blood foreigner." She looked upwards, contemplatively. "A proven warrior they might follow. Someone to rid the Ma'diin of the northern infestation once and for all."

R'en was fuming at this point. "The Ma'diin will never follow you. You would lead them to ruin."

"I will lead them to glory."

It was worse than Tamsin imagined. Much worse. She had expected Hazees not to support them, but she had not foreseen Hazees making her own plans to take over the Ma'diin. If Hazees tried to play their game, she would win. She could not let that happen.

"A duel then," Tamsin said. "Me and you."

Hazees let out a barking laugh and Numha and R'en exchanged a worried look.

"The Kazserii do not duel each other here," Hazees said. "We let the children have their fun. But if you still insist…" She raised an eyebrow.

"If you challenge her it's as good as declaring war. The best you could do is challenge her kazsiin," R'en said.

"Your best fighter then," Tamsin told Hazees.

"Tamsin…" Numha started.

"Set it up," Tamsin said without breaking Hazees's gaze.

Hazees grinned as if she had already won. That was her weakness and Tamsin would exploit it. A Kazsera like Hazees only responded to strength. Tamsin would give that to her.

"Mowlgra will be looking forward to it," Hazees said. "As will I."

The men on the outside of the tent straightened their spears, allowing them access out. Tamsin turned and left without a backward glance, leaving Numha and R'en to catch up.

"Enjoy the next few days, lu'Kazsera," Hazees called after her.

Tamsin kept going and didn't speak a word until they were back at their own camp, though R'en and Numha argued back and forth the whole way. Numha thought it best to leave the Hazees'diin alone. They would find a way to work around them. But R'en was pleased by Tamsin's show of courage. If they could duel against the Hazees'diin and win, the other Kazserii would fall into place in the blink of an eye.

Tamsin rubbed her temples, her headache starting to dissipate. She accepted a bowl of padi from one of the tribesmen and sat down to eat and think. Numha reminded her that they still had three Kazserii to visit today. It would be best to do so before Hazees got to them.

Tamsin agreed, but she wanted to do something first. She instructed them to gather all the Tamsin'diin together. Once everyone had assembled, she discussed her ideas. She wanted them to gather all the information they could on the Kazserii and the women she would be dueling. She wanted to know their strengths, their weaknesses, who their closest allies were, and anything else that would be useful in her upcoming duels and their greater cause. They were to report everything that night after they returned from visiting the Kazserii. Tamsin wanted to know exactly what she was up against and who she would be dealing with if their plan succeeded. She also told them to spread the stories of her survival of the mangroves despite Hazees's attempt to get rid of her and anything else that might flush out who was truly aligned with Hazees and who could be swayed.

After everyone had their orders, Tamsin, Numha, and R'en went to visit the last of the Kazserii. The first two were hesitant, as Tamsin expected, though they were much more cordial than Hazees had been. One had even heard of the challenge between Tamsin and Hazees and said if Tamsin were to win, then she would have her support.

As they made their way to the last, Tamsin remarked, "Half the Kazserii are only speaking to me because of my mother and the other half are too afraid of Hazees to take a stand. Even when the facts are plain as day that if they do nothing the marsh lands will be wiped out."

"Your mother was the only one Hazees ever feared," Numha said. "At the last Duels we attended, my mother lost to Hazees." Numha's eyes fell, the echo of a shadow still written there. "But she did not claim her because she wanted the chance to challenge your mother. Your mother won. She could have claimed Hazees, but she didn't."

"Why didn't she?"

"I don't know. Hazees was strong and maybe your mother thought her more useful as an ally. She never told me."

"The tribes only unite if they are feuding with other tribes," R'en commented. "Never have they all been on the same side. That's why allies are important."

"They will all wish they had us as an ally by the time the Duels are over," Tamsin muttered, stepping up to the muudhiif of Bakkrahkazsera.

The color of the Bakkrah'diin was a lush gold and displayed throughout the muudhiif in everything from the banners to pillows, dressings, jewelry, and even the birds that cheeped in several cages throughout. Numha had explained to her that the Bakkrah'diin lived the farthest inland and produced most of the weaponry for the Ma'diin, making them the wealthiest of the tribes by material standards. Though, they were the farthest removed from the problems the outer marsh tribes faced. Tamsin understood that they needed the Bakkrah'diin on their side. Going up against the northerners and the amon'jii was not something one did without a weapons supply.

Bakkrah was seated on a plush pile of pillows. Several of her kazsiin surrounded her, fanning her with large padi leaves and offering her bowls of different berries and nuts. Next to Bakkrah was a crossed wooden post with a large golden conure perched atop it. The small parrot had a long tail with green-tipped wings and dark, inquisitive eyes.

Bakkrah welcomed them, ushering them to have a seat by her and then offered a berry to the bird, which it plucked from her fingers.

"Do you like her?" Bakkrah asked them, petting the bird's tail feathers.

"She's lovely," Tamsin said, watching Bakkrah. The Kazsera was more than slightly overweight, with the bracelets on her arms looking like they pinched the skin. Her dark hair was tied back in a dozen large braids with little gold beads encasing the ends and her clothes fell in white waves over her plump figure with trails of gold and purple and green beaded throughout. It seemed Bakkrah's reign had been one of luxury, though Tamsin noticed her kazsiin wore only gold bracelets. The rest of their clothing was brown and coarse.

A teenage girl came forward with a golden pitcher, offering them some wine, but Tamsin politely declined. "I'm afraid we don't have time for that," she said. "We come to talk to you about an important matter."

"Ah yes," Bakkrah said, "I know why you're here. My kazsiin have talked to the other tribes. Numha, I don't think your new Kazsera understands the delicacies of negotiations." She indicated the wine once more.

"Do you not understand?" Tamsin asked harshly. "If we can't get to the dam and destroy it, then the rivers will dry up and there will be no more barrier between you and the amon'jii."

"The gods will provide," Bakkrah said, slowly offering the bird another berry.

Tamsin couldn't believe it. "You have to stop depending on your gods to solve your problems," she said. Numha put a hand on her shoulder to calm her down, but Tamsin shrugged her off and stomped out of the muudhiif.

"So much for not pissing anyone off," R'en muttered to Numha as they followed her out, but Tamsin didn't care.

"Wait up!"

They all turned to see one of Bakkrah's kazsiin jogging over to them. She was the one that had offered them the wine.

"Yes?" Tamsin asked.

She flicked her fingers off the back of her hand and nodded to each of them. "I am Calos," she said. "I believe you speak the truth."

Tamsin, R'en, and Numha looked at each other, confused. R'en crossed her arms. "Thanks for speaking up back there."

Calos dropped her eyes. "I am sorry," she said.

Tamsin believed her. Calos couldn't have been more than sixteen years old. She frowned. "It's alright Calos," she said. "I'm not sure you would've changed her mind anyways."

"That's what I thought," Calos said, her eyes twinkling. "So I've decided I'm going to challenge her tomorrow, for the title of Kazsera."

Numha beamed and R'en clapped her on the back, but Tamsin shook her head. "I can't ask you to do that, Calos."

Numha and R'en both gawked at her. "Don't be foolish, Tamsin," R'en said. "Calos is of age and when she wins, we will have an ally, which is why we are here."

Calos nodded eagerly. "I am a good fighter and tomorrow I will pledge my tribe to yours." She smiled, flicked her fingers again and returned back to the muudhiif.

"This is a good sign," R'en said. "If the Kazserii won't join us, then maybe their tribesmen will."

"We must be careful how we approach this, though," Numha said. "If the Kazserii think we are poaching their people or goading them to turn against them—."

"They won't," R'en said. "We will be discreet. If things don't look favorable with a Kazsera we can approach the others who show a differing opinion. *Our* opinion."

Tamsin turned and walked away, running her fingers through her hair. She wove through the tents without direction until she stopped to watch another duel taking place, though she barely saw any of the fighting.

Numha found her anyways, though she was alone. She stood silently next to Tamsin until the match was over, then she turned to her, waiting for an explanation.

Tamsin sighed. "She's just a child," she said, confessing her misgivings. "I can't ask a child to fight for me. To maybe even die." She clenched her fists at her side.

Numha didn't pat her reassuringly or give her any sympathetic words. The look in her eyes was hard, but not cold. "War is upon us, Tamsin. It shakes the ground beneath our feet and chokes the air we breathe. It shadows us everywhere we go. If we do not go to it, then it will surely meet us here. There are many, like Calos, who would rather not see their homes burn to ash."

Her eyes softened a little. "I do not have any desire to see children go into battle," she said, "but they have been trained since they could walk. They're better off than most."

Finally the days of trading and challenging and recruiting came to an end and it was time for the Duels to begin. The morning was filled with ceremony. All of the tribes assembled in the center of the dueling grounds, forming a circle around the Kazserii. They listened for a brief time as one of the sh'lomiin stood in the very center and recited the founding of the Kapu'era and the laws laid down at its inception. The Kapu'era was formed at the end of the *Alahkiin Zakar,* or the War of the Twelve, in which each of the twelve tribes had been at war with each other for over a decade. The Kazserii of the time had agreed to a truce, and to keep the truce they created the Kapu'era where every three years the tribes would reunite to settle their feuds. It had been a fragile truce for a long time, and many fights would still occur between tribes, but every time the Kapu'era were held the truce grew stronger, until eventually it became more tradition than an actual need to keep peace between the warring tribes. Here, inter-tribal debts were settled, marriage alliances were formed, and warriors were glorified. The Kapu'era became a symbol of strength among the Ma'diin, almost a rite of passage for those looking to improve their status in the tribe.

When the sh'lomiin had finished his recitation, twelve clay jars were brought forth by members of the sha'diin and placed before the Kazserii. One by one, the sh'lomiin went to each Kazsera, flicked his fingers off the back of his hand with a bow in respect, then dipped his fingers in the jar and drew a vertical line over the Kazsera's lips.

Tamsin noticed that each of the jars contained a colorful powder and each one was different. When the sh'lomiin came to her, Tamsin saw the powder in her jar was blue. As the sh'lomiin touched his fingers to her lips with the shimmery, sapphire dust, she suddenly remembered the tiny vial of blue powder she had pulled out of Irin's chest. She made a note to ask Numha about it later for the ceremony was not over.

There was one jar that had no owner and Tamsin was keenly aware of Ysallah's absence. Poma was nowhere in sight, for she had already left, and when the sh'lomiin called for the Kazsera to come forth there was no one to claim it.

Unsteady murmurs rippled through the crowd and then Hazees stepped forward.

"Darkness has fallen over the Ysallah'diin," Hazees shouted, silencing the questions. "I have given them refuge with the Hazees'diin, but they will not be attending the Kapu'era."

Again, murmurs spread throughout the crowd, but the sh'lomiin seemed to accept this without question and motioned for the jar to be taken away. A boy then came forward with a tall staff, decorated with brightly colored ribbons. The sh'lomiin took it and untied the crimson red one from it. The color that represented the Ysallah'diin.

Somewhere nearby drums began to sound. The sh'lomiin walked to the center of the ring with the colorful staff, the drums beating faster with each step he took. He held the staff up and the drums stopped. Then he slammed it into the dirt and cheers erupted from the Ma'diin.

The Duels had begun.

Each tribe had their own circle for the duels to take place with a staff similar to the one from the ceremony that was adorned with the colors of that tribe. The winner of each duel took a ribbon from the staff and wore it for the rest of the Kapu'era as a badge of honor. There were never any rematches.

Numha had explained to Tamsin the rules of each match. The sha'diin used reed sticks to spar with while the honor of swords was reserved to the kazsiin and the Kazserii. It was quite difficult to best a Kazsera, though the rules were the same. There were two ways to win a match: One was by forcing your opponent out of the ring and the other was by beating your opponent with your stick, or if lost, by hand until they conceded. There were no other rules inside the ring, but once someone stepped out, the match was over.

The first day was usually filled with duels within each tribe, so Tamsin spent the morning watching her tribe spar against each other. R'en was by far the most skilled fighter among them and took obvious pride in her victories. Nobody challenged Tamsin though, for it was all agreed that she was the rightful Kazsera. At midday they broke for lunch, but while the sha'diin chatted easily about the mornings duels, Tamsin could barely touch her bowl of padi. Her duels would begin that afternoon.

All their plans hinged on her winning. She was used to sparring with those of her tribe, even the Watchers, but what if she wasn't good enough to beat the others? If she failed—

Shouts erupted from the next camp over, calling Tamsin's nerves to attention. Numha stood up and motioned to one of the sha'diin to go investigate. There had been cheering and congratulations being exchanged throughout the morning, but the shouting going on now far exceeded the general clamor that had been heard so far.

The sha'diin returned shortly, panting from running, but he could not hide the huge grin stretching across his face.

"Calos has done it!" he exclaimed. "She's defeated Bakkrah!"

Excited murmurs spread throughout the camp; it was unheard of for a Kazsera to be challenged the very first day, let alone replaced.

Tamsin took off running, Numha and R'en close at her heels. She could not wait. She had to see for herself. She pushed her way through the exuberant crowd surrounding the dueling ring and saw Calos in the center, triumphantly shaking her staff at the sky. A gold sash was brought forth and someone tied it around Calos's waist. The crowd cheered again and Tamsin could feel the approval of the victory like a wave over her. She caught Calos's eye, who smiled and walked over to her.

Tamsin flicked her fingers off the back of her hand. "Congratulations, Calos!" she yelled over the din. "It pleases me to know I will be dueling the Calos'diin soon instead of the Bakkrah'diin."

"You do me great honor Tamsinkazsera," Calos yelled back. "But it is not necessary. The Calos'diin are with you!" She thrust her arm forward and Tamsin grasped it tightly.

The crowd surged forward then and they were separated. "Come to my muudhiif tonight!" Calos yelled as she was clapped on the back and embraced by dozens of arms. "We will celebrate together!"

Tamsin shouted back, but she doubted Calos heard her. She then disentangled herself from the crowd and found Numha and R'en, who followed her back to camp. They were thrilled that Calos was going to keep her word and side with them.

Only nine more to go, Tamsin thought, but her spirits were definitely higher than earlier.

Soon enough though it was time for her first duel. It was against Ajiinha of the Fataan'diin. She was one of Fataan's best fighters and a member of her kazsiin. Dueling the regular sha'diin was a matter of pride, but dueling with a member of the kazsiin held higher stakes. If one challenged another tribe's kazsiin and won, then they had the right to choose a mate from that tribe's sha'diin. If they lost however, then the Kazsera of the winning tribe could choose to assimilate that person into their tribe.

Ajiinha was a dark-skinned young woman, probably in her twenties. She was lean and had close-cropped hair. She had three orange ribbons tied around her arm, indicating her success at the duels so far. She was not much taller than Tamsin, but carried herself like a warrior, eyeing Tamsin from across the ring with the hint of a smile.

"I've fought Ajiinha before," R'en whispered to Tamsin, offering her a sword. "She'll try to unbalance you so stay on your feet."

Tamsin nodded, but she waved the sword away. "Give me the *tiika*," she said, using the Ma'diin word for the sticks they used to duel with. As Kazsera she knew it was her right to use a sword, but dueling with a sword and dueling with a stick were completely different.

R'en shrugged and shook her head, but she handed the *tiika* to Tamsin.

There were a few eyebrows raised at the choice, but she saw even more nod and murmur to their friends in approval. Tamsin would use a sword if she had to, but she wanted to show them that she did not think of herself as above them, especially when many of them still considered her an outsider. She would prove herself the same way the others had to:

from the ground up. And if Ajiinha was going to try and unbalance her, the weight of a sword would aid in that endeavor.

It got Ajiinha's attention and as the two women stepped into the ring, she acknowledged what Tamsin was doing with a graceful nod. Then she too held her sword out for someone to take and replaced it with a *tiika*.

True to R'en's warning, Ajiinha's first attack was aimed at Tamsin's feet. Tamsin struck down with her *tiika* and blocked Ajiinha's blow. But Ajiinha was fast and immediately swung her *tiika* around the other way, this one connecting with Tamsin's shoulder. There was enough force behind it to make her stagger, but she kept hold of her *tiika* and when Ajiinha came back around to swing at Tamsin's legs again, she was ready. Tamsin swung her *tiika* low to block and then before Ajiinha could come back around she went on the attack, alternately striking high and low. She could feel the momentum swing her way as Ajiinha was forced to take a step back and then another. They were nearing the edge of the ring. But then Ajiinha ducked a high blow from Tamsin and dove to the side, rolling up gracefully onto her feet. Tamsin whipped around to face her, but she knew she had fallen right into Ajiinha's plan to lure her out to the edge and then turn the tables so Ajiinha was on the inside. So instead, she let Ajiinha think she had the advantage, letting her go on the attack. They exchanged only four more blows and then on the fifth Tamsin dropped her own *tiika,* grabbed onto Ajiinha's, and *pulled*. Ajiinha was too slow in realizing what Tamsin was doing and before the look of surprise was even gone from her face, she was lying on the outside of the ring.

Tamsin froze for a moment, feeling as surprised as Ajiinha looked, and then the cheering started. Someone pulled her back to the center of the ring. Numha came forward with an orange ribbon and tied it around Tamsin's arm.

She had won. She looked around at the faces in the crowd. Some were shocked, others were exuberant. She expected to see the Fataan'diin looking annoyed or even angry, but all she saw on their faces was apprehension.

"Because you are Kazsera and because Ajiinha is kazsiin you hold a special power right now. Because you won, you may decide if you wish to bring Ajiinha into the Tamsin'diin. Her fate is in your hands," Numha explained.

Tamsin realized why the Fataan'diin looked so uneasy now, but Tamsin had not been expecting this. She was going to say how she didn't wish to claim anyone who did not want to be claimed, but she recognized that there was an opportunity here.

"I wish to speak to Fataankazsera," she said loudly.

There was a murmur from the Fataan'diin and then they parted suddenly to reveal Fataan herself. Fataan walked forward into the circle. Tamsin remembered she had been on the fence about allying her tribe to the Tamsin'diin, choosing instead to see what the consensus of the other Kazserii were first.

"You fight well, Tamsinkazsera," Fataan said. "Is it your intention then to take Ajiinha for your cause?"

"It is not my intention to take anyone," Tamsin replied, "but I will if you still will not join us."

Fataan looked offended at first, but then her expression softened. "I propose this instead, Tamsinkazsera: you will duel each of my kazsiin. If you win them all, I get to keep my kazsiin and I will pledge myself as your ally. If you lose, you may claim any kazsiin you have defeated, but you will cease your efforts to persuade me to join you. Do we have a deal?"

"How many kazsiin?" Tamsin asked.

Fataan smiled. "Seven."

Seven more duels, for one Kazsera, but Tamsin refused to let her concern show. "What are we waiting for then?"

By mid-afternoon, Tamsin was dripping with sweat, but she relished the ache in her muscles for it reminded her of her all-day sparring matches with Kellan and Oman and she knew she had the stamina to keep going. She had won the first five matches with the Fataan'diin with frightful ease, but the sixth proved to be the most challenging. It was not common to have a male kazsiin, but when the six foot giant of a man stepped into the circle, Tamsin knew she needed to adjust her expectations. It took her longer to find his weaknesses than the others, but eventually she found it. Their huge difference in height actually worked to her advantage for he was forced to try and use his body instead of his *tiika* to unbalance her, but it was he who ended up being unbalanced in the process and she exploited it with swift upward motion with her *tiika* when he tried to kick her.

She had used a lot of energy avoiding him in the ring, however, and she knew her last duel would be even more challenging. She took a few minutes to recover, taking measured drinks from her water skin

Tamsin stepped back into the ring, calming her breathing and sharpening her focus for the next challenger. She scanned the crowd, which had grown with each duel for word of Tamsin and Fataan's deal had spread and piqued the interest of the other tribes.

A young boy pushed his way through the crowd and stepped into the ring. He could not have been more than ten years old.

Tamsin raised her eyebrow. "You are my next challenger?"

The boy's eyes widened. "No, no," he said hastily. "I am Asmal. Fataankazsera sent me. She wanted me to tell you she will send no more challengers. She said she will tie her arms to yours."

Tamsin looked back at Numha quizzically. Her Ma'diinese was good, but some phrases she found were still lost on her.

Numha was smiling however. "It means Fataan has agreed to align with us."

The Tamsin'diin in the crowd started cheering, but Tamsin still had questions. She was tired, but she didn't want her mind or body to relax until she was convinced Fataan was truly surrendering.

"Why would she do that?" Tamsin asked.

"Either your prowess has given her confidence in our cause or she does not want to shame her tribe any further by losing her final kazsiin to you," Numha replied.

"Or she doesn't want to lose her lover," R'en said, referring to the male kazsiin Tamsin had just defeated. "Either way we have another ally."

Tamsin nodded. "Who else am I scheduled to duel today?"

"Two more before sunset with the Muula'diin, though I doubt you will have to duel each of her kazsiin. Between Calos and Fataan, news of your new allies will spread quickly."

Numha was right. After Tamsin won her duels with the Muula'diin, she was approached by members of both the Isilla'diin and the Carron'diin whose Kazserii wished to have another audience with her. R'en had uncovered rumors that their kazsiin had been inspired by Calos's defeat of her Kazsera and talk was growing of similar intentions within those tribes. Isilla and Carron were both smart enough to get ahead of the talk before they could become actions and by the time evening fell Tamsin had two more allies. Tamsin found out that even the threat of losing their station was enough to motivate some of the Kazserii to take sides.

The Tamsin'diin and the Calos'diin supped together that night, under Calos' invitation. Stories of the day's duels flooded the night air as platters of cooked buffalo and water skins of *aluuva* were passed around. Their previous Kazsera was nowhere to be seen, but the decadence she had displayed seemed to circulate freely amongst the tribesmen now. Those that had won their duels proudly displayed not only their ribbons, but gold bangles as well as beaded headdresses and daggers encrusted with jewels and gold filigree. Men brought drums out and dancers with colorful gauzy costumes moved barefoot around the fires. The dancers paired off with a partner, but unlike any of the elegant couples dances Tamsin knew from the Cities, these men and women never touched each other. Rather, they moved around each other, stepping side to side with the drum beats in crouched positions. One would raise his leg and swing it over the other's head while the other ducked low, stretching his leg out to the side and bringing his arms up in mock protection of his face. Calos told her the dances represented the Duels, mimicking the motions of battle, though in a far more graceful way. And as Tamsin observed, she agreed; every movement coincided with a counter-move from the other and both swayed to the rhythm of the drums. Some of the dancers were so skilled that they could leap clear across their partner or over the fires that bordered on acrobatics.

"Have you ever seen anything like it?" Calos asked, noticing Tamsin's mesmerized gaze.

"We dance in my country," Tamsin said, "but nothing like this. Can all the Ma'diin do that?"

"No," Calos shook her head with a smile. "Ma'diin children are taught the basic moves, but only those that show great skill move on. I could have, but I prefer to have a sword in my hand when I do."

Tamsin was blown away by the maturity in her voice and she knew she was going to make a great Kazsera, but she couldn't help but wonder if she would even get the chance. "Calos, I want you to understand something. I know you've agreed to help us, but I can't promise a good outcome."

Calos turned her attention away from the dancers. "What are you saying?"

"I don't know what's going to happen after the Duels, but I can't guarantee anyone's safety. People could die. You have your tribe to think of now."

"I made my decision when I chose to challenge my Kazsera and those that supported me did the same. I know I look young to you Tamsinkazsera, I can see it in your eyes, but I've been kazsiin for years now. I cannot let you stand alone in this fight, for it is all the Ma'diin's. You made your case clear to my Kazsera. Now I hope you hear mine."

Tamsin smiled gratefully at the young woman's sentiment. "I hear you Caloskazsera. And thank you."

Numha approached them then, flicking her fingers off her hand before taking a seat next to Tamsin. She leaned in and whispered, "The sha'diin are watching and you two look awfully serious over here. I hope the conversation is going well."

"Quite well," Tamsin said, making sure to smile. "Perhaps you and Calos would like to discuss the amount of weapons we will need constructed for our endeavor while I try my hand at the dancing?"

Numha raised her eyebrows and Calos smirked, but she waved her hand forward. "May the gods be with you," she said.

Tamsin walked over to where the dancers were, amidst hollers and oohing from the sha'diin. One of the dancers took her by the hands and then motioned for her to mimic him. She did her best to keep up, but she was soon laughing along with the other tribesmen at her attempts. She had to agree with Calos; she preferred a sword in her hand, though it felt good to laugh.

They laughed and danced and drank until the late hours of the night and for the first time in months Tamsin fell asleep with a smile on her face.

Tamsin's high spirits from the night before dissipated with the rising sun, but her focus was sharper than ever. She felt good about her victories and wore her ribbons proudly for not many could boast that many from the first day, but today was her duel with Hazees's kazsiin, Mowlgra. She knew she could not let her victories make her overconfident, for that was exactly how she had beaten many of her opponents. Everyone had underestimated the small Kazsera from the north and she had exploited it, but that was yesterday. It would be foolish to think that Hazees had not kept tabs on her, getting reports from her sha'diin on Tamsin's duels. Tamsin's own sha'diin had reported back that Mowlgra had also won all five of her duels yesterday.

Tamsin sparred with R'en in the morning to keep her muscles loose and her mind off the anticipation of the upcoming duel while Numha made the rounds with the other tribes to gauge their sentiments and if they had shifted one way or the other. When she returned though, it seemed the general opinion hung on the outcome of the next duel. Tamsin wished the Kazserii would make up their own minds; it seemed they were all afraid of siding against Hazees, though she couldn't come up with a good reason why Hazees wouldn't want to side with *her*. It was Hazees's lands that would be affected next if the dam was left to cut off the Elglas from the marsh lands. Hazees was being petty, using her ill-feelings towards Tamsin to cloud what was best for her people.

Tamsin had been on enough diplomatic missions with her father to know that everyone had their own agendas, though she firmly believed that if one was in a position of power then they should base their decisions on the good of those under their care.

A stray thought caught her off-guard and it allowed R'en to flick her *tiika* behind Tamsin's ankle and knock her onto her back. She lay on the ground, trying to catch her breath.

Did she not have a personal agenda as well? Wasn't all of this to get Haven back?

She accepted R'en's hand to help her up, though the realization left her shaken and she suggested they take a break. R'en asked if she was alright, but Tamsin waved her concern away, saying she just wanted some time to herself before the duel. She went inside her muudhiif, asking the sha'diin posted outside not to disturb her. She washed her face in the water basin and then sunk down into the pillows, knowing she had to get her head on straight if she was to have even a chance against Mowlgra.

If it came down to it, would she choose the Ma'diin over Haven? Or would she stay true to her original intentions and choose Haven? Was she supposed to become Kazsera and lead an assault against the dam? Or had she strayed too far and was getting further from rescuing Haven? Numha had assured her that this was necessary if she wanted any help getting Haven out of the Ravine, but by the time that happened would it be too late?

She wondered if this was how her father felt sometimes: torn between his loyalty to those he loved and the duty he had to his people.

Was there a way for them to coexist or did choosing one inevitably lead to the abandonment of the other?

When she finally emerged from her muudhiif, the others were waiting for her. It was time for the duel.

Chapter Twenty

Tamsin had lost track of time, though both she and Mowlgra dripped with sweat. Their movements were both getting slower; they were making more mistakes, but for as much as the two differed in size, their abilities were quite evenly matched. Where Tamsin was quick and good at anticipating Mowlgra's moves, Mowlgra was all muscle and seemed to have an endless supply of ferocity to back up her strength, making it difficult for Tamsin to get close enough to her without risking getting tossed out of the ring like a doll. Swords had taken the place of their *tiikas* and they had both received their fair share of damage though they now circled each other, simultaneously favoring their wounds while coming up with a strategy to break the other.

Both women panted heavily on their respective sides of the circle, taking the moment's respite to catch their breath, though neither one's eyes left the other. Mowlgra favored her left leg; if Tamsin could get a swift kick in to the knee she might be able to end this, but it was also opposite of Mowlgra's sword hand and she would not leave her left side exposed. Tamsin's own arm tingled from exhaustion and the amount of energy it took just to block Mowlgra's blows.

Mowlgra was definitely the hardest opponent she had faced yet, but Tamsin was hopeful that she could still win. If she could draw her out, force her to move and put weight on her bad leg…

She caught a glimpse of Hazees, whose face reflected barely concealed disgust at the match. Apparently she thought Mowlgra was going to lose as well. That look alone should have given Tamsin the last spurt of confidence she needed to finish it, but something about her expression made Tamsin realize something.

Even if she won, Hazees wouldn't agree to help them. She would never show that kind of subservience to another in front of her tribe. Seeing one of her tribeswomen lose, and to someone she considered a foreigner, would only anger her.

Tamsin took a few steps forward. She had no time to consider the risks of her idea, only time to act. She feinted to the left and jumped to the right. Mowlgra was a hair too slow in her recovery and Tamsin could have ended it there with a slash to her exposed leg, but instead she raised her sword high over her head as if she were going to bring it down square on Mowglra's shoulders. It gave Mowlgra just enough time to raise her own and she blocked Tamsin's strike easily and because Tamsin was smaller, her stance allowed Mowlgra to use her brute strength to shove her back and unbalance her.

Tamsin gritted her teeth and pretended that the blow had unsettled her more than it actually had and she was just slow enough to allow Mowlgra to send her reeling even further. People jumped out of the way as she fell onto her back.

"She's out! She's out!" she heard people yell.

Cheers and groans of dismay erupted through the crowd and Tamsin rolled on her side to see she had fallen outside of the ring. It was over. She had lost.

A different scream pierced the air then and Tamsin's eyes darted around trying to locate it. She saw Mowlgra charge at her and she was able to raise her sword just as Mowlgra brought hers down. She was able to block what would have been a killing blow, but the weight behind Mowlgra's swing was enough to pierce Tamsin's side just below her ribcage.

Pain exploded inside of her and her vision blurred momentarily. She tried to roll out of the way, but Mowlgra grabbed her by the throat and dragged her back into the ring. Tamsin lost her sword somewhere in the dirt as she blindly grappled with the hand around her neck. Mowlgra shoved her back into the dirt and this time Tamsin tasted blood in her mouth as Mowlgra's fist connected with the side of her face.

There were outraged cries throughout the crowd as Mowlgra continued to beat her and some rushed forward to intervene, but Mowlgra swung her sword around her in a wide arc, stopping them in their tracks. But it gave Tamsin a chance to breathe. Everyone sounded far away and she couldn't understand what they were saying, as if she was underwater, though it felt like someone had set her head on fire. It was hard to breathe and her hands seemed slow as they groped for something, anything to save her…

A laugh bubbled from her lips as she realized she had all she needed. She located Mowlgra's leg wound through the spots in her vision.

Mowlgra raised her sword…

…and Tamsin ignited a fire.

Mowlgra howled in pain, dropping her sword and falling to the ground. She clutched at her leg, clawing at the flesh around her wound as it burned from the inside. Tamsin could only hold her concentration for a few moments, but it was enough. She felt arms underneath her, pulling her up as Mowlgra continued to hiss and writhe on the ground.

Numha's face appeared before her, filled with fear, concern, and despair. Tamsin was sorry for that, knowing what Numha must be thinking, but she hadn't had time to explain herself. She tried to apologize, but her tongue felt swollen. She coughed few times and wiped the blood off her mouth with the back of her already bloodied hand. The ground swayed underneath her, though the hands still held her tight. Numha ordered them to get her back to the muudhiif, but Tamsin grabbed her arm and told her no.

Numha's look of confusion was short-lived, though, as Hazees separated herself from the crowd, her lips curled back in rage. Numha stood in front of Tamsin, ready to defend her, but Hazees stopped next to Mowlgra instead and picked up her fallen sword.

"You ignore the rules of Kapu'era. You should be beaten like an honor-less dog!" She grabbed Mowlgra's arm and cut off the colored cloths she had acquired with the sword, leaving a dark line of blood running down her arm. "You will return to the tribe and bear the shame on your flesh."

Everyone, most of all Mowlgra, knew Hazees was letting her off easy by sparing her life. She had shamed her Kazsera by breaking the rules and continuing to fight after Tamsin had already lost and could have easily killed her for doing so. But Hazees was not stupid; Mowlgra was still the strongest in her tribe and she would not throw away strength over pride. That was something Tamsin had counted on when she had made her decision to let Mowlgra win.

What she hadn't counted on was Mowlgra continuing to fight after she had won. It was almost like she had been set on killing her. Almost like she had been ordered to.

Tamsin's heart nearly stopped. This wouldn't be the first time Hazees had tried to have her killed.

Hazees turned towards Tamsin then, her snarl replaced with triumph.

Numha bristled. "Leave her alone, Hazees. She lost. Let it be."

"Yes, your champion lost," Hazees replied with a sneer. "Which means I get to decide what happens to her."

Numha's face hardened and Tamsin knew she was fighting back the impulse to throw one of her knives right between Hazees's condescending gaze.

Hazees smiled and raised her voice. "I, Kazsera of the Hazees'diin, claim Tamsin of the Tamsin'diin by right of the Kapu'era."

Numha's shoulders fell while shouts of awe, delight, and outrage echoed throughout the crowd.

"Welcome to the Hazees'diin," Hazees said. "You will make a fine trophy." She turned away and raised her arms, eliciting more cries from the Ma'diin.

But Tamsin had no interest in becoming one of Hazees's fighters or someone she could use and throw away as she pleased. She tried to push away the arms holding her, but Numha would not let her go that easily.

"Hazees!" she called out. She blinked a few times to clear her vision and then wiped her eyes as she realized it was blood dripping over them. Hazees turned back to her and the crowd quieted, making the pounding in Tamsin's head even louder. She tasted salt in her mouth and felt a burning energy gathering in her. "By right of the Kapu'era, I challenge you to the title of Kazsera."

The look in Hazees's eyes could have turned the sea to stone as hushed exclamations swept through the crowd like a swarm of bees. She moved closer, looking at her from the side and Tamsin almost wondered if she had the same ability to control fire for she could almost see fire running through her veins. She half expected Hazees to strike her down right then and there. She recognized that Tamsin had not only out-maneuvered her best fighter, but had anticipated her own decisions.

Tamsin's legs started to tremble, not from Hazees's gaze, but from exhaustion, and she felt another pair of arms join Numha's to support her. R'en, she thought, but she did not look to see. Instead, she kept her eyes locked on Hazees as this silent understanding passed between them. The understanding that the northern half-breed girl had outsmarted one of the most formidable Kazserii in the marsh lands.

Hazees's nostrils flared and then that sneer returned. "I will not fight someone who can't even stand on her own."

For a fearful moment, Tamsin thought that her plan had failed and the loophole she had found would be overturned. But Hazees wanted her dead and this would be her last chance without repercussions.

Then Hazees said, "Go back to your tribe and take the night to recover. I will meet your challenge tomorrow." Her lips curled back angrily and then she turned and marched away, the crowd parting quickly to make way.

The Tamsin'diin who had come to watch gathered swiftly around Tamsin, forming a protective cocoon and speeding her away to their campsite. Word was already spreading about the duel and curious men and women from the other tribes tried to catch a glimpse, but one flash from R'en's sword halted their advancement and silenced their questions.

The world was a blur and bloody haze to Tamsin and she was grateful when they reached her muudhiif for she was able to sit and everything didn't spin quite so fast. But the adrenaline from the fight was starting to wear off and she was slowly becoming more aware of her pains even as Numha barked orders at the others and told them to clear the tent.

Suddenly R'en's face was in front of her. "Tamsinkazsera, are you with me?"

"I'm...I'm..." Her tongue felt too big in her mouth and there seemed to be a heavy weight on her chest though she didn't know where it was coming from. The growing pain was starting to bring the world into better focus though and she was able to hold R'en's gaze for a few moments.

"There you are," R'en said with a quick reassuring smile. "Stay with us Kazsera. You're going to be just fine."

Tamsin groaned. She did not feel fine. She felt anything but fine. She felt like she was going to be ill.

A few of the sha'diin brought in fresh bowls of water, bandages, and bags of herbs. Numha started grinding them with a mortar and pestle as R'en washed the blood from Tamsin's face. Knowing that this was the best treatment available to the Ma'diin made Tamsin think of home for some reason. There was a healing center in Jalsai, though Tamsin had grown up with the privilege of healers coming to their home had the need for one ever arisen. It was an odd feeling, she concluded, because she never would have pictured herself in a situation like this. What would her mother have said if she'd been here to see her in this state?

When she was done, Numha applied the crushed herbs to the gash on Tamsin's head and wrapped it with a clean cloth. "It's not too deep," she said. "But the herbs should help stop the bleeding."

R'en hissed. "A little blood is nothing. Mowlgra beat her to a pulp though. She'll be lucky if she has a spot that isn't black by morning. Hazees should have stopped it. She's just as cowardly as that malicious brute."

Numha nodded, a sadder kind of anger in her eyes. "Your hurts will only worsen overnight," she said to Tamsin. "Hazees is giving you time to retract your challenge."

Numha's tone sounded to Tamsin like she wanted her to take it back, her eyes betraying just how hard it was for her to see Tamsin like this and Tamsin was sorry for her. "I won't."

"That's why it doesn't hurt her to give you time," R'en said. "She knows she has you beat either way."

"I won't lose…this time," Tamsin managed to get out between breaths.

"Skiishiv!" R'en cursed. "Look at you. Hazees could beat you like this blindfolded and with one hand tied behind her back!"

"Do you wish for the whole tribe to hear you?" Numha hissed at R'en.

R'en glared back, but lowered her voice. "If she loses tomorrow, she won't be given another chance. She will kill you," she said to Tamsin.

The muudhiif had started to tilt again. Tamsin cradled her head. "I will not lose tomorrow," she pushed out through gritted teeth.

The women looked blankly at her. R'en started to pace. "We'll come up with something," she said.

"We can go to Hazees's tribesmen. See if any are sympathetic to us," Numha said.

"They might tell us her weaknesses. Tamsin is a small target and good at adapting…"

"Do you doubt me?" Tamsin said, surprising them and herself with the force behind her words. "I'm not just your puppet. Losing to Mowlgra was my choice. I saw Hazees during the duel. Even if I had won she would not have joined us. She would only have thrown more people in to fight and we don't have time for that. And the Hazees'diin will never support anyone else as long as she is Kazsera."

"You lost on purpose," Numha said, realizing what Tamsin was saying.

Tamsin didn't have the strength to nod her head. Her speech had left her breathless. "My mistake was underestimating how far Hazees would go to see me dead."

Numha sunk to her knees, guilt and shame scarring her features. "I'm so sorry Tamsin," she cried. "I should've been the one to challenge her. I never should've let you—."

Tamsin wanted to take Numha's hands, but gripped the edge of the mat instead. "Do you believe in me?"

Numha blinked. "Of course I do."

Tamsin looked at R'en's blurry form. "And you?"

The scowl on R'en's face remained intact. "The bite of Hazees's sword will not care what I believe."

Tamsin knew that was probably as close to a pledge from R'en as she was going to get. She took a few raspy breaths, fighting against the pain and nausea that was coursing through her. She began to tremble from the effort and luckily R'en still had her senses about her and grabbed a reed basket just in time for Tamsin to retch into it. She had been able to ignore the pain in her side up until now, but it flared like a hot iron as her stomach contracted, ripping her apart with wicked teeth. She pressed her arm to her side, forcing herself to breathe until she could open her eyes. "If you can keep me alive until tomorrow," she gasped, "I promise you I won't let you down."

But the movement didn't go unnoticed by either of the women and Numha gently pulled Tamsin's arm away and untied the dark leather vest around her torso.

Tamsin's mouth opened in a silent cry and she squeezed her eyes shut again as Numha peeled her bloody tunic away from her side. She didn't need to see it or the horrified expressions on the women's faces to know it wasn't good. She could feel it. Mowlgra's sword had found its mark.

"Vas akru," R'en cursed under her breath.

Tamsin grinned, despite the pain. "You have a filthy mouth," she said, but her words sounded muffled and she barely heard Numha's frantic yell outside the muudhiif for a healer.

The hours stretched out long into the night, though Tamsin was unaware of most of it. Every time consciousness began to fade, someone was there with water or some herb to bring her back, though all she wanted to do was sleep and block out the pain completely. They seemed concerned about the blows to the head she had received and she seemed to lie in a timeless haze, forever on the brink between wakefulness and the warm blanket of oblivion.

She caught glimpses of her tribesmen outside as R'en and a few others left the muudhiif with dirty bandages and came back with bowls of clean water and other things. R'en made sure the flap was never open long enough for the others to get a good look inside and Tamsin was only able to snatch glimpses of their worried eyes as they lingered near the entrance. She thought she heard Numha say that everyone had stayed near and not partaken in any of the nightly festivities.

Her tribe's concern was the only thing keeping her torment in check and she realized just how much their support meant to her, but did they mean more to her or her more to them? She would grit her teeth and endure, for she did not have the strength to ponder it.

It seemed a long time before the healer left them alone and even then he was reluctant, waiting until Tamsin had stopped trembling from the exhaustion of fighting through the pain of her side being sewn back together. He said he would be back later to wrap it, giving her a short respite which Tamsin thought was more out of pity than giving her time to recover.

It was the quietness, though, that brought some coherency back to Tamsin. It must have been late. She could only hear the occasional crackle from the fires outside. R'en had disappeared and it was only Numha who remained with her. Numha was quiet too as she offered Tamsin some water, which she declined.

"Help me sit up," Tamsin said weakly.

"Tamsin—," Numha started to protest.

"I'm sick of lying in my own blood and sweat," Tamsin said, willing to endure a little more pain if it meant Numha wouldn't look at her like she was a lame horse that should be put out of its misery and Numha begrudgingly obliged. This time she accepted the water, wishing there was something a hair stronger in it.

"You should get some rest," she told Numha, who had dark circles under her eyes.

Numha chuckled and Tamsin realized how silly that must sound to her. "I'm not going anywhere," Numha said. "Your wounds won't be fatal as long as you don't do anything foolish. So I'm going to stay right here," she added with a quick smile.

"Foolish like challenging a Kazsera," Tamsin attempted to smile back.

Numha's smile vanished and that guilty look replaced it.

"What did I ask you before?"

"If I believed in you. I do," Numha said, "but I will not let you sacrifice yourself tomorrow. We will find another way."

"Sacrifice? You think that's what I plan to do?" Tamsin had to pause to catch her breath, finally understanding Numha's quiet distress. She thought Tamsin was going to martyr herself for the cause. Tamsin would gladly trade her life for the Ma'diin's salvation, for Haven, and her family here, but she had no intentions of doing that anytime soon. Her death, she was afraid, would only polarize the Ma'diin, not unite them. Not yet.

Tamsin knew there was only one way that she was going to ease Numha's fears and any nerves or reservations she had about revealing her secret had evaporated within the last few miserable hours. She was exhausted and simply did not have the energy to talk herself out of it. "I do have another way," she said. "Where's R'en?"

"She left a little while ago. I do not know where."

"Find her. I have to show both of you something."

Numha crossed over to the tent opening and whispered something to one of the girls outside. She was quiet until a few minutes later when R'en burst into the muudhiif. Upon seeing Tamsin alive and upright the panicked look on her face of someone who had been woken up abruptly to bad news disappeared.

"Thank the gods! I thought I was going to have to kill that brainless cow of a healer." Obviously she had thought Numha's summons had meant something else.

"I don't know if I should be worried or take comfort in your concern," Tamsin said wryly. It was well that R'en hadn't gone to the healer's buurda first.

R'en was not one to be visibly shaken and she quickly resumed her hard demeanor. "I see your terrible sense of humor has returned. If you're able you should go out and see your people. It would do them good to see you well."

"Well? Speak for yourself." She could see Numha's face relax a little at the banter between them and R'en chuckled, seeming to rid herself of any lingering worry. "You should be resting then for tomorrow Tamsinkazsera. What is this about?"

"She says she has a plan," Numha said.

Tamsin knew her physical ailments would make this difficult, but she also knew that if she couldn't do it now then her plan tomorrow would fail and Numha's fear of making a martyr of her might come true. She took a few small breaths, preparing herself. "I'm going to show you something that only two other people in the world have seen."

Chapter Twenty-One

The dueling grounds were charged with anxious energy that morning. The duels that would have taken place that day were suspended in lieu of Hazees and Tamsin's. No one expected it to be long fight; many had seen her duel with Mowlgra the previous day and the subsequent buzz of activity around Tamsin's tent that night did not bode well for the Tamsin'diin's camp. Time dueling had been exchanged for socializing amongst tribes, everyone trying to feel out where the other Kazserii stood, who had already pledged support for Tamsin, who was loyal to Hazees, and who were simply waiting to see what happened. There was even a rumor that Tamsin hadn't survived the night and the Tamsin'diin were going to be forced to join Hazees's tribe.

Tamsin laughed when R'en told her this. It could have been the herbs Numha had given her to numb the pain, though she had assured her they would not dull her mental senses. More likely, it was her own nerves bubbling out.

R'en shot her a look as she carefully tightened the laces of her jerkin, indicating she was not amused. "I'll wake you up from the dead and kick your hafakii myself if I have to join Hazees's tribe of idiots," she grumbled.

"That won't happen," Numha said. The awestruck smile she had since Tamsin had shown them her ability to create fire still played on her lips.

They had spent the morning hours going over different ideas on how to actually pull it off. R'en remained as prickly as ever and after Tamsin's display her first idea was to just set Hazees on fire and be done with her. But they knew it was going to take a little more covertness on Tamsin's part. They had finally settled on using Tamsin's power as a distraction, instead of maiming her like she had done with Mowlgra. There was no way, not in her current condition, that Tamsin was going to get close to Hazees without Hazees being distracted first. One opening: that was all Tamsin was going to get. It had to be enough.

When Tamsin had shown them, she was surprised by how easily it came. She was learning that the more easily something burned with real fire the easier it was for her to set it alight. But she was growing stronger. She had savored the feeling; she didn't need to be physically strong. She just needed enough to focus.

The only capricious part of the plan was the timing. Tamsin would have to let Hazees get close enough and then judge the exact moment. If she was off even a little…

Benuuk poked his head through the door flap "It is time Tamsinkazsera."

R'en made the final adjustments to Tamsin's wardrobe and nodded. "You ready?"

Tamsin had done little more than move from her mat to the center of the muudhiif, but she nodded and did her best not to wince as she followed them outside. Numha's herbs had helped, but her earlier prediction had come true: there was little part of Tamsin that wasn't bruised or wounded in some way.

She stepped out of the muudhiif and saw every single member of the Tamsin'diin camp on their feet. Everyone was looking at her. Everyone was silent. She couldn't tell from their expressions if they thought she had a fighting chance or if they saw a girl on her death bed.

She felt something cold in her hand and noticed R'en pressing her sword handle into it. She squinted at her and Tamsin nodded slightly and grasped it. Just holding it was enough to make her lip twitch in discomfort. Getting to the dueling circle might be the hardest part, she mused.

Then someone stepped forward and flicked his fingers over his hand. "We are proud to have you fight for us, Tamsinkazsera."

Then another spoke up: "Show those fuh'diin what the blood of Tamsin Irinbaat is worth!"

A cry rose up among them, drowning out the doubts that Tamsin had about their faith in her. Next to her, Numha squeezed her hand. Tamsin squeezed back, allowing the rumbling roars of support to fuel her. She needed it today.

She walked forward, her shoulders and teeth set, and the roars intensified, shattering the anxious buzz of the watching Ma'diin. She focused her gaze forward as she made her way to the dueling circle, letting the shouts fade into one rising hum. She could feel their fervor as surely as she could feel the wind on her face, so she harnessed it, forced it to strengthen her until all the hurts she had suffered previously were left in her wake.

A small boy caught her eye, peeling her focus away for a moment. Just old enough to stand on his own, he was naked except for a cloth diaper wrapped around his waist. He clutched his mother's leg uncertainly as Tamsin's entourage filed by. There weren't too many children at the Duels; just ones still too young to be away from their mothers. She had seen a few of them, but none had caught her eye quite like this one because she had only seen markings like his on two other people. She knew the others couldn't see them and the poor mother had no idea that he was already marked.

Twenty years ago, that could have been Haven.

She ripped her gaze away, but that wound she could not easily ignore.

Numha, always sensitive to her Kazsera's frame of mind, nudged her and whispered something in concern, but Tamsin could not make it out above the raucous or the slivers of pain slowly pressing into her heart.

"So, what do you have to say today?"

"I want to thank the Kazsera for being generous and giving me time to recover and that my challenge still stands."

Hazees's smile did not change, but Tamsin saw her eyes flash briefly, though she could not tell if it was out of anger or anticipation. Either way, Hazees was overconfident. Tamsin had not seen her fight, she didn't know what her style was, but she was betting it would be theatrical. Not that Tamsin doubted her skill, but Hazees wanted to make an example of Tamsin. She would draw it out, taunt her and puff up her own might at the same time.

Hazees held out her hand towards the ring. "Then let's begin."

The two women stepped into the ring as the crowds around them shouted and cheered.

"You look unwell," Hazees commented with false concern. "Did you not sleep well?"

Tamsin wasn't going to allow herself to get sucked in to Hazees's game, but she couldn't help but reply, "Even at my worst I look better than you."

Hazees's smile vanished. "At least I know what I am when I see my reflection. What are you? A half-breed? A mutt? Your mother was so mutilated after she turned the only one who would take her was an outsider. You are the unfortunate offspring."

Numha had prepared her for this. Hazees was going to try and get in her head, make her doubt herself and her birthright. The Tamsin'diin bristled behind her. Had Irin still been alive it would have been very much within their right to take Hazees's head right there.

Tamsin stopped the slow ring they had been pacing in the dirt. It was a useless waste of energy, something Tamsin had precious little of. "Well you better get used to this 'unfortunate offspring' because she's going to be your Kazsera."

Shouts from both sides of the crowd erupted around them and the two women glared at each other. Hazees took out her sword. The games were done and now the pain would begin.

One to keep her throne. The other to claim it.

As much as Tamsin wanted to, she waited for Hazees to strike first. Her lessons with Haven had taught her that: let your enemy show you how they fight first, then use that against them. And Hazees seemed happy to oblige, confident that she held the upper hand in every way. Hazees lunged forward and swung wide, high enough so Tamsin could duck and roll out of the way. The movement left Tamsin breathless, even with the numbing herbs helping her, and she was slower to get up than she usually was. But Hazees didn't attack again right away, but let Tamsin find her stance again. Hazees smiled and feinted another lunge, but sidestepped and swung from the right.

Tamsin fell for the feint, but got her sword up just in time to block Hazees's blow from the side, stepping back to avoid another shot.

Hazees laughed this time, waving her free hand up to incite the crowd to do the same.

Tamsin had guessed right. Hazees was theatrical, but Tamsin already knew her plan: to use Tamsin's injuries against her. Wear her down by making Tamsin move around more than necessary. Draw it out until Hazees was tired of the game and then make the killing blow. But even though Tamsin was not privy to her actual fighting style, she couldn't let Hazees have her way.

"It's almost not fair," Hazees said loudly. "It's like dueling a chil—."

Tamsin didn't let her finish. She charged forward, bolstered by the flash of surprise in Hazees's eyes. But Hazees was quick and blocked Tamsin's blow to her chest. Tamsin spun once, swinging low as she did, forcing Hazees off her feet. Tamsin came up and Hazees landed and the two locked swords. The theatrics were over. The real fight had begun.

The two went back and forth then in a seamless blur of metal, almost like it had been rehearsed. It was a thunderous meeting of sweat and strength, of agility and speed, of passion and reaction. There was barely a breath between them and they seemed to move with the skill and beauty of the Kapu'era dances.

The crowd was completely silent, entranced by the opposing forces.

Until finally the moment came. Hazees missed a strike to Tamsin's midsection, but instead of aiming at Hazees's exposed side, Tamsin took the opening to bring her own sword down on top of Hazees's, momentarily pinning it to the ground. *Perfect.*

Tamsin quieted her mind and hushed her breathing, then, with all the energy she could muster, set the dueling pole in the middle of the circle on fire.

Shrieks erupted from the nearest Ma'diin like lightening as they jumped away from the circle and gasps erupted all around them.

But it was only one whom Tamsin was concerned about.

Hazees's gaze flew to the flaming pole that was just inches from them, her eyes wide with confusion and shock.

Tamsin took her moment and spun to the side, their swords sliding apart. Hazees stumbled forward into the space Tamsin had just been, but before she could get her footing Tamsin slashed the back of Hazees's leg, sending a spray of blood across the dirt. Hazees howled and fell to all fours. Tamsin stomped on her wrist, eliciting another cry, and kicked her sword away out of the circle.

Tamsin held the pointed end of her blade at Hazees's throat, not taking her eyes off her despite the sweat glistening over her eyelashes. She didn't know which was more prominent on Hazees's face: rage or surprise. Her nostrils flared in anger and the edges of her jaw clenched as she clutched her leg.

"Do it," she whispered through gritted teeth, pressing farther into Tamsin's blade. "My sha'diin will avenge me."

"You think if I kill you, they will even care?" Tamsin hissed back. "They will forget you as soon as they've finished burying your body here in this dirt."

She saw a flicker of doubt in Hazees's eyes and pressed on. "If you truly want to lead them, you will help me save them. What's happening is bigger than either one of us. I'm giving you the chance to be a part of it."

"How do you know I won't try to kill you the first chance I get?"

"I don't."

"Then why?"

"Because you want to leave a legacy. And I want to make sure there are people still left to remember it. The two don't have to oppose each other."

She watched Hazees weigh the options. She had every right to just end Hazees right there, but even as horrible as Hazees was, Tamsin couldn't do it without giving Hazees an out.

And it seemed she was going to take it. The fight seemed to visibly leave Hazees's body as she let out a breath. Then she nodded.

Tamsin took her sword away and extended her hand, helping Hazees up. It seemed that Hazees could be reasoned with after all and that she might value some things more than her hatred of Tamsin.

The crowd around them didn't seem to know how to take the sudden truce between the two and the still burning pole in the center of the ring. Someone shouted *"Irinbaat!"* and it seemed to shake off the blanket of awe that smothered them and suddenly the Ma'diin around them came to life, shouting and jumping up and down in excitement. Others fell to their knees, not in despair, but rather in praise to the gods. *"It's a sign! It's a sign!"* they said, pointing to the burning pole.

Tamsin released her hold over the fire and the pole let out a sharp *crack* as the top portion broke off and fell to the dirt, leaving a burnt, jagged spike.

Hazees looked from Tamsin to the blackened pole and back to Tamsin, suspicion and awe fighting for dominance on her features. Tamsin had been the only one unfazed by the fire and Hazees was the only one close enough to notice.

"You did that, didn't you," she said.

"I don't harbor evil *jiin*," Tamsin said, "but I do possess something more powerful. And I'm going to use it to help our people."

Someone came forward and tied a strip of cloth around Tamsin's arm, signifying her as the winner of the duel. More happy cries erupted around them and Numha and R'en came forward, grinning wildly. But the adrenaline of the fight was wearing off, even as the realization that she had won sank in, and the pain from her previous injuries was growing quickly. She gave her sword to R'en.

"We will speak later," Tamsin said to Hazees, then to Numha and R'en, "Take me back." She was unable to hide a grimace as she clutched her side and they were on either side of her instantly.

But the storm had been rebuilding behind Hazees's eyes ever since the first shout of *Irinbaat* and even as Tamsin walked away from the ring she heard an enraged cry that sliced through the noise from the crowd. She turned around to see Hazees's face contorted in a snarl as she made a grab for her fallen blade.

Tamsin only had a moment to react, realizing that Hazees intended to finish what she had started, consequences be damned. As Hazees lunged at her again, instead of running Tamsin darted towards her, dropping to her knees just as she reached the center. She grabbed the charred remnants of the pole sticking out of the ground and thrust upwards just as Hazees was about to bring her sword down on her head.

The feeling of the pole sliding through Hazees's stomach mirrored the look of surprise on her face. The sword fell from her hands as she looked at the red stain spreading across her clothes and then at Tamsin.

Tamsin breathed heavily, still clutching the pole as Hazees's blood trickled down onto her own. Everyone around them had gone quiet and all she could hear was the pounding of her heart, flooding her ears with the heavy weight of what she done.

Hazees's gaze stayed locked onto hers as she stumbled back, the pole making a sickening wet sound as it came out. Hazees's eyes showed only disbelief as she staggered to her knees. She looked around her at the faces of the Ma'diin, but no one came forward to help her. No one showed any sympathy or grief. And this seemed to be the fatal blow.

Hazees fell forward into the dirt and did not move again.

Tamsin didn't know how long she stayed like that, staring at the body that had only minutes ago been alive and full of fight. But then Numha knelt down by her and peeled her fingers off the pole, helping her to her feet.

She didn't know what happened next, or what the Ma'diin did with Hazees's body, but she blinked and was back in her muudhiif. The healer was there, as well as Numha and R'en, but she didn't feel any pain. She just felt numb. The memory of the pole in her hands as it slid into Hazees with frightful ease replayed itself like an ocean tide.

She looked at her hands. They had been washed of Hazees's blood, but they were red from gripping the pole, as it had still been hot from the fire she started.

R'en's voice slowly broke through the fog as she paced around the muudhiif joyfully, praising Tamsin's skill and the fact that they were finally rid of the tyrant.

But Tamsin was far from joyful. She was far from everything. "R'en, shut up," she said quietly.

But R'en didn't hear and kept on.

"R'en!" Numha said loudly, watching Tamsin with concern.

R'en quieted then, but crossed her arms over her chest, clearly not happy with having to reign in her excitement. Then she sighed in annoyance and left the muudhiif, mumbling that they needed to lighten up.

Numha waved the healer out as well and then draped a blanket around Tamsin's shoulders.

"I know what it is you are feeling right now," Numha said. "Just breathe and it will eventually pass."

"Have you ever killed anyone?" Tamsin asked her softly.

Numha nodded. "Yes. It was a long time ago."

But Tamsin could see in her eyes that it was something that still haunted her. And Tamsin would have to bear this for the rest of her life, even as awful as Hazees had been.

"It wasn't your fault," Numha said. "It was either you or her. But I know that knowledge won't help right now." She got up and retrieved a water skin and gave it to Tamsin.

Tamsin took a drink and nearly spit it out. It definitely didn't contain water. She looked at the water skin: it was leathery brown, but had purple beads hanging from the bottom seam. And then she noticed the blanket around her was purple too.

"These aren't ours," Tamsin commented.

This prompted a smile from Numha. "They weren't, but now they are."

"What do you mean?"

"Can you stand? I want to show you something."

Tamsin did and followed Numha slowly outside, where the buzz of excitement still had not bated from the other Ma'diin. But just outside the door were piles of blankets, baskets, clothes, knives, jewelry, and dozens of other items. But what struck Tamsin was that they were all different colors. A rainbow of gifts was laid out before her.

"What is all this?" she asked.

"They are offerings from the other Kazserii to the new Kazsera," Numha said, "or should I say, the new *Kaz'ma'sha*."

Kaz'ma'sha. The leader of all. Tamsin was now the Kazsera of all the marsh lands.

"You have your army now."

The image of the solstice celebration in Empyria flitted through her memory; the blazing fires, people laughing and dancing all around, the smell of abundance simmering over the fires, smiles on everyone's faces. She had been an outsider then. Here, however, it was much of a celebration for Tamsin as it was for the end of the Duels. But she was still uncomfortable as the Ma'diin came up to congratulate her and offer her more gifts as the evening celebrations took place.

She had done it. She had accomplished their mission and won the Duels. And they had won the hearts and loyalties of the Ma'diin. So why could she not take one night and celebrate their victory?

Because you haven't accomplished what you set out to do, a voice whispered from within.

That realization hit her harder than any of the blows she had taken the last couple days and she had to fight back the ball of guilt that rose in her throat.

Numha, who had stayed protectively near to Tamsin most of the day and night and handled most of the conversations with other sha'diin, noticed the change in her demeanor. She leaned in. "Are you alright Kazsera?"

Tamsin nodded, a little too quickly because Numha's eyes narrowed suspiciously.

"There is no shame in retiring early Tamsin. Your injuries are-."

"My injuries are fine," Tamsin snapped. "It is all *this*," she indicated the festivities around her, "that is not." She looked Numha in the eyes so she would not mistake her frustration for an insult. "I cannot celebrate when I know I should still be fighting. Haven is still fighting. I can't—." The ball of guilt found its way up and choked her off then. She couldn't look at Numha anymore. She couldn't stand the shame she would see there. She was the winner of the Duels and she had never felt more helpless…

She felt the pressure and jumped up just before the fires went dark, ignoring the sharp stab in her side. All sense of guilt in her extinguished with the flames as her instincts took over. Cries of shock and confusion filled the air, replacing the sounds of the drums, and people huddled and bumped into each other in the darkness. Tamsin's hand was on her sword hilt, but she didn't move. She could have brushed away the other force that was holding down the flames with ease, but instead she waited, a smile touching the corners of her mouth.

Loud whispers spread throughout the people and then two fires, one on either side of Tamsin, reignited with a *fiss*, illuminating the dark shadow of a cloak that stood amongst them. Oman's silver eyes glowed brightly under the edge of his hood. The people closest to him jumped back as they were able to see again, another round of surprise ringing through them, but then shrank back even more. For it was not just one Watcher that stood among them in the firelight; he had brought a dozen more Watchers with him.

Though her elation at seeing Oman again did not disappear entirely, Tamsin's smile vanished. She had never seen so many Watchers gathered in one place before and from the looks on the faces of others around her, neither had they. Even Numha's face had gone pale in the ruby glow of the firelight. Oman stood in front, the only one whose n'qab was lowered. Tamsin walked forward until she could see all of Oman's face under his hood. She was not afraid of the Watchers as the others were, only of what had brought them here. She hoped it did not show.

"Oman," she said, barely above a whisper. "What are you doing here? What has happened?"

He did not answer right away. There was a hardness to his expression that she was unaccustomed to; he had a wall up and she was not used to one between them. But around so many Ma'diin, she realized he had to. Or the news he carried was graver than she expected.

He brushed his fingers over his hand, recognizing her rank. "Tamsin," his tone was low and took some of the hardness out of his expression, but set her instincts on edge. "The marshes are gone."

Chapter Twenty-Two

Numha stayed close to Tamsin as they walked to through the camps, making sure she did not push herself too quickly. Not all the Kazserii had been present for the Watchers' appearance, but word had spread quickly and they were to meet at Ysallah's unused muudhiif. A ring of Watchers stayed in step around them and a hoard of Ma'diin followed behind them. Oman walked on her other side. He said nothing about their pace and Tamsin said nothing about her injuries that slowed them down, though she knew that he remained silent out of respect and not ignorance. He knew one did not make it through the Duels unscathed.

"So you have won your duels?" Oman asked, but his tone was not questioning. The ribbons around Tamsin's waist and arms was a kaleidoscope map of her victories.

Tamsin nodded, but that consumed the least of her thoughts now.

"What do you mean 'the marshes are gone'?" she asked.

"We should wait for the others," Oman said. "They need to hear this too."

"Is Samih back from the north?" She glanced behind them at the Watchers following them, but she couldn't make out one from the other.

"He is here. And Kellan too. Though it might be best if only I spoke to the Kazserii."

"The others may use Hazees's old muudhiif in the meantime," Numha said. "Tamsin is Kaz'ma'sha now."

Oman raised an eyebrow, but Numha shook her head with a look that said she would explain later.

They reached the muudhiif and Oman instructed the Watchers to go to Hazees's muudhiif while they waited tensely for the other Kazserii to show up.

Once everyone was gathered, they all sat in a circle and listened to Oman explain what was happening on the northern edges of Ma'diin territory. None of the Kazserii were oblivious to the fact that the northerners had crept south and were building a wall, but the news of the dam's completion was a shock to those that lived in the deepest parts of the territory. Numha was correct when she had said those Ma'diin were experts at turning a blind eye to the dangers that faced the outer tribes.

But no longer. The village Samih and Tamsin had come upon was only the beginning. All of the villages along the border were no more than dried up mounds of reeds and streams of mud. Those that had not gone to the Duels had fled, choosing to abandon their homes for fear of the tragedy that had struck Ysallah's tribe.

"We have had dry seasons before," Lam, one of the Kazserii that had been allies with Hazees, spoke up. "It will pass just like it always has."

"This isn't a dry spell," Oman said. "The river is blocked completely. No amount of rain can make up for it."

"And what about the amon'jii?" another Kazsera asked; her name eluded Tamsin. "If the water is gone in the marshes then shouldn't you be out there instead of here?"

"There are not enough of us to cover the entire border," Oman said. Then he paused and looked directly at Tamsin. "The amon'jii attacked us. Not as individuals, but together. And after they attacked us, they disappeared. There has not been an amon'jii sighting in three days."

A murmur swept through the muudhiif. Tamsin held Oman's gaze, questioning him with her eyes, but he just shook his head. He had no more ideas about the amon'jii's activity than she did. There was something very wrong. Why would the amon'jii not take advantage of the lack of water?

"Maybe your slayer has killed them all," Isillah broke through the murmuring.

"Haven is not responsible for this," Oman said dismissively.

Tamsin froze. *Slayer.* She had not recognized the nickname, but Oman's words chilled her. She was never prepared when his name came up, just like she was never prepared when someone spoke of her mother.

"Are there stories about you?"

"Maybe one or two."

Her conversation with Haven months ago echoed in her ears. Haven was notorious among the Ma'diin, a notorious *killer*. Not killer, she scolded herself. Hunter. Protector. Guardian. But even so, it was no small feat for a Watcher.

She caught Oman staring at her and wondered what expression must have been on her face just then. She shook the chill away, before that cold, familiar hole of missing him widened any further, but she could not shake the feeling that something was off. She was missing something…

"Describe the amon'jii attack," Tamsin said.

"It seemed coordinated," Oman said, "like they were all working together. I've never seen anything like it. But as quickly as they struck they disappeared just as fast."

"Were there any casualties?" she asked, folding her hands under her chin.

"Two, but they were taken by surprise. The rest of us had enough warning. Once the amon'jii met resistance they left. It felt…strategic." Here he shook his head. "But I can't figure out what they wanted."

"We need to take advantage of the amon'jii's absence," K'al said. "We have the chance to take out the northerners' wall, but we have to act now while the amon'jii are not a threat."

And before there was no more water or Watchers left separating them at all, Tamsin thought, though she did not say that part out loud.

"Kaz'ma'sha," young Calos addressed her. She looked around at the others nervously as if expecting them to hush her. She had succeeded in winning her duel against Bakkrah and had earned her place in the muudhiif tonight, but her youth showed. "What do you want us to do?"

The time had come. Tamsin had won the Duels and gathered the support of nearly all of the Ma'diin. They were unpolished, unrefined, and the idea of being united under one Kazsera was strange to them, but the Watchers showing up had proved to them that what she had been campaigning for was true. The Watchers needed a weapon and now she had one for them.

Tamsin's pulse pounded in her ears. How could she hand over a weapon that was made up of children? What would happen to them if she sent them north to the dam? What would happen if she didn't.

"Perhaps the new Kaz'ma'sha needs more time," Isillah sneered.

But it turned out that it was the Kazserii that needed more time. Tamsin was about to tell them to get ready; that they were leaving at dawn, but K'al interjected before Tamsin could reply, sparking a long debate. The Ma'diin needed a united army if they were going to take on the northerners, that much was clear, but it seemed that some of the Kazserii were *seeking* a reason not to go. Concern after concern was listed: The Watchers could not be trusted, there were not enough of them, the sha'diin were untrained, Tamsin was from the north herself—why should they listen to her? Each was argued, both for and against, and eventually dismissed and Tamsin got a real clear view of who was truly ready to follow her and who needed more convincing.

Tamsin knew it was their fear talking more so than their lack of faith in her, but when talk began of what strategies would be best for each tribe doubt in herself began to take hold. It had seemed only logical and fair to Tamsin to let the Kazserii discuss amongst themselves at first. She did not want to start her reign by making the Kazserii feel like they had lost control; that would only lead to resentment. She wanted their opinions, but she felt like their support was already slipping through her fingers before she even had a chance to grab the rope. And with it the chance to get Haven back.

This isn't working. This isn't working. Oman had stopped talking an hour ago. She rubbed her knuckles into her palms. Her side was burning in waves and she was finding it harder and harder to tolerate the circular discussion. Droplets of sweat beaded her hairline. She had not come halfway across the desert for this. She had not faced an amon'jii up close for this. She had not nearly died in the mangroves for this. She was Kaz'ma'sha; she needed to act like it. But what should she do? What would Irin have done?

Oman leaned over to her as the others kept talking. "There is one more thing that you should know," he said, "but I can't tell you. I have to show you."

She nodded, eager to be away from the packed muudhiif. She stood up gingerly and followed him outside, ignoring the questions and confused stares that followed her. Dawn was many hours away yet, but no one was sleeping. Those that were not already standing or pacing jumped up at her sudden emergence. Numha and R'en were by her side in an instant and she saw many of the other Tamsin'diin nearby, though there was a ring of space between them and some of the Watchers that lingered around the muudhiif. She suddenly thought of the Ysallah'diin and the other tribes Oman had spoken of, displaced and homeless, and she realized, though they were used to wandering, the Watchers were now refugees as well.

She followed him away from the muudhiif, but one of the Watchers stepped in their way. It was Kellan.

Before she could speak, Kellan held up his hand, a displeased look in his eyes like he already knew where they were going. "Oman, you should take her back. She needs to rest." He looked her over uncertainly, as if he was waiting for her to tip over or something.

"She should see this," Oman retorted. "Then rest, I promise."

Kellan still looked doubtful, but now Tamsin was intrigued. She tucked her hands underneath her arms so they would not see them shaking. She was exhausted, but sleep would have to wait. "See what? Show me."

Kellan shook his head, but led them over to Hazees's large muudhiif anyways, with Numha and R'en following. Kellan held the flap back for her and she stepped inside. She was happy to see Kellan here and safe, but the smile fell from her lips as she beheld what was inside.

Tamsin wished she was anywhere else. There was nothing special or threatening about Hazees's old muudhiif, with a bare floor and supplies stacked along the walls. Either Hazees had used it for more practical purposes rather than comfort or the Hazees'diin had already rid it of its items. Each of the Kazserii's muudhiifs she had visited had their own unique extravagance to them, but this one was quite plain…save for one large detail.

As she stared at what they had brought her in disbelief, she thought back to a time before all of this; before she had become Kazsera, before she had known the Ma'diin, before she had fallen into the river. A time when she would sip tea on the balcony overlooking the gardens in Jalsai and all she had to worry about was her upcoming history lesson. A time before she knew the Empyrian witch woman kneeling in front of her.

If Mora's eyes were arrows, Tamsin would be dead. Mora's hands were bound in front of her, a gag stuffed in her mouth, and the two other Watchers in the muudhiif guarding her had their long knives out. Her face was smeared with grime and her clothes were an unrecognizable color. Her nails, the ones that had nearly left scars on the backs of Tamsin's hands, were either broken or ripped off completely.

"We found her stumbling through the marshes," Kellan said before Tamsin could even grasp one of the questions that was whirling around her mind.

She must not have been very cooperative when the Watchers found her, for it was not a priority of theirs to capture lone women in the marshes.

"What is she doing here?" Tamsin asked, not even ashamed that she couldn't bring her voice above a whisper.

"At first we thought she was an evacuee from the outer border, but she would not stop shouting and rambling...and then," Kellan paused here for a moment. "Then she said your name Tamsin."

Tamsin nodded. She could not break Mora's gaze.

"Tamsin, do you know her?" Oman asked.

Tamsin swallowed hard. "Yes. She is from Empyria."

Oman and Kellan exchanged a look. "What was an Alamorgrian doing in the north?" Kellan asked him.

Tamsin had heard that name before, but she could not remember where. "A what?"

"She has the markings of an Alamorgrian," Oman said, indicating her white lips and the blue veins showing under her eyes. "They were notorious blood stealers, but we thought that race long extinct."

Mora howled something then, and though the gag muffled what was said, the anger and bitterness behind it could not be silenced.

"Maybe she would like to tell us," Kellan said, moving forward to remove the gag.

"No," Tamsin said firmly, putting her hand on his arm. "Do not let her speak." She turned and walked out.

She let out a long, shaky breath, one she had not wanted Mora to see. She trembled from head to toe and though she had a thousand questions for the seer she needed to get her head on straight.

Kellan and Oman emerged a moment later. She didn't want to look at them. She knew they had questions too, but she couldn't answer them yet. They seemed to sense it too so they just stood there. When the silence became unbearable Tamsin told Numha and R'en to tell the other Kazserii to get some rest and they would reconvene in the morning and then she would explain.

All she wanted was to sleep; to sink into the warm safety of slumber and forget everything else. A sleep that was not plagued by nightmares or blurred by pain. She wanted it so desperately. Tears slipped from the corners of her eyes and all she saw was Mora. And Haven. And her father and mother. She was exhausted, but her ghosts would not let her rest. These weren't images caused by some firestone. These were her own demons, her own guilt haunting her.

She needed to confront them.

She wiped the tears away and straightened her shoulders, then told the Watchers that she wanted to talk to Mora alone. They were hesitant, but allowed her to go back in. Inside, Tamsin stood there for what seemed a long time, then she finally said, "What in the seven hells of old are you doing here?" The common tongue felt sticky, like honey, in her mouth after having not spoken it in so long.

Mora's eyes flashed wildly and her nostrils flared.

"Decided to come scare me with another prophecy of doom? Or reveal another secret about my family? Or did you just come to say I told you so?" Tamsin could feel her pulse pounding harder in her neck despite her efforts to control her temper. She knelt down so she was only a foot away. "Congratulations," she reached up and pulled the gag out of Mora's mouth. "You get your chance, but make it quick."

Mora moved her jaw back and forth and licked her cracked lips. Her face was nearly as pale as them, making the blue veins under her eyes look almost black. Then she sneered. "You think I came all the way here to this mud hole to speak to *you*?" Her voice was hoarse. "Though you have exceeded even my expectations...*Kazsera*."

"What, you did not see me leading the tribes against the north in your *visions*?"

Mora chuckled, a dry, splintered sound. "No, that you still do not see the greater threat gathering at your doorstep."

"My doorstep has widened since the last time we had the misfortune of meeting, but so have my allies. If you know of another threat speak of it now."

Mora's eyes crackled like lightning. "You dare dictate to me what I am to do?! My people have been persecuted by *him* for hundreds of years! I will not run away from one tyrant into the hands of another!"

Despite the ferocity of her words, Tamsin was able to keep a calm mask on, though she was beginning to wonder if her visit to Mora was again only going to lead to more questions than answers. "Who is *him*?" she asked.

"If you don't know by now, then it is too late for him. As it is for all of us."

Tamsin tried to riddle out what the mad woman was saying, though it was like trying to figure out what the starting point of a circle was. She kept saying 'him,' but she was using it in two different contexts. "The first 'him' you speak of is a threat. Who is the second?"

"You moon has fallen, but he will rise again. Though it will be his dark side rising."

"My moon...? Do you mean Haven?"

Her gaze had drifted somewhere else, as if she were seeing another vision or caught up in some memory. "I have seen him. He is there now, where I escaped from."

"You know where he is?" Tamsin had to shove down the urge to force the old woman to tell her where he was, or lest provoke her again into more conundrums. "Where, Mora, where were you? Where did you escape from?"

Mora's eyes suddenly glistened and Tamsin felt an irretrievable stab of pity. She had only known Mora to be fierce or fanatical, there had been no in between. Now she wondered why she had not asked herself why Mora was like that in the first place. What had made her this way?

"It was my home a long time ago," Mora said, "but it is not any more. Not since *he* came with his damnable beasts. I believe you call it…the *Ravine of Bones.*"

It was the same place Samih had mentioned all that time ago before they set out for the marshes. The only place they could've taken Haven. If they had taken Mora the same time they had taken Haven, then there was no doubt in Tamsin's mind now that that was where he was.

"Thank you, Mora. Truly."

Mora's eyes snapped up suddenly and she strained against her ties. "What you're planning to do, it will not work."

Tamsin's gratitude was brief. "What do you know of our plans?"

"These walls are thin and your people's tongues are loose. You will lead your people to extinction if you continue. You came for advice little Kazsera. This is mine: get as far away from here as you can."

"I'm going to save them," Tamsin insisted. "And I'm going to get Haven back. And when I've done that, I'll be the one telling you I told you so."

Mora laughed. "You know, there's a way you could see what I've seen. Then you would heed my words."

Tamsin had gotten up to leave, but she paused. "Excuse me?"

"You have so many veins around you. All you have to do is cut into one. Just a few drops." There was a gleam in Mora's eyes that was almost ravenous.

"You're talking about blood stealing? That's what they said you were. Is that how you tell the future?" Tamsin remembered all those bottles at Mora's home in Empyria. Were they all filled with blood? The thought suddenly sickened her. "Where did you get it all?"

"You can't imagine how many years it takes to get a collection like that," Mora replied, understanding perfectly what Tamsin was referring to. "But Empyria's a bit far. Especially when you're surrounded by a much fresher supply."

Tamsin had never liked the old woman, but this was despicable. Unforgivable. If Mora even thought about touching any of her people, she would—.

Then it hit her. Mora wasn't referring to the Ma'diin in general. She was talking about the Watchers. Poma had told her that first day with the Hazees'diin that Watcher blood was nothing to mess around with. It could cause blindness, paralysis, even…*visions.*

Tamsin leaned in closer to Mora. "Your gods will judge you for the things you've done," she whispered and then walked away.

"That day is closer than you think. For both of us," the seer replied.

But Tamsin flung the door flap open and this time kept on walking. She went back to Ysallah's muudhiif and luckily caught the Kazserii before they had left completely. They were talking outside, but stopped as they saw Tamsin approaching. She didn't tell them to go back in, but instead climbed up one of the sturdier corner beams on the muudhiif until she could see above everyone's heads. More Ma'diin started to gather to see what she was going to do and others waved their friends over.

She could feel the fire inside her, licking at her insides just waiting to be released, spurred on by her anger towards the seer. Instead of letting it blind her, she tightened her fists and forced it to strengthen her. These were her people now and she would guard them as fiercely as she guarded Haven in her heart. They looked to her, waiting for her to speak.

"Some of you may have heard," she shouted. "There are foes to the north that threaten us: the northerners' wall and the amon'jii. The Watchers cannot deal with this on their own. It's time that we all stand up and protect what we love."

She paused here, looking at all the faces watching her. "One of our own is there, in the Ravine of Bones, and as long as he fights I will fight to get him back. I do not ask you to come with me. I have no claims on you, though you have become my family."

Numha spoke up, "I will go with you, because I claim you as my Kazsera." She kneeled down and held her fingers to her lips and then touched the back of her hand.

Behind her, R'en did the same. "I will follow you Tamsinkazsera!"

One by one, the others did the same, until they were all kneeling before her, pledging themselves to their leader's cause. Only the other Kazserii remained standing, but the awe on their faces as they beheld their tribesmen pledging themselves to the Kaz'ma'sha was apparent.

Tamsin's nostrils flared in sudden pride, and her eyes burned brighter than the moon as she beheld her stars. "You have honored me more than I dare breathe and I desire nothing more than to stand next to each and every one of you and repel our foe. We all fight for each other. For our sisters and brothers, for our children and our mothers and fathers! For the ones we have lost and those we will lose in the coming struggle. But we fight together! The Ma'diin are truly united!"

A determined roar erupted from the crowd and they jumped up and thrust their fists at the sky. Cheers of '*Tamsinkazsera!*' and '*Irinbaat!*' reverberated throughout the marshes and it was more than an exclamation of loyalty from the Ma'diin, it was a cry of hope. It filled her, fueling the fire that coursed through her veins and surged to her fingertips.

Tamsin closed her eyes and raised her sword into the air, and though her last attempt to light metal on fire had failed, it came easily now, as if it had only been waiting for her to embrace it. When she reopened her eyes her tribesmen were gazing at her in wonder and when she smiled the cheers were even louder and more passionate than before. A line of flames sizzled with energy across the edge of her blade.

The Ma'diin would not forget this night for many years after and songs would be sung and passed down from the children who were there to witness Irin's daughter become Kaz'ma'sha, the girl who united the Ma'diin and could control fire.

She would be damned to the seven hells of old or banished to whatever underworld the Ma'diin believed in before she would let whatever Mora saw in her vision come to pass. If she could change the future, she would do everything she could to save his. That's what she had come for and if she believed in anything, she believed she wouldn't have made it this far just to fail.

She was going to get Haven back.

But she could not deny the rest she needed first. The energy that had consumed her during her speech to the Ma'diin had used up the rest of her reserves and when Numha suggested she rest, she could not even argue.

She pushed the flap open to her muudhiif and walked inside and froze.

In the middle of her muudhiif stood a man. His back was turned to her, but he was tall and lean and—and was wearing the uniform of an Empyrian soldier. It was grimy and torn in some places, but the details on the shoulders were unmistakable.

Tamsin grabbed the hilt of her sword. "Who are you?" she demanded to know.

The man turned around.

Tamsin's grip on her sword slackened and her jaw dropped open. *"Enrik?"*

A flood of emotions poured through her, making her want to laugh and cry all at once. "Enrik, what are you doing here? How did you get here?"

Enrik stood there silently. He was bent over slightly, as if there was great weight on his shoulders and his hair was slick with sweat that beaded his forehead. But his eyes were the strangest. He looked at her, but it was like he wasn't seeing her.

Something wasn't right. "Enrik," she took a cautious step forward. "You don't look well. Why don't you sit down and you can—." Then she noticed what he was holding in his hands: Haven's firestone.

"Enrik, what are you doing with that? Give it to me." She reached out her hand for it. She remembered her first experience with it and wondered if he was in its grip right now.

There was a rustling behind her as someone walked in. Tamsin glanced back.

"Tamsin, Numha told me you were here. I had to see y—," Samih started to say.

Tamsin felt a tug at her hand and looked back too late to stop Enrik from grabbing her sword. She tried to hang onto it, but he twisted it around and thrust the blade towards her.

But the sword never touched her. In that moment there was a swirl of black as Samih stepped in between them.

"Enrik, no!" Tamsin cried, but everything had happened in the blink of an eye.

Enrik dropped the sword and for a moment a look of horror crossed his face, but then he trembled violently and ran out of the muudhiif, still clutching Haven's firestone.

Samih looked down at his chest, to where a dark stain was slowly spreading across his tunic. He looked up at Tamsin, his eyes showing confusion. He inhaled once, shakily, and then pitched forward like a falling tree.

Tamsin's shock broke in time for her to catch him, but his weight sent both of them collapsing to the ground. She called for help, though her blood pumped deafeningly in her ears and she couldn't hear herself. Others came running in at her call, but came to a halt at the sight of the Watcher.

"Help him!" she cried. She put her hands over his wound to stop the bleeding and this seemed to break the trance the others were in. Someone jumped forward and grabbed her by the shoulders, pulling her back.

"You can't! His blood!" the person said.

Kellan and Oman rushed into the muudhiif then, and even Oman's always stoic expression seized for a moment in horror. They went over to Samih and quickly started administering to him.

"What happened?" Kellan asked.

"Enrik, he—he was here and he tried to—and Samih came in—please, you have to save him!"

"Someone was in here?" Kellan started barking orders at the others. "Go, start searching for the man who did this. And get the Kaz'ma'sha to safety."

Tamsin didn't want to go, but the arms around her pulled her away. It was too similar. Too similar, she kept thinking. This couldn't be happening again. And Samih was just a kid…

She wanted to shut out the old woman's words, but the harder she tried the more doubt seeped in. And waiting for news of Samih only made it worse. As much as she loathed Mora, she could not come up with a reason why Mora would hate *her*. Unless she truly believed that Tamsin was the harbinger of doom. And now with what had just happened to Samih, Tamsin was starting to believe her.

She pressed her palms together. She had made a vow to herself the day she and Samih decided to leave Empyria. She had promised never to let her life be controlled by anyone else; that she would no longer be a pawn in someone else's game. But she felt that way now more than she ever had in Empyria. But it wasn't a stranger or a mad old woman pulling the strings. It was Haven. Every decision she made was chained to him.

When she pulled her hands away she realized they were still covered in Samih's blood.

The blood of a Watcher is powerful...it could kill you.

Poma's warning drifted back to her, but it was too late to stop the idea that had ignited.

I'm powerful too, Tamsin thought. Her idea was reckless, but it might be the only way she could know if Mora was telling the truth. She had no idea how or if it actually worked, but she was alone in Ysallah's muudhiif and this might be her only chance. There were dozens of guards outside, but no one was allowed in and they would not let her leave. As Kaz'ma'sha her safety was the most important, especially with an assassin running around. All she had to do was mix Samih's blood with her own.

Before she could talk herself out of it she unwrapped herself from the colorful layers of fabric that enveloped her, discarded the leather jerkin, and pulled up her tunic to reveal the wound in her side. Numha had patched it with an herb mixture that now looked like moss growing out of her abdomen. She pressed her lips together as she peeled the dry spongy patch off her skin, cringing when it re-tore the edges that had just begun to heal. Tears pooled in the corners of her eyes, but she continued until a thin line of her own blood leaked from the wound. Once the mossy patch was sufficiently removed, Tamsin took her hand and pressed it to the wound, gritting her teeth against the flare of old pain and trying not to think of what had happened to get her this blood.

Numha was going to have her head for this if she ever found out. If it even worked. Worst case scenario nothing would happen and she would just have to tell Numha the patch dried and fell off, but best case—

White-hot pain exploded from her side and she gasped, the suddenness of it forcing all the air from her lungs. She doubled over, but refused to take her hand away, pressing her fingers against it, barely able to watch the blood seep through her fingers.

Then the pain turned cold and the very air seemed suddenly chilled because of it. The muudhiif had lost its vibrancy: the glittering beaded pillows to the richly-colored rugs had taken on a dull, greyish hue, as if the shadows had sucked in all the color and light from the space. The blood under her hand had turned as black as oil and her hands a ghostly shade of white.

She stared at her hands, horrified, but that was not the worst thing. They had made no sound, but she suddenly sensed that she was not alone and when she looked up she was surrounded by a dozen hooded figures. But these were not her Watchers; she wasn't even sure they were Watchers. The grey air shimmered under the blackness of their hoods and their cloaks ruffled about, though there was no wind. They stood completely still, their sleeves folded together in front of them as if they were waiting for something, but every time she tried to look directly at one it was like looking into a haze. They were clear when she didn't look directly at them, like when one looked at the stars one had to look *between* the brightness to see them clearly.

One of them cocked his head to the side and as she stared she felt long, cold fingers descend upon her shoulder from behind her, digging into her flesh like the talons of a harpy.

Then everything blurred into a grey haze and went dark.

Chapter Twenty-Three

It was as if the sky had cracked, shards of red splintering the dull grey like lightning bolts frozen in the clouds. Someone whispered that it was an ill omen, that the gods were divided.

She stared across the desert between them, at the wall of soldiers quickly approaching them and thought maybe he was right. There were too many of them. They had not expected the northerners to have this large of a defense. The wall of Empyrians reached them and the clash of metal rang out across the sand. One by one her protectors were forced to negotiate more than one assailant that forced them away from her. She was not afraid though. She parried the first attacker easily, using his surprise at a woman's presence on the battlefield to her advantage, and swung around behind him, slashing the backs of his unprotected legs. The ones that followed were not so easy, having seen their comrade fall to the deadly girl with the blade, and she quickly found she could not match them for strength. She had to dodge and sidestep the heavy blows to avoid being crushed by their massive shields. But where they were overconfident in their brute strength, she was quick and her size gave her the advantage because it gave them a smaller target.

She stopped seeing faces through the sweat in her eyes and listened to the swish of a sword cutting through the air, ducking just seconds before the blade sliced through the spot her head had been. The earth trembled where their footsteps fell and men screamed all around her, but she heard the sharp intake of breath right behind her and she whipped her blade over her back and felt the shuddering ring of steel on steel as she blocked the blow. She shoved it away and spun around, swinging low so her enemy had to jump back to avoid the strike. Another man charged from the side and she grabbed her knife and flung it at him as the first swung his sword for another blow. The second man fell, but she was forced to roll away from the other's attack and the sand slipped beneath her as she tried to come out of it on her feet. She threw another knife and he blocked it easily with his shield, but the brief moment he had his shield up covering his face she swung her feet around and connected with his legs, knocking him to the ground. She plunged her dagger in the soft spot underneath his helm and he shuddered once and was still.

She got to her feet, taking advantage of the momentary lull around her and scanned the area for the others. Amidst the clash of bodies and weapons she saw a dark cloak, whipping around with two deadly scimitars, cutting down those nearest him. She tried to see who it was; Kellan had been the last one nearest her. Something was wrong though. The cloaked man was fighting against the Ma'diin.

She cried out and staggered forward, but tripped, over a body, and coughed as sand filled her mouth. She looked up and trembled as the figure's head turned and the dark space under his hood stared at her. He started walking towards her, slowly, deliberately, killing anyone that crossed his path.

She heard her name being called and a moment later Oman was kneeling next to her.

"Are you hurt?" he asked.

"Look out!" she screamed and he looked and threw up his sword just as the cloaked figure brought his down upon them.

With a mighty heave, Oman pushed back and forced the attacker away and leapt to his feet. The two figures glared at each other and then, like lightning, they struck, the sound of their swords colliding echoing in Tamsin's skull. They attacked, blocked, spun, and attacked again, their movements reminding Tamsin of two hawks clawing at each other in the sky, a dizzying spiral of slashing and slicing. Movement behind her caught her attention and she rolled just as a large bludgeon impacted the earth where she had been. She tried to block with her sword, but the shield that came next hurled her several feet away. She tried to stand, but the ground pitched severely beneath her and she had to clench her eyes shut as she clutched the hilt of her sword, knowing the killing blow would be next. But it never came. Instead she felt hands underneath her, lifting her up.

She wiped her eyes, trying to clear her vision and her sleeve came away red.

"Can you stand?"

She recognized Kellan's voice, and was vaguely aware of being picked up. "Oman...where's Oman?" she asked, the taste of blood in her mouth. She tried to turn in his arms, but the jostling made her dizzy. She looked behind him as he ran away from the fighting and the last thing she saw before she passed out was a hoard of approaching amon'jii.

She had never been in a battle before. That was the peak of the mountain, what everyone had been working towards. It was the biggest thing any of them had ever done. But nobody had prepared her for the other side, for the cliff that awaited them after the battle was over. Nobody had told her what came in the aftermath, when the swords lay lifeless in the sand next to their masters, when the smell of dust and blood lingered like a thick, choking fog, when the eyes of the living looked duller than those of the dead. She knew it was possible that they might lose, but she had not been prepared to lose and live.

This world she had awoken into several hours later was foreign to her. She didn't know how she got there, but she was suddenly walking through the fallout, seeing the tired, slumping shoulders and the grim faces of those she could barely recognize through the layers of dirt and blood. The wails of the dying echoed through the air like ghostly howls, lingering in the eyes of those who sat near, motionless, as if they were permanent fixtures of the landscape. No one even seemed to notice her as she staggered through the devastation of the Ma'diin camp, too exhausted to be concerned with anything but breathing. There was music playing somewhere and she recognized it as a song her father used to play for her on the piano, a slow, melancholic song where, as each note fell, another filled the void of its fading sound, and she thought it strange that someone would be playing it now, though she did not guess that it was all in her head.

Before she realized where she was going she was inside the tent. Three heads turned to look at her and she had to blink several times to make sure she was seeing right. She felt like she was in some peculiar dream.

"Tamsinkazsera? What is she doing here?"

One of the sha'diin. She had seen him before, during the battle maybe.

"I thought she was still out. There were no signs from her since we came back."

Benuuk. He was alive, though he held his arm protectively against his body and had a bruise that covered the left side of his face.

"Tamsin, can you hear me?"

Kellan. She looked at him and his face told her the truth. Fatigue, grief, worry, pain: these were all chiseled into his features. Every swing of the sword, every blocked blow and near miss was etched there for her to read.

"What happened?" she asked.

"You should be resting, Tamsinkazsera," Benuuk said, moving to take her back to wherever she had been before, but she waved him away.

She closed her eyes for a few moments and when she opened them they were all watching her. "What happened?" she asked again, slowly, deliberately.

Kellan was the one who answered her, his chin sticking out slightly as he recalled to her what took place after she had lost consciousness. The northerners had sustained heavy losses at the hands of the Ma'diin, but they still outnumbered the tribesmen. Luckily for the Ma'diin, night fell before the northerners could wipe them out completely. Blind and vulnerable in the dark, it should have been an easy victory for the Ma'diin. But then the amon'jii had showed up, attacking them from behind. The Ma'diin had lost half of their original army and the other half were wounded and exhausted. Their only choice was to run.

"Our best option at this point would be to send the wounded back to the marsh lands while those still able to fight make an attack now, while it is yet dark and to our advantage," Kellan said.

"It would be suicide," the sha'diin said. "There are few still able to defend themselves and even less that possess the night vision." He glanced at the other two men worriedly.

"How many?" Tamsin asked. "How many would fight?"

Benuuk could not meet her eyes, but Kellan stared at her squarely. "We could hold our own for a little while, at least enough time so the others can get a head start."

Benuuk looked up at Kellan and after a moment, nodded. They would fight to the death if it meant giving the others a chance to live. It was no different than in the marshes against the amon'jii.

"Numha is still missing. I lost sight of her after I grabbed you," Kellan continued. "Demus and V'shgra may be able to fight yet, but I fear that Sinsha will not make it through the night. Ruvo, Igryn, and Kep'chlan are dead."

Tamsin counted the remaining Watchers in her head. "Oman? Did he...?"

Something dark flashed through Kellan's eyes and he trembled.

Tamsin knew what had happened. She hadn't seen it, but she could see it in Kellan's eyes now. Oman had protected her; he had saved her life at the cost of his own.

Kellan's hand opened and closed around the hilt of his sword several times before he had composure enough to speak again. "We will mourn the dead later. There is nothing else we can do for them."

"And what about the living?" *Tamsin asked.* "Is there no other choice?"

"If we can slow them down, even for a day, it will give the others a chance to escape. Tamsin, you must lead them back to the marshes."

She shook her head, feeling a chill breathe across her skin. "I will send them back, but I won't abandon you to your deaths." *With the last word, the air in the muudhiif seemed to go still and the colors appeared less potent.*

Something tickled the back of her mind, but she couldn't remember what. Kellan was saying something and she could see his lips moving, but he sounded far away. She looked between the faces, but they had gone grey. Like the faces of the dead, they had lost their color. But not their expressions or movements. Their lips kept moving and their foreheads scrunched together in concern.

She shook her head again, trying to dispel the déjà vu that swept through her. She backed away and stumbled back out of the muudhiif, shoving the flap out of the way...and stopped dead.

Standing in a semicircle outside the muudhiif were the twelve cloaked figures she had seen before. This time their cloaks were blazing red, standing out against the dull, grey landscape like the stars against the night sky. One moved toward her and laid his outstretched hand on her shoulder...

Slowly the blurriness went away and her vision returned, but the faces in front of her were different. It was bright out too. Had she passed out? She blinked, trying to determine where exactly she was, but the faces kept crowding her, making it difficult to see. Someone helped her sit up and she gripped their arm for support, her head feeling like someone had taken an ax to it. She squeezed her eyes shut against the sudden nausea that came with it.

"Tamsin? Tamsin! Kazsera, can you hear me?" an urgent voice asked.

"Yes, yes, I can hear you," she replied crossly, annoyed that someone thought that shouting was a good idea. "You don't need to—." She stopped, realizing then who that voice belonged to. She opened her eyes.

One of the faces hovering over her was Oman.

It took the kazsiin a good hour to calm her down before she would even listen to them. Oman left quickly after she woke up and the kazsiin tried to usher Kellan out of the muudhiif as well, but she refused to let go of him. He was her anchor, holding her to reality as she tried to reconcile what she was seeing with what she thought had happened. Everything had been so real, so painfully real that she thought the battle had really happened. And then she remembered: she had taken on the blood vision. It slowly started to make sense. The last thing she remembered before the battle was being alone in the muudhiif and Samih's blood on her hands.

Kellan's attention was required elsewhere and he left hesitantly, but returned a little while later, after the kazsiin had seen to her needs and confirmed that she was neither blind, paralyzed, or had lost her mind. They left her alone with him at her bidding, not wanting an audience for what she knew was going to be a scolding of epic proportions.

He knelt down next to her. "Are you alright?" His voice sounded pained.

She nodded, not knowing what to say.

"You're sure?"

"I'm okay. You can ask the kazsiin." Her gaze met his briefly before she dropped her eyes again.

He was quiet for a little while and she braced herself for his fury, but it never came. "Why did you do it, Tamsin?" he asked softly.

She tried to think back, before the battle, the battle that never happened her kazsiin assured her. "Because I was angry," she said. "And I didn't know what to do. I didn't think it would work."

"You can't take something like this lightly," he said. "The red sight has not been used in hundreds of years for a reason. Its effects are too unpredictable."

They even had a name for it. She nodded again. "I'm sorry Kellan. I didn't mean to disappoint you."

"Disappoint me?" He inched closer and tilted her head up so she had to look at him. "You *scared* me, Tamsin."

He wasn't lying. Fear still lingered in his eyes and the Watchers did not scare easily.

A different kind of fear settled in her stomach, one that had nothing to do with her vision. She suddenly wanted him to yell at her, to tell her how stupid she'd been and that he was locking her in this muudhiif until all the battles were over.

But he didn't.

"Kellan—" she started, but she couldn't get her thoughts together, not with him looking at her like that, like he wanted to…

He dropped his hand away from her chin. "I know," he said and moved away from her. He pulled his hood further over his face, but not before she saw the flicker of sadness there.

And then what she had seen in her vision returned to her: the dark figure stalking towards her on the battlefield, his hooded gaze burning into her skull. She knew the figure, she knew he was fighting for the wrong side, but she reached out anyways. She could bring him back, she could try and save him…

The hood fell away, but it wasn't Haven in front of her. It was Kellan and suddenly he was kissing her.

It was like a wave of warmth and sunlight washing over her. For the first time in months she felt a glimmer of happiness. She could feel it in the way his lips moved with hers, his longing, his desire. She could feel all of the feelings he had suppressed in the way his hands tightened around her waist, pulling her closer. He wanted her just as badly as she wanted someone too. He would be there to protect her, to hold her, to love her. She glimpsed all of the things she could have with him, of a future that she should've had with Haven…

The figure raised his weapon, casting a shadow over the whole sky, and struck.

She broke away, breathing heavily as if all the air had left her lungs. Her eyes darted around quickly, confirming that she was in fact in the muudhiif. Haven wasn't here.

Kellan looked at her worriedly. "What's wrong?" he asked.

She put her fist against his chest, partly to steady herself, partly to keep him from coming any closer and tried to ignore the pounding of his own frenzied heart. She shook her head. "I'm sorry, I can't, I can't."

His eyes darkened briefly. "Haven's not with us anymore, Tamsin. He's not coming back."

"How can you say that?" she said harsher than she wanted to. "He's still out there. I keep seeing him in my dreams. I saw him in my vision. He was going to—he tried—."

The worry in his eyes deepened and his forehead creased. "What was he going to do?"

She took a deep breath and relayed everything she could remember. They had been caught, she realized, between the Empyrians at the dam, which had a much bigger force than anyone had anticipated, and the amon'jii somewhere in the desert. And Haven had been there. He had killed Oman. The rest of the Ma'diin had been decimated. Kellan was going to lead a group to give the wounded time to get back to the marshes, but it was a suicide mission and everyone had known it.

Kellan shook his head when she had finished. "I believe you, Tamsin. But what I don't understand is how the amon'jii are involved in this. They are solitary creatures. Once in a while you see a pair of them, but never in the numbers you saw."

"But you saw them when they attacked you? All of them, together?"

"Something must have driven them all to the same place."

"And don't they live in the Ravine?"

"Scattered throughout the caves, I'm sure. But they rarely hunt together."

Tamsin rubbed her hands together, scouring her brain. What wasn't she seeing? What connection wasn't she making? But something else leapt to the forefront of her thoughts as she saw her hands. Someone had scrubbed them clean.

"How is Samih?" she asked with trepidation.

Kellan's eyes grew stormy. "You should come with me."

Tamsin stood on the bank at the edge of the dueling grounds, watching the single canoe drift slowly off into the water. The canoe that carried Samih's body. He had been wrapped in black cloth and laid in the canoe with boughs of pentiyan flowers surrounding him.

Hundreds of Ma'diin stood along the bank with her to honor the fallen Watcher. It was not custom for a Watcher to receive the funeral rights of a Kazsera, but it had unfolded without argument as he had died in the place of the Kaz'ma'sha.

Knowing she was the reason Samih was dead stung worse than killing Hazees. The bitter taste in her mouth made her want to be sick.

Next to her, Kellan held a blazing torch. "Was this part of your vision?" he asked.

"No," she said quietly. "It was not."

His nostrils flared and the muscles in his jaw clenched repeatedly. Finally, he walked out into the water, to the canoe, and lit it on fire. He threw the torch into the water and watched the canoe as it was engulfed in flames. Tamsin could see his shoulders heaving with emotion.

It wasn't long before the whole canoe was ablaze. The pentiyan flowers that had glowed blue the night of the sh'lomiin's storytelling now turned the flames to sapphire.

The giant, blue bonfire on the water reflected in all the eyes of the Ma'diin. Whether they loved the Watchers, revered them, or hated them, an understanding of what was at stake touched each of them. The hour of embers was upon them, where they each had the choice to pick up the torch and light the fire of purpose in their hearts or let the embers burn to ash.

And none felt the draw more so than Tamsin. The image of the canoe, burning bright as cobalt, stoked the fight in her. But it also stoked doubt.

"Why are these people so eager to follow me?" she asked Numha who stood on her other side.

"Would you rather they not?"

"No, we need them of course, but I just—I don't know."

Since her speech it seemed there was a constant stream of strangers, people from all tribes, wishing to see her and talk to her. Some were too shy to approach her, but they watched her from a distance and even then the admiration in their eyes was obvious. Most would flick her the sign of respect and say how honored they were to be in her presence. A few would even drop to their knees and kiss her feet. They looked at her like a god. Even now, as they watched the blazing canoe drift away, she could feel their eyes on her. And she wondered why they did not look at her with scorn, since it seemed to her that danger and death followed her like a shadow.

"But you understand love, do you not?"

"Sometimes I think I do and other times I don't, but I feel it."

"And they feel that love for you, similar to the kind they feel for the gods. It is called faith."

"I did nothing to deserve it. I am not worthy of it."

Then her breath caught and a twisted sense of deja'vu came over her.

"Haven used to tell me that," she said quietly. "He used to think he was unworthy of my affection, of any love at all."

Numha nodded understandingly. "And was he?"

"He was the most worthy of all."

Numha then knelt down and brushed her fingers over her hand and across the water. "To the fallen," she said.

"To the fallen," Tamsin said, and soon the echo was repeated throughout the Ma'diin.

"To the fallen."

It was a unanimous decision: all the Kazserii and the Watchers had agreed to send a full assault against the dam while the amon'jii were dormant. This meant every fighting man and woman, even those not at the Duels, would be marching towards the anasii hada. They could send word and get everyone assembled in three days' time. All they needed was the Kaz'ma'sha to give the all clear.

But Tamsin's sight was anything but clear. The images of the red sight lingered with her and she found she could not give the okay, especially when it might send them all to their deaths. She didn't know when or where or even if what she had seen would take place, but she was certain about the devastation she had witnessed. Haven had been fighting for the wrong side. The Ma'diin had been decimated. And right now she was the only thing preventing that.

Maybe Mora was right and she would be the cause the Ma'diin's demise. Not the dam. Not the amon'jii. Tamsin.

Her eyes drifted to the door flap, as if to look through it and to the Watchers' muudhiif where Mora was being held. She had done the red sight because of what Mora had said. She wondered if the seer had seen what she had. And if she could change it.

She stood up, grabbed her sword, and streamed out of the muudhiif, startling the sha'diin outside. She didn't say a word or offer any explanation as she made her way to the Watchers' muudhiif, hopefully leaving the last seeds of doubt from the red sight behind her. She shoved the flap aside and marched right in. Kellan and Kep'chlan were inside keeping an eye on Mora, but they seemed unfazed by Tamsin's sudden appearance.

"I need a moment alone," Tamsin said, looking squarely at Mora.

Kep'chlan nodded and left immediately, but Kellan paused at Tamsin's side. She could feel his mahogany eyes boring into her, though she didn't meet them to see if he was cautioning her or asking permission to stay. She didn't want to entertain either, especially after what had happened between them last night, so she stared ahead until he eventually shuffled outside, the edges of his cloak brushing up against her as he passed.

Once the muudhiif flap had settled again, Tamsin sat down where she had stood, so she and Mora were eye level with each other.

"What was in the bottle?" she asked slowly.

Mora's eyes narrowed. "I've seen many bottles in my life little Kazsera, you'll have to be more specific." She licked her lips.

Most of them were probably Arak bottles, Tamsin thought, but that was not what she was after. "When we first met. You had me pick a bottle and you spilt it over the coals and in the water. That was Watcher blood in that vial, wasn't it?"

Mora paused and her cheek twitched as if she had not expected such a deduction from the girl before her. Her eyes narrowed even further, but Tamsin saw the fire in them even brighter than before. "You took the red sight, didn't you?"

"Yes."

"A dangerous venture for one so untrained in its power, though you have grown stronger since our first meet…"

"Stay on track Mora," Tamsin snapped. She didn't have time to waste and she sure as seven hells wasn't going to let the old seer twist the conversation. She came here for answers, not more questions. "What did you see then?"

"The future is already set. The sight does not change that. It only gives us our perspective of it."

Tamsin was already running short of patience. "What did you see?" she asked again, accentuating each word.

"I only see death."

A chill settled in Tamsin's limbs and her tongue grew heavy.

"What you really want to know," Mora continued, "is if I saw all the bodies, the blood, the wounded, the song of defeat echoing in the air. You're leading these people to war Tamsin. There is only death in war."

Tamsin shook her head, trying to shake out the images that Mora's words conjured. But then she looked up, the answer springing to her mind as clear as the prisms on a chandelier. "I'm not leading them to war. I'm not leading them anywhere. I'm going alone."

Mora seemed to know what she was thinking. "If you go after him, you'll wish you had let him go."

"You told me when we first met that I was one of the soulless. What is more important: having no soul or having no love?"

"You put too much faith in love."

"And you put too much faith in your gods."

They glared at each other, contempt for the other being masked by a distant understanding.

"What is your decree, Kazsera?"

"I'm giving you a choice: you can either tell me how to get to the Ravine of Bones or you can show me."

Tamsin left the muudhiif some time later, replaying the seer's words. She felt a pressure on her shoulder and looked up to see Oman gazing down at her in concern. He was speaking, but her mind was already to the future. "What?"

"You shouldn't talk to her anymore," he said. "She's playing on your fears."

Tamsin shook her head, more to clear the remaining fog than to agree. "I'm not going to. You can release her. I've gotten what I need."

"Tamsin," the pressure on her shoulder increased with his concern. "She's a blood stealer. She would slit all our throats in a heartbeat just for a drop."

"Fine, then I'll leave it to the Watchers to figure out what to do with her." She saw Numha and R'en approaching so she slipped out of

Oman's grip and walked towards them. They parted and followed her when she didn't stop for them.

"Tamsin?" Numha trailed after her.

"We don't leave until I say, is that clear?" Tamsin asked, turning around to face them as she reached her muudhiif.

"Perfectly," R'en said, an eager smile on her face.

"Of course Kazsera," Numha said, a frown creasing her mouth. "Tamsin…"

"I wish to be alone right now." She waited a few moments until they finally turned and left. She let out a deep breath. It was much easier to pretend to be confident and decisive than to actually believe it herself. But she knew she would have to dig it up from somewhere if she was going to pull off what she intended. R'en obviously believed that they were going to act soon, but Numha's nature would only let her obey Tamsin's creed not to be disturbed up until a point. Tamsin hoped she would be long gone by the time that happened. Maybe her absence would cause enough of a delay that what she had seen in the red sight would just pass over like a storm cloud without releasing a single raindrop. And Samih's death would not have been for nothing.

Chapter Twenty-Four

Tamsin looked back, but the Ma'diin camp was long behind her already as were the marshes themselves. She was headed northeast, per Mora's directions, and if she followed them right then she figured she would be able to find Ib'n's Pass: the back door to the Ravine. She couldn't lead the others to the dam, that much was clear. If she went with them, then what happened in her vision would surely unfold all over again and she would be powerless to stop it. She didn't know if she could change what would happen to the others by leaving, but she knew she had to try.

She had two, maybe three, days before the others caught up to her and even less time for them to figure out she had left. She had to get to the Pass before they found her and tried to stop her. She owed it to Haven. She owed it to Samih now as well.

Tamsin took a break where the incline finally levelled off near the edge of the ridge. She sat on a ledge that jutted out near a scraggly clump of bushes whose branches were contorted and covered in thorns. The leaves were hardly bigger than her thumb and sprouted near the center, protected from birds and predators by the sharp points. The ledge she sat on was solid, but she could see the layers compacted together at the edges and it crumbled in little flakes under the pressure of her fingers. It was strange to think of the marsh lands as civilized country, but this was truly the wilds out here. She had found the ridge a couple of hours ago and was using it as a sort of guide as she continued, but the terrain was uncultivated and rough so she did her best to stay near it. She wondered if this was the same route Haven came when he had gone to the Ravine. Had his feet walked over the same stones?

She sighed deeply and winced. She loosened the strings on her jerkin and inspected the bandage around her side. A thick red line had permeated through the cloth. It was the third time it had soaked through since she left. She scowled and hissed as she peeled the cloth off. Trekking through the wilderness was not helping the gash from Mowlgra's sword heal fast enough and as much as Tamsin tried to play it down to discomfort, the pain it caused was enough to slow her down. At this rate if the Ma'diin were tracking her they would find her before she even got to the Ravine.

She rummaged through her bag of meager supplies. The poultice that Numha had put on the wound had long dried up and caked off and she was out of bandage cloths.

She raised her face to the sky and fought back the tightening of her throat. She would just have to keep going and deal with the pain. She had no other choice.

"I could use a little help right now," she whispered into the empty air. Clenching her fists in fiery resolve, she stood up and started again.

But she only went a few steps before she faltered. Pain lanced through her side and she could feel the tearing bite of Mowlgra's sword all over again. Her trembling hands hovered over her side, too afraid to touch it and make the burning worse.

She staggered back over to the ledge she had just vacated and slowly sat down, breathing as if she had ran for three leagues instead of walking three feet. She had to do something. What would the Ma'diin do? They were so adept at using the resources they had; she had to think like them. Her gaze fell on the thorny bush next to her. Some of the thorns were long enough to be needles. She broke one off and studied it. The tip was so fine she could barely see it. She was only barely decent at needlepoint, but she had stitched up more than one of Haven's garments before. She didn't have any thread, but she could pull apart the pieces of cloth that weren't soaked in her blood and use those strands. It's what the M'adiin would do, but her stomach turned at the thought of what actually doing it would feel like.

It's what the Ma'diin would do...

She stared at the thorn, a terrifying idea forming in her mind. The Ma'diin used what resources they had, but she was forgetting that she possessed a resource far beyond anything in the natural world. It would be painful, but it would be quick. She had tested it on Mowlgra and it had worked.

She instantly broke out in a chilling sweat, but she knew she had to do it. She tore her jerkin off and rolled up her tunic, revealing the bloody gash. She tried to take calmer breaths and focus her thoughts. This would be the most precise use of her power she had ever attempted and it scared her to death.

She grabbed her water skin and took a long drink, wishing that it had something stronger in it. She set it aside and took out her short knife from her boot. She placed the leather-bound handle between her teeth before she could change her mind. Her hands still shook as she placed her fingers along the gash line and pressed her skin together.

Tears leaked out of the corners of her eyes, but she didn't let go. She bit down harder on the knife handle and forced herself to focus…

It was as if she had taken a hot iron and branded herself. She screamed through her teeth as she felt the fire cauterizing her wound. The image of a snake flashed through her mind, sinking its fangs into her and injecting its searing poison. She doubled over as all of her muscles contracted in protest, but she didn't stop it until it was completely sealed. The entire ordeal only took a few heartbeats, but it left her trembling from head to toe like a lamb facing a lion.

She placed her palms down on the cool rock, steadying herself. She spit the knife out into the dirt and looked down to inspect the aftermath. Blood still smeared her skin, but the wound had turned into a vigorous pink welt. She could cross bleeding to death off her list.

She lifted her face back up to the sky and waited for the pain to subside. Once it was back to a tolerable level, she put her jerkin back on, picked up her knife and put it back in her boot, and started off once again. Gingerly at first, wincing with every step, but eventually getting into a rhythm that worked.

As she continued up the ridge, a funny thought hummed in between her ears. During her studies, back in Delmar, they had learned about the seven hells of the old religion. Though the books were careful not to be too detailed, she did remember that the fourth, or fifth, hell was walking through a sea of burning coals.

She laughed out loud, startling a pair of birds in a nearby bush. *Close enough*, she thought.

Chapter Twenty-Five

Emilia looked out the window at the two carriages lined outside in front of the Urbane manor. One to take Lavinia away to their country house near Alstair and one to take Emilia to her aunt's estate in Fairmoore. After Brunos's assassination attempt it was decided that the women should leave, even though he had been caught. Lord Urbane was preparing his case for the Lord's Council and Jalsai was about to become a political battleground. Secretly, Emilia wondered if Lavinia just wanted to get away from Lord Urbane after everything she had learned. But as she watched Lavinia get into the first carriage without even a backward glance, she wondered how she could just turn her back on a life that she had spent years building and had given her so much. She had a title, wealth, servants, a family. But Emilia had all of those things too, back in Empyria. And she had left too.

Emilia turned her attention back inside to the lone suitcase on the bed. Everything she had brought with her was in that case. Everything else was Tamsin's. But she had inherited her aunt's estate and once she reached Fairmoore she would have more than enough to make a comfortable life. A new life.

She was about to head downstairs when she heard the crunch of gravel outside getting louder. She went back to the window, expecting to see Lavinia's carriage leaving, but saw a different carriage pull up behind the other. She didn't have to wonder who it was for very long for moments later she saw Lady Allard and Madame Corinthia step out.

Emilia's feet barely hit the floor as she flew downstairs, her head spinning with questions. She rushed outside, knocking Mr. Brandstone out of the way as he was about to get the door. She no longer wore her veil and the look on the two women's faces as she ran up to them was pure surprise.

"Emilia," Lady Allard said. "We weren't expecting you here. Is this the right place?"

"If you came to see Lavinia, yes it's the right place. You got here just in time."

Lavinia stepped out of her own carriage, a look of confusion plastered on her face as she beheld the others.

"Lady Allard? Madame Corinthia? What are you doing here?"

The two women tried to smile, but neither one looked happy. In fact, Emilia noticed, they looked exhausted. Especially Madame Corinthia who was heavily pregnant. Emilia knew just how toilsome the journey from Empyria to the Cities was, but these women looked as if they had made the journey twice over. They were well-dressed and their hair was well-placed, but their faces appeared gaunt and pale.

"I wish we came under better circumstances," Lady Allard said. "But Empyria is not a safe place anymore. We had to leave."

"Your husband is not with you?" Lavinia asked her. "Your servants?"

Lady Allard shook her head, her eyes downcast.

"Are my parents alright?" Emilia asked, fear rising in her voice.

The two women exchanged a look.

"I'm sorry, Emilia. We—we left very suddenly," Lady Allard said. She pulled out a piece of parchment from the pocket in her skirt. "I do have a letter for Tamsin, though. Is she here?"

"I can give it to her," Emilia said, but Lavinia snatched it before she could, giving her a reproachful look.

Lavinia opened the letter and scanned it quickly, but the farther she went the more her eyes betrayed her. Finally, she put the letter down and handed it to Emilia. She smoothed the front of her skirt. "Perhaps you should give it to her," she told Emilia. "In a little while."

Her tone scared her, but she nodded.

Lavinia took a deep breath and then seemed to collect herself. "We were just about to leave, as you can see," she said, indicating the carriages, "but I think you two could use a hot cup of tea."

"Please, we don't want to intrude," Madame Corinthia said, but even as she said it, she grimaced and rubbed her belly.

"Nonsense," Lavinia said, taking her by the elbow and directing her inside. She told Mr. Brandstone who had been waiting by the door to get some tea made and then unpack her carriage. She would be staying.

"Thank you," Lady Allard said, following them. "She shouldn't be travelling in her condition, but I couldn't leave her there."

Lavinia nodded knowingly. "And she shouldn't travel anymore. Not until the baby is born. And you are welcome to stay as long as you like."

Lady Allard thanked her again and then put her hand on Emilia's arm. "We should talk later."

Emilia watched them disappear inside, but she didn't want to wait until later to read the letter meant for Tamsin. The handwriting was poor and hastily done, but good enough to make out yet.

Tamsin,

Things have gotten much worse here. I don't know if my other letters have reached you, but I hope Lady Allard gets this to you safely. It's too late for my father, but we're helping her get out of the city. It might be too late for us too. I mean the resistance. Cornelius and his men; they've started hunting those in the resistance. They imprisoned my father, but now it's worse. They're killing people without even a trial. I know this because I saw him, I saw Cornelius kill Lord Regoran.

Emilia dropped the letter, not caring to read any more. Whatever was in the rest of it didn't matter. Her father was dead. Cornelius had killed him. Guilt and anger and grief coursed through her trembling hands. She had left Empyria, left her parents behind, but she had never imagined not seeing them again. But that chance had just been ripped away forever. The courtyard around her was the same as it had been seconds ago, with the carriage horses chewing on their bits and the breeze brushing through the trees, but it had also irreversibly changed. The world without her father was much duller. The guilt of never even saying goodbye to them before she left crawled into her stomach, sinking its sickening claws into her. But she hadn't lost both of them.

She reached for the letter again, scanning its contents again for any word about her mother, but there was nothing.

"Miss?" the carriage driver interrupted her. "Are you ready?"

"Do I look like I'm ready?" she answered hotly, wiping her eyes with the back of her hand. She picked up her skirt, ignoring the shocked look on the driver's face and took her flask out of her stocking. She went to take a drink, but all she got was one drop.

Letting out a frustrated cry, she was about to throw it on the ground, but then saw the letter clutched in her other hand. Still trembling, she realized this moment right now would either break her or build her. It would be so easy to give in and let the grief and guilt consume her. But she thought of everyone that had fought and everyone that was fighting right now. Tamsin had gone off completely on her own in search of the man she loved. Lord Urbane had survived and was getting ready to convince the Council to go to war. Even Lavinia, who had every right to be angry at the people around her put a smile on her face and carried on. Her father, Lord Regoran, had given his life trying to overthrow a tyrant. These were people who didn't get their strength and courage from a flask. It was a choice.

After taking a moment to calm herself, she folded the letter and put it in her pocket with a shaky breath. Though this letter was about her father, it was not intended for Emilia to keep it a secret. This was firsthand evidence of the corruptness in Empyria and Lord Urbane would need all the help he could get when he went to the Council. Emilia then tossed the flask at the driver and smoothed the front of her skirt with her hands, just as Lavinia had done.

"I won't be needing this anymore," she told him. "And you can unpack this one as well. I'm staying."

Chapter Twenty-Six

Tamsin was reminded of the entrance to the anasii hada as she stared across the stone bridge that crossed the canyon over the river. The bridge had formed naturally from the ridges, arching slightly in the center and spanning about the length of her outstretched arms at its widest. Where it connected on the other side there was a wide plateau that stretched out from the ridge, but across it was a large cavern that Tamsin knew to be the gateway to the Ravine.

This was it, the place Mora had told her about. Somewhere in those murky tunnels was Haven. All she had to do was cross the bridge, find him, and get him out. It sounded so simple, but as she took her first step onto the bridge, doubt pushed upon her with such force it felt like she had anvils attached to her feet. She hadn't doubted her decision to come here since she had made it, but looking ahead at the dreadful entrance made her chest heavy with fear.

Deep down, she had known it would come to this: to her facing Haven's captors alone. She had come to the Ma'diin for help, because Samih thought they would need an army to storm the Ravine and rescue Haven. It was their best chance of course, and she had exceeded even her hopes with every tribe supporting her.

She was here. But she was alone.

The water churned a ways below, reminding her of another time when she sat on a ledge overlooking the Elglas, a certain Watcher by her side telling her about the stars. Thinking of him helped shed some of the fear and she took another step. She made it to the middle and the wind picked up, not enough to make her falter, but she paused anyway. It could have been the wind, but a foul smell suddenly filled the air like…sulfur.

Her eyes moved from the water and focused on the handle of her sword hanging at her hip. Slowly, she pulled it out and looked up.

Standing in the shadows underneath the opening to the cavern was an amon'jii. It stood with statuesque stillness, which was impressive given that the hunger shining in its eyes was very much alive and eager.

It was the second amon'jii she had seen in her life. She had very nearly lost her life to the first, but she was not about to let her fear get in the way, especially when she had a massive monster already in front of her to deal with. The amon'jii were creatures of stealth, despite their size, and preferred to surprise their prey at the last second, but the way this one watched her suggested an even deeper level of strategy. It seemed to understand that she wanted to get across the bridge, which was why it hadn't attacked yet. It was in no hurry. Tamsin would come to him.

"No fear," she whispered and took another step closer.

The amon'jii arched its neck, its gaze still zeroed in on her. Its nostrils flared in and out and its lip twitched in anticipation. It thought it was getting an easy meal.

Such a little she-hunter, but she will be deliciousss...

Tamsin froze just as she reached the end of the bridge and put her foot on the plateau. The voice was back: the one she had heard in the marshes the night she went looking for Cairn. She had thought then that she was hearing fear-induced voices. Her mind had a terrible knack for playing on her terror at the worst times.

"I am not afraid," she whispered through clenched teeth. She would not let fear rule her or distract her. Not this time. She gripped her sword in both hands and stepped completely off the bridge, only yards away from the amon'jii. She took even breaths, steadying herself, forcing the pounding of her heart to work for her, not against her. She stretched her senses and felt the beating of the amon'jii's own heart, hot and strong. A calmness settled upon her, knowing she had control of its fire. It was going to get a wicked surprise when it tried to burn her and realized it couldn't. It thought the element of surprise was lost. But only for one of them. The amon'jii would feel the bite of her sword long before she felt the heat of its fire.

She circled slowly to the side, every step an inch closer. The amon'jii turned with her, neither one of them taking their eyes off the other. Tamsin feigned an attack, lunging forward just enough to get the amon'jii to react. She jumped back just as quickly when it swung out with its long, clawed arm, missing her by a brush of air. It didn't pursue her, but held its ground, blocking the opening to the cave.

C'mon, Tamsin thought. She needed it to try and burn her. Then, when it was surprised, she would slit its throat. Haven would've believed her to be out of her mind, trying to incite an amon'jii to attack.

She lunged again and rolled out of the way when the amon'jii swung, but this time it was ready for her retreat and made its own lunge toward her. She saw its claws descending and rolled again, dirt and rock flying up from the spot she had just been. She rolled up onto her feet, grabbing her dagger from her boot as she came up and threw it at the creature. The amon'jii drew back and swatted it away, giving Tamsin an opening. She charged, slashing her sword at its head, but missed as the amon'jii flung itself back and spun around. Its tail came around and crashed into her back, causing her to fall forward into the mouth of the cave, but she managed to hang onto her sword. The amon'jii whirled back around to face her and this time she saw the white gleam of its teeth as it snapped at her. She wielded her sword like a shield and the amon'jii's teeth clamped down on the blade instead of her head. It shrieked and whipped its head to the side. Tamsin, not willing to let go of her only weapon, was flung across the plateau, skidding to a stop just before the edge of the canyon. She gasped as her ribs buckled under the impact, but brought her sword up, ready for another attack.

She stared at her sword in horror. The force of the amon'jii's bite had reduced it to a handle and five inches of broken blade.

The amon'jii hissed at her several yards away, blood dripping out of the corner of its mouth. Tamsin smiled and the amon'jii curled its lips back, baring its dagger-sharp fangs.

Our teeth are the same size now little she-hunter.

Yes, but mine are sharper than yours, Tamsin hissed back.

The amon'jii stopped mid-step and Tamsin froze. She exhaled, the air coming out of her lungs like a fading fog.

The amon'jii had spoken to her. That was the voice she heard. But that wasn't the worst part. She had spoken back.

The amon'jii seemed just as stunned as she was, but recovered faster. It charged at her, and just as Tamsin thought her throat was going to be ripped out, it stopped. Its long snout hovered over her so close she could feel its breath blowing her hair back and she could see the individual scales along the ridge of its forehead. Its slanted eyes bored into her with singular malice, as if daring her to move while it figured her out.

From a distance, the skin appeared seamless, glossy almost. But up close she could see the edges of the diamond shaped scales, rippling with its movement. The horns that curled back behind its ears reminded her of a ram's. They looked as dead as bone, but looked as if they had grown through the skin. Its teeth were about as thick as her wrist at their widest and dripped with saliva. It could easily snap her like a twig.

Tamsin still couldn't fathom how she could communicate with it. The amon'jii were animals, beastly predators with no concept of morality…just like the Ma'diin were to the northerners.

These were not just animals. They were something terrifyingly more.

It panted on her and the sulfur smell engulfed her. Past its row of mountain range fangs she could almost see down its long throat. The inner inferno it contained burned like an ember. Its eyes burned with that same fire, aimed at her like two golden arrows. But the conflict was making it angry; torn between instinct and curiosity. The former always trumped the latter, however.

Its mouth turned back into a snarl and the soft thrumming in its throat as it breathed turned into a roaring shriek.

Chapter Twenty-Seven

He didn't know much about the gods, even less about how to pray to them. He knew the story of course of the world's creation and the rise of the Ma'diin and the fall of I'bn and the Lumierii. It was the story of his creation, after all. And he had heard snippets of stories from the sh'lomiin and from Lu'sa who had loved to tell him her latest discoveries of Mahiri's prophecy or of Baat the daughter savior. But his knowledge of the Q'atorii was like Lu'sa's: childlike and incomplete. Whenever he had heard a new story he could remember feeling like he was just on the verge of figuring it all out, that he was this close to uncovering the secrets. Just one more story, one more sign of their omnipotent power and he would have unconditional faith. He wanted desperately to believe that there was a place for him in the afterlife, that the suffering of this life would end and he would be received into the gardens of Edan.

But as it was spoken, Edan was reserved for Mahiri's children. 'After Mahiri's mortal death, her immortal life passed into bliss and there she created a new paradise: Edan. There she awaits each one of her children in the bosom of eternity, free from all evil and abominations.'

That's why his mantra was 'no fear,' for it's what he had to tell himself every day in order to keep his biggest fear from crippling him. He had always feared being rejected from the holy waterfalls because he knew what he was and what was not allowed there. It was impossible not to wonder what would happen to him at the end.

But standing here, he couldn't pinpoint what he felt. Fear? No, something more like awe. Horror without actually being frightened. This was the moment he had anticipated so many times. The moment of knowing and believing. It was a strange clarity, something he had not felt in months, and yet he couldn't remember the moment he died. But he believed now that it had happened. For his biggest fear had manifested right before his very eyes and yet he felt nothing. Not peace exactly, but the fear was gone. Somehow knowing what his eternal afterlife was like left nothing else in his way. His afterlife was exactly what he deserved.

He fell to his knees under the burning glare of his creator. Not Mahiri or Behrun, but the one who created the stars, the amon'jii, and...the Lumierii. His creator, the god of the Watchers. He raised his *head, daring to look at the face that contained thousands of years of hatred, simmering in his immortalized prison of sinew and bone.*

He barely heard the footsteps coming towards him, then suddenly stopping. Out of the corner of his eye he saw Monstran's white hair fall forward as he bent his head in reverence.

"I bring good news, Master," Monstran said. "The boy has returned with the firestone."

"Bring it to me." The Master's command was calm, but boomed throughout the cavern.

Monstran bowed even lower. Then another pair of footsteps came forward and Haven saw the boy. It was the one who had tried to help him. Why was he here?

The boy gave something to Monstran who then held it up for the Master to see.

Haven's heart pounded, making him think that maybe he wasn't dead after all. Monstran held a firestone. His firestone. But it wasn't the firestone that made his pulse race. It was the blood stains on the boy's jacket.

Something cracked inside of him as he connected the blood stains to who he had given his firestone to. No...

The Master sighed. "He is ready."

Monstran looked at Haven and then back to the Master. "Are you certain, Master?"

The Master arched his enormous neck, clearly offended by his defiance and Monstran fell to his knees next to Haven.

The two exchanged a glance, and Haven guessed Monstran realized the irony of the situation.

Haven looked up again. At the Master. At his creator.

At I'bn.

"Take this soul. Do with it what you will."

Here Ends Book Two of An Empyrian Odyssey

Pronunciation Guide

Afain'jii (ah-fane-<u>jee</u>)
Alahkiin Zakar (ah-lah-<u>keen</u> zah-<u>kar</u>)
Aluuva (ah-<u>loo</u>-vah)
Amon'jii (ah-mahn-<u>jee</u>)
Anasii hada (ah-nah-<u>see</u> <u>hah</u>-dah)
Baagh (bahg)
Baagh'dovuurii (bahg doh-<u>voo</u>-ree)
Baat (baht)
Buurda (<u>boor</u>-dah)
Cavahst (kah-<u>vahst</u>)
Empyria (em-<u>peer</u>-ree-ah)
Fairmoore (<u>fair</u>-moor)
Fluazan (<u>flaw</u>-zahn)
Fuh'diin (<u>foo</u>-deen)
Haava (<u>hah</u>-vah)
Hafakii (hah-fah-kee)
Halcyona (hall-see-oh-nah)
Haniis (hah-nees)
Havakkii (hah-vah-<u>kee</u>)
Hiita (<u>hee</u>-tah)
Ib'n (<u>ee</u>-bin)
Ireczburg (<u>ear</u>-ex-berg)
Jalsai (jahl-sa-<u>ee</u>)
Jiin mughaif (jeen moo-<u>gah</u>-eef)

Kapu'era (kah-poo-<u>air</u>-ah)
Kaz'ma'sha (kahz-mah-<u>shah</u>)
Kazsera (kah-<u>zay</u>-rah)
Kazserii (kah-<u>zay</u>-ree)
Kazsiin (kah-<u>zeen</u>)
Kazszura'asha (kah-<u>zoo</u>-rah-<u>ah</u>-shah)
Kor'diin (kor-<u>deen</u>)
Lumierii (loo-mee-<u>air</u>-ee)
Lumii veritaas (<u>loo</u>-mee vay-ree-<u>tahs</u>)
Ma'diin (mah-<u>deen</u>)
Muudhiif (moo-<u>deef</u>)
N'qab (nee-<u>kob</u>)
Pa'shiia (pah-<u>shee</u>-ah)
Pak'kriin (pahk-ee-<u>kreen</u>)
Pentiyan (pehn-tee-<u>yahn</u>)
Q'atorii (kah-<u>toh</u>-ree)
Sh'lomiin (<u>shee</u>-lo-meen)
Sh'pav'danya (shih-<u>pahv</u>-dahn-yah)
Sha'diin (shah-<u>deen</u>)
Shafaii (shah-<u>fah</u>-ee)
Shriiski (<u>shree</u>-skeh)
Skiishiv (<u>skee</u>-shehv)
Tiika (<u>tee</u>-kah)
Vas'akru (vahs-ah-<u>kroo</u>)

The completion of this book would not be possible without the support of my family. The last two years have brought a lot of change and without their love and sacrifices this book might still be unfinished. So all my thanks and gratitude goes to my family, my faith, my friends, my reviewers, editors, babysitters, and everyone who read *The Dark Solstice* and choose to follow Tamsin and Haven on their journey. For their story is far from over.

> "But in the end it's only a passing thing, this shadow; even darkness must pass."
>
> -J.R.R. Tolkien

ABOUT THE AUTHOR

Nikki Leigh Willcome lives in northeastern Wisconsin with her husband, Bill, and her son, Kypling. She received a B.A. in English Literature from the University of Wisconsin – Madison in 2011 and is now a work-from-home mom and writer. *The Hour of Embers* is her second novel and the sequel to *The Dark Solstice*.

Nlwillcomeauthor.wordpress.com

Facebook.com/NikkiWillcome

Goodreads.com/nlwillcome

Made in the USA
Columbia, SC
26 May 2023